In a World Apart

Lauren Amanda Shepherd

In this book are several small black and white samples of over 50 color illustrations for **In a World Apart** *that you can order in a 9"X12" size.*

You can find them on my website:

http://www.lauren-amanda-shepherd.com/home-page.html

Go to:

Giclée Art

Illustrations by the author.

Prologue

"Set yourself on fire and people will come to watch you burn."

~ Dr. Martin Luther King, Jr.~

"My last memory is of the plane roaring down the runway and lifting in a perfect ascent.

I remember thinking at the time that the plane was a slender streak of steel, angling upward, its wings reflecting the light before it banked to the left and passed through a low-lying cloud.

Then, without warning, there was a bright flash and an eerie silence before a thunderous clap, and the front section where the pilot, my mother, and my father were sitting, became flaming debris shredding the sky."

HEH

~ Hayley Elizabeth Hamilton~

~1~

The men with the muckrake are often indispensable to the well-being of society, but only if they know when to stop raking the muck.
~Theodore Roosevelt~

Fitchburg Massachusetts Municipal Airport
FAA News Conference
May 21, 1999

A tall man with a grim expression strode across the airport terminal entrance to a makeshift podium. Glancing at the waiting crowd of reporters, he took his place beside the Fitchburg Public Relations representative at the microphone. Leaning to the side and pointing to the crowd, he handed a stack of papers to his assistants. He scanned a copy of the paper, cleared his throat, and held up his hand for quiet.

"Good evening ladies and gentlemen of the press. I'm Jimmy Pederson, a Federal Aviation Administration representative. This is Bobby Moran, Fitchburg Public Relations. We're here to update you on a small plane that crashed shortly after takeoff this afternoon from the Fitchburg Municipal Airport.

My staff is circulating a preliminary fact sheet and press release for you. These are the facts at this time, but, as you know, things often change from moment to moment as additional information emerges. I would ask you, please, to hold your questions until the end.

Today, May 21, 1999, at 4:00 PM, a privately owned Learjet went down leaving a young woman without both parents. After taking off from Fitchburg Massachusetts Municipal Airport, the plane crashed, resulting in the deaths of New York attorney, John A. Hamilton, his wife, Lady Elizabeth Hayles-Townsend Hamilton, and their pilot, Marshall K. George. The lone survivor was the Hamilton's daughter and their only child, nineteen year-old Hayley Elizabeth. The family had attended Miss Hamilton's Wellesley College graduation. They were on route to Southampton, New York before going home to England where Ms. Hamilton planned to attend classes at Oxford University.

Airport traffic control reports that there was no problem on takeoff. The plane was lifting to cruising altitude when, according to eyewitnesses, unknown assailants shot a rocket into the left wing, sabotaging the plane. The wing burst into flames and the aircraft nose-dived into a wooded area a short distance from Fitchburg. The tail section split from the front on impact with the ground. Subsequently, the front section burned into unrecognizable debris. Apparently, Miss Hamilton survived because she had not buckled her seatbelt on takeoff and we assume the explosion threw her into the rear of the plane. In spite of multiple injuries, she held on to the family dog, and managed to crawl away from the fire before losing consciousness. She's currently in surgery and doctors say it's too soon to speculate on her recovery.

At this time, the attack is under investigation by various federal and state entities. Mister Moran and I will take your questions now.

Yes?"

For two weeks, the British press, as well as the American press, droned on about the Hamilton's tragedy. John Hamilton was a well-known New York attorney, a descendent of Alexander Hamilton, the solitary delegate from New York to sign the U.S.

Constitution. His wife, Lady Elizabeth Hayles-Townsend, was the daughter of Lord Townsend Brandley, Earl of Circencester. They hauled out colorful stories of family history to show the origin of the Earldom. Tabloids dug deep for dirt, but the family came up spotless. Finally, after all their digging, they resorted to outrageous speculative questions for their headlines with inference and supposition in the articles. The two-week whirlwind of coverage ended with the memorial service in New York City's Saint Patrick's Cathedral.

New York's popular cable news channel, Savvy News, produced a program about marriages between wealthy Americans and British nobility in the nineteenth and twentieth century. Most, they said, were *nouveau riche* Americans marrying for a title and titled landowners taking wealthy American wives to bolster their impoverished British estates.

London's American owned cable news channel, Airway News, produced a program speculating whether or not Hayley Hamilton, Lady Elizabeth's daughter, would walk the halls of Oxford University in her mother's footsteps. Zara Chandler, a technical consultant for the university, fielded questions as she was leaving the Rhodes scholarship office.

"Ms. Chandler," asked Airway News reporter, Calvin Chaser, "How well did you know Lady Hayles-Townsend?"

"Lizzy and I were students here at Oxford, actually. Lizzy stopped by to say hello when she and her daughter, Hayley, were here on a recent visit to the university. It was brilliant to see Lizzy and talk over old times. We were *such* good friends. Mind you, her little girl was *thrilled* to be taking classes here at Oxford.

"What will happen now?"

Zara's thin fingers preened her spiky red hair.

"Oh, well... poor Miss Hamilton may be unable to start reading in the autumn. I've heard she has not come out of her coma, so it appears that will be the case. Perhaps she will recover and be able to go on with her plans, but I'm not hopeful," she sighed. "*Tsk, tsk,*" she clicked her tongue; "she'll be *frightfully* disappointed, then, won't she? That is, if she lives. Such a disaster, isn't it?"

She spoke fast and appeared rushed. She wore a pained expression, but it merely reflected her impatience to end the interview. She didn't want to be late for her lunch meeting with Peter Gabriel-Johns, a potential client.

"Thank you, Ms. Chandler. We can see this tragedy has far-reaching implications. For Airway News, this is Cal Chaser reporting from Oxford University. Now, over to you in the studio for coverage of the memorial service from Saint Patrick's Cathedral in New York City, an update on Hayley Hamilton's progress, and more on Lady Elizabeth's story."

Doctor Peter Gabriel-Johns watched Zara Chandler's interview on Airway News from his office near the University's campus. *I wonder how my mother is taking Lady Elizabeth's death.* While he waited for Chandler to arrive, Peter cleared his desk and then rang his mother at their Oxfordshire estate, Seven Valleys. Barbara Gabriel-Johns answered on the first ring.

"Mum, how are you and Dad? What are you two up to today?"

"Oh, we're good, Peter. Your father is meeting with the architects and builders today to reconstruct the old chapel for his winery. This new venture is taking on a life of its own. As for me, I just finished a large canvas, now I'm cleaning brushes," she sighed deeply, "and I've been watching the memorial service for Lady Elizabeth and her husband, John Hamilton. I can't believe this happened. But, how are you, Peter?"

"Oh, I'm all right; busy though. I've been watching the memorial service, too, Mum. I know you and Lady Elizabeth were becoming good friends."

"Oh, yes, Peter, we were." Barbara's voice cracked and Peter knew his mother was grieving. "Is that why you've called, Dear? To see how I'm taking this horrible news?"

"Yes, I had a minute to talk, Mum, and I wondered how you were taking it. I'm waiting for a woman who I might hire to help me design my research project software. We're going to tackle it over lunch. An Airway News correspondent just interviewed her about Elizabeth. She said that she and Lady Elizabeth were friends. Let me ask you something, Mum. Did anyone ever call Elizabeth, 'Lizzy'?"

"No, Peter," she chuckled softly, "her school friends called her *Snugglebuns*, but no one who didn't know her well would ever *dare* to call her Snugglebuns, or Lizzy, for that matter. She hated it.

The last time I saw her, which was just last month, actually, we arranged to meet at the NobleArtist Gallery. She was picking up three more of my paintings for her clients in New York, but her interior design expertise was only one outlet for her creativity. She'd established an *atelier*, *Antiqué de Classiquite*, in Buddinghill's Department Store in New York City. She designed fashions for her own collection of vintage and classic couture. She was on her way to becoming an acclaimed designer. While she was here last, she told me she found some antiques, objects d'art, and paintings by European artists for the shop, too."

"Were you able to spend some time with her, Mum?

"Yes, fortunately, she suggested tea in the Colonnade Room at the London Ritton Hotel. They have a wonderful new tea menu and we had a grand visit. Hayley was with Elizabeth that day. She's a lovely young woman, Peter. She said she was looking forward to starting her classes at Oxford. This is just my opinion, but there was something in Hayley's voice that told me she was going on to Oxford only to please her mother. You know, while we talked, I realized you and Hayley had a lot in common. Of course, she's a few years behind you, but I would have liked you to meet her. I told her all about you."

"I wonder...do you know if their daughter is still in a coma, Mum?"

"Yes, last I heard, she is, and I've wired flowers to her at the hospital. Oh, Peter, I'm terribly upset about Hayley; she's too young to be all alone. Elizabeth and John doted on that child. Personally, I thought they suffocated her."

Peter heard tears in his mother's voice. "I know this is a dreadful loss for you. I know you're mourning her death, but also the long and warm friendship that could have been. And now..."

"I simply cannot believe I'll never see her again. Elizabeth planned to return to Belgravia late in June. I invited her to the July Wolds-on-Thames Arts Festival. I asked her to spend a week with the family at Seven Valleys as our guest. The invitation delighted her. Hayley would have been in London at that time as well. Elizabeth had asked many questions about you, William, and Matthew. I gathered she had designs on my sons and planned to look you all over as a potential match for her daughter." Barbara chuckled when Peter scoffed. "Peter, you've helped so many people as a grief counselor and through trauma therapy. I want you to arrange to go to New York to see Hayley when she comes out of the coma. She's going to need a great deal of compassion and support when she regains consciousness -- if she's lucky enough to survive."

"I'm not sure going to New York is such a good idea, Mum," Peter shook his head, his hand rubbing the back of his neck. "First of all, she, or her doctors, may not want me there. Furthermore, she doesn't know me. I'm neither her friend nor her therapist. What do you suggest I tell them?"

"I don't know what to tell them, Peter; you'll think of something."

Although he couldn't see her, Peter knew from her tone of voice that his mother's mind was set. It was what *she* wanted and as far as she was concerned, her son would go.

Squirming in his chair, he said, "All right, Mum. I'll do it for *you*, but let's wait and see, shall we, before you go buying any plane tickets. When she wakes, I'll call her doctors, or that attorney, and arrange to see her, if possible."

"Thank you, Peter, and thanks for ringing me. Talking about my feelings for Elizabeth has helped lift the sadness weighing on me. It will make me happy for you to go to Hayley. The least I can do for Elizabeth is to make sure her daughter is all right." She paused; "Will we see you on Sunday for family dinner?"

"Yes, Mum. I'll be there. I'm going for a run on Sunday morning with some men I met at the London Marathon this year. I'll see you a bit early, though. I want to discuss an investment for Aunt Pat's trust with dad."

Peter hung up the receiver and pressed his fingertips against his eyes. He took a deep breath and became aware that a faint musky scent had drifted into the room. Turning his head toward the doorway, he was startled to see Zara Chandler standing there and he wondered how long she'd been eavesdropping on his conversation.

She wore an odd expression on her face when she said,

"Are you ready for me?"

~2~

"The language of friendship is not words,
but meanings."
~ Henry David Thoreau~

Stanford University
Palo Alto, California
May 1999

Across the world from Oxfordshire, England, in northern California, Christine Horowitz slouched in front of an antiquated TV watching the Hamilton's memorial service. In her hand, she held an invitation from Hayley to join her for a vacation in Southampton when she arrived on the east coast before starting her new job. When the ceremony concluded, she wiped her eyes, blew her nose, and snapped off the television set.

Folding the invitation and stuffing it into her jeans pocket along with her wet tissue, she stretched, took in a deep breath, and exhaled slowly. She still had some work to do and only a few hours left.

A recent Stanford Journalism and Communications graduate, Chris was the last of six roommates to clear out of an off-campus apartment. One by one, they departed, removing their personal belongings, until nothing remained except a few last-minute items of hers. They agreed to leave behind the old television set and a few pieces of shoddy junkshop furniture. A newly minted group of freshmen would start arriving any day.

The gloomy apartment needed one final check and she walked through the rooms gathering trash. Each room reminded her of the students who shared the space. She found scraps of torn sheet music from a temperamental music student, the butt of a hand-rolled joint stuck on a toothpick, and a tear-stained brown teddy bear losing its stuffing that had fallen behind a bed. She could still see them all in her mind's eye. She pressed her palm against the dusty wall and willed them to return so she could once again hear the laughter, the crying, the singing, and even the hip-hop music they played too loud.

"I'm getting maudlin," she chided herself, trying to shake off her mood.

Chris walked down three flights of stairs and shoved the bag of trash into an overflowing dumpster. She loaded her meager belongings into a 1947 red Oldsmobile Woodie with faded tie-dyed undershirts covering the seat backs. She planned to leave at daybreak, driving alone across the country to start her first job as a low-level production assistant at a local TV station in Buffalo, New York.

She'd cleaned out the refrigerator and cabinets, and had thrown away all the leftovers. Deciding to splurge and treat herself to some comfort food, she hopped in the car and headed for Starbucks, where she bought a deli-stacked sandwich, a blueberry nut muffin, and a tall white chocolate mocha cappuccino.

At twilight, Chris sat on the seat of an open bay window inhaling the steam wafting from the top of the hot liquid bliss, while at the same time a cool breeze drifted over her face. She always enjoyed the colorful panorama of sunset in the evening sky.

The roommates had crowded around this large bay window many times at the end of the day to toast the setting sun. The literature and poetry student had described the sunset as clouds laying in streaks, the colors changing from rose and lavender to violet, spreading across the darkening azure sky. They'd raise their drinks to the low-lying banks of fog rolling in and to the setting sun that cast shafts of light into the room.

Now, as the lone observer, Chris held up the steaming cup and brought out their toast one final time to celebrate her personal milestone and to observe the passage of time. With a deep sigh, as the very last glimpse of the sun slowly dipped behind the mountains, she whispered, "*Going...going...gone.*"

Rising, she walked to the bathroom to prepare for bed and stumbled over a well-worn scale. She'd spent three years with roommates whose education and career were secondary. They faithfully watched their diets and killer-dressed to attract college men. They spent agonizing hours in front of the bathroom mirror, picking at their faces, plucking eyebrows, applying moisturizers and makeup, slathering their bodies with fake tan, coloring and styling their hair, staring at their youthful faces, wishing their breasts were bigger, their bodies thinner, and they were more beautiful.

Chris stared at herself in the mirror. She knew the girl looking back at her was a misfit. She didn't bother about her appearance, or care that she was overweight. Christine wasn't into attracting boys; she was only into her career.

She laid out her travel clothes taking no notice of how large and shabby they were. Chris was frugal and considered it a challenge to save a dime. She shopped at thrift stores, wore her clothes until they were threadbare, and never paid full-price for anything. The car was an exception; it was a collectible in perfect condition when her parents bought it and was the only car she'd accept. Her parent's mechanic taught her to make engine repairs and she maintained the body with meticulous care. She took greater pride in the vehicle's appearance than she did in her own and the Woodie still looked like new.

Although Chris was friendly, outgoing, and could easily make acquaintances, she'd made very few friends. The differences between her and most people meant they didn't enter her heart and make it into the big, empty space within, where she could truly care about them. Let's see, she thought, sitting cross-legged on her bed and facing into the room; how many am I going to miss from this apartment? She made a circle with her thumb and forefinger and held up her hand in front of one eye like a spyglass, circling the room. "Zero," she sighed, feeling quite alone and empty.

Of all her peers, the one person who had ever managed to wriggle into Chris's heart was Hayley Hamilton, who now lay in a hospital bed, clinging to life. She was feeling a great deal of compassion for Hayley.

"Oh, God, what if she doesn't survive?" she whispered into the silent room. "We're both just short of twenty, our lives are only beginning. Her life will be over before she's even had a chance to live. But, what happens to her if she does come out of the coma? Who will be there for her? I know how close she was to her parents -- what in God's name will she do without them?"

~3~

"The world is a stage, but the play is badly cast."
~Oscar Wilde~

Stanford University
Palo Alto, California
May 1999

Christine slept fitfully that night. She lay in the dark mulling her life before Stanford and going over her plans for the trip. It was a long drive from Stanford to Buffalo. She'd already mapped out the quickest route across the country and planned to sleep in the car to save money. Christine didn't need to economize; it was one of the ways she chose to be different.

Upon graduation, her parents released a trust fund they shrewdly managed over the years. She chose not to use the money and asked them to continue investing the funds. However, the trust wasn't the only reason Christine had no need to economize. Her parents were famous, wealthy, and powerful.

She rarely discussed her family, but one night, she dropped her guard and told one of her roommates that although she was an only child, she wasn't her parents' natural child.

"When my mother died from an aneurism during childbirth, her sister, and her sister's husband, adopted me. They named me after my birth mother. You might remember her, Christine Wyndham, a Hollywood starlet who nearly made it big before her sudden death. Well, I caused her death. I was an accident. She hid her pregnancy from the public and I'll never know who my father was. She carried that secret to the grave."

Her adoptive mother was Diane Wyndham, an award-winning scriptwriter and occasional actor, and her adoptive father was Ben

Horowitz, a mega-hit producer and director. She grew up in her parents' Laurel Canyon compound, north of Los Angeles, a bastion of old Hollywood wealth and celebrity. Ben and Diane were so influential that the entertainment industry baptized their partnership the *POW! Factory* and dubbed their compound, the *Powerhouse.*

"My mother and father have a loving marriage and successful business partnership that takes all of their attention," she told people who asked about them. She kept to herself that she thought their relationship was so big and so tight, there really wasn't room for her to squeeze inside their box with them.

From the time she looked outside herself at her parent's world, she astutely watched them from the sidelines taking cover from the radiance they cast over an industry where the electricity they generated lighted the way for the stars. Chris chose to exist in the shadow of their brilliance, developing a keen interest in literature and cultivating her writing. She spent time absorbing the classics, reading her mother's scripts, and sharpening her skills on the best writing the industry had to offer. Although her parent's celebrity made them fair game for the paparazzi, she stayed out of sight, hiding in the background, watching, listening, and learning.

Chris would appear at Ben's office door several times a day and begin chattering, "What is this? What does it mean? Who did that? Why? Why not?"

"*Tch*, Christine, you're such a nudge," he'd groan, holding his head in his hands. "Stop interrupting my train of thought with your incessant jibber jabber."

One day, fed up with the interruptions and inquisitions, Ben scoffed, "Christine, you can be so pushy at times, I wouldn't be surprised if you became a scandal-chasing reporter or an ambulance-chasing lawyer from the insensitive way you pose questions."

Then at sixteen, Chris nailed it down. She stomped into their conference room after a meeting.

"May I have your attention, please?" She stood at the head of the long table and rapped. "I have an announcement to make. Are you ready?" Then, she said smugly, "I've won a full-paid scholarship to Stanford to study journalism and communications. I'm going to be a reporter."

"That's wonderful, Christine, but you're not even sixteen yet," Ben said. Are you *sure* you're ready to live away from home? You know it's not going to be easy being responsible for yourself. You're used to dropping your crap everywhere and having someone else bend over and pick up after you."

"Well, totally, yeah. I'm ready. I'm excited!"

"But, Christine, why take a scholarship away from someone who can't pay for their education? We can afford..."

"Because I won it; I did it myself," she sniffed defiantly, crossing her arms across her chest.

Diane looked down at the table for a long moment. "Yes, that's wonderful, Christine, but bottom line...I'm not sure I want you living away from home yet, and like your dad said, you'll be a lot younger than the other students. First thing you know, you'll be..."

"*Yeah, yeah, yeah*, I know," she interrupted her mother. "Damn it, just for once, can't you two be happy for me?" She scowled at them. "Oh, and by the way, Dad; I'm already sixteen," she scoffed and flounced out of the room.

Nevertheless, Ben and Diane were indeed happy for her and pleased by her talent and initiative. They secretly hoped someday she would make her mark by their side. They never told her of their dream; she was so pigheaded, they were afraid that telling her would jinx it.

~4~

"I can't believe that God plays dice with the universe."
~ Albert Einstein~

~ On the Road ~
Palo Alto, California ~ to ~Buffalo, New York
May 1999

Rising at daybreak, Christine threw the last of her belongings onto the back seat of her Woodie. On top of the pile was a worn turquoise western-style suede jacket. *My lucky jacket*, she thought. She left the Bay area and headed east toward Yosemite on autopilot, still brooding over Hayley and lost in reverie about the day they spent together.

At that time, Christine commuted from the family's 80-acre compound to attend an accelerated private girls' school. Chris edited the school's newspaper and she won an award for three articles she had written for *Teen's Personal Best Magazine*. The magazine espoused the best of the teen scene in America. One of those articles was about Hayley Elizabeth Hamilton. She had heard about Hayley from her school's music teacher.

"Christine, she's a gifted pianist studying with the Juilliard pre-college program. She often gives concerts for the students in Harlem's elementary schools. She's one of ten Juilliard students who were honored by the City of New York and she's involved in fundraising for the Harlem school district to encourage students to play musical instruments."

"She sounds perfect for my *Dream Teen* articles. How can I contact her?"

"I can arrange a personal interview with Hayley through the Julliard Director if your parents would allow you to fly to New York from Los Angeles."

"Of course, you can go, Christine," her father agreed, "but your mother will accompany you. You cannot go alone."

"*What*? No! I don't need a babysitter!" Chris sat down hard with a frown on her face. "Please don't do this to me, Dad," she begged, acting as forlorn as she could. "If she goes, it will turn into a paparazzi feeding frenzy."

"If you want to go kiddo, that's the condition."

"Please, Dad, I won't do anything dumb, I promise. I can take care of myself. I'm not a kid," she whined."

Ben snorted and scoffed, "*Puh*...You're only fourteen, Christine. What do you mean, you're not a kid?"

After days of arguing and pleading, Ben and Diane grew tired of the melodrama, the pouting, the scathing glances, and the shedding of hot, angry tears. They grimly relented, although against their better judgment.

"We can't take this anymore, Christine, screw that!"

"No crap, Christine, you make our lives a living hell when you don't get your own way. You can go, but please try not to play in traffic, all right?" Diane scoffed and walked out of the bedroom.

"*M-o-o-o-m*, that's mean," Christine pretended her feelings were hurt.

As soon as they were out of earshot, she skipped around in circles punching the air doing a "*yes-yes-yes*" happy dance, collapsing on her bed hugging herself, and kicking her feet in the air.

Ben's staff made a reservation for Christine at the Plaza Hotel. They imposed one firm condition; she would use the Plaza's limo and driver they arranged for her from the time she arrived in New York until she returned to La Guardia.

She balked at flying first class and insisted on flying standby.

"Christine, you are driving us crackers!" Ben warned her, "If you haul out one more obstacle, I'm calling it off."

"Come on, Dad," she whined and looked at him pitifully.

Frowning, Ben glowered at the floor and then glared at her.

"All right, Christine, we'll negotiate this. You can fly standby on the way to New York, but you'll wait with us in the first class lounge and you'll fly First Class on the way back to L.A. Deal?"

"Oh, all right, I suppose," she pouted. "I can do this all by myself, you know."

"*Pffft*...Don't push it, kid. We're taking a risk by dropping your leash and letting you wander off the reservation alone."

Diane threw up her hands and glared at them. "I am not *pleased* Ben. This is a bad idea, but it's just too much to buck both of you. You're a spoiled brat, Christine, and if anything happens to you, I'm holding your father responsible," she huffed, and stomped out of the room.

They drove Chris to the airport and waited with her so she could fly standby to La Guardia. When she boarded, Ben and Diane stood with gritted teeth and white knuckles at the Jetway entrance, making her vow to call when she arrived.

"And I want you to call home three times a day, Christine, or there will be hell to pay. You got that, your highness?" Ben's eyes burned into hers while he shook her by the shoulders.

"*Yeah, yeah, yeah; I'll call, I'll call*," she mumbled.

Diane whispered in her ear and air-kissed her goodbye. "Don't forget to *wash* while you're away. *Hug, hug, kiss, kiss. Love ya, baby."*

"Geez, *M-o-o-o-m*," Chris rolled her eyes.

A flight attendant escorted Chris to her seat. Halfway down the Jet way, she glanced back over her shoulder to wave and saw a camera flash and a reporter sticking a microphone in her parents' faces.

"Yeah, I'll call the help," she scoffed, "Neither of you will be around to pick up the phone."

Driving through Cheyenne, Wyoming, Chris passed a store called Cowgirls of the West. It reminded her of how Hayley had dressed the day they met. Chris arrived first at their arranged meeting place, the Park East Café in Central Park not far from the Plaza Hotel. Heads turned when Hayley entered the café. Tall, slim and graceful, she carried herself like a dancer. I can see her performing Swan Lake, Christine mused.

She was surprised to see Hayley wearing a plain black tee shirt, jeans, cowboy boots, and a western-style jacket. She had a fringed black suede pouch slung over her shoulder. She wore no jewelry with the exception of a wide, black leather belt around her narrow hips decorated with silver Conchos and turquoise stones. Something about the way she wore her clothes made them look stylish and expensive. Hayley wore her blonde hair in a short, boyish style. Chris thought her features were soft and delicate, her smile was engaging, but most outstanding to Chris was her aura of tranquility.

Hayley looked around the café and Chris stood up to attract her attention. With a bold black marker on a yellow writing pad she had written, 'CHRIS,' in huge letters above a downward arrow and held it over her head. The sign made Hayley chuckle and waving, she moved toward Chris, who also had dressed in black.

Chris wore a stovepipe hat and black boots that laced up to her knees. Silver and rhinestone stars studded her tee shirt and she had loaded her arms and fingers with silver jewelry. Chris used dark and dramatic makeup. She'd dyed her hair black and clipped on streaks of magenta and bright blue accents around her face.

Within minutes, the girls were chatting comfortably with each other. Chris wrote while they talked and she could feel Hayley studying her. Chris's teeth were perfect and white. Her lips were full, curved and feminine, but she knew her upper lip was far too short. When she smiled the excessive amount of gums that showed was distracting. Her heavy, hooded upper eyelids made her feel like a frog and she could sense that Hayley's eyes hadn't moved from her nose. Most people found the unsightly, ridged hump on her nose off-putting. For Chris, the worst was the twisted septum blocking the inside and causing her to sniff.

"You're looking at my nose, aren't you?" She spoke abruptly, not lifting her eyes while she took a sip of her Coke. *Sniff.*

"Oh, I'm sorry, Christine. I apologize," Hayley spoke softly and looked away.

"That's all right," Chris inclined her head and chuckled, "I'm used to it. I was a tomboy when I was a kid. A baseball hit me head on and banged up my face. That was the end of what my parents called my *Tom-Brat* phase. They begged me to have my nose fixed, but I refused. I gave in on the braces, which have just come off, but a nose job would make me just like all the other Bratz Dolls in Hollywood. They've been stamped out by Beverly Hills' Lop-Offs with their plastic cookie-cutters."

Hayley appeared to have none of the Upper East Side New York pretentiousness Chris expected and she was without a touch of snobbery. She had a charming voice and cultured British accent that mesmerized Chris.

"Hayley, you have, like, a posh accent. Why is that?"

"*Oh...*" Hayley chuckled softly, "Yes, my Mum is British. We spend a lot of time at our home in London Belgravia. I was born there, actually, and she often travels to England because of her business."

"Will you tell me more about your parents, Hayley? They sound interesting."

"Christine, please don't write about them in your article. I'd rather you focus on what I'm doing with the Harlem project and not on my family."

"I so get it, Hayley, I don't like to discuss my parents either. I'll keep your family out of it, I promise." *Sniff.*

Hayley impressed Chris with her commitment to provide children of low-income families with musical instruments. She described the youngsters touching reactions when they received their instruments and how sheepish and amused they were on their first attempt at playing them.

Chris wrote furiously and when they finished the interview and their Cokes, the girls slid off the café's leather sofa and left together to stroll around Central Park. It occurred to Chris that their lives were poles apart, but they chatted amicably like long-lost friends, talking off-the-record about their aspirations and dreams.

"I'm actually torn, Chris. My dad, John Hamilton, is American and is an attorney working here in the city, and since I'm an only child, I've always suspected he'd like me to join him in his practice. On the other hand, I enjoy the stock market and comparing corporate financials and annual reports. Daddy says I'm actually very good at it and calls me *Buttonwood*," she laughed. "He says I'm his star stock-picker and that it's part understanding the flow of business, the economy, and part intuition."

"You and I are, like, so different, Hayley. You approach money from the position of making it and I approach it from the position of saving it. I was probably shopping in a thrift store while you were researching a company's annual report. How did you learn so much about the stock market?"

"My dad saw I was interested. Daddy said that most kids my age grab the cartoon page when the morning paper comes in, but I fight him for the business section. My favorite is the Wall Street Journal and I fight him for the Sunday New York Times, too. So, one day he arranged with his financial advisor to escort me to Wall Street with Uncle Arthur. We spent a day on the New York Stock Exchange Trader's Floor. It was fascinating; so noisy and frantic and so exciting. I love doing the research on company's financials and comparing them, following the rise and fall of their stock, and deciding which ones I think will jump.

"You're weird, Hayley, but I like that about a person," Chris snickered shaking her head. "And you're way too smart and way too old for your age. But, you're teaching me what I need to do with the money I've saved. Okay, a question; why does your dad call you Buttonwood? I'm sorry, but it doesn't ring a bell with me."

Hayley laughed, "Because it was under a Buttonwood tree that a Constitution was signed to create the New York Stock and Exchange Board."

"Oh, I get it, yeah," she chuckled. "Hayley, who is Uncle Arthur? Is he famous? Should I know him?"

"Arthur Symington, who prefers to be called, 'Symington,' is not really my Uncle. It's a term of respect and endearment. I love him as though he were part of the family. No, he's not famous. He was my grandfather's manservant, his personal valet, you see, and when my grandfather died, he was bereft. Grandfather was Lord Weston Hayles Townsend-Brandley, Earl of Circencester. My mother, Lady Elizabeth Hayles-Townsend, asked him if he'd like to come to America to be here in New York with us. She told him we didn't need him as a manservant, but asked him if he would like to look after me, 'cause I was just a little kid at the time. He said he'd be a glorified nanny," she laughed, "but it turned out that he looked after the whole family the same way he looked after my grandfather. I did actually have a nanny for a while, though. He saw to it that she did her job, believe me," Hayley chuckled.

"Does your Uncle Arthur – *Symington* - live with you, Hayley?"

"Well, yes...and no, Chris. My mother bought a small apartment one floor below us, so he'd have his own private space, but he spends most of his time in the penthouse. Symington and I have a special relationship. He picked up after my parents, but made me pick up after myself, read bedtime stories to me, played games with me, and made me keep my nose in my studies. He taught me how to hold a knife, to use the right forks, not to eat with my elbows on the table, or with my mouth open, and always say please and thank you," she smiled, reminiscing. "He taught me how to manage myself in British society. We did an in-depth study of British history that turned into world history, because England's long reach circles the globe."

"Did he pick you up from school, too, with all the nannies?"

"No, I've been home-schooled all my life, but, when I got to be a teenager and didn't need close supervision any longer, he was bored and didn't know what to do. All he'd ever known was taking care of someone else's needs. My mother was concerned about idleness making him feel useless and suggested the doorman's position, either full-time or as a fill in."

"Seems like quite a come down for him, Hayley. Why would he do that?"

"He saw it as an opportunity, because it would give him something to do, and in a way, he could still look after us. It's part time. He fills in for other door attendants when we aren't traveling and he takes it seriously, actually.

Symington's quite an equestrian and he taught me to ride. We ride almost every Sunday on the bridal path around Central Park's Reservoir. When he travels with us to London, he takes me to polo matches and accompanies us to Ascot. Uncle Arthur and I will always be very close."

"How did you manage being home-schooled and traveling so much?"

"Tutors came to the penthouse, which is very large and has a schoolroom, among other things. My parents hired tutors who were experts in their fields and they designed my classes depending on where we were traveling and what was going on at the time. I have already completed the requirements for high school graduation and I could go on to college, but I want to wait. Fourteen may be too soon. I'd be too much younger than the other students and I like what I'm doing at Juilliard."

Chris remembered Hayley told her that because she was home-schooled by tutors, it made life easier in one way and harder in another. Her parents traveled all over the globe. Homeschooling made it possible for her to travel with them, but impossible to establish friendships.

"Then, I started at Juilliard in the fall last year. I wasn't with kids my age until I went into the pre-college program, you see, but I think there's no comparison between a regular school and Juilliard. So, I've never spent much time with other kids. When I did, except for the music, I found their interests and lifestyles were far different from mine."

"Do you have a boyfriend at Juilliard, Hayley? I don't. The school I go to is all girls and the teenage boys I meet want to be actors. They're used to being idolized by hot California girls and they love themselves more than anyone else ever could."

"No, no boyfriend yet, but maybe I'll meet someone when I go away to college."

"Oh, definitely, yeah. Hayley, do you know where you'd like to go to college? I do, and I have a plan."

"I've given that a lot of thought, actually, Christine. I want to go to Wellesley for my undergrad work, maybe when I turn seventeen. My paternal grandmother graduated from Wellesley and I want to feel that I'm in touch with my father's family, too. If I decide to go into finance, I may take my master's at Wharton; if I decide to become an attorney, I'll choose Harvard, Yale or Columbia Law. I think my mother would like me to consider Oxford, too. I'll always have my music, but I'm not looking at it as a career. Where do you go to school, Chris, and what do you want to do?"

"I'm a day student at an accelerated private school and I've covered the basic high school curriculum already. I love to write. I've read all the classics. Of course, I love movies. I get to go to the premieres of all the latest films."

"I think I spend more time reading newspapers and keeping up on current events, but I do enjoy reading the classics, too." Hayley glanced at Chris. "My mother and Symington see to it that I practice the piano a lot. My piano teacher plays with the New York Philharmonic and comes to the penthouse to give me lessons. He thought it was worth his time since my parents are patrons, if you know what I mean," she laughed.

"My music teacher is teaching me an instrument to keep me busy and, like, *out of trouble*. When I told her I chose the sitar, she snickered and said sarcastically, 'Of course you did.'" Chris giggled. "I love Donovan. He has soul for an old person and he plays the sitar. I'm actually not very good - *yet*, but I've just started and I'm still learning. Have you heard 'Teen Angel,' or 'Catch the Wind?' Oh, look where we are, Hayley. Is this the mosaic about John Lennon's song, Imagine?

"Yes, we've walked a long way, Christine. We're on the west side of the Park in a section called *Strawberry Fields*."

"Look at all the flowers and guitars, Hayley. I still can't believe someone would shoot him. This is a crazy world, yeah."

"It's so sad, Christine. I..."

Chris saw that Hayley was filling up with tears and changed the subject. "So, like, what were your favorite subjects, Hayley; music, of course, and what else?"

"I guess I'd have to say foreign language. My Spanish language tutor was young and cute. Uncle Arthur sat nearby pretending to read during every lesson, but he never took his eyes off Reynaldo," Hayley chuckled. "My Mum would have preferred that I study French, but I can always do that later."

"Really? You could start now, Hayley. I know! Let's study together in France!" Chris reached out and touched Hayley's arm. "Come on; what if we, like, went to Paris and studied at the Sorbonne? What do you think?"

"I think you're a maniac, Christine. But, oh, wouldn't that be fantastic?" Hayley's voice sounded wistful.

They laughed, but Chris was aware of a dreamy and faraway look in Hayley's eyes.

"I've started studying French now that I'm fluent in Spanish. It's so much fun eavesdropping on people who are speaking in a foreign language!" Chris snickered, "It's amazing what they say about you when they don't know you understand. Especially the help who have come up from Mexico; they rip us up one side and down the other.

I've gotten the scoop on a lot of celebrities, because I eavesdrop and they gossip like crazy."

"Yes, I know...I love eavesdropping, too!"

They peeped at each other like conspirators. Chris snorted, threw her head back and guffawed. Her hat fell off and Hayley caught it in mid-air. She put on the hat and hugged Chris. Their laughter was contagious and every time they glanced at each other, they giggled and laughed until they were breathless and red-faced, tears streamed down their faces.

Finally, Chris managed to control her laughter. "I want to be a writer, Hayley. I think I'd like to be an investigative reporter. I like snooping into other people's lives. I wonder about lots of things. For instance, Hayley, I've been admiring your turquoise suede jacket. I've never cared very much about trendy or expensive clothes," she rolled her eyes, "but I must be honest, the jacket is so scrumptious it's making my mouth water. I never expected you'd be dressed in western style. I guess I thought you'd be, well, more *big-city chic*." *Sniff.*

"You're right, actually, Christine. I don't normally dress this way. We just returned from Tucson, Arizona, where my father roughed it for a week at the Red Stallion Dude Ranch with his Millionaire's Club. They went on cattle drives, slept under the stars on the desert, and ate meals prepared on a chuck wagon. They get together to play poker once a month, but they got the idea to play poker and have an adventure at the same time. They liked it so much that they're planning to go whitewater rafting down the Colorado River through the Grand Canyon next year. I wish I could go with them on that trip."

"Did your mother go to the dude ranch, too?"

"No," she chuckled, "if you knew my mother, you'd know how absurd that would be. My mother's idea of roughing is to suffer a week of spa treatments and do some serious dieting. We went to the elite Canyon Ranch in Tucson while my dad was playing cowboy on the desert. I couldn't let her suffer alone, could I?" Hayley grinned and slid her eyes toward Chris. "My mother bought these duds at the gift shop. She thought the soft suede and color were exquisite, and I liked the western style with its fringes, the silver Conchos, and beading."

"Your mother has, like, excellent taste, Hayley."

"Thanks, Christine," Hayley beamed. "What are your parents doing while you're with me?"

"Oh, they're not here, *yeah* - they're back in Los Angeles. I wrapped them around my little finger, as usual, and got to come alone," she shifted her eyes toward Hayley and giggled.

"Oh, you're so lucky, Christine! My mother *never, ever,* lets me go anywhere alone. She's the quintessential over-protective parent. I'm going to work on finger wrapping! Got any tips?"

"Sure, it's simple; you just wear them down with your brattiness and whine until you get your own way. And, if that doesn't work, you, like, stomp around, and at the top of your lungs, you invoke the granddaddy of all tyrannical teenager mantras, '*You never let me do anything!*' Or, if it's appropriate, you whine the grandma mantra, '*All the other kid's parents are letting them do it!*' You have to start early; sometimes it depends on how long they can stand the pouting and whining before they give in."

"Oh, my God, Christine; you make me laugh so hard!"

"*You didn't know that*? I mean, like, what kind of teen-ager are you, anyway?"

"*I - I'm* not sure that will work with her." Hayley lowered her eyes. "But I'll give it a try. Thanks for being my inspiration," she wrapped her arm around Chris's shoulders and hugged her.

Chris snickered, "Show me your knuckle." Hayley lifted her knuckle and Chris tapped her. "That's called a *knuckle-bump.* It's the new high-five; a show of support."

They walked around the park; a tall, slim girl in a black top hat and a turquoise western jacket, and a short, stocky girl dressed in Goth style. Now and then, they paused to give money to homeless people and directed them to where they could find a meal and lodging.

"Aren't we just encouraging them, Hayley? I mean, won't they, like, spend it on booze or drugs?"

"Well, Christine, maybe," she shrugged. "But what if that small amount of money is the difference between life and death? What if they didn't know where to go for a meal?" Hayley spoke so primly, Chris thought she might be hearing Lady Hayles-Townsend's voice channeled through her daughter. *Hayley's not a child; she's much too mature for fourteen. I wonder if she's ever had a childhood.*

The day continued sunny and mild and they walked out of Central Park, across Fifth Avenue, and onto Lexington. As they strolled, Chris took two steps with her short legs to keep up with each one of Hayley's long strides and was out of breath and puffing.

"Hey, Hayley, how tall are you anyway, like, s*even feet, eight feet*?"

"All right, I'll slow down," she laughed.

Walking up Lexington, Chris saw their images reflected in Buddinghill's window and noticed the irregular shadow of her nose on her cheek.

"Would you like to go into Buddinghill's, Christine? We can check out my mother's favorite departments."

"Sure, Hayley, let's go in and get perfume samples, yeah." Chris chuckled, grabbed Hayley's hand, and pulled her through the revolving door. "I love free stuff."

Once inside the store, they entertained each other with sidelong whispered comments about other shoppers.

"Hayley, see that little girl with the chocolate candy bar zipping in and out between the racks? Her name is *Helen Wheels*. Oh, and see that man over there with the thick glasses? His name is *I.C. Clearly* and he owns a windshield replacement company called, *Pain in the Glass*. See the man over there in the orange and green shirt? His name is *Walter Melon*. That tall guy? His name is *Tim Burr*."

"Look there, Christine," Hayley whispered, breathless from giggling, "see that guy looking up at the ceiling? I think his name is *Hal Lee Luja*. "Do you see that girl with the dirty hair? Her name is *Anita Bath*." They walked past the Evening and Special Occasion Shoppe. "Christine, see that young woman trying on the pink cocktail dress? Her name is *Bella d'Ball*."

They invented clever stories about what they would be if they weren't themselves that they called, "*In My New-fangled Life*," and entertained each other by putting on wild combinations of clothes from Buddinghill's *Garb-Grabber* sale racks. They explored Buddinghill's exclusive departments and without explanation, Hayley took Christine to *Antiqué de Classiquite*. Chris observed the sales staff called Hayley, "Miss Hamilton," and they asked about her mother. Hayley bought a white lace lavender-scented sachet pillow, embroidered with lavender flowers. They wrapped it in tissue paper with perfume samples of Lady Elizabeth's signature blends, *Rhapsody* and *Rhapsody in Blue* and placed them into a metallic gold fabric bag with a card from the shop.

"This is a memento of the occasion for you, Christine, and I wanted to make sure you got your perfume sample," she chuckled. "Someday, when we study together at the Sorbonne, we'll take time off to walk through fields of lavender in the south of France."

Only later did Chris realize the shop was Lady Elizabeth's *atelier*.

One after another, Chris rattled off blonde jokes that made Hayley weak with laughter and regaled her with stories about the antics of Hollywood kids whose parents made tons of money in the entertainment industry.

"Their wild kids smoke pot; they take drugs; most of the girls are anorexic; they're promiscuous; they drive too fast; and they accumulate useless, expensive possessions. All they care about is their appearance, especially their skimpy, sexy clothes and hair."

After the girls left Buddinghill's, Hayley walked Chris back to the Plaza. When they passed the carriages lined up along the edge of the park, Chris suggested a carriage ride and an ice cream cone, hoping they could spend more time together.

"I'd love to, Christine. You may not believe this, but I've never been on a carriage ride in Central Park!"

Chris literally bit her lip to keep from blurting out that she did, in fact, believe it, and that she thought Hayley lived in privileged captivity.

The early spring weather stayed sunny and dry as the horse clip-clopped around the park along its familiar trail. The girls enjoyed the fresh air and the colorful flowers along the tree-lined paths.

"Hayley, I've never met anyone like you before."

"Christine, you are special and fun," Hayley flashed a bright smile. "I love your sense of humor and your wit. You bring out my lighter side and you've tickled a funny bone I didn't know I had! This was one of the best days of my life, and I wish I could have you around all the time."

When the carriage returned to the Plaza, Chris didn't want Hayley to leave. *There's so much to this girl.*

"We can't let this be goodbye, Hayley. Let's hope our future holds another meeting between us. There's always Paris," she giggled, "so this will be just *au revoir*. I know! Let's meet at the top of the Eiffel tower, or in New York at the Empire State Building, yeah."

"Yes, Christine, let's make a pact that we'll meet at...the Plaza...*say*...in ten years!"

"That would be like *totally awesome*, Hayley. *Yeah*, I'm up for it! Ten years from now will be 2004; we'll be old women, married with a baby on our hip, and carrying diaper bags instead of backpacks," she laughed. "It's a deal!" Chris reached out and gave Hayley's hand one quick shake.

Both girls sighed when they parted and wished each other the best of luck. Hayley walked into the park and Chris walked in the opposite direction toward the Plaza. When Chris turned around to glance back, Hayley was standing amidst shadowy trees talking to a silver haired man wearing a tan trench coat. They reminded Chris of a scene from a bad spy movie. The man nodded; Hayley turned and ran toward Chris pulling off her jacket.

"Christine, I want you to have this," Hayley was breathless and thrust the jacket at her.

"*What?* Like, are you *totally insane*? I can't take that, Hayley."

"I want you to have it, Christine, to remember me! Wear it when we meet in ten years. *Promise*?"

Chris put on the jacket and pulled off her ruby birthstone signet ring. She handed it to Hayley, who accepted the ring and placed it on her finger.

"Now the "H" stands for Horowitz *and* Hamilton!" Chris beamed. Hayley held up her knuckle for a bump.

When we left each other that day, I realized that although we were both good kids, Hayley and I were the yin and yang of teendom. I felt regretful and sad; I thought she needed someone like me in her life to keep her awake. It's too bad we waited so long to seek each other out again, but our busy lives intervened.

While Chris drove through Columbus, Ohio, she remembered thinking that although Hayley was only fourteen, she possessed substance, initiative and commitment. Hayley had made a long-lasting impact on her. From their brief encounter, Chris realized that being born into the British peerage made the difference between Hayley's world and hers. Snobbery, *old* money, and upper-crust society filled Hayley's world. Snobbery, *new* money and prejudice filled her world. In both cases, it didn't take scratching very far below the surface to find class differences.

The first time I saw Hayley, she was standing in the doorway of the dim coffee shop backlit by bright sunlight and I had merely an impression of her. On the surface, everything about Hayley, her skin, her hair, and even her voice, was as smooth as silk. That day, I peeled back layer upon silky layer to get to the core of her substance and found that she was already a highly polished adult. Compared to her I was childlike and I felt raucous and coarse. Walking beside Hayley, so graceful and serene, with every step I took, I felt like a noisy one-man band with clattery cymbals between my knees, tooting my own Oompah, and banging a big drum on my back.

I was still a child, but not her. When I look back at fourteen-year old Hayley, I wonder if her parents ever allowed her to be a child, to bang her drum, or toot an Oompah. I could blather, make all the clatter, and create all the chaos I wanted. My parents didn't care what I did as long as I did nothing to jangle their perfect partnership.

The Hamilton's catastrophe brought Christine too close to her own sense of mortality. Driving over long, straight interstate highways, she wondered about God and questioned the likelihood of the existence of an all-knowing being that allowed such things to happen. Ben was Jewish, Diane was Christian, but although neither practiced their religion, they lived their spiritual beliefs. She thought there wasn't any perceptible difference in their moral values. While she grew up, they allowed her to seek her own spiritual faith. Although she intellectualized religion and philosophy, she thought little about the meaning and nature of God as it related to her own life. *Until now.*

Having driven through the breathtaking crests and waterfalls of Yosemite Valley, over the rugged Rocky Mountains, and miles and miles of big sky, she wondered how something as beautiful and complex as this planet could exist unless created by a higher being that planned the order of the universe. *Who knows, maybe there is a God and when the Rapture comes, He'll appear to those left standing and they'll hear Him say,*

"Puh... I washed my hands of you a long time ago.
I gave you this beautiful planet and look what you did to it.
Trust me; I had no control over the havoc you've created.
You did it all by yourselves!"

But, then, what of destiny? Does this God of ours plan our individual destiny as well? Are we bound by destiny because of God's great plan for us? Does God know the end from the beginning? Does he actually plan to destroy good people through horrendous acts? If so, how does he choose who will be the persecutors and who will be the victims or martyrs? Why would a just and loving God allow innocent people to suffer so? What about diseases and disasters? Let's face it; this planet is beautiful, but most of it is inhospitable and plague ridden. What if you can get off your preordained track and not follow your destiny? What if the Hamiltons weren't supposed to die in a plane disaster; that somehow that day they got off track and they were actually supposed to live long lives? Will God make it right? Will they have another shot at life? Will Hayley?

I'm going around in circles. She shook her head. *Maybe its cause and effect and we create our own destiny through the choices we make. Somebody does something that causes something else to happen and it's all a chain of events. Maybe we don't know when we make a choice that it will likely turn out badly, or we know when we do it we're taking a risk, like placing that last card on a house of cards and not being able to do anything but sit and watch as they all fall down.*

"They all fall down." She heaved a sigh and began to sing –

"Ring around the rosie,
Pocket full of posies,
A-choo, a-choo,
They all fall down."

As soon as I get to Buffalo, I'll send flowers to Hayley at the hospital. She wiped her nose on the back of her hand, and with her fingertips, she brushed away the tears that trickled down her cheeks.

Chris realized she'd brooded about the Hamiltons all the way across the country. She questioned the unanswerable mysteries of life that philosophers contemplated through the millennia, but she also pondered a solvable crime.

Whether it's fate, destiny, God's will, or cause and effect, the fact is someone harbored a grudge big enough to want them all dead. Who hated the family enough to destroy them? I want answers to these two questions:

Who and why?

"I felt like a noisy one-man band with clattery cymbals between my knees, tooting my own Oompah, and banging a big drum on my back."

Christine

~5~

"We understand death for the first time when he puts his hand upon one whom we love."
~Madame de Stael~

Stony Point Trauma Recovery Center
Rockland, New York
July 1999

Phillip Capshaw, John and Elizabeth's trusted attorney, took responsibility for Hayley until she awoke from the coma and could make decisions for herself. John had given Capshaw power of attorney over all financial, legal, and health issues in case of his death or incapacitation. John was a thoughtful and thorough man and placed the utmost trust in his friend.

Capshaw was also the executor of John and Elizabeth's wills and estates. Irritated when their distant relatives swooped in and began to circle Hayley, he decided to get them out of the picture by calling them together to read the wills. Learning they would receive nothing from either estate, they floated away like dust in the wind.

Several weeks after the reading of the wills, NYPD detectives met with Capshaw and reported the status of their investigation.

"We interviewed all possible suspects. We found no active rocketry clubs in the area and ruled out a stray rocket. We believe it was intentional.

We interviewed the Hamiltons' associates, acquaintances, and family members, and everyone accounted for their whereabouts. After intensive investigation, there are no clues or leads to follow. Nothing tells us who shot the rocket or why. There are no serial murders connected to it, and frankly, this case has stymied our investigators and profilers. The case is going cold," they told him, "but we'll keep it open for the time being."

During the weeks of media frenzy, the reading of the wills, the police investigation, and the memorial service held for John and Elizabeth, doctors consulted Capshaw when orthopedists set Hayley's broken bones, a plastic surgeon reconstructed her shattered cheekbone, and her bruises, scrapes, and burns were healing.

"The concussion appeared not to have left any brain damage and her vital signs are stable," a doctor told Capshaw. "We believe it will be only a short time before she wakes. Of course, there is no way of knowing."

"Doctor, what is her condition? How do you know there is no brain damage?"

"We've performed tests...EEG and CAT scans. They show everything is normal with her brain function."

"Then, I don't understand, Doctor. Why is she still in a coma?"

"We don't know, Mr. Capshaw; you must be patient. Sometimes they just don't *want* to wake up. They're happier flying among the fairies."

"I see. I suppose I'm anxious. Tell me; what will happen when she awakes? Will she remember what happened? She'll be in a bad way, I fear."

"When coming out of a coma, a person will often be confused and can only slowly respond to what's going on. It will take time for the person to start feeling better. Whether someone fully returns to normal after being in a coma depends on what caused the coma and how badly the brain may have been affected."

"In Ms. Hamilton's case, Doctor, can you speculate on what she'll have to deal with when she awakens? I refuse to contemplate her not coming out of it."

"To be honest, Mr. Capshaw, it's complete and utter hell. There are tubes in her bladder and throat and anywhere else we could manage to put a tube to put things in or take things out of her body. However, patients don't feel too much while they are flying with the fairies, but when they start to wake up and become more responsive, that's when it becomes hell on earth... especially when everything is pulled out."

Capshaw's stomach lurched. "Please go on, Doctor. This is difficult, but I want to hear your prognosis."

"Sometimes people who come out of comas are just as they were before. They can remember what happened to them before the coma and can do everything they used to do. Other people might need therapy to relearn basic things like walking all over again. They may also have problems with speaking or remembering things. She hasn't stirred, so we don't know the extent...*but*, in Hayley's case, the good news is that there are perceptible internal signs of improvement. So, we're not looking for a miracle - *yet*."

Later that evening, Capshaw slumped into his worn leather recliner. With the tiny Yorkie in his arms, he whispered a prayer for Hayley's recovery.

"Perhaps she'll make it, Diva, and wake up from this nightmare." He held her up and sadly looked into the puppy's face. "But, I fear when she does, she'll be thrown into a nightmarish world."

"*Doctor, she moved!* I think she's coming out of the coma...Hayley? Hayley, can you open your eyes?"

That voice is close...so close...it doesn't echo inside the bubbles like the others...

So thirsty...how long have I been sleeping? Eyes feel heavy...can't force them open.

Oh, God...please stop the pounding in my ears. Cymbals banging - clang...clang...clang-clang-clang...

How long have I been sleeping? Where was I when I fell asleep? What was I doing? Thinking? Oh, yes...I was thinking about Christine. I have to get up now. I have to be there when she arrives in Southampton... Want to get up...can't move. My body aches...arms heavy...head hurts...What happened to me?

"Hayley...Hayley...*dear, can you hear me?* Doctor...her eyelids are fluttering..."

Fluttering? Oh, yes...I see butterflies fluttering...beautiful colors...and frogs, jumping and floating on the bubbles. Does she see the bubbles, too?

"She's trying to say something, Doctor."

The doctor removed the tube from Hayley's throat so that she could speak.

"Her voice is so faint that it's hard to understand her." The nurse turned her ear closer to Hayley's lips. "Tell me again, Darlin'."

"Well, what did she say?"

The nurse's somber face broke into a grin. She giggled when she straightened up and faced the doctor.

"Well, it sounded like she wants to know if I saw her butterfly bubble gum."

The hushed room came alive after the doctor buzzed the staff with the good news. The nurse standing bedside held on to Hayley's hand as though fearing that if she let go, the young woman would slip away from her grasp and slide once again into oblivion.

There was exhilaration in the doctor's voice when he clapped his hand on the nurse's shoulder.

"Well, woman, don't just stand there; go and get the young lady her damned bubble gum! And, I know someone else who will want to celebrate this awakening, too. Get Capshaw a big box of Bubbalicious cigars!"

When Hayley awoke, Capshaw sped to the hospital to question her doctor.

"Unfortunately, she's in a profound state of confusion, not knowing how she got here...and she's crying for her mother. She's suffering from mild dysphasia; *uh*...that's difficulty articulating speech. She did try to utter a few words when she awoke, but nothing comprehensible – something about bubbles and butterflies. She'll need physical therapy and psychotherapy. We can recommend a private facility where she'll spend time in therapy under the care of staff psychiatrists skilled in working with patients who suffered trauma from violence and tragedies."

Before long, Hayley was fully awake and aware of what happened. She fell into a deep depression. Her mental state was of chief concern to doctors and nurses who advised Capshaw that she was traumatized and emotionally unresponsive. Seven weeks later, when they were sure her bones had healed well enough that she was ready for physical therapy, Capshaw had Hayley moved to Stony Point Trauma Recovery Center in Rockland, New York.

Barbara Gabriel-Johns had called Capshaw while Hayley lay in the hospital, but he was not forthcoming with information. Hayley had been at Stony Point for several days when she spoke to Capshaw again. After their conversation, she rang her son.

"Peter, I have explained my connection to the family, but that attorney, Capshaw, will only give me carefully worded updates on Hayley's progress. I can tell he's hedging and I have concluded that Hayley isn't doing all that well. You must fly to New York to visit her in the recovery center."

"Mum, you know I respect your wishes and I have the utmost regard for your insight and judgment, but this time I'm not altogether sure that I should do what you're asking. The young woman's doctors might see me as meddlesome, or fear a clash of professional opinions."

"You *must* go to her, Peter. I will not take *no* for an answer! I can't get anything straight from that attorney and I want some assurance that she's all right."

To please his mother, Peter contacted Hayley's doctors and explained that his mother was a friend of Elizabeth's and that she thought it might benefit Hayley for him to visit.

The psychiatrist on her therapy team presented the request to Hayley and saw a brief spark when he mentioned her mother's artist friend, Barbara.

He returned Peter's call, telling him, "She didn't say no, so you might as well come ahead. But don't expect too much from her."

A few days later, Peter sat on the plane mulling over how to approach the patient, wishing his mother hadn't forced him into this uncomfortable position. What can I tell her about why I'm there? My Mum sent me, he scoffed. Certainly, I'm not making this visit in any official capacity, even though I admit I'm interested in the case as a clinician. I'm not going as a friend. We've never met. Using my mother's connection as a friend of her mother's is best after all.

The staff psychiatrist assigned to Hayley was coming out of her room when Peter arrived at the hospital. He nodded, offered his hand, and the doctor barely acknowledged him. The man kept his hands in his pockets, not shaking Peter's hand or recognizing him as a colleague.

"I'm not sure what your expectations are, or even if she's up to a visit just now, but you can try your luck."

The doctor rolled his shoulders as though shrugging off an unwanted burden. Tall, sallow and bald, he dressed in black and wore a gloomy expression. *Doctor Doom*, Peter thought.

Peter inclined his head toward the door, "Can you describe to me what's happening with Miss Hamilton right now?"

"Neurologically, the slight brain trauma that caused the coma has healed, but frankly, she's terrified of strangers and panics when the staff tries to go into her room. She's terrorized when a new face shows up. I've warned them repeatedly; they need to let me prepare her for new people. She refuses to see anyone from the outside and won't allow mail or flower delivery." Leaning his back against the wall, the doctor glanced up at Peter, peering at him through narrow black slits over the dark bags under his eyes. "Actually, I was surprised when she agreed to allow this visit. You are the exception."

"I see," Peter nodded. "I'll be very careful how I approach her. I understand her mental state, but how have her physical injuries healed?"

"They used ultrasound bone growth stimulator and the breaks have healed well. She says the physical therapists are trying to torture her and won't let them near her. She won't talk to any of the other psychotherapists or to me; she says we're trying to brainwash her. We simply haven't been able to get through to her," he sighed and shook his head. "I'd hate to think she might wind up cloistered in an institution," he mumbled, looking at the floor.

"Oh, I think not; there may be a long way to go, but she's young and has so much to live for. I've no doubt she'll eventually come round."

"Hmmm," the doctor looked into the distance, "you haven't seen her yet. She's very agitated. She just awakened from a horrendous nightmare and before you arrived, she was wailing and crying out for her mother. I've given her a sedative to calm her. I hope you've polished up your bedside manner, Doctor. You're going to need it."

"Perhaps I can distract her for a few minutes," Peter turned his face away, thinking the man needed to work on his own bedside manner. He requested that the doctor precede him to prepare her for his visit. He agreed and then came out and advised Peter that he could go in. Peter thanked the doctor, took a deep breath, set his jaw, and went into the room.

What Peter found behind the closed door dismayed him. The slight young woman was hyperventilating and shivering. Although the room felt chilly, her short blonde hair was dark with perspiration. Her face was pale and expressionless from the sedative, but her skin was smooth and clear without a hint of the cuts and bruising she'd suffered.

The room was dim and austere with walls painted a mind numbing military green and contained only a bed, an overbed tray, a cushionless wooden side chair, and a dresser. Outside the day was sunny and bright, but there were no windows in the dismal room. A single fluorescent light above the bed was the only illumination and it made the corners of the dreary room dark and shadowy. There were no personal items of any kind -- no flowers or cards, nothing cheerful -- except for one lone picture on the wall opposite the bed, which seemed to absorb the patient's attention. The room was silent except for her ragged, staccato breathing.

"Hullo, Hayley, I'm Peter Gabriel-Johns," he spoke in a soft voice and slowly approached the bed. You assured your doctor that you would see me."

"Yes," she whispered, her voice weak from sedation and exhaustion. "Why have you come?"

"I'm here on a mission for Barbara Gabriel-Johns in England. We're glad you remembered meeting her. She's sent me to cheer you. She insisted that you'd love me, so I said, 'Brilliant! I'm off to New York to see Hayley."

"Brilliant," she murmured, repeating the word without expression or emotion. Her eyes slid sideways to glance at him and then drifted back to the landscape on the wall in front of her.

"What do you think about the picture, Hayley?"

"The road is going over the hill," she whispered, "I can't tell where it's going."

"What else can you tell me about it?"

"It's going into the unknown. Like me. I don't know where I'm going. I'm lost and alone, you see."

Hayley remained motionless except for visibly shivering and trembling.

"Yes, I do see," he replied softly and sighed deeply.

Peter stood in front of the picture so that Hayley would focus on him. He looked into her eyes then, the deepest, clearest pools of aquamarine he'd ever seen. She continued to stare ahead and he felt as though she was looking through him, lost in the unknown.

"Hayley, I'll come and sit beside you, if that's all right."

"Yes, all right," she murmured, and lay motionless when he moved toward her.

Peter brought the chair to her bedside and she tugged at the sheet with her frail hands. It seemed impossible for those fragile fingers to play the kind of music she performed. He tried to help her adjust the covers and she recoiled when he accidently touched her hand.

"You're shivering, Hayley, and your skin feels icy. Do you feel warm enough?"

"I don't know... No. I'm cold. I'm *always* so cold."

"I'd like to get another blanket to cover you."

"No. Please don't bother. I don't want to be any trouble."

"It's no trouble at all and I'll tell you what we'll do. I'm off for a moment to find more blankets. When I return, I'll tap three times, so you'll know I'm at the door. I'll cover you, and whilst I sit beside the bed, I'll hold your hands in mine. My hands are warm and toasty."

Peter returned with warmed blankets and a dry pillow. He tucked the blankets around her, replaced the sweat-soaked pillow, and gently brushed away the damp hair clinging to her forehead. He sat bedside and placed her hand in his open palm. She flinched as though contact with his flesh shocked her, but then, her long, slim fingers relaxed and his touch seemed welcome to her. He covered her hand with his and she glanced at him again. After a few moments, she inhaled deeply and her body relaxed for the first time that morning.

They sat together for two hours while he warmed her hands, first one, and then the other. He hummed classical melodies and themes from musical stage plays and when he stopped, the room was so silent and empty he could hear her swallow. Sometimes she appeared far away and he wasn't sure she remembered he was there.

An attendant tapped at the door and brought in a lunch tray. He took the tray and rolled the overbed table closer to Hayley. After a few minutes, Peter felt that if he weren't there, she might eat. It was time for him to leave. He cleared his throat and asked if she wanted anything.

"No. There is nothing I want." Her face was drained and passive, and the lunch tray sat untouched.

"Suppose there is something I want you to have, Hayley, may I bring it to you?"

"No. Please; I don't want anything."

"Well, then. It's time for you to eat and rest, so I'll be going."

"Will you come back?" She looked like a frightened child whose parent was abandoning her to the care of strangers. It was the first time he saw any expression on her face, but then, her eyes drifted back to the picture.

"Will you talk to me if I come back?"

"Yes, I'll talk to you tomorrow."

"Good, then I'll come back and stay longer so we can talk. But if I do, you'll have to share your lunch with me."

"You can have it all, but you won't like it." Hayley said, glancing at him. He saw the slightest smile curving her lips. "What do you want to talk about?"

"Well, let's see. You think about something happy tonight and so will I. We'll talk about that, all right?"

She turned her pale face toward him. "Promise me you'll come back tomorrow?" Her voice was timid and she pleaded with her eyes.

"Absolutely, I'll see you bright and early, all right?"

"Yes," she murmured, her voice husky, and for the first time she looked into his eyes.

"But you must promise me you'll eat what's on this lunch tray." He pulled it toward her and took off the dish covers.

"I'll try," she said faintly, looking into his eyes again.

"Before I go, Hayley, I want to tell you something about my youngest brother, Matthew." Peter took her hands and held them, pleased that they were much warmer now. "Matthew can be very astute at times. He has always enjoyed reading Shakespeare and he fancies himself an actor. I remember this so well. Matthew cried buckets when we lost our beloved old bulldog, Churchill. My brother, William, and I were keeping a British stiff upper lip. We refused to cry, talk about our grief, or our love for Churchill, but then Matthew said something to us that helped us express our feelings."

He looked into her eyes and quoted Matthew's passage from Shakespeare:

"'*Give sorrow words. The grief that does not speak whispers the o'er-fraught heart and bids it break.*'

I'll leave you with that thought, then, Hayley. Now, you eat your lunch, get some rest and let's look forward to a pleasant talk tomorrow."

Peter didn't want to break the upsetting news about Hayley's condition to Barbara, but he'd promised to ring her that evening.

"Mum, you were right to send me. She's a lovely young woman, and I'm sorry to report this, but she's beyond despair, so traumatized and withdrawn that she isn't able to respond to those around her." Peter's jaw tightened thinking about her bleak existence. "She's all but institutionalized and entombed in a barren room. The frustrating thing is that it's her choice; she's too frightened to allowed caregivers to help her. I must say, they're a dismal lot from what I've seen. They lack sensitivity and the warmth she needs. Her own doctor is a caricature of an undertaker."

"Peter, I'm aghast," Barbara sat down, worried and upset. "You *must* help her. How long can you stay with her, Darling?"

"A couple of days, Mum; I have an important research project deadline looming over me and I have patients waiting."

"Then make the most of the time you have, Peter, dear. *Please help her,*" Barbara sobbed, her eyes flowing with tears.

"I'll do my best, Mum," Peter replied softly. "Give Dad my love."

When Barbara hung up the telephone, she went into her husband's arms and wept.

On the second day, Peter returned wearing a new shirt that he'd found in a shop selling colorful men's summer clothes. He had brought only grey and blue tailored shirts with him. He wanted to add something bright to her room, even if it were only a sunny yellow, red, and orange plaid sport shirt.

He tapped on Hayley's door and when he stepped inside, she greeted him.

"Oh, I hoped you'd be here soon."

He smiled warmly; her eagerness delighted him. "Yes, I've arrived a tad later than I intended. I stopped on the way to do a little shopping. How are you today? Did they adjust the thermostat as I asked? The room's temperature seems pleasant compared to yesterday."

"Yes, my hands aren't so cold. Feel them."

He gazed for a moment at her outstretched hands and her skin appeared translucent in the dim, blue-white light.

"That's wonderful news, Hayley," he sat on the edge of the chair and leaned toward her. "Oh, and this is for you." He reached into a shopping bag. "I have a warm jumper to keep the chill off your shoulders. I've brought flowers, too. Do you mind?"

"You brought flowers?"

"Yes, a vase of pink rosebuds." He stood to help her into the jumper and then pulled off the green florist's paper from the flowers.

"They're lovely. You are the first one to bring flowers since I woke from the coma. They said there were hundreds delivered to the hospital, but I haven't allowed anyone to bring anything from the outside into the room since I arrived here, you see."

"If there were a window in your room, we could open the curtains and we'd be better able to see the bouquet. This room is dreary, Hayley, and it's a beautiful summer day. The sun is shining, the sky is bright blue, and the clouds are billowy and white. There are birds singing in the trees outside the building."

Her hand came up to protest. "No! I don't want a window in my room."

"Hayley, an outside room would be more pleasant. The sunshine might raise your spirits."

"No, please. The outside scares me. Someone might get in."

"You're on the third floor, Hayley. No one is able to get in."

"Oh, I know," she bowed her head, "but I'm afraid they might shoot something through the window."

Peter couldn't argue with her logic considering what had happened. He decided to change the subject and asked her, "Hayley, do you remember who I am and why I'm here?"

"I know that you were sent by my mother's artist friend, Barbara. I remember meeting her in London at the gallery and having tea with her at the Ritton. She's beautiful and charming; her paintings are treasures. Of course, I remember your name is Peter," and she added, "like Peter Rabbit." A hint of a smile played on her lips; she turned her head toward him to see his reaction and gazed at him from under lowered eyelids.

"Yes, just like Peter Rabbit." She took him by surprise and his hearty laugh echoed in the silent room. "You're teasing me, aren't you Hayley? That's all right. You can tease me all you like, but be forewarned; I've had a lot of practice verbally fencing with my two brothers."

Pleased to see a spark of humor rising through some of the layers of her gloom and grief, Peter was delighted that his visit was having a positive effect on her morale.

"Hayley, Barbara Gabriel-Johns is my mother. My father's name is Edward. I'm the eldest of their three sons. My father and mother live on a 1,200-acre estate in Oxfordshire called, Seven Valleys, which they refer to as the farm -- and it is a working farm, actually. My father's hobbies are making wine from his vineyards and growing roses. Here, I have brought with me a book about roses for you." Peter reached into the bag and withdrew a large, colorful book.

A slow, spreading smile tiptoed across Hayley's face. "Thank you, Peter Rabbit. May I see the book?"

He helped her hold it as it was quite large and they shared the book for some time. Peter described the Seven Valleys estate, their mansion, the farmland and parkland. He told her about his father's prized rose gardens and the acres of vineyards.

"Hayley, it looks to me like pink roses have begun to leave these pages and are flying up to your cheeks," he teased.

She smiled at him when he touched her cheek. "You know, my mother was quite fond of roses and grew many varieties around our home in Belgravia."

Peter glanced at her when she mentioned her mother to gauge her reaction to the thought. She seemed all right and he decided to push ahead.

"Hayley, how did your parents meet? Do you feel up to talking about it?"

"Oh...yes, I try, Peter," she said softly and looked down at her hands. "They met at Oxford, actually. My father was attending a seminar and my mother was a student who volunteered as a guide for anyone wanting to tour the university. My father said he took one look at my mother and she swept him off his feet. He waited for her to graduate and then came back to see her in London. He courted her and when he proposed, he promised her she could have the freedom to do whatever she liked with her life. After a very short engagement, they married in Westminster.

She established her design business in New York and travelled to England and Europe to work with clients. After I was born, she didn't travel as much until I got a little older. Something happened during my birth; I know it made her unhappy that she was never able to have more children.

I was very close to my parents. We were inseparable and to be honest, I found their company far more satisfying than casual friendships with other young people. Your turn, Peter," she exhaled deeply.

"All right, then." He shifted in the hard chair and leaned against the bed closer to her. "Well, I've heard this story so many times. It was my favorite at bedtime, actually. The story goes that my Aunt Patricia wanted to visit England and my mother had promised to go with her. Toward the end of their vacation, the two girls received an invitation to a polo match. Patricia was a bit bored, but my mother, an art student, entertained herself by filling a sketchbook with action drawings of horses and players. She still has that sketchbook; I love looking at those drawings. Even then, she was a skilled artist.

Well, it came time to replace the divots. After patting a divot into place on the lawn, my mother stood up and backed into a tall, blonde young man who was standing too close behind her. When he turned round to apologize, he was dumbstruck. It was love at first sight when my father met my mother. His heart fluttered and flip-flopped, he said, 'when I saw a virtual prima ballerina in a pink ruffled dress stuffed with crinolines underneath.' He wasted no time in asking for her hand in marriage.

When my mother told the story, she'd say, 'I went to Seven Valleys to live with your father like a princess in a fairy tale.' They had no luck having children and then ten years after they married, the three of us came along, one right after the other. I was first, then William, then Matthew. Theirs has been a brilliant, loving marriage. They are both extraordinary people and I love them dearly. And you know, I understand what you mean when you say that you found their company satisfying. I have always enjoyed being with my parents...while as a child, and now as an adult. Although I am fully able to care for myself, they are my rock."

At the end of the day, Peter asked if she'd like him to bring anything to her. She thought for a moment.

"Yes, I would like music. I miss hearing music."

"What would you most like to hear?"

Hayley's expression froze. She turned her head away and began to weep silently. After a moment, she spoke through her tears. "I would...*most* like to hear...the sound of...my mother's voice." Her expression crumbled and she dissolved into racking sobs.

Peter sighed deeply and his voice broke. "Ah, Hayley, I'm so sorry, of course you would." He wanted to gather her in his arms to comfort her, but merely cupped her hands in his. "Can you think of something beautiful about your mother? What about a happy memory of a time or place that you shared together?"

"Peter, when I think of my mother, my mind is flooded with memories of the last time I saw her. It was just before the explosion. I remember her loving smile when I took her puppy out of the carrier." Hayley's expression was bereft and she swallowed hard. "I have been over this so often in my mind that I've committed to memory every word...every gesture...every nuance. I never want to forget those happy last moments with my parents.

We had just attended my Wellesley graduation and were flying to Southampton for a few weeks of sun and relaxation before we were off to England. I remember my dad took off his jacket and reached into the pocket for a purple velvet jewelry box tied with a pink satin ribbon. He said, 'Hayley, before we take off, your mother and I want you to have this token of our affection. We hope it will always be a reminder of our pride in you, Darling.'

I said, 'Oh, Father,' and pulled off the ribbon. There was a wide gold bracelet studded with diamonds twinkling in the purple satin lining. It had my initials, H.E.H. engraved on it. I thanked them and asked my dad to clasp it on my arm. They haven't retrieved it, so I suppose it was lost in the debris.

Mother enjoyed serving gourmet *hors d'ouvres* on short afternoon flights. I filled a small plate with poached pears stuffed with goat cheese wrapped with Parma ham, and several toast points spread with Beluga caviar and truffled fois gras. When I returned to my seat, I looked at the adorable Yorkie puppy lying in the carrier and asked my mother if I could hold her, 'because I want her to get to know me,' I said.

She said, 'Of course, Lamb, come and get Diva now, before Marshall starts to taxi to the runway.'

I hurried, because the pilot was just beginning to move the plane. 'I love her name, Mum,' I said, and murmured to the puppy while I lifted her out of the carrying case. I held Diva up to look into her face and I giggled when she licked my nose. I snuggled her into my arms, kissed the top of her head, and turned to make my way back to my seat.

'Wait one moment, Hayley,' my dad held up his hand, and said, 'I'd like you to join us for a glass of champagne.'

Marshall taxied the plane at the top of the runway and waited for clearance. I stood in the aisle bracing myself against the seat back. Dad popped the cork, poured *Dom Pérignon* into three crystal flutes and handed a glass to my mother and me. We raised our glasses and my dad said, 'Here's to our daughter; you are your mother's and my pride and joy. We're happy that you chose to walk in the footsteps of another wonderful woman from Oxford University - your mother. The future holds our greatest pleasure, Darling, and that will be to see you grow into a strong and independent woman.' When I think about what he said...and know what I know now..."

Hayley fell silent and Peter saw tears welling in her eyes. She sighed and continued, "At the time, I thought how unlikely that was. My close relationship with my parents and their tight grip on my life precluded that I ever would be liberated and self-determining. I think my mother took advantage of my eagerness to please her and she controlled my life.

I remember thinking that I am so unlike Chris Horowitz, who is my ideal independent woman. I couldn't imagine anyone telling Christine what to do; she'd defy the saints." Hayley chuckled softly and glanced at Peter. "I remember thinking about the day we spent together in Central Park. We were both only fourteen at the time. There never were two girls so different, but we were different in all the right ways. Our peculiarities made us misfits within our own groups, but together, we were a perfect fit.

Just before the crash, Chris sent me an announcement telling me that she graduated from Stanford University. When I received it, I wrote inviting her to our Southampton beach house to vacation with me before we left for England. I was more excited at the prospect of seeing Chris again than I was about going to Oxford.

I knew your mother had invited us to the celebration at Seven Valleys. I was to go with her, of course. My mother planned and scheduled everything according to her wishes and I assumed she had an ulterior motive. It wouldn't have surprised me if she had something cooked up with Barbara.

Peter, the memories of the crash and my horrible loss, fill my days and haunt my nights. I thought if I didn't talk about it, it would be as though it never happened, but it's always there, you see. I'm so afraid, Peter. I'm afraid to even talk about it."

"Hayley, please go on; tell me your memories. I'm here for you...to listen. You don't have to be afraid to talk to me. I promise you, talking about it will help."

She tearfully related her agonizing memories of the inferno that took her parents from her. Peter nodded and held her hand. He didn't speak, so that he didn't stop her momentum.

She sighed, "I'm never really alone, because fear is my constant companion. If only they'd find who did it; if only I *knew* who did it, because in not knowing, I fear something will pounce upon me at any moment and it could be anyone or anything. I'm afraid to trust anyone. And I'm angry, Peter! I don't understand why, but I'm angry with my mother and father for leaving me all alone! Yes, they gave me principles, a moral upbringing, and an appreciation for the finer things in life, but I'm angry that they didn't prepare me for what lies ahead. And I'm so angry that someone took everything from me that mattered in my life."

"Hayley, you've suffered a horrendous, life-altering trauma. I'm not sure anyone or anything could have prepared you for what will be your future. Your fear and mistrust are understandable. Humans fear change and the unknown – it's normal. The important thing is what we do about it. The best antidote to fear is to know all we can about a situation and find ways to adapt.

I'm sure the police are continuing their investigation to find whoever did this, but in the meantime, you can't shut everyone out; it's not healthy. Hayley, fear of the unknown is harmful when we permit it to paralyze us and let it interfere with our proper reaction. Your fear of one unknown is why you're shutting everyone out. You aren't afraid of me; I know you trust me. Isn't there someone else you trust who you'd like to visit with you? Haven't you friends your own age you'd like to see?"

"No, I can't trust anyone. There is no one left except Symington who doesn't drive, but I haven't asked him to come. What will I do without them, Peter?" she sobbed, "This is not the world I expected and I don't know how to go about creating a new life for myself. Above all, I don't want to live in a world without my mother and father."

Peter left Stony Point weary that day. Although it had been difficult and painful for her to break her silence, she'd been able to express her mourning and talk about her fears. It was a major breakthrough. Trust was another issue. Peter knew it wasn't enough to *tell* her there were people in her life she could trust; he'd have to prove it to her.

Later he called Barbara to report the day.

"Mum, this has been too hard; I've gotten too close. I sensed her pain when she describe the ordeal as if I had been there, feeling it myself." Peter knew that he had to soften the message, or his mother would break down. "She became much more alert as the day wore on, and to my surprise, I discovered she has a keen sense of humor. We talked all afternoon about our families and she had a breakthrough. She discussed her memories of the crash and her fear about the future. I found her intelligent and sensitive...rather poetic, actually. Earlier we had discussed music and theory, composers and their lives, and compared centuries of musical styles. She discussed the topics with enthusiasm. I told her that someday we must play a violin and piano duet."

"Oh, Peter; I think this is all wonderful. When I met her, I found her quite knowledgeable on many subjects and although I couldn't say we indulged in witty repartee, I found she does have a keen sense of humor."

"Yes," Peter chuckled, "she does. Our conversation was stimulating and enjoyable to me and we discovered interests in common and found we share many of the same ideals."

"I knew it!" Barbara smiled at her husband after she hung up the phone.

The next day would be Peter's last day in New York. His practice and his studies at Oxford were awaiting his return. After he hung up the phone from his call to his mother, he placed a call to Phillip Capshaw and made special arrangements for the following day.

When Peter arrived at Stony Point the next morning, he found Capshaw waiting for him in the lobby eating a donut and drinking coffee out of a container. Peter was surprised; he looked nothing like a successful New York attorney with his straggly red brows and bushy red mustache. He wore a green paisley bow tie and a red plaid vest with its buttons straining over his rotund middle. He cuddled the family's puppy in his arms and the dog was trying to catch the crumbs from his donut when they fell from his moustache. Capshaw told him on the phone that the dog had fully recovered from a broken rib and multiple lacerations.

The two men spoke cordially while walking down the corridor.

"Hayley doesn't know I've asked you to meet me here, so I think I should go in first, Mr. Capshaw, and prepare her for your visit."

They met the doctor coming from her room.

"I don't know what magic you've performed, Dr. Gabriel-Johns, but she slept through the night for the first time without waking from a nightmare. She's eaten her breakfast and requested two comfortable chairs for her room. I believe she's waiting for you."

Peter tapped on the door and poked in his head. Hayley looked rested and was in far better spirits than the day before. The dark circles under her eyes had vanished and her skin had a healthier glow. She was out of bed, dressed, and sitting in an armchair wearing her new jumper.

"Hayley, look at you! I'm delighted." He paused and cleared his throat, "My dear, I know better than to surprise you, but I've brought someone with me who has something lovely for you. I'm positive you're going to be pleased."

Protesting, Hayley began to rise, but Peter stopped her and folded her hands into his.

"Please trust me, Hayley. Do you trust me?"

She stared at the floor and for a brief moment, Peter held his breath, fearing she'd refuse him.

She sighed deeply, "*Y-Yes*, I think so, Peter."

He breathed an imperceptible sigh of relief. "Do you remember your father's attorney, Phillip Capshaw? He's been working on healthcare, legal issues, and estate matters on your behalf."

"Yes, of course I remember Phillip. I always called him *Lippy* because of his wild moustache." She smiled faintly at him, "Oh, it's all right then; yes, I'll see Lippy."

"He's also been a caretaker for someone we thought you'd enjoy seeing." Peter strode to the door and gave Capshaw a high sign.

"Hello, Hayley, my dear girl," Capshaw grinned as he entered the room. "Surprise! I've brought Diva with me. She's all better now and we thought you'd like to see her. After all, you are responsible for saving her life."

Hayley gasped when she saw the curious dog observing her from the safety of Capshaw's arms.

"*Oh, Diva, Diva*! Oh, thank you, Lippy!" Tears sprung to Hayley's eyes, but at the same time, her smile widened, "I've longed to see her and hold her. May I?"

"Of course, Dear; if only we'd have known," Capshaw's wide smile was hidden beneath his moustache. Hayley's face brightened when he placed Diva into her outstretched arms. "I'll bring Diva twice a week to see you if I may. I'll take good care of her until you're well enough to care for her yourself."

When Capshaw left with Diva, Peter told Hayley it was time for him to return to England.

"And now, that leads me to my last gifts, Hayley. I have brought you a CD player with an earpiece and a few discs as well. I rather assumed you'd enjoy piano and violin concertos."

She took the gifts and a smile curled up the corners of her mouth. "Thank you, Peter; this selection is perfect."

Peter saw it as a good sign that she accepted his gifts.

"Please ask Capshaw…um…*Lippy* for any other discs you'd like to hear and he'll bring them when he brings Diva to see you. I've fixed it with him. Your father's trust in Capshaw was implicit, Hayley; I feel you can place your trust in him, too."

"All right, Peter. He's trustworthy, I'll admit," she said seriously, nodding her head.

"Please open this box, Hayley. I looked everywhere for what I wanted and finally had them specially made. I think you'll see why when you open it."

"Peter! A box of white chocolate roses, so delicately made. The pastel colors are lovely. They're too pretty to eat. I don't know what to say."

"You don't have to say anything, Hayley. Just enjoy them. And this gift is from my mother. She wrapped it in Christmas paper but she'd like you to open it now, please, Hayley."

"Oh, thank you, Peter. I wonder what it could be," she glanced at him while she opened the box.

"She sent me pink mittens and a pink cashmere Pashmina." She stroked the soft wool and rubbed it against her cheek.

"My mother thought you'd like the color and that you might need them when you leave here."

"Please thank Barbara for me, will you, Peter? She's been very thoughtful."

"I will, Hayley." With a lopsided grin, he said, "I've one last gift for you, so you will remember me and my visit." He brought out a little book from behind his back. "Here is Beatrix Potter's, *The Tale of Peter Rabbit*."

"Thank you, Peter…*Rabbit*, but I know I'll always remember you."

Hayley turned the book over in her hands while a lone tear slid down her pale cheek.

"Hayley, I must get back to my work in England, but..."

"Peter, Take me *with* you. I'm not safe among these strangers! Please don't leave me here," she pleaded miserably. "When you leave I'll be so alone! Peter, I have *never* been so alone."

Peter's heart thumped in his chest, his hands trembled, but he willed himself to be strong. When he spoke, he struggled to keep his voice from cracking.

"You must try to bear in mind, Hayley; these people are here to help you. When you get to know them, they will no longer be strangers and you will trust them. I've an idea; before I go, let's call in the doctor I met and talk to him. We'll start with him; he doesn't frighten you, does he?"

"No, he's all right, I guess. He's just so...*dour*," she rolled her eyes.

"Good. Yes. Well, then." Peter couldn't help but agree. "We'll ask him to introduce someone he trusts to you and so on, until you've met everyone. Perhaps you'll meet someone with an actual sense of humor," he quipped. "Hayley, the sooner you work with the therapists and allow them to help you regain your emotional and physical strength, the sooner you can return home. You'll be able to leave when everyone agrees you can take care of yourself."

On his return to England, Peter sat comfortably in First Class on British Air. He tried to sleep or think about other things, but his thoughts continually returned to Hayley. When she opened herself to him, she went from a childlike and unresponsive state to an intelligent, eloquent and talented young woman. Someone, for some reason, destroyed her family, and her whole world was gone. She would no longer live in the world she knew; from now on, she would live in a world apart.

Hayley's qualities deeply affected Peter; they resonated within him and his emotional reaction to her caught him off guard. Her words entered through a tender spot in his mind and heart and something about Hayley drew him into a transcendent connection that never happened before. When he touched her, held her hands, and kept her warm, he shared her healing almost as if their hearts were beating as one.

Hayley's distress and pleading in their last moments together were agonizing to him and leaving her in that gloomy place wrenched his emotions. His desire to take her with him and protect her was palpable, but it wasn't possible. She would need a period of recovery and who knew how long that would take?

Confused and weary, he lay back drifting on a sea of melancholy. *I'm not sure if I've left my heart with Hayley, or if I've carried her heart away with me in my heart. All I know is that I didn't want to leave her.* He closed his eyes and wondered; *what does my mother know that I do not?*

Landing at Heathrow, his father, Edward, met Peter and drove him to Seven Valley's to pick up his Bentley. Over dinner, he gave his parents an in-depth report about the three days he'd spent with Hayley. Barbara was pleased with Hayley's progress, Peter's success, and with herself for standing her ground.

"It was love at first sight when my father met my mother. His heart fluttered and flip-flopped, he said, 'when I saw a virtual prima ballerina in a pink ruffled dress stuffed with crinolines underneath.' He wasted no time in asking for her hand in marriage."

Barbara Gabriel-Johns

~6~

"And how am I to face the odds
of man's bedevilment and God's?
I, a stranger and afraid in a world I never made."
~ A. E. Housman~

Stony Point Trauma Recovery Center
Rockland, New York ~ to ~ New York City
December 1999

Thanks to Peter's efforts in bringing them together, Hayley and Lippy forged a friendship of their own while he brought Diva to see her twice a week. The attorney was a caring and gentle guardian and she depended on him.

Gradually, Hayley began to trust and respond to those who were there to help her and after several months of therapy, the staff assured Capshaw that she was far enough along in her recovery to leave Stony Point. Capshaw felt ambivalent. He knew that Hayley still relived the fiery crash in flashbacks and in moments of melancholy. Recurring nightmares often robbed her of nights of sleep and he knew that whoever destroyed her life was still out there.

He couldn't think of anyone who would want to harm the Hamiltons for any reason. Who was the target? Was it John? Elizabeth? If it's Hayley, then she's still in danger, and until they apprehended the person behind this heinous act, she would always feel afraid. He wasn't sure she should be on her own. She was pale and still in a fragile emotional state, but she wanted to leave. She told him she chose to go to her parents' Manhattan penthouse on Park Avenue and trusted him to arrange for her return.

"I want to go home, Lippy," she had said, "now where would that be? *Home* isn't really a place, after all. It's a *feeling* and it's in my parents' penthouse where I will feel their presence and love. That's what will make it home."

On a bleak, overcast December day, Capshaw drove to Stony Point for the last time. His mission was to deliver Hayley safely to the Top of the Turret. When he picked her up at Stony Point, she was wearing a long black coat, her pink mittens, and the Pashmina.

Hayley was quiet during the drive, watching the scenery change from country, to suburbs, to city. Lippy had brought Diva with him and holding the little dog in her arms comforted Hayley, but her thoughts were far from cheerful. *The world is stark and grey, just the way I feel inside.*

Looking at him with a sidelong glance, she broke the silence. "It was July the last time I rode in a car, Lippy. The weather was hot and sunny, trees were green, and there were flowers everywhere. Today it's cold and the trees are barren. Six months, Lippy, six months of my life are gone, along with my beloved parents, all my hopes, dreams and stability," she sighed deeply, "now I'm going home." *I'll be home soon, but it will be an empty, lonely world.*

Again, she sat silent and motionless until she said, "Lippy, I want to thank you for opening the penthouse and getting it ready for me. My mother's housekeeper left for England right after her death and it's been closed up until now."

"Of course, my dear; it was my pleasure. The couple you and my secretary found as a housekeeper and bodyguard pleased her, and she said they have made an outstanding effort to make the penthouse welcoming for you. Who are they exactly, Hayley?"

"Their names are Marisol and Miguel Alvero. They were born in Puerto Rico and moved to New York with their families. They were married one month before their interviews. They speak some English and I'm fluent in Spanish, so there won't be a language problem. Your secretary hired an investigator to look into their background and families. They were perfect, so we hired them."

Marisol and Miguel Alvero assumed their responsibilities of caring for and protecting Hayley by preparing for her arrival. Hayley established a routine once she settled inside the penthouse, but she was determined to shut out the world. She trusted only Miguel, Marisol, and those few outsiders who came in to provide services.

Capshaw followed Hayley's orders not to forward requests to contact her. He rebuffed reporters who continued to seek an interview. At first, Peter and Barbara called Capshaw often to inquire about Hayley and requested to speak to her. He assured them she was doing well, but he was unauthorized either to arrange a meeting, a phone call, or to deliver personal correspondence.

"She's just not receptive, Dr. Gabriel-Johns. I have to admit, this puzzles me. You were instrumental in breaking through to her while at Stony Point. I should think she'd welcome a call from you and your mother. She just doesn't seem responsive; I'm sorry."

Christine Horowitz tried to reach Hayley. "Tell her it's Chris Horowitz. I just want to see her. Remind Hayley we met in high school when I wrote an article about her. Ask her if she still has the signet ring with "H" for Horowitz and Hamilton. Tell her I still wear her jacket. She invited me to vacation with her in May in Southampton. Maybe she'll see me if you remind her of that."

"I'm sorry, Ms. Horowitz, I have strict orders from Ms. Hamil-"

"*I don't care*, Mr. Capshaw! She *needs* me. Please; I *must* go to her."

Capshaw had to disappoint Christine and rebuffed everyone who contacted him by phone and mail. Symington turned away anyone unauthorized by Hayley at the entrance to the building. Therefore, with the exception of those in her employ, no one ever made it to the twentieth floor of the residence tower.

The penthouse was far more spacious and luxurious than Hayley needed, but her life wasn't about space or luxury; it was about a link to her parents and her need for safety. When she walked through the rooms, it was as if their spirits surrounded her. There, twenty stories above the streets of New York City with the rest of the world locked out, she felt safe. She existed inside the walls of a sanctuary that buffered her from the menace of the outside world, the fear of the unknown, but most of all, the fear of whoever shot down the plane.

She knew the monster was still out there...waiting.

~7~

"Happiness is the only sanction of life;
where happiness fails,
existence remains a mad and lamentable experience."
~ George Santayana~

Top of the Turret Residence Tower
Park Avenue
Manhattan, New York
May 2004

Hayley moved into the penthouse in December 1999. Although she lived in a cloister, she was constantly aware of the world outside through television news, newspapers, and magazines. A study of the stock market was a reflection of the global economy and the world situation.

Three years after her parent's death, not only had her world changed, the entire world changed after the horror of Al-Qaida terrorists crashed two commercial passenger airliners into the New York World Trade Center's Twin Towers. She watched televised events unfold in disbelief while the media replayed the human drama like a recurring nightmare.

After 9/11, she wondered if a random terrorist attack had brought down the Learjet. Nightmares of the explosion that killed her parents returned, and in the aftermath, she wondered if she ever wanted to live again outside her sanctuary in a world of terrorism, war, and intolerance.

By 2004, Hayley had become a habitual recluse. She continued to shut out everyone who wasn't necessary to provide services, or to make her life comfortable inside her sanctuary. Those who worked with Hayley called the penthouse, *Command Central*, and it bustled with activity most days with people coming and going providing business, household, and personal services to Hayley, Symington, Marisol, and Miguel. Hayley reestablished her life in a familiar pattern, recreated much as her parents structured their lives using the penthouse as a home business address.

Shortly before Hayley completed her senior year at Wellesley, John hired an architect to modify the 9,000 square foot penthouse as a residence to serve as their home and a business place to suit their needs and his wife's tastes. A separate entrance in the foyer served employees and professionals who entered their offices. The spacious business suite was equipped with a library for John's collections of law books and literature, conference rooms, Elizabeth's studio, office, and personal service areas. The family used the penthouse as their own personal community and as the nerve center for their many business and charitable enterprises. Everyone had come to them to provide services.

Hayley saw the renovation for the first time when she arrived home after leaving Stony Point. She wasn't surprised that Elizabeth had added a gym, a Jacuzzi and sauna with a spa for private services that she had arranged including a personal trainer, a masseuse, a stylist, a nail technician, and dog groomer. Hayley arranged for these people to continue providing the same services.

For all her public work, Hayley knew her mother was a very private person. It was obvious that her mother not only enjoyed her privacy, but was an elitist who organized her life to avoid rubbing against the *hoi polloi*.

Hayley's social life as she knew it before the tragedy was gone. After she moved into the penthouse, her parents' former associates offered many invitations that she declined. The family had been involved in philanthropic and cultural events, held soirées and parties for Elizabeth and John's clients, supported many artists at gallery exhibits, and fund-raised on behalf of politicians. They never missed the opening night of a new Broadway play. Elizabeth and Hayley attended designer collection shows in New York, Rome, and Paris. Hayley no longer desired designer clothes, or new shoes, or to eat in the best restaurants, or any of the other things privileged young women like to have or like to do.

Other than a violin student from Juilliard who came in weekly to practice piano and string duets, only people she hired surrounded her. In that regard, she didn't live a simple life; she lived a structured life with many responsibilities. Hayley worked hard with her stockbroker overseeing estate investments. Lippy and an accountant met with her in the penthouse office to work on legal and financial matters.

A member of her accountant's staff worked with Buddinghill's to add *Antiqué de Classiquite* to their on-line store. Buddinghill's was one of the first department stores to realize the sales potential of the internet. Lady Elizabeth's dressmakers were still selling her made to order classic designs on Buddinghill's website. They added the *atelier's* signature blends, *Rhapsody and Rhapsody in Blue* to their on-line products for sale. They came packaged as perfume, cologne, body lotion, and bath oil, sold alone and in sets. The products were some of the store's leading sellers.

Hayley used the profits from the sale of the fragrance products to purchase musical instruments for children in the Harlem School District and funded the Lady Elizabeth Hayles-Townsend annual scholarships given to students at Pratt Institute for the study of Fashion and Interior Design. Recently, she'd forced herself to accept an invitation to honor a Pratt Institute scholarship recipient. However, when it was time to go, staying home with a good book seemed a more appealing alternative.

By far the most important people in Hayley's life beside Arthur Symington were Marisol and Miguel Alvero. Hayley provided them with a two-bedroom furnished apartment one floor below the penthouse next door to Symington's one-bedroom and she respected their privacy. She made no demands on them other than what she hired them to do and they were free to live their lives as they pleased.

They respected Hayley's choice to live a reclusive life, managed her household, cared for her needs, and protected her. With the exception of Symington and those who provided for her or worked with her, Hayley was alone in the world with only a tiny Yorkshire terrier to love.

If it were not for Diva, Hayley would find little reason to leave the penthouse. Clarissa, a young college student, walked Diva afternoons, evenings, and weekends, but Hayley needed motivation to get up in the morning.

Accompanied by Miguel, she walked Diva to the Park East Café each weekday morning. The café was a familiar and comfortable place to sit and enjoy coffee, or other specialized delicacies and beverage concoctions prepared by the owners. For Hayley, it was a pleasant link to the past. The hustle and bustle of the Café felt good to Hayley and she felt safe with Miguel walking beside her and sitting nearby. She avoided conversation or eye contact and ordered coffee to take back to Symington for his morning break.

On any morning, the café was crowded and noisy with friendly chatter and lively conversations of men and women stopping for a break after an early run in Central Park. They sat in groups on sofas, or alone on comfortable chairs, turned on their computers, or chatted on cell phones. They enjoyed their morning coffee and some bought take-out for work, or like Hayley, walked their dogs to this welcoming and cozy Café.

Hayley was not someone you would notice as she drank a *café au lait* and browsed on her Vaio notebook computer. She blended into the coterie like any other young woman in her mid-twenties with her long hair tucked under a black New York Yankee's ball cap with her large sunglasses placed above the brim. She wore a faded black Wellesley sweatshirt and worn out jeans frayed at the cuffs above her worn Reeboks. She carried a small, black leather backpack.

Hayley was lost in thought as she sat at a table with little Diva on her lap. She gazed out a window at a world of which she no longer felt a part; a world of fashionable streets already crowded with upscale shoppers and of young people leading their happy, sad, frantic lives with jobs, plans, and friends.

At an adjoining table, a bearded, middle-aged tourist with a Georgia accent sat with two women. He read aloud from an opinion column about the Upper East Side in a newspaper taken from a stand outside the door. The words fell dully on Hayley's ears.

> "*These verdant, tree-lined neighborhoods, with their multitude of cultural attractions, famous Museum Mile, exclusive luxury apartments and trendy restaurants, are home to many celebrities and politicians. This secluded world of privilege and affluence is separated from the rest of society not only by the artificial boundaries of streets, parks and rivers, but its residents couldn't live in a more class-built fortress if they were protected by high, thick walls. This privileged class is shielded from peril by private security guards and polite doormen with impressive gold-braid stripes on their military style uniforms.*"

The man wore a brightly colored Hawaiian shirt and straw hat. Hayley noticed that slung around his neck was a clunky old Canon camera with a huge telephoto lens. He paused, and out of the corner of her eye, she saw one of the women flip her nose with her finger, and say, "*Well, la-de-dah.*"

She watched the women snicker and slyly glance about the Café comparing themselves to other customers. Then, the three tourists discussed their next stop -- Ground Zero. They left the café to continue their journey, but while they sat there, they hadn't taken notice of Hayley, a young woman who by some measure was typical of the well-to-do who dwelled in the haven about which they just read.

One Friday morning on their return, Hayley and Miguel walked toward Symington standing guard and protecting the entrance to the exclusive Top of the Turret Residence Tower. Not ten-feet away was the entrance to an adjacent building undergoing reconstruction. The crew temporarily barred the main public ingress to prevent access to the work site and the building's foyer was last in the order of renovation. A homeless woman had crept inside the dark entrance to take refuge. Even in sections of the city such as the Upper East Side, vagrants crawled into unused spaces to find shelter. No one bothered her and she considered this dank, stale doorway her home.

Wrinkles threaded and crisscrossed this shriveled old woman's face much like a dried-up apple. The knees on her thin legs bulged like tight knots in ropes. She carried a red backpack and wore someone's cast off red running shoes that were too large, making her look like a whimsical bobbing bird toy with its big red feet and long, white legs.

When she ventured out, she wore round, black glasses frames with no lenses, usually dangled an unlit cigar from her lips, and wore a battered Aussie hat on her head. Most of the time she stayed behind the loosened raw board barrier, but every day, through slits in the loosened boards, the little beggar peeked out to watch Hayley and Miguel going back and forth on their morning walk. She could smell the aroma of hot, fresh coffee Hayley brought to Symington. She wished Hayley were bringing the coffee to her, but she knew after they'd gone inside, Symington would pour some of his coffee into her little tin cup. The coffee was good, but oh, how she longed for a delicious cherry and cheese sweet roll from the Park East Café. The money Hayley gave to Symington wrapped around his coffee cup - she wanted that, too.

On this balmy Friday morning in April, as Hayley and Miguel approached Symington, the wiry little vagrant popped out of the doorway. In a flash, her scrawny legs carried her to within an inch of

Hayley, stopping short in front of her and waving a dirty, crinkled paper under Hayley's nose.

Startled, Hayley exhaled sharply and jumped, splashing hot coffee on her hands and clothes. She scooped Diva into her arms, but the woman teetered and nearly fell against her, causing the frightened dog to snarl and bark. In a flash, Miguel was between them using his well-muscled body as a barrier. The woman lost her balance and her head thumped against Miguel's chest.

Screeching, she crumpled to the ground. Lying flat on her stomach, she kicked the ground with the toes of her big red sneakers and pounded the sidewalk with her fists, whining and pleading with Hayley.

"*No! No! Please...please take this paper. You must take it. I know this. I saw it in my dream. You must have it,*" she wailed. "*You are the swan!*"

Hayley ran to stand beside Symington. Gaining her composure, she called to Miguel, "Please accept the paper and give her some money."

Frowning and grumbling, Miguel helped the woman to her feet, not wanting to touch her or the paper. "Do not approach *Señorita* Hamilton again," he growled, holding out a five-dollar bill.

The eccentric little vagrant snatched the money from Miguel's hand and shoved the paper at him. Relieved that she completed her mission, she turned to face Hayley and Symington with a grin of satisfaction. She glared at Miguel, drew her heavy gray eyebrows into a frown, and pursed her thick lips into a pout. Then, with a loud, "*humph,*" she yanked the filthy Aussie hat over her matted hair. Turning away from Miguel, she scurried through the cracks into her refuge.

"It's all right, my dear," Symington said to Hayley, while he used a clean handkerchief to blot up the spilled coffee, "don't be afraid. She's harmless. I've kept my eye on her since she showed up. I've occasionally shared my morning coffee with her. I was sure you wouldn't mind."

Relieved to be safely inside the penthouse, Hayley plopped on a sofa and slowly filled her lungs with air. She hadn't realized she was holding her breath. She glanced at the paper in Miguel's hand.

"Miguel, I'm sorry you had to touch that paper, but will you please ask Marisol to wrap it in plastic so we can read it?"

Miguel returned with the sealed paper and sat on the arm of the sofa.

"See," he pointed to the scrawled writing. "It looks like *un niño* write this."

"Yes, it does appear as though written by a young child with a black crayon. Look how the lines overlap. She'd said it was from a dream and to me it reads like some kind of dreamscape language. Why would that woman dream about me? Is this a premonition, or some imagery from the past?"

Cold chills ran along her arms while she read the words –

the black Panther casts its shadow on the horse and swan
the snake will come but the swan is not afraid
the swan will help the snake shed its skin
the snakes rise will help the swan mount the winged horse
the swan must stay on the horses back
the black Panther and the ravens will find the swan
the ravens beaks break its wings and the swan cannot fly
the ravens take the black Panther into the fire

Hayley sat in her sanctuary contemplating the meaning of the cryptic imagery and listened to her favorite Strauss opera, Der Rosenkavalier. As a child, she'd gaily waltzed and twirled around the room with Symington, delighted by the enchanting confection of melodies. Like Hayley's life, the way of life that once glistened in the world of Vienna so lovingly depicted in Strauss' opera, soon died in the trenches of death and destruction.

Melodies filled the rooms of the penthouse and while she sat listening, Hayley compared herself to the Rose Knight. Someone had thrust a sword into her and she ceased to exist.

By late afternoon, the waning springtime sunlight lent a golden glow to the walls of the gracious room. Hayley contemplated with sadness how these possessions came to be hers. *Really, what are they? All this material wealth is a constant reminder of my terrible loss.*

Shrill police sirens seeped through the music from twenty stories below. The wailing from the street nudged the place where the terror lurked. It was a chilling reminder of a time she was desperate to forget.

"Why?" she whispered, "For God's sake, why?"

Hayley would give it all up – she would give up everything - if she could only feel her beloved parents' arms around her again.

"She wore round black glasses frames with no lenses, dangled an unlit cigar from her lips, and wore a battered Aussie hat on her head."

Dream-Girl

~ 8 ~

"So let me assert my firm belief
that the only thing we have to fear is fear itself –
nameless, unreasoning, unjustified terror which paralyzes
needed efforts to convert retreat into advance."
~Franklin Delano Roosevelt~

New York City ~ Oxford City
May 21, 2004

Hayley often thought about Peter Gabriel-Johns during the years since they'd met at Stony Point. Up until now, she didn't want to see anyone or think about anything to remind her of that terrible time in her life, but she had thought about him. She remembered his words and that she'd begged him to take her with him that last day –

> *"Hayley, fear of the unknown is harmful when we permit it to paralyze us and let it interfere with our proper reaction. Your fear of one unknown is why you're shutting everyone out."*

She knew he was right, but the fear had been too great. Then, in May, she'd searched for his name and discovered Peter's website, exactly five years after the crash. She now had a link to the person who jump-started her recovery. Peter listed symptoms, treatment overview, coping skills, lifestyle choices, and therapy choices for people suffering from agoraphobia and traumatic stress disorder. He wrote that he was currently the head of Oxford's Simon Wessely College for research in Traumatic Shock and Panic Disorder. He earned his MD in Psychiatry at Cambridge, went on to earn his PhD in Psychology at Oxford, accepted a consulting position at Wessely, and became head in 2002.

There was an image of Peter on the website. Disconnected when they met, Hayley hadn't notice how handsome he was. She remembered she thought his eyes were kind and his gentle smile was comforting. His voice was calming and there was the familiarity of his well-bred British accent. That wasn't all; there was something else familiar about Peter. She couldn't define it -- she couldn't explain it -- she could only feel it.

She got up from the computer and walked to the bedroom to find the box she had tucked away in the top of her bedroom closet. Standing on a chair, she pulled down a hatbox from the shelf and sat on the edge of the bed. She emptied the box and Barbara Gabriel-Johns' card, the mittens, Pashmina, and Peter's books tumbled out.

On the card, Barbara wrote of her fondness for Elizabeth. She said that she grieved for her friend and felt a terrible personal loss. She invited Hayley to turn to her and come to her for comfort and support when she recovered.

There was a small book, *The Story of Peter Rabbit.* Hayley chuckled when she remembered she called Dr. Gabriel-Johns, "Peter Rabbit," and that he'd given her the book when he left Stony Point.

Of course, at the time she had no idea about his profession. He told her only that his mother sent him to cheer her, but his visit turned the tide for her. She regretted not being able to respond to calls from Peter and Barbara, but until now, she was too withdrawn from the outside world.

After considering whether to ask Lippy to contact them, she decided to take a direct approach and write to him on his website address. She wanted the communication to be less official by emailing him at the address on his website.

In her first message to Peter, Hayley wrote --

"Dear Dr. Gabriel-Johns,

I wanted to tell you that I have thought many times how much you helped me when you came to Stony Point and how much it meant to me.

It's been five years since my parent's tragic death and I have become a virtual recluse, sequestering myself in their home. Now I am searching for answers to help me escape from the existential prison I have built in my mind that now has become my physical prison. I have been happy here, though, because this place reflects my mother's spirit and my father's ideals, you see, and it's here that I feel their presence and love.

I saved the little Peter Rabbit book, the book about roses, the mittens and Pashmina, and your mother's card. Please tell Barbara that I appreciate her sending you to me.

Hayley Elizabeth Hamilton"

"Dear Hayley,

I'm delighted to receive your message and have wondered many times over the past five years how you were getting on. I contacted your attorney, who I remember you called Lippy, and my mother urged me repeatedly to contact you. She will be happy as am I, that you have found my website and have reached out to me.

Hayley, I would like to continue to help you, but not in any official capacity. I would rather reach out to you as a friend. However, I can recommend a sensitive and intuitive therapist in New York City for you when you are ready.

Please write to me any time, or call me at the University or at home. My numbers are at the bottom of this message in the signature. I will always be delighted to hear from you and perhaps together we shall find a way for you to recover from this tragedy.

Peter"

~9~

"Lust's passion will be served;
It demands, it militates, it tyrannizes."
~ Marquis De Sade~

Oxfordshire, England
May 2004

Peter went for an early run on Saturday morning. When he returned to the house, he made a cup of tea and logged into his website's email account. He was pleased to see a new e-mail from Hayley. He felt sad and dismayed after reading her first message and was determined to do anything he could to help her. While he was reading, his work mobile phone rang, interrupting his concentration.

"Hullo, this is Dr. Gabriel-Johns, speaking."

"Peter, Sean here. I'm sorry to disturb you on a Saturday, but I rang to tell you that somehow I created a glitch in Zara's new computer program and it's skewed a student's project making the results unreliable."

"Thanks, Sean. Don't worry; we'll sort it out. I'm on it."

First, Peter decided, I'll call Zara and then I'll take some time to write to Hayley. With that, he rang Zara Chandler, now his college's technical consultant who was an expert in computer technology, network management, web design and development. Zara was up to speed on all new programs and in demand whenever the young tekkies mishandled their computer network's hardware and software.

While Peter worked with Zara for five years he had sensed -- *well, more than sensed* -- she'd like more of him and his free time than he was willing to give. She was an excellent technician, always dependable, and so he overlooked her interest in him for the good of the college. *It's Saturday, but maybe she's available.*

Zara Chandler rolled out of bed and stumbled to the bathroom sink. Groggy, hung over, and nauseated by a foul taste in her mouth, she turned on the water tap and grabbed her toothbrush and toothpaste. While she fumbled to open the cap, she examined the ravages of last night's binge in the mirror. Her eyes were swollen and bloodshot. Her skin was blotchy; here it was sallow, there it was red, several deep creases etched in her cheek from sleeping with her bloated face in a pillow, and her hair spiked like spring crabgrass.

"Ugh," she grunted at her reflection and grumbled in a raspy voice, "Sodding bloody hell; not an altogether pretty picture, Zara, my dear."

She scowled, slumped forward, and rested her forehead on the mirror, trying not to gag while she brushed away the beastly taste from the night before. It was almost noon; she had slept far too long after a late night of trolling from pub to pub on the outskirts of Oxfordshire. The locals she knew in the pubs were always there on Friday nights and when she became bored with her mates in one pub, she took off for another, until in a back alley, she moved to the twisting, gyrating music that only she and her lover-of-the-night could hear.

Even in her early forties, Zara's physical appeal was considerable to men who looked for a sexual liaison, but had no interest in a relationship. She knew she could always find a bloke who, at the end of the night, would follow her to a dark corner for a quick bang. Zara kept people at arm's length unless it was her idea to make an acquaintance. Friday nights were an exception. On Friday nights, she'd take it where she could get it.

Earlier in her youth, she bewitched, married, and recently divorced her last husband who turned into a lazy, insufferable bore. He'd grown fat and she was disappointed that he replaced his desire for her with cravings for sausage rolls, pasties, trifle, and soccer on the Tele. Now, there were no men in her life, except for a few strays she used for sex.

Saturday is an easy day, Zara thought, while she splashed cold water on her face. She grabbed a damp towel from the dirty wash and wiped off the water. When she held the musty towel against her face, she breathed in a scent that reminded her of her mother's home in London. She sighed, tossed the towel in the laundry basket, and tried to remember where she'd left a new bottle of aspirin. She decided it must be in the kitchen. An aspirin bottle and a Bloody Mary were her best friends on Saturday morning after a late Friday night binge with a different kind of bottle.

Clumsy and unsteady from the hangover, she lumbered down the steep staircase in bare feet to the kitchen below, squinting and wrinkling her nose as the bright sun reflected off the polished wood floor of the foyer. She headed to the kitchen of the fifteenth-century cottage.

The kitchen was stuffy and the foul smell of rotting fruit sitting in a bowl on the counter prickled her nose. When she opened the French doors to the garden, the brightness of the midday sun made her eyes water. She gasped as a rush of cold air hit her face.

It was chilly spring weather for England. Roses were late to bloom as were the usual profusion of flowers and climbers on trellises and ivy-covered walls surrounding the garden. Zara's head pounded and she didn't notice the cold weather, the lack of flowers, or the rotting fruit.

"Where is that bloody analgesic," she moaned.

She found them on the counter under a magazine, then poured tomato juice and a jigger of Vodka into a tumbler, popped three aspirin in her mouth and washed them down. She padded to the front door where the newspapers and yesterday's mail collected on the floor. Bending over, she gathered them and returned to the kitchen, tossing them on the table.

After making a pot of coffee and slathering a piece of toast with Marmite, she lit a cigarette and slid onto a bench at the kitchen counter in front of her laptop computer. Hunching over it, she booted it up and logged onto her forum, On Board the Great Escape, to read the members' current posts.

The forum was Zara's toy, a plaything. As an administrator on the forum, she hid like the Great Wizard of Oz as though working behind a curtain, pulling all the levers, making others believe what she wanted them to believe just as she did in her real life.

The program accepted her password and after she viewed new messages on the front page, she validated two new members, Jacques Bonnier from London, who chose the forum name, "Frenchtoast," and Christine Horowitz from Cleveland, who chose the forum name, "Witzend." Then, after sending acceptance e-mails, she returned to the New Members page, posted a stock welcome to them, and began to read new posts.

Zara was one of three administrators who contacted experts to moderate discussion rooms in various sections on the forums.

"Oh, bloody hell," she groaned, her hand went to her aching forehead when she remembered a promise to find a moderator for a one-time discussion requested by people with stress-related disorders. There were many who posted on the Relationships and Lifestyles section that could benefit from professional advice and counsel but could ill-afford it.

"It has to be Peter," she muttered. "I'll ring him today. Peter would be perfect and I must convince him to do it."

It was fortunate for Zara that Peter's call came in at that moment.

"Hullo," she grimaced, the ringing of the 'phone jangled in her head.

"Zara, this is Peter Gabriel-Johns. I'm glad you're at home."

"Peter! I was just thinking about you," she forced a bright perkiness into her voice.

"Oh? Well, Zara, Sean's having a bit of a problem with a software program for a student's research. Would you be a dear and see about sorting it on Monday? He's trying to work with the results and he's stuck."

"Of course, Love," chirped Zara, "I'll see to it straightaway. There's no need to wait until Monday and then Sean won't be held up." She went on; "Oh, Peter, I was going to ring you today, actually. I have a small favor to ask," she took advantage of the unexpected opportunity.

Peter thanked her for offering to sort the problem on the weekend and waited to hear what she wanted.

Zara hesitated for a moment deciding how to put it to him -- "Peter, I was thinking; would you fancy discussing this favor over dinner? Are you free tonight? Can you meet me? Mind you, it will be my treat! It will be easier to discuss this bit in a relaxed atmosphere."

"I suppose I can, Zara, but it will have to be an early evening. I have an important family obligation tomorrow morning."

"Oh, that's brilliant," she twittered. "I'll see you at the Cygnet round eight then, Peter!"

Zara hung up the phone before Peter objected to her choice of venue. This dinner played into a personal agenda she launched that began with casual lunches and meetings with him after she had designed a program for one of his research projects. Zara was obsessed with Peter and now focused her undivided attention on him. She enjoyed having a man in her life for obvious reasons and she'd already chosen Peter Gabriel-Johns as Mr. Zara Chandler, the fourth.

Peter had been in her sights for years. She'd schemed and tried every maneuver with him she'd used on her conquests in the past, but failed to make headway. Oh, yes, they jogged together on an occasional weekend morning, but Peter was a marathon runner and her pace was too slow for him. Several years ago, he told her to find another running partner.

Peter was different from her other conquests; his father was descended from Baronet Saint-John of Basing, a title created by King Edward the First in the year 1299, a title that was now extinct. Through centuries of marriages, the family name had evolved into

Gabriel-Johns. She knew his wealthy parents lived in a seventeenth century manor and they'd given him the house in Oxford City on woodsy Cranmer Close when he became a Don.

Smug and self-assured, she murmured, "It's time to move forward to the big payoff." Using her wit and charm, she would make this a fantastic evening of dining, wining and seducing, after which she would entice him to join her in a room at the Cygnet for the night, or preferably in her own cozy bed at home.

She sighed, first a little troubleshooting on the research software and then a lot of repair work on herself before she met Peter for dinner. The day would not be as carefree as she'd hoped, but perhaps at its end, it would yield a heavenly reward.

After his discussion with Zara, Peter sat at his file-cluttered desk listening to Dvorak's Romance for Violin and Piano. He removed his glasses, rubbed between his eyes where they pinched his nose, and reflected on her.

He first encountered Zara when he planned his own research project, and later he contacted her to review his college's computer programs. Since then he'd hired Sean to manage their research programs and in-house software, but in the meantime, she'd located empty space in the Psych Department and pitched a tent.

As time went by, he realized it might have been a mistake to allow her the privilege of setting up an on campus office in the building. She made him uneasy with her coquettish glances, flirtatious smile, and too many prying personal questions into his romantic life, but he kept putting off asking her to find space in another building. He couldn't find a suitable explanation other than to say, you irritate me, which seemed a tad too rude.

Peter was not happy with himself for accepting her invitation. Zara never before requested a dinner meeting, but tonight seemed a special occasion in her mind. I should have pushed her to tell me what she wanted and let it go at that. He suspected she had an agenda behind this meeting and he didn't want to encourage any romantic schemes.

Because he was part of an elite group, she'd made obvious overtures letting him know she fancied him taking her as his date to upper social class fundraising events, university social gatherings, or private dinners that were by invitation only.

He'd already put a stop to an occasional weekend run or ride when she tried to manipulate him to ride the horses on the family's estate. He saw it as a blatant maneuver to introduce her to his family.

This request was a new and different horse from Zara's stable.

"Well," he heaved a resolute sigh, raised an eyebrow, and muttered, "I'll ride her horse out and see where she plans to lead me."

~10~

"One thing I've learned in all these years is not to make love when you really don't feel it; there's probably nothing worse you can do to yourself than that."
~ Norman Mailer~

Wolds-on-Thames
Oxfordshire, England
May 2004

Zara arrived early at the Cygnet, a picturesque Inn that sat upon a rise overlooking a pleasant inlet in Wolds-on-Thames, South Oxfordshire. She chose this hotel for its elegant haute cuisine, mellow candlelight, and romantic atmosphere. The hotel required formal dress for men after six o'clock in the dining room. She knew Peter's good breeding would oblige him to wear proper formal attire and she had worn what she thought was her most stylish and sophisticated dress to be his equal.

It was nearly dark when she walked from the carpark over a fifteenth century stone bridge that spanned a waterfall. She shimmered from head to toe wearing a sequined silver lamé cocktail dress, her ears sparkling with dazzling diamond jewelry. Rhinestones studded the clear plastic stiletto heels of her silver shoes. She wore her spiky red hair slicked back into a pompadour and held with a small diamond clip.

Pleased with herself for maneuvering this rendezvous, she wanted to assure there were no distractions while she wove her spell. Approaching the maitre d', she asked for a secluded table inside a private cove in the back of the dining room. He escorted her through the maze of tables, set with sparkling crystal and white linen. The

Inn's renowned chef created delectable entrées that he served on elegant English bone china.

Aware that she attracted covert glances from other diners, Zara played it to the hilt and shimmied with a hip rolling gait. Always one to savor the limelight, she vamped like a flashy showgirl, or a glittering celebrity.

Seated and waiting for Peter, Zara admired her carefully applied makeup in a small gold compact. Her breath caught in her throat when she saw him striding through the front door. In the few seconds that he stood at the entrance searching for her through the roomful of diners, myriad impressions and reflections went through her mind.

The overhead halo lights illuminating the entrance shone on his full head of sandy blonde hair. An unconscious mannerism, he ran his fingers through an unruly lock that fell over his forehead. The halo cast shadows on his face and highlighted his chiseled features, wide forehead and square jaw. He was tall, well built, and possessed the essence of a Hollywood matinee idol. Lesser circles would consider Peter a hunk, Zara mused. He had expressive light blue eyes and a beautiful smile. She admired his straight, even white teeth and a tingle of excitement went through her as she imagined how later in the evening his curved, masculine lips would feel pressed against hers, first soft, tantalizing, then hard and passionate...his tongue trailing down her neck...on her nipples...kissing her breasts...

He was handsome and had a *caché* that appealed to her. Yes, she thought with satisfaction, sizing-up this handsome, distinguished man, I should be well-sorted married to Peter Gabriel-Johns.

Peter spotted Zara and nodded, gesturing that he saw her. While he made his way to her table, he greeted other diners and chatted briefly to delay the inevitable.

"Good evening, Zara," Peter reached her table and extended his hand. She ignored his greeting and clutched his neck. She pulled him forward and sought his mouth, but he twisted his cheek toward her. He heard her inhale deeply when she air-kissed him on both cheeks, but quickly backed away when her scent assaulted him; the musky perfume mixed with the smell of alcohol and cigarette smoke that clung to her.

"Charming frock, Zara," he glanced at her plunging *décolleté* while he took his seat. It left little to his imagination.

"Thank you, Peter." Zara stroked her slicked-back hair and puckered her lips. "You're quite posh yourself tonight. I like the subtle stripe of silver in your tie with your blue shirt. It sets off your...*and oh*, your monogrammed cuff links are *smashing*, Peter!" Zara lifted Peter's hand to look at a cufflink, holding on far too long for his comfort.

The waiter approached the table and greeted them politely while offering a wine list and menus.

"Good evening, Antony," Peter greeted the waiter cordially. He knew the young man well. When he'd returned from Afghanistan, Peter saw Antony professionally to help him through a difficult bout of traumatic stress.

"Good evening, Dr. Gabriel-Johns." Inclining his head toward Zara, he smiled and said, "Ma'am."

Antony recited the specials of the evening and asked if they were ready to order drinks. Zara gazed sweetly at Peter and reluctantly freed his hand.

"Why don't we choose our entrées before we select our wine?"

Peter agreed and they skimmed their menus. Zara chose her entrée.

"I'll have almond and truffle-crusted pavé of halibut and white asparagus. Ask the chef to sauté the asparagus in extra-virgin olive oil. I want them well coated. Are they fresh? If they're not fresh-cut today, then serve me ratatouille nicoise. I'll have pomme dauphine as well."

Zara looked away from the menu with a haughty tilt of her chin. She gestured toward Peter as if to say, "Your turn." Antony chuckled faintly when Peter rolled his eyes.

"And for you, Doctor?"

Peter read from his menu, "Roast hand diver caught scallops and grilled cauliflower beignets sprinkled with fresh parmesan. That sounds quite delicious to me, Antony."

"May I suggest a wine selection to go with your fish entrée, Doctor?"

"*No!*" Zara's sharp voice cut him off. "I think we should have a French *Voignier*. Do you agree with me, Peter?"

Peter shrugged and Antony agreed, "An excellent selection, Madame."

Antony happened to have been standing at the window when Zara crossed the bridge from the parking lot. To him, she appeared like a glowing wraith caught in the reflected light from the Inn. He was surprised when he saw Peter Gabriel-Johns was the woman's companion, but he supposed the Doctor had his own good reason.

He took their menus and left the table sniggering. Standing beside the maitre d', Antony continued to observe the woman from across the room. Turning his head, he whispered behind his hand. "Mate, that arrogant wench's dress is so tight, if she sneezes, sequins will explode all over the dining room." Smirking, he turned his back to Zara and muttered, "The tart has all the appeal of a dolly peg, you know? A wooden clothespin doll, the face painted on the knob, the top dipped in bright red paint, and the pin rolled in silver glitter." He stole a glance at Peter; "Yup, the good Doctor thinks she's a dolly peg, too," he swallowed a chuckle, "but he's keepin' a stiff upper lip."

Considering Zara's staging, Peter knew there was more to this evening than just a request for a simple favor to command a dinner here; an Inn with guestrooms. He braced himself, because he suspected she was about to whip her horse into a lather.

The Sommelier served their wine and Peter sat back in his chair willing himself to relax.

"I'm certain you'll enjoy the wine, Peter. It has a creamy flavor that goes well with seafood. Her smile was coy and she added, "I happen to like a creamy feel in my mouth."

Whoa, Peter thought, when he caught the deep throat allusion; *off and running already, are we?* He'd suspected this was where she wanted to lead his horse, but he controlled his reaction with a well-practiced façade.

He raised an eyebrow and cleared his throat. "All right, Zara, time to share your request."

Without speaking, she sipped her wine, peering at him over the rim of her glass. Peter studied her while she engaged in seductive posturing. Her bright red lipstick made her lips look like a thin, bloody gash. Even with all the dramatic make-up, her eyes lacked depth, like flat, unpolished green tourmaline stone. *This woman hides many secrets behind those eyes.*

"Come now, Zara; the favor...what is it?" His throat was tight and his voice sounded strained.

She swirled the wine in the glass and her voice was husky with lust. "First you promise to do me a favor and then I'll do you a favor. I know you find me tempting, Peter. Give in to your desire and I will show you a night that will fire your hottest dreams."

Peter gulped wine, nearly choking on his impulse to laugh. The woman was crude and had no finesse; he wondered if she expected him to take her tawdry performance seriously and if this vulgarity worked for her in the past. He had hoped she wouldn't push him to the point of a flat rejection, but she'd already dashed that hope.

Throughout dinner, Zara purred; she postured; and she consumed another bottle of wine. The more she drank, the more shamelessly she responded to him with sexual innuendo, and the more uncomfortable Peter became.

Almost through dinner, Peter asked again about her favor. She infuriated him; his thin veneer of patience was cracking and falling away. His voice was scratchy from irritation.

"This is becoming quite tiresome, Zara. If you don't tell me straightaway what you want, my answer will be no."

"Oh, very well." She exhaled a long sigh of final defeat. She described the forum and their need for a moderator to hold a discussion for people with traumatic disorders.

"We need someone who understands how and why this lot can't deal with the pressures of our fast-paced society, how they've been traumatized, why they become reclusive and all the other odd bits. It's a one-time thing, Peter, and I think you'd enjoy it, actually."

"Oh, *please*, Zara," he shook his head. "I'm familiar with forums and whilst many find the activity enjoyable, I find them redundant and a bit of a bore. I don't see how I can possibly be of any help to you."

"But Peter, yes, you can! All you need to do is lead the discussion and suggest a few coping skills. Mind, you can hold the session at your convenience from the office or at home because it's all computer-based. Please," she wheedled, "will you consider it as a favor to me, Peter?"

"I'll most certainly think about this as a favor to you, Zara. I'll give you my answer on Monday after I've perused the forum."

"Oh, that's brilliant, Peter. I'm so pleased."

So...that was it. He breathed out with a *whoosh* that relieved the tightness between his shoulder blades. *Thank God this damned excruciating evening is over.*

Peter refused a third bottle of wine. He wanted to handle any situation that arose. Zara wanted coffee and a dessert of creamed rice pudding with poached figs. Once served, Peter insisted on taking the check. He paid Antony and rose for a quick getaway.

Zara put her hand on his arm to delay him. He deftly moved it and placed his hand under her elbow while he lifted her from her seat. She wobbled unsteadily and grabbed on to his sleeve. He picked up her small rhinestone purse from the table while he patted her on the back as if to say, "We're finished here."

His actions were adroit and swift and she knew she'd run out of time, unless...

"Did you drive, Peter?"

"No, I organized a car."

"Oh, that's clever of you. I drove; would you fancy a nightcap? Cancel your driver and come to my place." She gazed into his eyes enticingly. "I'll drop you off at home...*afterw-*."

"No, Zara," his response was terse, "thank you all the same, but my driver will be waiting."

"Oh, but Peter..."

Ignoring her protest, Peter ushered Zara through the dining room and out the door. Walking through the foyer, he saw disappointment and humiliation on her face when the halo light shone on her from above, the effect of his flat rejection to her seduction.

Once outside the restaurant, they found the pleasant weather had changed into a drizzling rain. As he'd hoped, his driver was waiting. Before she could delay him further, he roughly removed his arm from her possessive grasp.

"Perhaps I'll see you at the office next week, Zara. It was – *uh* – charming." He sprinted from the entrance, jumped in the car, slammed the door, and shoved a twenty-pound note into the driver's hand. "Thank God you're here early. Move it fast, mate!"

The wheels screeched on the rain-slicked cobblestones as the driver sped away from the curb.

Zara ducked through the spattering rain to the carpark, started the car, and slumped behind the wheel. She had been so sure of herself; so positive about her ability to entice him. Gazing at him all evening, she tingled looking at his parted lips, and imagined how his tongue would feel on hers. She ached thinking how he would respond under her fingertips. She envisioned how he would look, feel, and taste while she kissed and caressed every part of his body.

Steering her black Jaguar from the car park, her face wore a grotesque mask of mounting fury. She pounded the steering wheel with the heel of her hand while she sped over the slippery road. She was barely able to maneuver the twisted, winding turns.

Arriving at home, Zara slammed the door with such force that a wall full of valuable antique china plates tumbled and shattered on the floor. If she'd owned a cat, she'd have kicked it.

"Hell! Bloody hell!" she screamed, "God damned bloody hell!"

Hands shaking, she managed to pour herself a tumbler of scotch, toss it down her throat, and stumble blindly up the stairs to her bedroom. Yanking off her jewelry, she hurled the exquisite diamonds against the wall. Uncontrollable fury surged in her again. She ripped off the sheer silver lamé dress and tore the delicate garment to shreds. She splashed cold water on her face and looked in the mirror. Earlier, she'd lavishly applied makeup to seductive eyes that were a smoldering green; now they looked as though they'd been burnt to charred, black coals.

Zara crawled into the shower and sat on the floor. Scalding beads pelted her until the water ran cold and the emotions that threatened to consume her washed away.

Drained by her rage and the edge of her gut-wrenching disappointment placated with more alcohol, she wrapped her hair in a towel, threw on a robe, grabbed her tumbler and bottle of scotch, and stumbled down the stairs to her study adjacent to the kitchen. Brooding, she sought distraction and plopped in front of her desktop computer. She lit a cigarette and logged onto the forum to view new posts from the day. There was a message from the new member, Witzend, in the Welcome New Members section.

"I'm an American journalist living in Ohio," she wrote. "I'm looking forward to hearing opinions from others on current events, but most of all, I'm anxious to make new acquaintances."

"Anxious to make *new* acquaintances, are you?" Zara snarled, "You think you're anxious? I set out to get shagged tonight by an *old* acquaintance and missed by a mile."

Snapping off the computer, she grabbed the scotch bottle -- her solace for the evening -- intending to drink until her wrath vanished into oblivion.

While Zara groped her way up the stairs to bed, Peter was on the computer in his study reading the On Board the Great Escape forum. In the Lifestyles section, he read messages written by people traumatized by difficult life experiences and left on their own to pick up the pieces. Peter realized there was, in fact, an opportunity for him to offer help. His decision made, he signed up for membership using the login name, "DPGJ." Having that accomplished, he planned to tell Zara on Monday that he was in for a one-time, one-hour event.

He thought about tonight's dinner with Zara. He'd never led her to believe there could be anything between them. They were workplace associates, but not friends. They would *never* be friends. Tonight confirmed his suspicions.

Something about her just isn't right. Obviously, she lacks a proper upbringing. She lives well, but she doesn't know how to conduct herself with social grace.

I want no part in her agenda. From here on out, I will be even more guarded in my dealings with that woman. I'm anxious to have the whole ordeal over, so that I have no reason to cross paths with her again. I'll drop that hot potato in Sean's lap.

After reading the forum, Peter logged on to his website, reviewed his email correspondence, and reread Hayley's messages. He wrote to her about the section on the forum where she might safely link with others who suffered from traumatic experiences and told her that he planned a discussion she might find encouraging.

Hayley was pleased to find a new message from Peter when she opened her emails on Saturday afternoon. She followed the link he suggested and previewed the forum. He was right; this would be a new and different undertaking and she clicked the menu to register for membership. She glanced at little Diva sprawled on a chair by her desk and entered *Diva* as her forum name.

"I wonder," she spoke aloud, lifting the dog onto her lap to stroke her, "if this could possibly change my life."

"Why?" she whispered, "For God's sake, why?"

Hayley would give it all up – she would give up everything - if she could only feel her beloved parents' arms around her again."

Hayley

~11~

"It has become appallingly obvious
that our technology has exceeded our humanity."
~ Albert Einstein~

Oxford University
Oxfordshire, England
May 2004

Zara lay curled up in bed on Sunday morning reliving the dinner with Peter the night before. *Damn and blast, he should be waking up beside me this morning.*

Although it didn't turn out as she'd planned this time, she wanted him and she would have him. She found him sexy. Granted, he was a tad stodgy and serious, but she would loosen him up. She suspected he might be even sexier with the right partner. She was anxious for the opportunity to find out just how sexy. Peter was worth any risk in the future. With ruthless determination, she would reach out and grab the big prize. She smirked, *sooner or later Peter will be mine. Slowly, slowly catchee monkey.*

When the fuzziness cleared from her mind and she remembered her humiliation, she knew she couldn't face the day until she had a drink. She picked up the bottle from the floor and turned it upside down. Not one drop fell. Rising, she held her pounding head. Her stomach was queasy, but she had no choice but to go downstairs for another bottle.

Tripping over several empty glasses beside the bed, she saw the torn fabric from her dress, and the strewn jewelry that cluttered the room. Annoyed and angry with Peter for making her destroy the beautiful dress and ruining her plans for the evening, she grabbed her robe and stumbled down the stairs to the kitchen where she poured tomato juice and a jigger of Vodka into a tumbler, popped three strong analgesic in her mouth, and washed them down. She lit a cigarette, carried a fresh pot of coffee to the kitchen counter and placed it in front of her laptop computer. Sliding onto a bench, she booted it up and logged onto her forum where she went directly to the page for new members waiting approval. Another administrator had approved a new member calling herself, "Diva," but Zara's only interest was Peter, and she didn't take the time to read the member's profile.

"Crikey! There he is!" she squealed. "The bloke is bloody well going to do it!"

With her spirits rising, she validated Peter's membership and congratulated herself on capturing him to do the forum discussion. Trembling with excitement, she rang Peter at home and was disappointed that the call went to voicemail. She left a message telling him that she had approved his membership request. She sighed wearily, switched off the computer, went back to bed, and slept until the next day.

The weekend rain had stopped by Sunday night. The mists lifted early on Monday morning, giving Oxfordshire another welcome burst of bright and sunny weather to dry up the dewy landscape. Zara drove to the university singing along with the radio, happy that at least she'd accomplished one of her goals on Saturday night. It wasn't her preferred one, but she planned to set that right given enough time. Zara saw the truth as she wanted to see it, but this time she admitted to herself that she overplayed her hand and came on far too strong to snag a refined man like Peter. She would be more careful how she handled herself...*and him*...in the future.

She walked into the Wessely Building with a bouncy step. Once inside she went to look for him and found him already sitting at his desk.

"Good morning, Zara." Peter stood when she entered his office. She smiled appealingly at him while he spoke.

"I trust your Sunday was pleasant. I...*uh*...thank you for the dinner invitation and for thinking of me to assist you on your forum. It's an interesting opportunity and I think this venture is well worth an hour of my time."

"Oh, Peter, it's my pleasure," she purred. "I'm so delighted that you can take the time to help these poor, unfortunate people."

"Do you have a moment? If so, I'd like to discuss what the members' expectations are for this discussion."

Her heart leapt, "Brilliant, Peter! Unfortunately, I'm off to an appointment, but I'd fancy lunch today. I'll meet you at...well, you choose the time and place."

"Let's wait until you can meet in my office, Zara. I'd prefer to discuss it here. It will take only a moment."

"Oh, right. Well, then, how about meeting in the campus cafeteria?"

"No, it can wait until it's convenient for you to meet here. Tomorrow, perhaps, then?"

Any time, any place, would have worked for Zara, but she was in it to win and was cautious not to overplay her hand again.

At the brief meeting the next afternoon, Zara was businesslike explaining the forum and Peter's role in detail. She gave no hint her real objective was that she expected the forum to open fresh opportunities to get closer to him.

Later, she logged on and saw that he'd already begun working toward the group meeting.

She read his open message --

"A group message to all members of the
Health and Wellness Advice forums
Regarding: A World Apart
Hello Forum Members,

I'm pleased that you chose to join A World Apart discussion group. This discussion is open

```
to anyone suffering from symptoms of anxiety,
agoraphobia, and traumatic shock disorder. This
will be a single online group counseling session
on Thursday, commencing at 17:00 GMT and lasting
for one hour. I'll fix availability for one of
the forum's private chat rooms, so please sign
up for access. I have linked you to my website
for more information.

   Peter Gabriel-Johns, MD, PhD
   http://www.dp-gabrieljohns.co.uk"
```

By Thursday, a full house had registered for *A World Apart* including two new members, Witzend and Diva. Peter conferred with Zara before he logged on and asked her if there were any last minute instructions.

"Suppose something goes wrong; I really should sit with you during the session. Then, I can take care of any problems."

"Very well, Zara. That's a valid suggestion. I'll see you then."

At five o'clock, Peter and Zara sat together peering at the computer screen while the member's messages flowed. They were eager to discuss their symptoms with him and amongst themselves, comparing their own reactions against each other's when they talked about confronting their fears.

Peter fielded their questions and gave them suggestions. He kept it simple, reminding himself they are not his patients. He asked them to keep a journal of what was happening when they became anxious and gave them many links to informative websites he thought would be helpful.

Halfway through the session, Zara said off-hand, "After this bit is over, we can enjoy dinner together."

"*Hmm...*sorry, Zara, I'm afraid not. Sean will be waiting. We've planned to meet after the discussion. *No...sorry.*"

"Oh, well, all right, then Peter," she agreed. *We'll just see about that. I'll plan on it.* Outwardly, Zara remained cool, but her mind and blood were racing with anticipation. She was determined to have this opportunity and nothing was going to stop her.

After the session, Zara thanked him, leaned forward, kissed his cheek, and left the room. Lurking outside the doorway, she heard him pick up the phone.

"Sean, Peter here. Yes, I'm delighted with the outcome of the discussion. I'm feeling a bit peckish, actually. Are you up for a meal? Me, too. Let's walk over to the Turf Tavern for supper. It's my favorite Oxford pub. Yes, all right, then. I'm ready to leave. I'll meet you in the lobby."

Zara maneuvered to walk out the door at the same moment.

"Well, I'm starving; where are you going, Sean? I'll join you."

"Well, Zara, we're headed for the Turf Tavern," Sean replied. "I'm not sure..." He glanced at Peter, who broke in.

"Sean's briefing me on some research statistics and I'll brief him on tonight's event. We'd prefer..."

"Brilliant!" she gushed. "Now that I'm here, Sean, there's no need for you to tag along, actually."

Zara had no interest in discussing the event, having just sat through a boring hour of the tedious bloke's bleating. She wanted a cozier discussion; more personal. It was a perfect opportunity to talk about her...about them.

Sean appeared confused and looked to Peter. "*Uh*...well, I thought..."

"Sean, if you'd like to go home now, I'll keep Peter compa-..."

"Actually…no, Zara," Peter cut her off, "Sean and I have a date, don't we Sean?" Peter's harsh laugh didn't conceal his irritation. "We'd rather be alone, wouldn't we Sean?

"Oh, all right, then," she ignored the brush off trying to hide her petulance. "We'll all walk there and eat together."

Sean didn't get the message. Frustrated, Zara pursed her lips and glared at him. *I'll get even with him for this*.

They walked past the Bodleian Library, under the Bridge of Sighs, and down the narrow Hell's Passage to the Pub. Peter knew to put off Zara he needed to develop a harder shell. He gave in for the moment and broke the prickly silence.

"Did either of you tekkies know Thomas Hardy wrote in *Jude the Obscure* that Jude got drunk at the Turf Tavern and recited the Creed in Latin while standing on a table? It's Colin Dexter's *Inspector Morse's* boozery hangout and Evelyn Waugh wrote about the Turf Tavern in *Brideshead Revisited*."

"How do you know all that, Peter? I knew about Inspector Morse, though."

"Well, Sean, my brother, Matthew, is a World Lit graduate of Cambridge. According to him, Oxford is known as the 'city of dreaming spires,' a term coined by the poet Matthew Arnold when he spoke of Oxford's harmonious architecture. Hundreds of authors have chosen Oxford for their setting and mentioned the university in fiction very early in England's creative imagination. In 1400, Chaucer, in his *Canterbury Tales*, referred to the 'Clerk of Oxenford.' So much history; so many famous literary works." He paused and looked far away. "Oxford is so deep in the soul of England that it becomes another character in their books."

They continued walking through the narrow alleyway around doglegs to the pub. Zara stifled a yawn. *Oh, blah – blah – blah, who bloody well cares? Damn and blast, Peter can be so stuffy and pedantic.*

Peter rambled on, filling the deadly silence. "I picked up an appreciation for great literature and the classics sitting around the table after family dinners while Matthew read aloud. Ah, here we are now," he opened the door for Zara.

The pub was crowded and noisy with students and tourists, but they found a small table at the far side of the room and they each ordered hearty chicken, ham, and leek pie with a pint of ale. While they ate, Peter raised his glass and told Zara, "I'm thoroughly satisfied with the event and I want to thank you for suggesting the idea."

After some time, the discussion got around to Hayley Hamilton.

"I'm sure you know, as an administrator who can see every member's name as well as their login, that Diva's name is Hayley Hamilton. I met Hayley when she was in a New York recovery center five years ago after the plane crash that killed her parents. Now that I think of it, Zara, I remember your interview on the Tele about your friendship with Lady Elizabeth."

Sodding hell; I never looked. Diva is Hayley bloody Hamilton! Zara shuddered; a wave of shock struck her and left her trembling.

"Of course, Peter; Elizabeth and I were close friends." She forced a grimace into a smile. "We became friends as students here at Oxford. Terrible business, that crash."

"I have an interest in Hayley, Zara. I am working with her, not as a therapist, but as her friend. She emailed me recently on my website and I suggested that she might find the session helpful. She signed on as Diva."

"Yes, of course; I know everyone's name and login." *Blimey, I had no interest; I'm only interested in you, you blinkered prat. I didn't care who the hell Diva was.*

"Hayley has become a recluse," he went on. "For the last five years she has rarely left her home. I plan to help her by continuing to offer my friendship."

"Oh, I don't know, Peter. Mind, she might think you're prying. I think you're going too far. Maybe she'd prefer to be left alone, actually." Her voice was thin and reedy and she strived to hide the malice she felt toward Hayley Hamilton at that moment.

Peter shook his head and snapped, "No, Zara; you have no idea what you're talking about. I'll use my own judgment, thank you. Hayley is very special to me and she needs a great deal of help. I intend to do whatever I can for as long as it takes."

His words pierced Zara like a dagger. She had clenched her fists so tight that her nails cut bloody crescents into her palms.

Over my dead body will I allow that rich bitch cow to take Peter's attention away from me.

The next morning, Zara was at the Wessely Building before first light. She stole into Peter's office and covertly applied spyware onto his computer.

If Peter had arrived at his office a mere ten seconds earlier, he'd have caught her sitting at his desk. Zara heard his footsteps and scrambled to tuck herself into a secluded vantage point. She watched until his back was turned and slipped out the door.

Secure in the knowledge that he was not at home, she drove to Cranmer Close. Hidden by tall bushes, she picked the lock on a side door and entered the house. Then, as fast as she applied the spyware to Peter's university office computer, she put it on his home computer. And for good measure, she embedded a pin-dot surveillance webcam in his home office wall with a wireless signal picked up on a hidden recorder. When she finished, she let herself out and walked through the dense foliage to her car.

"There. Now, we'll bloody well see, won't we?"

On the first Saturday morning after she hacked Peter's computers, Zara was already lurking near his house. She sat crouched in her black Jaguar, concealed by shrubs and trees while she spied on Peter through the camera bug in his office wall. She watched him making calls and working at his desk. Too bad I didn't think of planting a listening device in the telephone. Then I could keep track of his phone calls, too. Oh, well, there's always tomorrow.

Peter walked away from his desk and was out of her view. About an hour later, he left the house with a camel-colored cashmere jumper tied over his shoulders, walked to his Bentley and drove from his carpark out to the road. From the direction he headed, she guessed he was off to his parents' estate to spend the day with his family. There was no use following. The gated mansion grounds of the estate were out of view and electronically monitored. *Someday, I'll be Mrs. Peter*

Gabriel-Johns sitting pretty in his Bentley and I'll ride through those gates with him.

Driving back to Burford, she reminisced about one early spring afternoon when she stole through the bushes surrounding the Seven Valleys' manor and gardens. She wandered the luxurious grounds under ancient trees, over manicured lawns, across small stone bridges spanning rippling streams, through rose gardens and flowerbeds. From the top of a knoll, she could see the beautifully restored stone manor house with its seven chimneys and gables.

As careful as she'd been, she'd gotten too close to the manor and one of the gardeners spotted her. It was then Edward and Barbara made the decision to protect themselves from snoopers and electronically secured the parkland and gardens close to the manor with electrified wire, cameras, and sensors.

In Zara's mind, she was justified in spying on Peter to protect her future, the one that existed only in her mind, unfounded in reality. She would put a stop to his membership on the forum and turn his attention back to her, but until then, she thought it best to keep an eye on his activities. She returned home and logged on with his passwords to access Peter's home computer.

She poured herself a tall scotch and water from the liquor cabinet and sat at the computer. She spent the rest of the day drinking, smoking, reading the forum, and Peter's computer files.

This may take some time, but...slowly, slowly catchee monkey.

~12~

"Friends will keep you sane; love could fill your heart.
A lover can warm your bed,
but lonely is the soul without a mate."
~ David Pratt~

Seven Valleys Estate
Wolds-on-Thames, Oxfordshire
May 2004

Peter rose early on a Saturday morning and ran along the River Cherwell from the boathouse through the Botanic Gardens and Christ Church Meadow. An overnight rain refreshed the spring air and the warm sun felt pleasant on his skin. When he returned, he showered and changed from an Oxford University tee and running shorts to a light blue denim shirt, khaki pants, and loafers.

He lowered the top on his blue Bentley and placed a gift-wrapped package on the passenger's seat. Heading out the secluded driveway to the street and down the M40, he covered the fifteen miles from Oxford to historic Wolds-on-Thames, a walled Saxon village on the River. Going home to Seven Valleys always lifted his spirits and made him feel well grounded.

The road turned to enter the village and Peter drove over the stone bridge, past the Cygnet Hotel and through the village, a major conservation area with an abbey and castle ruins. Wolds-on-Thames grew up around an inlet with architecture dating back to the eighth century. They built a rocky dam in the fifteenth century, creating a waterfall that spills into a recreational lake, which flows back into the river Thames. At this place, the river was one of many of England's sites designated as an area of outstanding natural beauty.

High above the village was the Gabriel-Johns' estate with its secluded manor, gardens, and parkland. Driving along the tree-lined edge of the estate, he could see that his father's prized roses were responding to the mild weather. Blossoms that only a week ago were tight buds were now beginning to bloom.

Approaching the entrance, he used his remote to open the gates and headed his car toward his parents' home. He drove through the rolling hills and vales of the estate, along a sunny horse pasture, and weaved the Bentley through huge, old trees that lined the gravel road to the manor gracing the top of a knoll.

His favorite spot on the estate was halfway between the entrance and the manor. Peter stopped the car and got out for a moment. He walked to the edge of the road and leaned against a tree, so that he could enjoy the vistas of the Wolds and the River Thames. A warm breeze rustled the leaves in the treetops and his father's walled rose garden scented the air. At this distance, the picturesque village appeared to be one with the estate and it looked closer than it was from where he stood. Fast moving clouds created shifting patterns of dappled color and light over the distant countryside. Through his eyes, everything paled in comparison to this corner of the world so steeped in history and natural beauty. He could see that his mother didn't have far to go for inspiration to paint her landscapes. He never stood on this spot without thinking of Tolkien's *The Path to the Top of the Valley* –

'Still round the corner there may wait
A new road or a secret gate;
And though I oft have passed them by,
A day will come at last when I
Shall take the hidden paths that run
West of the Moon, East of the Sun.'

Time spent here with his family was precious to him. Everything else in his life, including his music and hobbies, were lonely pursuits.

He enjoyed his practice and his position with Oxford University. He worked with dedication and intensity to get where he was professionally and sacrificed all else in his life to accomplish his goals. Many in his field regarded Peter as a leading authority. The psychology community received his book well, his research papers were given a great deal of credibility, and that gave him a great degree of satisfaction. He worked hard to achieve his accomplishments and enjoyed the opportunities his profession afforded him, especially those that took him to faraway places and gave him new experiences. However, all of this dedication spelled loneliness.

For him, Wolds-on-Thames and Seven Valleys meant home and family; it meant England and he longed for someone to share it with him. Although he was fond of the women with whom he'd established relationships, he knew he wasn't in love with them. The necessary chemistry wasn't there and they lacked a certain *je ne sais quoi*. His past romances, never robust anyway, all ended with merely a whispered farewell. Now thirty-five and enmeshed in his career, he supposed many considered him a crusty old bachelor, although he felt the life he was destined for had not yet begun.

During the years he spent looking, he'd envisioned the woman who would be his soul mate...the love of his life. He stood in the dappled sunlight surrounded by the one place that made him happy. *Perhaps I've waited too long to find her, or I have already let her go. Will I recognize her when I find her?* His mind flashed to Hayley Hamilton.

He looked toward the exquisite walled rose garden his father had created for his mother, filled his lungs with the perfumed air, and got back in the car. Approaching the manor house, the sun reflected off the blue surface of their swimming pool and glinted in his eyes. He chuckled thinking how his mother stubbornly insisted on the pool. Edward had told her well-bred Englishmen considered swimming pools in poor taste.

"I don't care one whit about anyone else's considered opinion, Edward." Peter had overheard his mother telling him petulantly, "This is for the boys; I want it for the boys. If we lived stateside, there would be no question. Shall we move stateside?"

Peter knew his free-spirited American mother well enough to know she would start packing just to get her way, or prove a point. His father knew he stood on shaky ground and acquiesced. At times like this, standing on ceremony never worked in their house.

Later, Edward told Peter he was glad he'd agreed when he realized how much pleasure it gave her to watch their sons swimming. Now, their grandchildren splashed about in the pool.

Rounding the final curve to the car park in front of a long garage that was previously part of the estate's carriage house, Peter saw his parents on the back terrace overlooking the heated pool. He carefully drove inside and parked in his designated spot. He took the stone path from the garage and strode across the landscaped parterres behind the immense stone mansion.

Englishmen are subject to capricious weather, but the day was sunny and pleasant enough for the family to sit outside. As he crossed the manicured lawns and raised stone terraces toward them, their Cavalier King Charles spaniels, Maggie and Lizzie, bounded toward him, barking and prancing around in happy circles making sure he got a proper welcome. Barbara and Edward rose when the dogs shot across the lawn to greet him.

Barbara called out to him, "Peter, you're the first to arrive. We're delighted to see you so early." She beamed, "Isn't this weather grand? Come sit by me, Darling! I'll have Emily bring out a fresh pot of coffee."

"Happy Birthday, Mum; you're still a bonnie lass, aren't you?" Peter's hug lifted his mother off her feet. "Why is it you never look one minute older?"

"Hullo, Dad," he said affectionately, and the two men, who resemble each other with their sandy blonde hair, broad shoulders and tall frame, bear-hugged and slapped each other's backs.

When William, a London surgeon, Jessica, his wife, and their two young children, James and Sarah, arrived, they kissed and hugged their parents and grandparents. James and Sarah both wanted to sit on their Uncle Peter's lap first. For a while, he held both of them, hugging them, and bouncing one on each knee while they chanted, "Ride a Cock Horse."

Matthew, who arrived shortly thereafter, zoomed up the road in his baby, a classic silver Aston Martin, and nearly hit the back wall of the garage before coming to a screeching halt. The family wondered if he had delusions of being the next James Bond. Edward once remarked to Barbara that Matthew's playing Romeo in summer stock might have colored his perception of his place in the family and his purpose in the world.

"One of these days, Matthew is going to miss," Edward growled, "and if he does, he'll pay through the nose for the damages."

"Right," Barbara grumbled, "he'll come to me begging for a handout to do it, then."

"Tar and feather the bloody git!" William sniggered.

"Take it out of his hide, Dad, and if you want help, I'm willing." Peter winked at his brother. "I see he's still wearing the cowboy hat and boots he bought last year in Utah."

William elbowed Peter, "I wonder if those boots still smell of horse manure."

"It's the only horse scents Matthew has," Peter twisted his mouth into a wry smile.

Matthew Gabriel-Johns sauntered across the lawn and stopped to pick up the dogs that were jumping against his legs. He held one under each arm, nuzzling them whilst he crossed the terrace to greet his family.

On his arrival, Emily Thirtle, their live-in housekeeper, appeared in the doorway offering hot coffee or cold drinks.

"Emily, how are you, dear lady?" Matthew stood up and hugged the grim, sparse woman. "Still trying to get everyone in the household's avoirdupois up?" He took off his hat and dropped it onto her head.

"Strewth, get on with you, Matthew. You're trouble," she simpered, pursing her lips and placed the tray of drinks on the table. "Who knows where you plunked that dirty thing before?"

Matthew laughed when Emily swiped the hat at him before standing on tiptoes to place it back on his head.

Peter watched Emily, who cooked and managed the household day staff. She was a sullen, late middle-aged woman with bad teeth, thinning, frizzy white hair, and a tiny, spindly body, who didn't bathe often enough. Her sallow, pinched face always looked as if she smelt something rotten. Even in her youth, she had never been particularly happy or attractive. Small boned and wiry, she had a permanent scowl on her long face, making her appear always disgruntled. When she stood up to place the hat on Matthew's head, Peter noticed a stiff white hair growing out of her neck just under her chin. The family had not requested that she wear a uniform; she chose to wear a plain, black dress with a gray apron and soft, but serviceable black shoes. She'd said that anything else was frivolous, but her real reason was that she could withdraw into the shadows undetected and eavesdrop on private conversations.

Emily had never married, and although she devoted herself to serving the family, the truth was that she lacked any talent or marketable skills other than performing mundane household chores. Even her cooking lacked skillfulness and imagination.

She arrived in the household only a short time before Edward's mother died. Barbara, then the woman of the house, battled wits with Emily to reach an understanding about who was actually the boss in the household.

When the boys came along, Emily endeared herself with secrets and hidden sweets in her apron pocket. Until he went away to school, she was Matthew's co-conspirator and helped him carry out impish tricks he'd devised to play on his brothers and the household staff. She was his audience while he was a little boy, when he dressed up in funny clothes and entertained her with comical voices. She was the ghost who stole and hid their toys and was the one responsible when Peter and William found their books at the bottom of the pool.

"Dad, you're looking well," said William. "That was quite a scare you gave us. I'm glad I was at the hospital when you came in with chest pains. I had just walked out of the operating room when they brought you in to emergency." William stole a glance at his father with a doctor's practiced eye. "You're doing a great job with him, Mum. He's leaner, healthier and his color is better for your efforts."

"I was beside myself with worry," Barbara said, "and I'm grateful that all of you were able to join me so quickly. Jess, it's lovely to have another woman in the family to hold on to, otherwise I'd be alone amongst all these sniveling men."

The men laughed uncomfortably, because they knew she was right about their sniveling.

"But, wasn't it fortunate that it was nothing more than a bad case of indigestion? Believe me, I've insisted on taking a more active role in your dad's diet from now on."

Peter watched his mother and father together. They still held hands and their love for each other touched and inspired him. Peter sipped his wine, lost in reverie.

It's so right for this family to gather amongst these beautiful gardens to share our love for mother on her birthday. My mother is a devoted wife and an ageless woman. Her face and figure seem only to improve no matter how the years attempt to steal away her youth. She's still slim and beautiful, still has a smooth complexion and honey colored hair without a hint of grey. The only sign of aging is a few lacy wrinkles under her eyes. That old straw hat... she was wearing it the day she met dad.

Family history was important to Peter and he thought about his mother and father's chance meeting. They often told the story and said if they hadn't both been at that particular place, at that particular time, it would have been... well... perhaps his mother was right; fate had a hand in it.

Barbara Jaclyn Van Der Piel met Edward William Andrew Gabriel-Johns on a tour of England with her sister, Patricia. Barbara was going into her senior year studying art at Vassar, when Julie Quinlan, Barbara's college roommate, invited Barbara to spend the summer at her family's Malibu beach house. Her family was in the theater and movies and Julie fascinated Barbara because she was imperious and headstrong, creative and theatrical. Like a sorceress, she beguiled Barbara and conjured up ideas that the gentle and steady Barbara never could have imagined. Barbara was a stabilizing influence on Julie, because left on her own, Julie never would have graduated.

Julie had set her sights on Bob Wagner and she became hysterical when she heard he'd married Natalie Wood. Barbara spent her junior year consoling her broken-hearted friend, listening to hours of angst and melodrama worthy of an academy award. To repay Barbara for her friendship, Julie promised a summer of parties at the Malibu beach house with Troy Donohue, Tab Hunter, Fabian, and a host of other Hollywood teen idols.

Patricia had worried that the lure of Julie's celebrity connections would be too strong for Barbara to resist, but Barbara wouldn't disappoint Patricia. Barbara was willing to sacrifice this summer of fun and excitement, and asked Julie to go with them on the trip. Julie couldn't imagine wasting the summer with two wimpy girls schlepping around dusty, crumbling ruins when they could spend every day sunbathing on the beach, drinking a tall, frosty Tom Collins, sneaking around studio sets, or driving to the in-spots of Hollywood and Beverly Hills in her new red corvette convertible.

"You mean you'd give up a chance to meet these Hollywood dream-boats?" Julie chided Barbara, who had no recourse but to stand and take it. "You'd pass up sunbathing on the beach and tooling around Hollywood, Malibu and Beverly Hills? What is wrong with you, Kid?"

"I'm sorry, Julie, I can't disappoint Patricia. I owe it to her."

"You're really a drag, Van Der Piel," she pouted.

"I understand how you feel, Julie. I'm not free to explain it to you, but I simply have to go with Patricia."

"Well, better you than me, party pooper," Julie said, with a dramatic toss of her hand. She angrily blew out smoke and ground out the cigarette under her foot.

Barbara often told Peter she desperately wanted to go to Malibu, but her older sister's wishes took priority. Even then, loyalty to her family was important to her. She never lost the values she'd learned early in life that were central to her family's happiness and well-being.

Toward the end of their vacation in England, the two girls received an invitation to a polo match. After patting a divot into place on the lawn, Barbara stood up and backed into a tall, blonde young man who was standing too close behind her. He was dumbstruck when he turned around to apologize.

Edward's heart fluttered when he saw Barbara. Overwhelmed by a desire to kiss her full, pouty lips, it was love at first sight for Edward William Andrew Gabriel-Johns. She was a vision with her straw hat framing her blonde pageboy, her fair skin, rosy cheeks, and dreamy blue eyes. He thought she was a true classic beauty; a virginal angel. And she was.

They laughed at the mishap and shy Edward asked the sweet young Americans to take tea with him. That day, Barbara and Edward found their destiny. Her sister, Patricia, knew her destiny; she'd already made secret plans of her own.

The aristocratic Edward wouldn't have cared if Barbara happened to be the offspring of peasants, but both Barbara and Patricia inherited trust funds from their grandfather's diamond mines in Namibia. It was an inheritance considered a large fortune in the days of their youth. Barbara's father bequeathed the mines to her and the attorney deeded them over soon after he died. At the time they met, Edward knew nothing about Barbara's healthy financial situation. Only a few days after their tea, he confessed that he couldn't live without her and ardently begged her to be his bride.

At the end of the summer, Barbara returned to Vassar to finish her senior year, wistful and dreamy over her handsome fiancé. She told Julie that Malibu wasn't the only place to find dreamboats; she'd found one of her own in England.

Barbara and Edward were married in the estate's old stone chapel. Theirs was a marriage for love; Edward had no need to enter into a marriage to support the estate. The family made good investments, sometimes not altogether on the up and up, but they parlayed their wealth and they had done well. Edward hadn't yet inherited Seven Valleys, but the family's wealth had held through the wars and there was no need for their only child to marry for money. Seven Valleys' estate was self-supporting for as long as it existed and gave employment to many local villagers.

Simon de Valle, the seventh Baronet Saint-Johns of Basing, through service to King James acquired the land and built the manor. He called the estate, Seventh Valle, and over the centuries, it became known in the village as Seven Valleys. Sir Simon was educated at Oxford in law, but he accumulated his wealth through privateering. From accounts in Sir Simon's own diaries, he commissioned three speedy sloops, the *Wind Rover*, the *Wild Wind*, and the *Raging Wind.* He spent much of his youth cruising the Caribbean and sailing off the coast of the colonies. King James mildly reproached him for his excesses aboard the Raging Wind when he took an enormous amount of booty on the sea as well as from fortifications on land.

When Sir Simon married, he'd commissioned the architect, Inigo Jones, to design the mansion and gardens. Jones' confident handling of detail and proportion set him apart from other designers of the period. Sir Simon's young wife bore him a daughter, but died giving birth to a stillborn son while he was landing his privateers ashore off the coast of Spain attacking land fortifications. He died at sea in 1625 on the Raging Wind from sickness during the failed Cádiz Expedition under King Charles. Edward's ancestor, Thomas Gabriel-Johns, a distant cousin of Sir Simon, inherited the estate in 1630 through marriage to Lady Catherine de Valle, Sir Simon's daughter, without gaining Sir Simon's title.

Many nights at bedtime, Edward thrilled the boys with flamboyant stories of the derring-do of Privateer Simon de Valle. According to Edward's version, he was a flashy, dangerous, swashbuckling buccaneer.

Today, the family sat on the terrace where the three young boys spent many a day fighting over which brother would play Simon de Valle, battling with their homemade wooden swords, and racing their toy sloops in the pool.

"Are you still with us?" Edward nudged Peter's arm, returning his attention to the present.

"Oh, right, Dad; I was lost in the past for a moment," he chuckled. "Sorry. Were you talking to me?"

"I asked you if you want more wine."

"Oh, yes, please. Is this a new varietal then, Dad? It's quite nice."

"Do try and keep up, Peter. I just explained it to you," Edward scoffed, refilling his glass.

The weather held and the family sat together on the terrace all afternoon. Peter was usually reticent about his work, because so much of it was private and confidential, but today he shared his successful discussion on the internet forum.

"Oh such a trivial pursuit," chided William. "I thought you were above using all that technology."

"Now, now, old man," Matthew smirked, "we mustn't tease Peter. We don't want to traumatize him and have him lock himself away like his agoraphobic patients. Tell us, *puh...puh...Peter puh...puh...Procrastinator*, have any of them gone out to play after you've mucked about in their lives, actually?" Matthew looked extremely self-satisfied with his new label for Peter, as if he'd taken a giant down a notch. He silently, but visibly, mouthed the words mocking Peter several times more, adding little head wags for an extra taunting effect.

Unlike William, whose teasing was only in jest, Peter was aware that Matthew was mean spirited and there was a nasty edge to his comment. He meant to belittle him and his profession. Matthew, like Peter, hadn't yet married, but unlike Peter, hadn't bothered to pursue a career. Instead, he lived on generous handouts from his mother, acted in amateur theatre productions, and made it his mission to enjoy the favors of far too many comely women.

"Who knows, I may make bloomin' extroverts given enough time, but putting that aside, Matthew, I'm curious. Tell me...who is the *babe-du-jour*? Or have your love affairs gathered such momentum that you are now dumping them by the hour? Are there any women left in the kingdom you haven't deflowered?"

"Bollocks, Peter," Matthew sneered. "At least I'm loveable, unlike you, whose stuffiness so puts off women they fear they'll suffocate from sheer lack of air. And I might add, your choice of women is dire at best. I can remember some who Maggie and Lizzie put to shame." He stroked the dogs. "I don't recall you shagging anyone lately. Has the supply dried up? If you find you're in desperate need to dig someone up, I suggest that you try cemeteries. Oh, but make it easier on yourself; first try the morgue. I believe they'd already be stiff enough for you. *Oi, phwoar!* Blow-up dolls. That's it! *Fabbity-fab and double cool with knobs*, Peter. They'll send one in a plain, brown wrap-...."

"*A-hah*, yes, *Romeo;* did I touch a raw nerve? God, that was a full-on monologue; you certainly do love listening to the sound of your own voice."

"*A-hah*, no, Peter, Bang away all you want, but I see the well of your witticism has gone quite as dry as your luck with women. I remain untouched by your lack of humor and what you've dredged up with your feeble attempt at kidding."

"*Who's kidding, Romeo*?" Peter snorted.

"Certainly not me, Professor Pompous," Matthew shot back with his lip curled.

"I don't think it's amusing at all, actually." Peter took on a patronizing tone of voice. "I should think *you'd* be worried, though. You're almost 30 years old, Matthew. Time will fly by and the audience will laugh you off the stage playing Romeo with Sir Adrian's troupe of rank amateurs. Or," he paused, "here's a novel thought for you, *Matthew the Moocher.* Perhaps you can actually get a *real* job for the first time in your life, then you can be self supporting and stop hitting Mum up for handou-..."

"Stop it, boys!" Barbara slammed her hand on the table cutting Peter off. She rose abruptly, "I'll have no more squabbling from you lot! I've had enough of your slagging matches to last my lifetime." Patting her husband's arm she softened her tone, "Jessica and I are going inside to talk to Emily. I hope the gardeners have brought her vegetables and herbs for dinner. When James and Sarah finish splashing all the water out of the pool, we'll have birthday cake with our tea here on the terrace and then Emily will see to a lovely late supper for us in the dining room. In the meantime, Edward and William, please sit here, enjoy your wine, mind the children, and that includes these two aging brats. And for heaven's sake," she huffed, "will you hooligans try to behave like gentlemen?"

There was a brief silence amongst the four men while they drank their wine and stared off in the distance. No apologies were forthcoming from Peter or Matthew.

"Clearly, you blithering idiots owe your mum an apology," Edward glared from one to the other. "Save your pettiness for another time, will you? This is her birthday party, after all."

"Matthew started it," Peter sniggered, flipping his hand dismissively at his brother.

"*Sod you, Peter, you tosser,*" Matthew grumbled and got up from his seat to top off his glass of wine. "You infuriate me, with your highbrow plummy voice, condescending superiority, and judgmental attitude."

Peter scoffed with a lopsided grin, "*Oh, boo-bloody-hoo,* Matthew; you reap what you sow."

"*Enough.* Take it from me, *yobbos*; one is well-advised not to twist your mother's tail." Edward chuckled, "I can show you the scars to prove it."

Barbara, the cornerstone of the family, was a sweet and loving woman, but she was also snappish and domineering when she disapproved or, on rare occasion, wanted her own way. The men gathered here today could attest to it.

After tea, Edward took the children for a ride through the vineyard on the estate's work train, Jessica and William rode through the pastures to exercise William's sadly neglected horses, Matthew looked on the bookshelves for his annotated copy of Shakespeare's *Tempest,* and Peter took his mother aside and told her about the emails from Hayley Hamilton. She was pleased and told Peter to keep her apprised of Hayley's progress.

"As you know, Peter, I always thought Hayley was a very special young woman." She glanced at him with a self-satisfied grin and let it go at that. "Don't forget to take the toy schooners to the pool for James; when he gets back from his train ride through the vineyard, he'll be waiting for you to play Simon de Valle. Did I mention Sarah will entertain us with a song and dance after dinner?"

Peter returned home that evening instead of staying overnight at Seven Valleys as he'd planned. He had allowed Matthew to unhinge his self-control and his tolerance for his wayward brother had worn thin. He poured a glass of Bacchus wine that he brought home from his dad's wine cellar, before he went upstairs to bed for the night.

He lay there, but his mind wouldn't shut off and he tossed and turned, unable to fall asleep. His thoughts drifted to Hayley. He arose, went to his desk, and sent an email to her:

"Dear Hayley,

How are you getting on after the discussion session? Did you find it helpful? I hope you will be able to use some of the recommended coping skills that we discussed. Please continue to write to me, or you can call me anytime on the office and mobile numbers I gave you.

Today was my mother's birthday and I spent the day with my family at Seven Valleys. She was pleased that we have been in touch with each other.

I'm here for you, Hayley.
Peter"

"Dear Peter,

Thank you for including me in the discussion. I'll review what you recommended, but I keep my life calm and insulated from anything that would be a threat to me.

Please give my regards to Barbara and wish her a Happy Birthday for me.

I want to thank you for reaching out to me in friendship. I need an understanding friend. I'll look forward to further exchanges with you, too.

Hayley"

~ 13~

*"And we find at the end of a perfect day,
the soul of a friend we've made."
~Carrie Jacobs Bond~*

*CableCoNews Studio
Cleveland, Ohio
May 2004*

Christine Horowitz and her production assistant, Kalia-Malika McKee, were working overtime on a Saturday night at CableCoNews in Cleveland, Ohio. They were brainstorming about programming changes for their half-hour, Sunday morning news program. Everyone began calling Kalia, Pookie, when Chris started the trend after she wore a puka shell necklace every day for luck.

They decided to take a break and Chris logged on to the Great Escape forum.

"So, you called yourself, *Witzend*?" Pookie was looking over Chris' shoulder while she typed in her login name and password.

"Yeah, *Witzend;* I love it! That's such a fun name. I don't know if this will amount to anything, Pookie, but it's worth a try." *Sniff.*

"Waste of time, Chrissy; nothing good will come from this. It's a giant waste if you ask me."

"Now, now, you have to give it a chance, Pookie. Let me poke around and see if I can stir up some snakes. This is a well-established forum with thousands of members from all over the world. I might be able to get a good feel for opinions and attitudes of normal people on international issues." *Sniff.*

"You're assuming people who frequent those forums are normal. And stop *sniffing*." Pookie wrinkled her nose and snorted. When she backed away, she crossed her eyes and twisted her fingers in her dimples.

Chris snickered, "This is science fiction, Pookie. For the most part we're all disembodied brains."

"Thanks for that swell image, Chrissy," Pookie rolled her eyes.

Chris giggled. "You know what I mean, Pookie. We're trying to understand each other while lacking facial expression and body language to help gauge the meaning of each other's messages. Of course, the funny little smiley faces help."

"Let's see," Chris mumbled to herself, "Okay, I've already posted on the Welcome New Members thread. I'll start with the Political Debate Forum and read the Current Events topics. Afterward, I'll look for interesting members and send some Private Messages."

"I really don't see the need for you to join a forum. We're doing well without any outside help and I see it as a distraction."

Pookie received no response from Chris.

"Yawn. All right then, wake me when it's over."

"Do I *have* to?"

After a lot of head shaking and eye rolling, Pookie threw up her hands and went into the production booth to run through Sunday morning's segment line-up.

Chris was deep in thought about what to write and absent-mindedly chewed on a dry spot of skin on her lip. She could write that she was married to her job; that it took five years of single-minded dedication and brutal, competitive pushing to work her way up from production assistant to production manager even with her talent, outstanding education, and credentials. She moved from station to station around the country and Hawaii. She finally landed at the CableCoNews Affiliate in Cleveland producing the local early Sunday morning news. She took Kalia with her from KHLU in Honolulu when she moved to CableCoNews. It was a *too-fer* deal. No Kalia; no Chris. She wouldn't mention that she was extremely overweight and aware that some at the station ridiculed the way she dressed and called her Frumpy-Dumpy behind her back. Instead, she wrote that she was in her mid-twenties, single, lived in Midwest America, and wanted new perspectives on international politics and current events.

Another new member, Frenchtoast, logged on the forum while Christine was writing her messages. A French expatriate living in London, Jacques Bonnier, wrote his own message on the Welcome New Members thread. He wrote that he chose the forum name *Frenchtoast*, because at the time he was hungry and eating a slice of toast. It was as simple as that. Jacques wrote that he was against the war in Iraq and he hated America and everything she stood for. He wrote that George Bush, or the *Shrub*, as he called him, was not worthy of wiping his feet on him. He wrote that he collected antique French wine glasses with rooster designs.

Jacques joined this forum to troll for women. To him, women were all birds of a feather. Although he claimed an interest in politics and international affairs, the last thing Jacques Bonnier would tell you on his welcome thread was that his real interest was in affairs of a different kind.

The forum's new members, DPGJ, Witzend, Frenchtoast, and Diva, hadn't spent much time on the forum messageboard, but what one reading the board couldn't see was the flurry of Private Messages among them behind the scenes.

Private Message from Witzend to Frenchtoast:

"Hi, Frenchtoast!

My real name is Christine. I live in Cleveland, in the Midwest of America. I'm in my mid-twenties and I work in TV. I read that you collect wineglasses with rooster designs. Why is that? I also noticed that you are very anti-American. Why is that? What do you do for a living and where do you live? What is your real name? Let's get acquainted!

Christine"

Private Message from Frenchtoast to Witzend:

"*Bonjour, ma petite amie*, Christine!

My real name is Jacques Bonnier, but you must call me Jaxx. I collect antique wine glasses with roosters because the cockerel is the national bird of France. I am French and a wine distributor. I have a successful business and live in London. This is my web address: http://www.JAXXAN.distribution.com.

I am single and a hard worker. I am anti-American because Americans have no culture, unlike France, the center of culture in the world. America's foreign politics are *merde* and Americans are warmongers. Jaxx apologizes if he hurts your feelings, but *c'est la vie, n'est-ce pas*?

Jaxx also is attaching his picture standing in front of the terrible Eiffel Tower and there is another photo of Jaxx with his wine and beer on his website. Would you send one of yourself to Jaxx, svp?

Maybe between us we can work out how to solve our country's differences. Write soon, *ma petit cherie*.

Bisous, Jaxx"

Jaxx was very pleased with himself. In his own mind, he was bigger than life and loved talking about himself in the third person. He earned his living through an online Import/Export business that he named JAXXAN International Liquors, Wines and Beers. According to his website, he sold and distributed French, British, Australian, and German wines and beers worldwide. His business was very successful and he handled it competently.

Logging off the forum, he stretched and spoke aloud.

"Ah, now it is time to take a break and find a pub to quench Jaxx' thirst and to feed Jaxx' appetite."

Chris was pleased that Jaxx replied and she went to his website. She was impressed by his business, but amused by the picture taken in a way that it appeared the Eiffel Tower was growing out of his head. She found his email address on the website and wrote her response in fluent French.

Jaxx woke up the next morning to Chris's e-mail message. He thought Christine must be very intelligent to have become so fluent. Any American who learned to speak French must be a *cultivee, elegante et charmante petit parakeet.*

Hayley logged back on to the forum later that day and found a private message from Witzend. *I remember that name; she's a new member, too.*

Private Message from Witzend to Diva:

"Hiya Diva,

I saw your message in the Welcome New Member section. I'm new here, too. I see we are both single and both Americans. How did you like the discussion with Dr. Gabriel-Johns? Did it help you? I hope so. I joined the group to see what he had to say. I thought he was brilliant.

I'm in Cleveland and my real name is Chris. I'm in my mid-twenties and I'm a Producer for CableCoNews. I got my forum name from my last name. Horowitz - Witz-end. What is your real name and where are you located?

Chris"

Private Message from Diva to Witzend:

"Hi Witzend-Chris, I'm Hayley.

Nice to meet you my fellow American. I once knew a girl named Chris Horowitz, but she was from California.

Hayley"

Private Message from Witzend to Diva:

"Hi Hayley!

I am originally from California. I noticed the spelling of your name is different from the usual way people spell it - Hailey, Haley - and I once knew someone who spelled her name Hayley and she was from New York City. Do you live in New York, Hayley?

Chris"

Private Message from Diva to Witzend:

"Hi Chris,

I live on Manhattan's Upper East Side. I have a Yorkshire terrier named Diva and I borrowed her name for the forum. I'm in my mid-twenties, too. I was born in England, but I grew up in America. I met my Christine Horowitz approximately ten years ago. I'm hoping by some outrageous coincidence you are that same Chris.

Hayley"

Private Message from Witzend to Diva:

Dear Hayley,

Yay! I am that same Chris! Yes, we met almost ten years ago in Central Park so that I could write an article about you. I gave you a signet ring and you gave me a jacket. My lucky jacket. I contacted you five years ago and your attorney wouldn't give you my messages. You can't imagine how excited I am!

Chris ♥"

Private Message from Diva to Witzend:

Dear Chris,
"This is unbelievable and wonderful, Christine! I'm happy to find you again, too. I remember how much fun that day was for me. Do you remember that you talked about us studying French together at the Sorbonne? Whenever I daydreamed after that, it was always about going to France with you. I wear your signet ring to this day. We were going to vacation in Southampton after graduation. Do you remember? It was the first thing I thought about when I woke from the coma. Let's rekindle our friendship through this forum.
Hayley"

"Pookie, I'm so excited! You could never guess who is a member of this forum. Do you remember Hayley Hamilton, the young heiress from Manhattan who survived the small plane crash that killed her parents about five years ago? I met Hayley when we were teenagers and wrote an article about her. I've been having private message conversations with her. I can't tell you how happy I am being in touch with her again."

"Really? I remember that, Chris. It was ghastly. Do you know if they ever found out who did it?"

"No, Pookie, the police have never found the killer. I've always wanted to dig into that story, but never took the time after the first couple of years. I tried to get to see Hayley again, but her attorney wrote that she wasn't receptive. Do you still think the forum is a waste of time?"

"Well, it might not be a *totally* bad idea."

"Told ya so." *Sniff.*

"*Yeah, yeah, yeah.* We'll see. '*It ain't over till the fat lady sings'*."

Chris caught the look on Pookie's face after the fat lady remark. It said, *Damn-how-could-I-be-so-dumb*, so she ignored the comment.

"I want to find good news to mix up with the bad news and I want to mix things up a bit. Most of the local news is bad. Bad weather, fires, accidents, crimes, murders. *Death. Death. Death.* How do we fix it so it's not all so damned depressing?" *Sniff.*

"How 'bout putting something in the water that'll make everybody turn nice?"

"Great idea, Pookie," Chris laughed, "that's probably what it'll take. Some new mind-altering elixir that will turn humanoids into the advanced beings we mistakenly believe we are."

"Actually, I've been thinking about some innovative programming and jotted down a couple of ideas." Pookie took a pad of paper from her desk. "Have you come up with anything yet, Chrissy?"

"Yup. What do you think of this?" Chris spun around in her chair to face Pookie and rattled off a number of ideas. "And I'll develop ideas for expanding our website. It's not as chock-a-block as it could be."

Pookie snickered. "*Chock-a-block*? Is that your *wacky word* for the day, Chrissy?"

The women put their suggestions together to work up a presentation for the next production meeting. They were sure they'd hit on a good formula with potential for expansion to an hour format. They worked until eleven o'clock, when, exhausted, Pookie left the studio. Chris left after midnight having worked late in the control room. Hungry and tired, she looked forward to a good meal and dropping into bed.

Juggling her jacket, purse, cell phone, and laptop computer, Christine let the door close behind her and walked to her old Woodie. Hers was the only car left on the darkened parking lot. She tossed everything onto the passenger's seat and got in. She put the key in the ignition and on the first try, the engine would only grind. She tried starting it for so long the battery died.

Frustrated, Chris walked back to the building. She had forgotten that at midnight, the door automatically locked until five o'clock in the morning.

"*Damn.* Note to self: Add a night security guard to that list," she muttered. She called Pookie on her cell, but her call rolled to voicemail. "I should have gotten Triple-A." She mentally kicked herself for always being so cheap.

Heaving a sigh, Chris resigned herself to sleeping in the car overnight. *Well, it won't be the first time I've slept in that old car.* She returned to the Woodie, got in, and locked the doors. The inside of the car looked like a trash heap. She rummaged through the pile on passenger's seat for something to eat. In a crushed McDonald's sack, she found a stale carton of fries, a half-eaten cheeseburger, and a half-full bottle of water. Under a pile of papers and folders, she found a sticky breath mint.

"*Ah-hah*! Dinner *and* a toothbrush." *Sniff.*

Having climbed over the passenger's seat into the back, Chris spread her lucky jacket over her legs and turned on her laptop. The computer got a wireless signal from the studio. Then, to entertain herself, she logged onto the forum and sent a chatty private message to Jaxx.

She sent an email to Pookie explaining what happened and asked her to wake her when she got there in the morning. She called her mom and dad to say hello but never intended to tell them she was sleeping in the car because she was too cheap to call a taxi. She thought the call would roll to voicemail, but Ben picked up.

"Oh, hi, Dad! I thought you'd be fast asleep, but I'm glad you're there. I was going to leave a message. I had a minute..."

"What's wrong, Christine? It's late in that godforsaken city and I can tell from your voice..."

"Nothing's wrong, Dad. I can't start my car is all, so I'm sleeping in it overnight. No big deal," she giggled nervously.

"Really? No big deal, 'eh? Any sane person wouldn't sleep in her car all night in a dangerous and open parking lot with her cell phone and expensive laptop computer around her." She heard exasperation in his voice and his long, deep sigh. "*Oy vey*, Christine," he huffed, "you're *meshuggaas,* kid. Do me a favor; call a cab, please. You need money? Tell me if you need money. If you're so desperate that you can't call a cab, I'll send you money."

"I'm fine, Dad. Honest, I don't need money and I'm safe. Don't worry. I shouldn't have called," she rolled her eyes.

"You're going backwards, Christine; we thought you had common sense. Time to come home kiddo, where we can keep our eyes on you while you finish growing up."

"*Yeah, yeah, yeah*, Dad, how come you never kept your eyes on me when I was a kid*?" A little fancy footwork and dagger twirling here*. "Hey, Dad; do you remember Hayley Hamilton? You know; the young pianist at Julliard I wrote about who survived that horrible plane disaster? Well, I've found her again and we've been staying in touch."

"That's great, kiddo! Yeah, I remember that episode. Your mother is still pissed at me for letting you fly across the country alone."

"I lived," she snorted. "What I remember most is thinking that her borg-parents assimilated her and completely controlled her life. They forged her into their idea of a perfect child and I have no doubt they adored her. They were the ultimate overprotective parents, but that's how they showed they adored her."

"You think we *don't* adore you, Christine? We protected you as best we could."

"I supposed so, about as much as adoptive parents could. I always felt thrust upon you because of the circumstance of my birth. I always considered myself an intruder in your hectic daily lives. And why not?" She sighed, "I'm one of those plain little things nobody notices, like that ugly dog-doo-doo gift Aunt Bessie scraped off her shoe and bronzed that you stash in a dark place ready to haul out when she comes for a visit."

"What is this? Your own little pity party? That drek's beneath you, Christine. Of *course* we adored you. We still do and always will. That was an ungrateful, rotten thing to say about your mother and me," Ben spat out. "You judge Hayley's parents as showing their adoration through over protectiveness, but you mistake our long lead of trust for disinterest. You'd have screamed child abuse if we'd tried to control you," he scoffed. "You wouldn't cooperate when we tried to reason with you to do things in your own best interest. Christine, you are still a pig-headed, super-brat with a crap attitude and you damned well know it. All you can think about is yourself. You haven't once mentioned your mother's new movie, *Regardless of the Rumor*. I suppose you haven't bothered to see it. And another thi-..."

Oh, *crap. He's on a roll.* Chris's exhales were short and raspy and her eyes were brimming with tears. "Listen, Dad. This is not going well. I'm hanging up now. Tell Mom I love her."

"All right, Christine. If you need anythi-..."

"I don't. I'm fine. Don't worry; I'll call soon. *Hug. Hug. Kiss. Kiss. Love ya.*" She sighed and hung up.

Ben squished her like a bug, but he always felt bad after he'd stomped her. She left the cell turned on thinking he might call back to make nice. *I'll see Diane's film when it comes to the dollar movie, or I'll rent the Video.*

Later, while sitting in the dark, reading the forum, and eating the cold burger and fries by the eerie glow of an old LCD computer screen, Chris was still thinking about changes to the program. Eating the miserable, cold food gave her another idea. *We could add a contest segment where we have some overweight women start diets, follow their progress, have some expert nutritionists give advice and give a reward, like a makeover or cash gift, to the woman with the best weekly progress. We could feature them on our website.*

With this in mind, she thought about making some serious changes to her own lifestyle.

Exhausted from putting in long hours, Chris fell asleep with her computer and cell phone turned on. After sleeping off and on all night, she awoke to Pookie tapping on the window. Stiff and sore from the cramped position, she stood outside the car, stretching and yawning. Her laptop and cell phone batteries were dead.

Gathering her belongings, Chris wearily shuffled into the building. Pookie and several others were already working in the production room. She popped the breath mint into her mouth and went inside the control booth to prepare sound bites and final copy for the Sunday morning edition of the news. She dropped into the chair and slumped forward over the controls. Rubbing her neck, she closed her bleary eyes, stretched, and yawned.

"I'll kiss the first gnome who brings me a cup of coffee."

~14~

"The universe is change;
our life is what our thoughts make it."
~ Marcus Aurelius Antonius~

CableCoNews Studio
Cleveland, Ohio
September 2004

Two weeks after they started the hour-long MetroMakers of the Week Sunday program, Christine ran into the production booth waving the morning newspaper.

*"We're a hit!"*She grabbed Pookie's arm and held on, flapping the newspaper in front of her. "*We did it, Pooks!* Listen to this review in the Entertainment Section –

> "CableCoNews' new format for their Sunday local news program, MetroMakers of the Week, is dynamic, attention grabbing, and wildly applauded by the local audience. Ratings for the station's Sunday morning program jumped from the lowest to the highest in only a matter of weeks."

Chris and Pookie had presented their ideas to the news director and the executive producer. They called a meeting with the station managers, who were so pleased with the new format and ideas for the website that they gave the Sunday morning news an hour to start the new season. They renamed the program, CableCoNews' MetroMakers of the Week, and bumped a paid commercial for a bogus face cream that was supposed to make women appear twenty years younger. The new sponsors they attracted made up for the lost income ten-fold.

Chris developed new program graphics and a segment lineup. Her favorite idea, a health and fitness program for a thirteen-week weight loss segment called, the *Chub-Club,* was all the rage with the public. The website would have a section showing before and after comparisons. Local salons vied for a spot to do a makeover for the winners and a local men's fashion store provided a new look for the male winners. Oscar Bluette, from Cold Spring, Colorado, sponsored the Chub-Club with his Rocky Mountain ale called, *Ol' Chubbs.* Oscar sent the winner's family on a weeklong, all-expense paid winter ski vacation to Aspen as his guest.

The Chub-Club members produced a motivating cookbook of their favorite low-calorie recipes. Chris worked with each member who wrote a section about how their lives and health had improved by getting their weight under control. Chris wrote the introduction to the book and she'd included her own success story.

The response was overwhelming for the segment, *Anchor's Away*, a weekly contest with a handsome and popular male desk anchor on the street they renamed, Jay Walker, giving clues to his location. The first person to find him and give the password for the day from the station's website was the winner. Crowds formed around him and onlookers were elbowing their way in front of the camera. Chris and Pookie were onsite when the crowd grew so large that they had to rope off the space where he stood to update the news.

Sponsors and advertisers were beginning to ante up prizes such as laptop computers, cruises, trips, cell phones, and other somewhat expensive electronic gifts, gadgets, and gizmos.

The station petitioned local schools for names of students who formed music groups and featured them each Sunday for ten weeks. Viewers voted for their favorite groups by texting in and scoring them from one to ten. The winning group won an expense-paid gig in Las Vegas at Caesar's Palace who put them up in their famous Rainman Suite. Pookie and a CableCoNews camera crew followed them around from beginning to end capturing their reactions and filming their performances to use throughout the show. Finally, they performed live onsite during the Anchor's Away segment.

Chris expanded the channel's website with a messageboard for viewers to discuss current events, the program, the anchors, Chub-Club, and student bands.

The production crew set up a webcam in the studio so that the voyeurs in the audience could watch the anchors and technicians while they made the set ready for the program. At first, the staff was self-conscious about the webcam, but then they ignored it. It was eventually left on twenty-four seven as the studio was used around the clock and they set up a live feed from the website for those who were sitting at their desks working at their computers.

However, all of these changes meant twice as much work for the production staff -- namely, Chris and Pookie. Their increased budget made it possible to pay a competitive salary and they were able to attract a popular news anchor from another local news channel for the program. Both women got a raise, a big bonus, the promise of two additional production staff members, and someone to manage the website.

Chris's reputation soared with the successful transition and she was beginning to get nibbles from local affiliates. She was flattered, but she wanted the whole *megillah*; the top-rated cable news channel, Savvy News, in New York City. She decided to act while attention was on her. She sent her résumé weeks ago, but still hadn't received a response.

This move wasn't about money, but if her parents knew how small her salary at CableCoNews was, they'd want her to give it up and come home. The reality was that she knew if she ever needed anything, they'd be there for her. All she had to do was ask. From the time Chris graduated from college, she'd never asked them for financial help and never tapped the trust fund that her parents' broker managed. She prided herself on paying her own way and compensated by living small. She learned the value of investing the day she spent with Hayley and now owned a good-sized portfolio. She reinvested her Certificates of Deposit, stocks picks were doing well, and her 401-K was performing better than she expected.

Chris felt confident that dipping into her savings was an investment in her career and thus, her future. Because she was frugal, she'd accumulated a reserve of ready money in her passbook savings account and planned to use some of it for her new wardrobe. She was determined to go to New York to perform a magical image makeover, because for Chris, in the end, New York was where she wanted to be.

Chris couldn't have been happier. Not only was her star rising over Cleveland, she had lost her heart to Jaxx, who wrote to her every day with fanciful vows of endless love and devotion.

After the *Night-In-The-Car Episode*, as Pookie called it, Christine made a conscious effort to get her life organized. She'd gotten Triple-A and never wanted to eat McVictuals out of the backseat of her car again. She began to grocery shop differently and was much more conscious about what she ate, even if the meals were from McDonalds. She chose salads and healthier fare. She hit the produce section and avoided the snack foods. She sandwiched her favorite cookbook, Pig Out, between Atkins for Life and the South Beach Diet. She took time to prepare healthy meals and found she preferred the taste of these foods to the junk food and fast food that was her staple diet for so long. She was surprised that she could afford simple healthy food and stay within her meager budget. In the evening, she exercised to her mother's old Jane Fonda Workout videotape.

Now that she was on a health and self-improvement kick, her unattractive clothes were baggier and looked shabbier than ever and she wanted to go shopping for some new outfits.

"New York, *Pee-Oookie!*" she exclaimed to Pookie. "I want to go to New York for fall clothes! Buddinghill's, my friend; *Shopper's Paradise*!" *Sniff*.

"Yeah, right, Chrissy," scoffed Pookie, "You're a makeover waiting to happen."

Chris ignored her comment. "I'm doing this thing right. I don't care what it costs."

"What's that I hear?" Pookie curved her hand around her ear, "*Ka-ching*! What bank are you going to rob, Chrissy? Or did you find some loose change in the break room sofa cushions?" Pookie pursed her lips, "You know, there are perfectly good clothing stores here in Cleveland. Oh, *tsk tsk*, silly me; but how would you know? You've limited your shopping to Goodwill and thrift stores, if I'm not mistaken."

"Yeah, but that just proves I support charities, Pook-annihilator," Chris snickered and turned off her computer for the day. "How about keeping me company tonight while I replace my fan belt? I've got Ol' Chubbs ale on ice and a veggie pizza."

Chris still maintained her Woodie. She changed the oil and made all the engine repairs by herself. When the red color began to fade, she decided to have it repainted and chose yellow, opening herself to more ridicule. The staff at CableCoNews called her car, the *Yellow Submarine*.

Pookie sat on a wooden crate in the driveway drinking Ol' Chubbs ale from the can, while Chris replaced the worn fan belt. Chris wore her favorite black tee shirt, on which was written, *I See Dumb People,* in big white letters. Pookie wore a faded Hawaiian shirt of blue and yellow flowers and a pair of cut-off jeans.

Chris glanced at Pookie, a tall and slim young woman who dressed well. She was striking with her mellow skin, lush features, and waist length, wavy black hair. The last time Pookie kept her company while Chris worked on the car, she told Chris that her mother was Hawaiian and her father was white and came from the mainland.

"I grew up on Kauai with loads of good-looking brothers and sisters." She'd laughed. "Sometimes we'd get up early in the morning to sneak up on our mother and father. We'd find them hiding on the beach, in coves, or among rocks showing each other just how much they enjoyed making all us kids."

Pookie took a long swig of her beer.

"Chrissy, you are a sexy little greasy-monkey."

"Do I smell like eau de sweaty-garage-mechanic?"

"*Hey...yeah!* Sweaty Garage Mechanic cologne for guys?"

"Or would calling it toilet water be more appropriate?"

"When you go to Buddinghill's, Chrissy, ask them if we can market Sweaty Garage Mechanic cologne through their catalog. I'll bet more women than men would buy it."

"I wouldn't turn up my nose at that!" Chris grinned. "Do guys turn you on with their bulging muscles?"

"Turn me on, Chrissy?" Pookie snorted. Her dark eyes sparkling merrily, she jumped up and made the muscles in her arms bulge.

"Woo-Woo!" Chris hooted as she dropped the car hood and wiped her hands on an old towel. She hopped around Pookie in circles making gestures that she thought men believed were virile and masculine.

"Actually, your arms are slim and shapely from your diet, Chrissy. Normally it's difficult to see any change because of your baggy, shapeless clothes."

Pookie tossed an empty Ol' Chubb beer can to Chris and she balanced it on her head. The last dregs of beer trickled down her forehead and dripped off the end of her nose.

Later that evening, Chris mulled over Pookie's comment about her baggy, shapeless clothes. That cinched it. She would go to New York to shop and decided to send a message to Hayley.

<u>Private Message from Witzend to Diva:</u>

"Hi Hayley,

You know our Sunday Morning News program is going gangbusters. Well, I've been working so hard that I actually shed pounds and I need some new fall clothes. I want to shop at Buddinghill's and I would like you to go with me. I'll bet you have excellent taste.

By the way, Hayley, you may know On Board the Great Escape administrators are planning to have a meeting in New York City in December. I told them I would help. Would you like to plan it with me?

Will you go shopping with me? Please?

Chris ♥"

<u>Private Message from Diva to Witzend:</u>

"Hi Chris,

When are you coming to New York? You might think about using the store's personal shopper to help you. Buddinghill's personal shopper's service is free. All you have to do is make an appointment. Her name is Lydia. Tell her I sent you.

Hayley"

<u>Private Message from Witzend to Diva:</u>

"Hiya Hayley,

I want you to know I'll be in New York City next week on Monday and Tuesday. I have contacted the Personal Shopper, Lydia, at Buddy's and have an appointment with her. I dropped your name and she remembers you. I can't wait! Can't you go with me? Please? I hope you will. I would like very much to see you. Have you made a decision about helping to plan the forum Meeting in NYC? It would be fun to work together. Please write soon.

XOX♥

Chris"

<u>Private Message from Diva to Witzend</u>:

"Hi Chris,

I have appointments with my accountant and financial advisor that day, so I'll not be able to shop with you. I hope you aren't too disappointed. However, I'm extending an invitation to you to come for dinner after you shop. Will you accept? Monday night would be perfect for me. I'll help you any way I can to plan the meeting.

Hayley"

<u>Private Message from Diva to DPGJ:</u>

"Dear Peter,

I found an old acquaintance on the forum. Her name is Christine Horowitz and she calls herself Witzend. Christine is coming to New York next week to shop and I asked her to dinner here in the penthouse.

I've been talking to Dr. Sydney Lawton, your colleague, who has been sorting out my fears and helping me to gain perspective. Thank you for putting her in touch with me. The therapy is working.

I know you play violin, Peter, we once discussed music, but may I ask what composers and styles you prefer? At this moment, I'm enjoying Mahler's First Symphony, on a CD that the New York Philharmonic released in 1998. I enjoy sentimental music such as this and I find his style intellectually stimulating yet romantic. I love the counterpoint of his melodies.

Peter, your friendship and support has meant so much to me over these weeks and months.

Hayley"

<u>Private Message from DPGJ to Diva:</u>

"Hayley, my Dear,

I'm so pleased that you have taken this step to open yourself to new experiences. Seeing Christine again and working with her on the forum meeting, even though you don't plan to attend, is good progress and Dr. Lawton is a fine therapist. She will help you to put everything in perspective.

Hayley, I also want to share with you something I read. On December 18, the New York Philharmonic will be playing a record-setting 14,000th concert. That is a remarkable achievement for the orchestra. Isn't this the same date as the forum meeting? If so, I have a plan to suggest to you. I know you are an aficionado of the Philharmonic and if you would be willing, I would like you to accompany me to this once-in-a-lifetime concert. I'll come to New York and stay at the Plaza. We can spend the afternoon together before the concert. I suggest High Tea in the Palm Court. Please think it over, Hayley, and then let's discuss arrangements via telephone.

Peter"

~15~

"Falling in love consists merely in uncorking the imagination and bottling the common-sense."
~ Helen Rowland~

CableCoNews Studio
Cleveland, Ohio
September 2004

Pookie shook Christine by her shoulders and looked her squarely in the eyes.

"Chrissy, you think this shopping trip to Buddinghill's is all about your career, don't you?"

"Well, yes. What's your point, *McPook-a-lator?"* Chris shrugged off Pookie's grasp and avoided her eyes. "You know I've never spent money on clothes to attract the opposite sex. No, this is a career makeover about appearance and first impressions, Pookie. When Margaret Thatcher was Prime Minister, she said, 'Appearance is the first impression people get of you. It does matter.'"

"Wow, from Maggie's lips to your ears and it only took -- *how long* -- for you to get it?

"What makes you think I haven't *got* it?"

"I'd bet your life on it."

"Nah, this is about my career, Pookie."

"Listen Chris; my point is that you can delude yourself, but you aren't fooling me. I've read some of this Jaxx troll's drivel and he has a vision of you as '*elegante et charmante.*' More than anything, you want to turn yourself into his Fantasy Cyberbabe."

"But Pookie, he said he's totally in love with me. I'm his sweetheart, his baby, his one and only love. He said he can't wait to throw me down and ravish me." She snickered. "Okay, yeah; all but that last part."

"*Oh, gag me*, Christine. You can be such an *idiot!*"

Pookie thought it was unlike Chris to delude herself. It *was* about Jaxx, but then, everything about Jaxx was delusional and an illusion. Throughout the day, Chris exchanged ten or twelve messages with Jaxx and she had left the office with his last message on the screen hidden behind a crawl that Chris had programmed to read -- *Yawn...wake me when Pookie shuts up.*

She rolled her chair over to Chris's desk, jiggled the mouse to wake up the computer, and read his message --

Private Message from Frenchtoast to Witzend:

"Ma chéri,

You have pulled yourself deep into my heart and make my heart beat in a way I never thought possible. Ma *petite bébé,* I love having you there. You are my precious one. You are unique; so elegant, cultured, and beautiful. You have my love. You have my spirit. Your spirit lives within me. I want to take you away and make love with you forever.

Tout mon amour."

Jaxx

"Oh, blaach. How can she believe this rubbish?"

Pookie hit her forehead with her hand. *He's never even met her, or seen a picture of her for that matter, and yet he says she's elegant... cultured... beautiful. What a freakazoid.*

She shook her head and left the room.

Chris returned to her desk and responded to Jaxx --

Private Message from Witzend to Frenchtoast:

"*Oh-la-la,* Jaxx!

You are turning my head. I think you already have my heart and it feels like home. I find you so exciting. You are precious to me, too. *Mon chér*, are you going to the December forum meeting, Onboard the Great Escape's New York City Getaway? If you go, we can meet. I want to meet you so much. Won't that be exciting? *Merveilleux! Très heureux*! What fun! I live for the day we can be together body to body and spirit to spirit!

Love,

Chris"

Private Message from Frenchtoast to Witzend:

"*Ma amour, très belle,*

Day in and day out, Jaxx thinks of nothing but his glorious Christine, in far off America, out of reach of Jaxx loving hands. He cannot touch you. He wants to feel your skin, look into your eyes and whisper all the words that tumble in his head about the feelings in his heart. *Ma belle amour*, Jaxx is so in love, he must see you, hold you, feel your beating heart against his.

Je t'adore,

Jaxx

Private Message from Witzend to Frenchtoast:

"*Mon Cher* Jaxx,

Your sweet words are so exciting. You mean so much to me. I'm head over heels in love. I can't wait to meet you and for us to be together. You must come to New York City to the forum meeting. Please promise me you'll come. I need you. I must be with you.

Tout mon amour,

Christine"

Pookie walked back into the production room. "Still playing lothario footsie on your electronic forum game, Chrissy?"

Chris jumped; she'd focused all her attention on the love she poured out to Jaxx through her computer.

"*Sheesh*, Pookie. You startled me!" She frowned and glared. "Stop sneaking up on me like that." *Sniff.*

"Me? I didn't sneak. And don't give *me* the stink-eye. You aren't aware of anything once you start mooning over Casanova, who, by the way, you have never met."

"He's my *Cracker-Jaxx,* Pookie," she laughed, "and I have just asked him to meet me in December in New York. When I read his messages, it's as though I'm right there in his arms. He's as yummy as a great, big box of chocolates!"

Pookie stuck out her tongue as though she'd just tasted something bitter.

"Yeah and he's about as substantial as chocolate is nourishing," she muttered and shook her head. Her waist-length black hair bounced on her back and her gold coin earrings jingled. "Oh, good grief, Chris, get a grip. It's bizarre and just not possible. There's not a shred of sincerity in a single word he's written. Why can't you see what I see? Don't you realize how creepy all of this is?"

"It isn't creepy at all, Pookie." *Sniff.* Chris looked at her defensively. "I've fallen in love. I feel as close to him as if I were with him every day in the flesh."

"*Whatever.*" Pookie shrugged with resignation. "You make me want to bite my knuckle." She shook her head, thinking Chris was asking for heartbreak. She was more convinced than ever that Chris's makeover *was* about Jaxx. "I'm heading out, Chrissy. See you in the morning."

Sitting alone in the gloom, Chris' computer dinged. She'd received a response from Jaxx to her plea to come to New York.

Private Message from Frenchtoast to Witzend:

"My dearest,

You have entwined your heart with mine. Your love makes me happy and your sincerity and commitment give me strength. All I can say is that Jaxx returns your love and will always be here for you.

But, these are only words. Yes, you will see Jaxx in December. You will hear him and feel him. I promise you one thing; As soon as we embrace, Jaxx will melt deep in your heart and touch your soul when he utters the words he is yearning to say to you -

"*Ma cherie* Christine, *Je t'aime*."

Jaxx took pleasure in the attention of any woman whether in writing or in person. On the forum, he began a flirtation after their initial response to him and in stages; he entwined them in an emotional or sexually driven on-line relationship. But most of Jaxx' attention was still on Christine. He fantasized about Christine's American beauty. In New York, they would both have hotel rooms, he reminded himself smugly. However, for that event, Jaxx knew many of his birds would be flocking to New York and *oui, ils veulent rencontrer Jaxx,* he chuckled to himself. They cannot wait to meet their beloved.

In Jaxx' London studio flat, there was a battered and rusty birdcage that he'd found in a junkyard. Inside the cage were dozens of colorful origami birds with all the forum women's names, including Chris,' written on them. Each day, he shook up the cage, reached in the door, and pulled out three brightly colored birds.

"These, then, are the lucky little birds that have won my JAXX-POT for tomorrow. *Jusqu'au demain mes joiles petits poules et canards chanceux*." His laugh was sly and throaty. "Until tomorrow, my lucky ducks, *vous avez de la chance sacres!"*

~16~

"They always say time changes things,
but you actually have to change them yourself."
~ Andy Warhol~

New York City, New York
October 2004

All her life, Christine had placed utmost value on her intellectual pursuit. She relied on what she believed were the madcap qualities of her personality to influence others and get attention for herself. She sought validation through her ability to communicate. Generally, when it counted, Chris said all the right things. It finally occurred to her that was only half of what decision-makers were looking for.

In an industry where looking your best was central to success, she was beginning to accept the reality that her appearance would make or break her prospect to influence people who might consider her for better jobs. In those first thirty-seconds a person had to form an impression of her, how she looked was saying, "I won't fit in." No matter how brilliant her thoughts, or astute her words, her appearance spoke volumes and was saying all the wrong things.

Her successful implementation of the Sunday morning program gave Christine's career greater potential than ever before. Local channels were pursuing her, but she set her sights much higher. And, of course, there was Jaxx, who would see her for the first time in December. Now was the time, or maybe the time was long past due.

Private Message from Witzend to Diva:

"Hi Hayley!

I've booked a flight from Akron to LaGuardia leaving tomorrow morning. When I arrive, I'll go to Buddy's and I'll be with the personal shopper all day. I'll check into my hotel, leave my bags, and go from there to the Top of the Turret. Thank you for your kind dinner invitation. I have the address and I'll try to arrive for dinner about five o'clock PM. I'm truly excited about seeing you again.

Jaxx says he's coming to be with me in New York. I'm so excited, that I need to clone myself; one of me to do my work and one of me to jump up and down with glee!

XOX♥

Chris"

Private Message from Diva to Witzend:

"Hi, Chris,

When you arrive at the entrance to the Top of the Turret, tell my Uncle Arthur (Symington, he'll be on duty), who you are. I'll tell him to expect you. He'll let me know when you've arrived and I'll send Miguel to escort you upstairs.

I'm happy for you that Jaxx is coming to NYC to see you. Perhaps you and Jaxx will join Peter and me for tea at the Plaza?

Hugs,

Hayley"

Hayley found herself humming and walking with a quicker, lighter step on the morning of Chris's arrival. Miguel was walking Diva and she moved her little legs as fast as she could to keep up with them. She gave up and sat on the sidewalk as if to say, "*Carry me.*" Hayley asked Miguel to pick Diva up because she was carrying a cardboard tray with a bag of sweet rolls and two cups of coffee in her hands.

As they approached the residence, Hayley stopped at the boarded up building next door. In front of the doorway, she placed the tray with a bag of sweet rolls and coffee with a five-dollar bill under it. It barely touched the ground before two scrawny hands reached out and snatched up the treats.

Symington and Hayley went through their morning ritual after Hayley handed him coffee with the usual fifty-dollar bill wrapped around the cup. At first, he'd refused the money, but Hayley convinced him to take it for his retirement fund. She gave generously to him because he looked out for her all those years and because Symington said he wanted to retire early. He planned to return to England to seek his roots, connect with his brothers and sisters, and find distant relatives.

Arthur's father, distantly related to the Symington port family, was an English genealogist with very little in his estate to share with all his progeny. Symington's income had always been paltry. He'd saved most of it, having very few expenses as a gentleman's gentleman. When he immigrated to America, Elizabeth wanted to set up a trust for him, but his pride would not allow him to accept her generosity. Hayley convinced him that these gifts gave her pleasure.

"Behold, King Arthur," Hayley smiled at Symington.

"Behold, Princess Sunshine!" Symington beamed, opening the door for her. "Thank you, my dear. You're far too generous."

"Not at all; you're welcome, my liege," Hayley grinned broadly. "Uncle Arthur, will you be on the lookout for Christine Horowitz, a friend, about five o'clock in the evening? I'm having my first dinner guest tonight."

Symington added Chris's name to a list and assured Hayley he would ring Miguel when her guest arrived.

Smiling at this sign of progress in Hayley, he watched her as she walked through the lobby to the waiting penthouse elevator and stepped inside with tiny Diva cradled in her arms. Miguel entered a code on a hidden keypad and Hayley waved to Symington as the doors closed.

Stepping off the elevator, Hayley thought about impressions Chris would have when she saw the penthouse for the first time. She regarded the foyer of the penthouse with new vision. In the center of the polished marble floor, her father had added a gleaming medallion. In the center was the crest of the Hamilton's ancestral Coat of Arms; a fruited oak tree springing from a ducal crown, symbolizing how the first Hamilton cleverly avoided death and escaped into Scotland in 1323.

She remembered an article in *Architectural Digest* written in 1999 after the renovation was completed. Hayley pulled off her ball cap, took the well-worn magazine off the shelf, and reread the article. It was a five-page color spread, with several smaller captioned color pictures of the family and a sidebar about John and Elizabeth's businesses. The author wrote –

> "When exiting the private elevator into the pink marble foyer of Lady Elizabeth Hayles-Townsend Hamilton's Park Avenue penthouse, one feels magically transported from the bustling, noisy American city below to a luxurious European chateau. In the foyer are two doorways -- one to the left and one to the right. The door to the right is the entrance to the Hamilton's businesses. Through this door, one enters into a constant hub of activity. They have designated nearly one-half of their home as office space for each of their businesses.
>
> Many people come and go, working behind the door to the right, but it's through the door to the left that takes visitors to the Hamilton's private chateau.
>
> Privileged few people enter the Hamilton's kingdom, but those so privileged are filled with awe by its elegance and palatial beauty."

Hayley closed the magazine and looked around the room.

"Nothing's changed and everything's changed since then," she whispered, rising from the chair and walking to her office. She switched on her computer, preparing to spend the day going over her income and expenses. The family had been moderately wealthy when

John became a consultant to the Microsoft legal team handling the suit with Apple Computer. Microsoft agreed to pay him with stock, and on Hayley's advice, he'd sold at its apex. Over the past five years, through keen insight and her uncanny knack for choosing stocks and investments that paid off, she tripled the size of the estate. Hayley decided to increase Marisol and Miguel's salaries again. She could afford to do that now.

While Chris shopped at Buddinghill's, Hayley met with her stockbroker, accountant, and financial advisor. It was nearly five o'clock when they left. She peeked in on Marisol when delicious aromas coming from the kitchen made her hungry. Because this was the first time in five years that Hayley invited a real guest to the penthouse, Marisol planned the menu carefully following all the recipes to assure everything was superb.

"Marisol, have you have prepared enough for everyone?"

"Oh, yes, I have already taken three dinners downstairs. I left Symington's warming in his oven. Your guest should be here soon, *si*? This is exciting, *Señorita* Hayley!"

"Yes; I'm excited, too, Marisol. I wonder how much Christine has changed."

Christine arrived at Buddinghill's upscale store on Lexington Avenue about ten o'clock in the morning. She was tempted to stop at the Garb-Grabber sale racks, but instead went directly to women's fashions. She told the receptionist that the Personal Shopper for Women's Clothing was expecting her. When Lydia came out of her office, she walked past Chris, who watched her trotting around the department, her high heels tip tapping on the terrazzo floor. Finally, she stopped in front of the receptionist.

"Pardon me; didn't you announce that there was someone waiting for the personal shopper?"

Christine stood up and approached her; "Hi, I'm Christine Horowitz. If you're Lydia, you are looking for me," but under her breath she mumbled, "What am I...chopped liver?" *Sniff.*

"Oh!" Lydia paused imperceptibly before introducing herself. "I'm so sorry, Ms. Horowitz. I was expecting someone... Madame Lydia Sorrel, at your service." She smiled warmly at Chris, trying to cover her gaff.

Lydia's eyes scrutinized her, while Chris admired Lydia's appearance. The woman was tall and slender; her asymmetrically cut brown hair was skillfully highlighted with blonde highlights and brunette lowlights. Her pumpkin-colored suit was definitely expensive haute couture and so were her tan crocodile shoes. Chris knew the stones in Lydia's whimsical jewelry were amber, turquoise, and jasper artfully entwined with gold beads.

"I'll tell you what," Chris said, with a cockeyed smile, "just bag up what you're wearing, Lydia, and I'll take it with me. *Oh-la-la*, your outfit is *très chic*," she put her fingertips to her mouth and threw a kiss. "I want to be drop dead gorgeous when I leave here, so please make me over in your image!"

Lydia showed no reaction to Chris's comment, but responded, "*Ah, oui*, Buddinghill's is the pinnacle of fashion for women who are the *crème de la crème* of style."

Oy vey, I feel like Lydia just spritzed me with her canned presentation.

The two women spent the morning selecting pieces from designer collections and the afternoon outfitting Chris with flattering, fashionable business attire and accessories. They worked well together to arrange outfits for work, meetings, and interviews. Chris was quick to grasp the basics of putting together a collection of outfits that flattered her figure and she responded well to Lydia's tutelage. They chose pieces from less expensive but classic American designer lines such as Ralph Lauren, Liz Claiborne, Jones of New York, and Calvin Klein. Lydia convinced Chris to include accent pieces from exclusive lines such as Bill Blass, Donna Karan, and Dolce & Gabbana that added a designer *caché* to her wardrobe.

Polite and accommodating throughout the day, Lydia provided a small fruit tray, sparkling water, and anything else necessary to make Chris's excursion productive.

"Lydia, I'm very pleased with what we've chosen. Thank you. I couldn't have done this without your help."

"Ms. Horowitz, I would like to recommend that you return tomorrow for a facial, compliments of Buddinghill's Elite Women's Spa, as a thank you for using our shopper's service. A makeup application with the Lancôme specialists is included. They will show you how to care for your skin and you will be pleased by the way it brightens your face. And they're having a special gift with a makeover tomorrow. You can choose seven free trial products *à la carte* to fill their signature bag."

"Well," Chris paused, "maybe. Oh, all right. I planned to do some sightseeing, but that might be a better use of my time. Yeah, I'll do it. I like free stuff," she laughed.

Chris left the *haute couture* department in the clothes she had worn into the city. Her arms were loaded with her travel backpack, a brown satchel she used as a handbag, a stack of shoeboxes and several of Buddinghill's Big Buddy Bags. On her way out, she caught a glimpse of herself in a full-length mirror. At first, she thought it was someone else, a homeless person or a bag lady. Shocked, she gasped, and stood in front of the mirror staring at her reflection. The baggy gray sweater hung on her body; the tan and grey plaid skirt was too long, too big, and looked like a horse blanket; the scuffed, clunky brown boots made her feet look huge; and her limp brown hair hung lifelessly down her back.

Negative impressions swirled through her mind -- *dowdy, stringy, dull, unkempt, and colorless.* "Give me a break! That's me? That can't be me," she muttered, "I look like a damned derelict!"

Having just spent hours in front of a mirror trying on stylish fashions that flattered her figure, the contrast made her feel as though she was seeing herself for the first time. She was appalled, turning from side to side to view all angles. The realization of what her appearance had been saying about her began to sink in and her stomach burned. *On top of this, it's late and I won't have time to go to the Plaza to change into my new clothes.* Feeling miserable, she gathered her packages and went out the door.

Several vacant cabs whizzed by and finally an empty cab stopped. She yanked open the door and literally threw herself in the back. A multitude of packages, boxes, and her backpack flew all over the seat.

"Take me here, please," she handed the driver a scrap of paper with the address for the Top of the Turret Residence Tower.

"Are you sure this is the right place? This is Park Avenue on the Upper East Side." The skeptical driver turned and eyed Chris up and down. "It's not far; you could walk."

She glanced at him annoyed. "Yes, I know." Her eyes narrowed. "I don't *want* to walk. Just go there, please. Don't worry; I'll pay you."

Dispirited, she sank back into the seat. They were nearly there when rush hour traffic stalled and Chris asked the driver to drop her up the street from the building. Struggling to get out of the taxi with her backpack and the packages, she glared at the driver when she paid him tossing the fare on the front seat.

Chris headed up the street checking addresses as she went. The packages were unwieldy and heavy. She was grumpy and it showed on her face. She passed the old woman's doorway and the wiry old vagrant silently slid out. Crouching on her haunches and hands, she crept along behind Chris making a hissing noise.

"You're the snake...I know you," she hissed, jabbing her finger toward Chris. "You are the snake!"

"Go away, you batty old woman!" Chris yelled over her shoulder, "You're scaring me!"

Chris's bulky parcels bounced against her body while she hurried up the street. She trotted past Symington, unaware that she was passing her destination.

The vagrant kept up with her, hissing and making weird noises in her throat. "Snake," she rasped as she skittered behind Chris.

Nearly to the corner, Chris saw the building numbers were too high. She turned around to backtrack and pushed the hissing old magpie out of her way. Glancing at her for the first time, Chris gaped in disbelief at the shriveled old woman in her filthy Aussie hat.

Chris ran as fast as she could to get away. Checking building numbers, she located the Top of the Turret and approached Symington. She felt exasperated and disheveled. The old woman hissed and glared. With her hands together, her arms undulating, she continued to prance in circles around Christine.

"*Go away*!" Symington commanded the vexatious woman, clapping his hands and waving her off.

She scurried back to her doorway, glaring, and making hissing noises while she ran. "You are the snake," she spat out, jabbing her finger at Chris while she slipped through the boards.

"Do you know Hayley Hamilton?" Chris sniffed and heaved a tired sigh. "Does she live here?"

Symington's hesitation alarmed Chris. *Is this address wrong?*

"Let me ask this in a different way; are you Symington, Hayley Hamilton's Uncle Arthur?"

"Yes, Madam, I am," replied Symington, looking askance at Chris.

"Then I *do* have the right building. I'm Christine Horowitz and Hayley is expecting me."

Symington asked Chris for her driver's license to verify her identity.

"Ms. Horowitz, please remain outside momentarily and I will call upstairs." He went into the building and rang Miguel's cell phone. "Miguel," he spoke in a low voice, "Hayley's guest has arrived. It's October and I believe she may be wearing a Halloween costume, as she's dressed as a charwoman." He chuckled, "Please hurry down to escort her. I'll attempt to store her packages in the lobby."

"On my way as we speak."

Symington turned and bumped into Chris standing at his elbow. She had overheard his rude comments and her face was red with embarrassment.

Miguel exited the elevator and strode toward them. He stopped short when he saw Chris.

"*Dios mio*," he mumbled. Symington caught Miguel's eye and his expression said, "*Tread softly.*"

By that time, Chris was exhausted and miserable; her shoulders sagged from the weight of the packages. Humiliated by their attitude, she decided to leave. Her chin raised, she glared from one to the other.

With an imperious toss of her hand, she said, "Please tell Ms. Hamilton that Christine Horowitz stopped by." *Sniff.*

Miguel answered his pager. He held up a finger to signal Chris to wait while he responded to Hayley and assured her they were on their way.

"Do you mind if we stored your packages in the lobby, Miss Horowitz?"

Chris gathered the packages close to her body. "I most certainly *do* mind, Mr. Symington. I'll not let them out of my sight," she replied, frowning and shaking her head, her stringy hair swishing on her back.

"*Señorita* Hamilton has sent me to escort you to the penthouse, *Señorita* Horowitz," Miguel said politely. "May I assist you with your packages?"

"Yes, thank you." Chris sniffed and relinquished her burden to Miguel's strong arms.

"Who *are* you?" questioned Chris, glancing up at him under her heavy eyelids.

"I am Miguel," he smiled soothingly. "I am Miss Hamilton's private security guard," he said, while he took numerous packages from her.

"Hayley never mentioned a private security guard."

Miguel gently guided Chris toward the penthouse elevator. She watched his fingers as he entered the code. To her it appeared as though he just lightly tapped the wall. The elevator silently glided without perceptible movement to the 20th floor.

The elevator doors parted soundlessly and Christine stepped into the pink marble world of Hayley Elizabeth Hamilton. She touched her fingers to her lips and whispered, "What kind of altered reality have I entered since I got out of that taxi?"

The exquisite marble columned foyer, the antique French period furniture, and the enormous bouquet of pink, apricot, and yellow roses awed Chris. She was walking toward the flowers to see if they were real, when one of the penthouse doors opened and there stood Hayley.

Chris gaped at her in disbelief and goose bumps rose on her arms. Hayley had grown more beautiful than Chris could have imagined. She'd changed from a merely pretty teenager with a no-nonsense haircut to a classic beauty.

Hayley went the short distance to Chris with open arms. They hugged and kissed each other on both cheeks. Chris watched Hayley's wavy blonde tresses cascade over her shoulders as she scooped up Diva to stop her yapping and from dancing around Chris's feet. Hayley was dressed simply in a fuchsia cashmere sweater with an antique amethyst brooch pinned to the turtleneck, black pants, and black suede boots, but standing there, holding the silky gold and tan Yorkshire terrier, she looked as delicate as an alabaster figurine.

"Hayley, you look somewhat like I remember, but of course that was nearly ten years ago when we were just kids. You've grown even lovelier."

Hayley prattled nervously, “It’s wonderful to see you again. Christine. You’re taller and slimmer, no longer a girl dressed in Goth clothing with streaks of magenta and blue in your hair. Other than that, you’ve changed very little. Hold up your knuckle.”

Chris grinned while they knuckle-bumped.

“You remembered all of that, Hayley?”

“Yes, Chris, I remember important things.”

Christine looked around the foyer. “Wow, this is so beautiful that I can’t imagine what the inside of the penthouse will look like.”

“You must be exhausted after your day of shopping. How ‘bout coming inside – Let’s catch up on the past ten years.” Hayley spoke softly, leading Chris by the hand inside her sanctuary.

“This looks like a palace,” Chris murmured, looking around the living room. “This place, Hayley; this place is incredibly celestial. Do you live here alone?” *Sniff.*

“Yes, I do live alone, but my housekeeper and security guard are here all day. They live one floor below and so does Uncle Arthur. There’s a backstairs, so we’re kind of connected. And of course, this is Diva,” she sat the little dog on the floor. “Don’t be fooled; this side of the penthouse is lovely and serene, but every day the other side becomes a hectic business place, actually. Please, come and sit in front of the fire. We’ll relax and you can put your feet up. You must be exhausted. Marisol, my housekeeper, is also the cook and is Miguel’s wife. She has some wine and starters ready and has prepared a wonderful dinner for us.”

Miguel took Chris’s sweater and the two women sat together in the living room in front of the fire. At that moment, Marisol approached them with a tray holding two wine glasses and a plate of *hors d’oeuvres.*

Hayley introduced her to Chris.

“*Con mucho gusto, Señorita* Horowitz. It’s a pleasure to meet you.”

“Mucho gusto en conocerle, Marisol. The pleasure is mine. Please call me Chris, Marisol.”

"Excúseme por favor, Señorita Hayley. Estoy apesadumbrado de interrumpir a le y a su huésped," Marisol said shyly, "I have found a bottle of Hogue Cellars Reserve Merlot 2002 to serve with *el aperitivo y entrée.*" She poured wine into the glasses.

Marisol placed the silver tray on the table in front of the two women.

"I hope you like seafood, *Señorita* Horowitz. I have prepared lobster, shrimp, crabmeat and a spicy dipping sauce with slices of avocado and lemon wedges."

"Oh, yes, this is wonderful, Marisol, thank you," Chris said, "I have eaten very little today and I really will enjoy it."

"Let's sit here in the living room to enjoy the starters, then, Chris."

Her energy drained from the hectic day, Chris relaxed for the first time since she left home that morning. Diva jumped up on the sofa, Chris picked her up, and kissed the top of her head. Chris smile at her and Diva studied her face. The dog snuggled down making herself comfortable on Chris's lap.

Hayley handed Chris her glass of wine. "To my first real friend; may we never lose touch again in our lives," her eyes sparkled as she lifted her glass. "*Cheers*."

Chris swirled the wine and said, "This is my father's favorite toast -- *L' Chaim...to life!"* Raising the glass to her lips, she sipped it, savoring the fruity flavors. "That's excellent wine, Hayley. My parents are connoisseurs and they taught me to recognize and enjoy the flavors and nose of fine wines."

They sampled the exquisitely prepared *hors d'oeuvres*. Then, Hayley sat forward on the edge of the sofa.

"It been a long time since I've played before an audience, but I would like to play the piano for you, Chris. Is there a composer you especially like?"

"No, no particular composer, Hayley. My taste in music has changed over the years and tonight I'd favor sentimental music."

"Yes, I do, too, Christine. I'm particularly fond of John Barry's romantic movie scores, and my favorite is the hauntingly beautiful theme based on Paganini from the movie, *Somewhere in Time*. I think it fits our mood tonight."

Hayley slid onto the piano seat and sat for a moment. She lifted her hands gracefully and began to play the poignant romantic melody that always filled Christine with nostalgia.

Chris could sense the affect the music was having on Hayley. She knew that what she was witnessing was more than just talent; it was coming from deep within. As her hands moved over the keys, the rich, mellifluous tones of the Steinway filled the magnificent room, and propelled Chris into a melancholy place.

She began to reflect on herself, her life, and on the exceptionally beautiful woman before her. The light from an overhead crystal chandelier cast a warm glow on Hayley's luminous skin and her face was flawless even without a hint of makeup. She studied Hayley's delicate features and noticed that her lips were arched, full, and rosy. *My high lip line that shows my gums looks like a dentist's ad for how you shouldn't smile.*

Hayley's nose was short and slim; Chris thought about her broken nose and that she'd stubbornly refused to have it fixed. *For years, that unsightly rock pile brought ridicule from people whispering behind my back.*

Hayley's blonde tresses were like long, glossy strands of silk shimmering in the light as her hands moved up and down the keyboard. Chris recalled the shock she felt when she saw her own appalling mane earlier in the day. *It looked like gunky brown seaweed clinging to my back.*

Only an hour ago, Symington's cruel words had cut her painfully. She'd always been able to rise above scorn, but lately it was a source of emotional pain. When she compared what she saw in the mirror at Buddinghill's with Hayley's remarkable beauty, she felt wretched about her own physical shortcomings.

Christine had never before observed the outside of herself through the eyes of her hopes and dreams. She had only ever looked on the inside of herself. Tears of emotion mixed with self-pity trickled down her cheeks. Until now, she lacked understanding of the importance of conforming to acceptable standards of good looks and placed too much importance on her individuality. *Being different is all right, but I have allowed myself to be different in the wrong way. Ben is right; I am pig-headed.*

The various interconnecting themes of the music died away. Hayley neared the last few notes and the walls echoed the peaceful ending. The room was silent. Both women sat motionless and then with a long sigh, Chris returned to the moment leaving her brooding for another time.

"I wish I could present you with a bouquet of roses, Hayley. That was a virtuoso performance." Chris sighed. "I'm a little moody tonight and the music affected me in a way that I hadn't expected." *More than moody -- I'm freaking depressed.*

"Maybe Marisol's delicious dinner will lift your spirit." Hayley sat down beside her. "Chris, I didn't know how much your being here would mean to me. I have been shutting out the good because I fear the bad. It's what Peter tried to tell me. He encouraged me to rejoin the world. That's what I want and I think your being here today shows me how profoundly I want it and how very much I need to do that."

"I understand, Hayley, we all need others in our lives. I'm here because when I saw you for the first time in the Park ten years ago, I knew that you were someone I wanted in my life."

"Yes, I felt the same way, Chris. I know exactly what you mean."

Chris's emotions were on overdrive; she picked up her wine and walked toward the windows not wanting Hayley to see that her eyes were overflowing with tears. The living room extended beyond the rest of the penthouse and Hayley had opened the drapes on all three sides.

"This is a fabulous view, Hayley. I can see all over the city from here. It's like there are a million black towers of shimmering white lights. I find New York so enthralling that I hope one day to live here."

Her thoughts returned to the old woman who accosted her on the street. "When I arrived this evening, your Uncle Arthur rescued me from a goofy homeless woman who, I swear, sprung up out of the pavement and kept crawling after me hissing and telling me that I'm a snake! She scared the wits out of me!"

"Yes, Chris, I know she can be scary." Hayley nodded and chuckled softly. "She doesn't respect personal boundaries. I had an experience with her, too, but Uncle Arthur assured me she's harmless and he watches out for her. She likes coffee and sweet rolls from the Park Central Café, so I bring them to her on mornings when Miguel and I take Diva for a walk. It's such a little thing, you see, and it makes her happy, although she'd never let on. She came at me out of nowhere one morning and was adamant that I take a list she wrote about her dream. She told me I'm the swan."

Hayley found the list and showed it to Chris.

"*A snake!* This is spooky. Let's find a dream symbol website." *Sniff.*

They went into Hayley's office and found a website on her computer.

"Oh, look, Chris; it represents change, like when a snake sheds its skin."

"I hope so. I've got a lot of résumés out there and I'm up for a change." *There's nothing I can do to change the past. I can't brainwash everybody to remember me differently, but I can change; will change who I am in the future.*

Marisol came into the room and announced that she was ready to serve dinner. Hayley and Chris proceeded to the dining room. The glazed, rose-colored walls were aglow from the soft light of the crystal chandelier centered within the dining rotunda. The mahogany Georgian dining table was set with pristine white linen, sparkling

Waterford crystal, and heavy ornate silver. The two women sat opposite each other at one end of the table.

Marisol arranged an entrée of pan-roasted chicken breast with Marsala mushroom sauce on a bed of saffron rice with slivers of red and green pepper and leaves of baby spinach. She arranged it artistically to please the eye and served on the meal Elizabeth's antique Minton bone china.

"*Mmm...*scrumptious," Chris said when they finished eating. "I can't remember when I've eaten a more exquisitely prepared meal. I'm enjoying myself so much that I forgot how miserable I was when I arrived."

"Chris, tell me about yourself; tell me about your job and about Jaxx."

"All right, Hayley, but you first. You promised to tell me what happened over the past ten years and I want to hear all about Peter." She smirked and slid her eyes sideways.

Marisol cleared the plates and brought an a*rugula salad* with shallots and tomato truffle with a champagne vinaigrette dressing, double cream brie, and French bread to the table.

"Here is a bottle of red *Lou Coucardie* 2001 to enjoy with the salad, bread, and cheese. It was recommended by my teacher."

"Marisol is taking gourmet-cooking classes at the Art Institute of New York. She's an excellent student."

"The meal was prepared so beautifully. I've been impressed, Marisol."

"Save room for the wonderful *lemon crème brulée* with fresh raspberries that she made for dessert. We just bought a torch for her. We'd better be sure to compliment her, or she may bring it out to show us how it's done by setting our hair on fire," Hayley's eyes danced while she teased Marisol.

"C*laro, que si*!" Marisol laughed, "No, your hair is safe from my blowtorch, but I will accept your compliments on behalf of my teacher."

"Her teacher insists that wines must be appropriate for the food and he taught his students to refer to the wine by the vineyard. You may have noticed Marisol's dedication to that when she referred to the wine she was serving, Hayley grinned. "All joking aside, you can see what an excellent and imaginative chef she is and she's quite knowledgeable about wines."

Marisol poured the wine into their glasses. She was pleased and glanced at Chris, delighted that she enjoyed the meal.

"*Si*, I enjoy the wines. Someday, I would like to visit a winery. *Señorita* Horowitz, would you like coffee now?"

"*Oh, Dios mio!* I'm not sure I can hold any more, but yes, that would be lovely. S*u cena era deliciosa, excelente y excepcional* and Marisol, please call me Chris, just Chris, all right? And Marisol, there are some beautiful wineries in New York State. Maybe someday, Miguel can drive you there." *Sniff.*

"*Oh, si, gracias*, *Señorita Ho-...Chris.*" Marisol appeared flustered to have been the topic of conversation and hurried from the room to pour the coffee and serve it.

During dinner, Chris and Hayley discussed the December Eighteenth Great Escape Getaway to New York City meeting.

"Lots of people are signing up from all over the world, Hayley. It's going to be a great weekend."

"I know New York City well; I'll do some research and plan where to go, if you'll make the arrangements. I think you should consider having tour guides available."

"Thank you, Hayley. I'll enjoy working on this project with you. I'm especially excited because Jaxx is coming to be with me."

"Chris, that's wonderful! Peter is coming to New York the same weekend as the meeting. We'll have our own plans, but we would like all of us to have high tea at the Plaza on Saturday afternoon. Do you think Jaxx and you would like that?"

"Oh, won't that be fabulous? I can't wait!" *Sniff.*

The two women talked and laughed all evening while they caught up the ten years they had been apart. When dinner was over and she was ready to leave, Miguel helped Christine with her bags and escorted her to the lobby. It had begun to rain while she was with Hayley, but the taxi was waiting at the curb. Miguel paid the driver and gave him the address of the Plaza Hotel.

Chris's hotel window overlooked Central Park. She was tired and emotionally drained, but before she climbed into bed, she stood at the rain spotted window silhouetted against the glittering towers of lights. She sighed, her thoughts rambling --

I grew up where reality is a razzle-dazzle make-believe world, but I have just emerged from Hayley Hamilton's rarified world, a place with a dazzle all its own.

It's so satisfying to have Hayley back in my life. Hayley and I have lived our lives so differently. Although I may not always have chosen wisely, nothing in my world has kept me from doing what I wanted to do. Unlike Hayley, who has lived her life in fear for the past five years and had no choice but to create her own world. Her fear and suffering are real; her isolation is real, as is her determination to reenter the world as a whole, complete person. She has a difficult challenge facing her and I intend to help if she'll let me.

Hayley and I both have challenges before us. I know I can help and support her, but no one can help me. I have to fight my battle alone. I'm responsible for my failure to understand what I needed to do to be a success in my life. Now that I know, I must devote my efforts to recreating myself in an image that will help me move forward to where I want to go.

~17~

"Men show their characters in nothing more clearly
Than in what they think laughable"
~ Johann Wolfgang von Goethe~

CableCoNews Studio
Cleveland, Ohio
October 2004

"Hey, Chrissy!"

Pookie plopped into the chair beside Chris's desk. "Tell me about Hayley...the penthouse...*oh*, and Buddinghill's! I'm excited to hear about everything. I wish I could have gone with you. I've never been in a penthouse. What's it like? What's Hayley like?"

"Well, *Pook-a-Snoopy*, Hayley is thc Howard Hughes of Manhattan's Upper East Side. Fear made her place herself in exile after her parents died and she practically buried herself alive. She lives with their spirits in that penthouse. We hope that after five years without further threats, there is no longer anything to fear, and her life can turn around."

"Is Hayley like you remembered her? Oh, well, I don't suppose she is; you met her almost ten years ago."

"Hayley is astonishingly beautiful now. When I met her she was tall and graceful and I remember thinking she was silky-smooth. Even at fourteen, she turned heads when she entered the café. Being with her that day was like walking in sunlight, but she said it was only because I brought something out in her she didn't know was there. After shutting herself off from the world for so long, she virtually glows with angelic innocence and purity. She made me feel like I wanted to protect her from harm. Perhaps with my friendship,

Peter's encouragement, and her therapist's guidance, she'll be like a walk in the sunlight again."

"Wow, I wish I could meet her. Maybe...*someday*. Tell me more about Hayley and about the penthouse."

Pookie sat down with her face propped on her hands.

"Oh, God, Pooks, *Chez Hayley* is like a fairy tale castle in the air. I saw rooms so exquisitely decorated with so many beautiful pieces of authentic antique furniture that I wished I could have a day alone to explore. On my way to the bathroom, I drifted into one large room full of books, toys, and dolls. It must have been Hayley's playroom or childhood schoolroom. I saw a dollhouse that was fascinating in its miniaturized detail. It reminded me of the one in the Smithsonian Institute, but I think it's a replica of her mother's mansion in Belgravia. I guess it's her mansion now."

"Oh, Chrissy! I can't wait to see your new wardrobe. I thought you'd be wearing something new today."

"The personal shopper at Buddinghill's was a little snobby, but she knows her stuff. I have an entire new image. You'll see!"

"Chrissy, I want to hear more, but I have to arrange the set for the new anchor." Pookie rolled her eyes and smirked, "Where can I find a big, hand-held vanity mirror? Her highness requires a *huge* one on the desk. I'm thinkin' floor to ceiling. Heaven forbid there should be a hair out of place. I'll be back in a minute and you can tell me more, all right?"

"Okay, Pookie. I'm going to send a private message to Jaxx while you're gone."

"*Pffft...* Oh, *big whoopee*, Christine." Pookie grimaced and shuddered when she left the room.

`Private Message from Witzend to Frenchtoast:`

`"Bonjour mon cher amour,`

`Je me suis très bien amuse tandis à New York. J'ai acheté beaucoup de beaux vêtements et j'ai rencontré mon ami, Hayley. I've missed you so` much! I've seen Hayley again, you know, Diva from the forum, and I bought some beautiful clothes in Buddinghill's; New York's answer to Harrod's in London.

Hayley is going to help me plan the New York City Great Escape Getaway. I can't wait to see you in New York, Jaxx. You have stolen my heart. Hayley has invited us to tea at the Plaza before the getaway dinner. Won't that be très chic?

I really, really love you. Bisous, bisous, bisous and even sexier French kisses!

Je t'adore,
Chris"

"Okay, Chrissy..."

"Good grief, McSpookie! You startled me. Don't sneak up on me like that."

Pookie shook her head. "Sorry, Christine." She had a stony expression and Chris heard a flat edge to her voice. "Just to remind you in case you've gone totally Witless, you scheduled a meeting to review Sunday's program and tie up loose ends with our new anchor this morning before we go on the air. Our meeting with her starts in fifteen minutes."

"I'm almost ready." *Sniff.* "I'll clean up here and be on the set. And that's Wit...*zend*, not Wit...*less*."

"Wit...*ever*." Pookie threw up her hands. "Listen Chris, this Jaxx thing is just disgusting and speaking of cleaning up, how long will you wait before you wear your new clothes...till they go out of style?" Pookie turned and started out the door.

"*Yak, yak, yak*; okay, soon, and will you stop whistling *Falling in Love with Love*; you're a pain in the butt."

Irritated by her friend's attitude, Chris held up her finger, "Oh, Pookie," wait just a minute!" She jotted a few words on a yellow sheet. "Before you go, will you read this statement for me?"

"Sure, Chrissy." She took the page and read aloud, "*Zip-it-up, Poo-ki-io*."

"*Bite me, But-ter-cup.*" She balled up the sheet and bounced it off Chris's head.

Chris smirked, "Okay, I'm going to make a pit stop. I'll meet you in the studio."

Chris was in a lavatory daydreaming about meeting Jaxx when she heard the rapid, self-assured tip tapping and click clacking of two pairs of stiletto heels. The ladies' room door opened with a whoosh.

"Why don't they say something; she looks like a damned tramp. What's her name? Christine? She doesn't present a good image for this station, that's for sure."

From inside the stall, Chris recognized the sultry voice of the newly hired Sunday morning news anchor; a shapely, dark-haired beauty, with a cosmetically enhanced smile that lit up the television screen. The local audience loved her, the camera loved every inch of her, and according to rumors, her last married co-anchor did, too.

"Yup," replied the station manager's secretary, a young, blonde type with big breasts and a tiny waist with brainpower to match. "Around here she's called, Frumpy-Dumpy, or the Dumpster. We used to call her the Blubster until she lost a ton of weight." They snickered conspiratorially.

Wide-eyed, Chris mouthed, "*The Dumpster*? *The Blubster*?" Her breathing was shallow and her heart pounded against her ribs. She held her nose to stop the urge to sniff and watched them through a small crack in the doorframe.

If that weren't enough, they continued trashing her.

"I don't know which is worse; her baggy, colorless clothes, or the stringy, colorless hair. With any less color, she'd fade into transparency."

"Oh, and don't forget the sniffing; that damned constant sniffing. It's driving me crazy," the secretary said from inside the stall beside Chris.

"And why doesn't she do something about that huge rumpity-bumpity-bump on her nose? Maybe it's as big on the inside as the outside and she can't breathe," said the new anchor with a long, drawn out, *s-n-i-f-f.*

The secretary snickered; "Have you seen Frumpy-Dumpy's Yellow Submarine car? It's an old bucket of bolts that used to be red and now it's painted bright yellow. It's the landmark we use to tell people where to find the studio. I mean, on what other parking lot would you find another one of those?"

The new anchor doubled over laughing, "Oh, stop," she sighed, trying to catch her breath and regain her composure. "Well, I've primped enough." She carefully dabbed away tears of laughter with a filmy white lace hanky. "I'd better go to the meeting with Dumpy-Frumpy and her Pet Pookie, or is Rumpity-Bumpity Pookie's pet Frump?"

They were still cackling when they left the room and the two women, full of self-importance and now having bonded, went down the corridor with their expensively clad feet trotting in unison.

Chris felt slashed open and eviscerated. She trembled and nausea rose in her throat.

"*Damn...* I've just been drawn and quartered," her voice quavered.

There's no time to cry, I'm due in a meeting with that odious woman in five minutes. Shaking from the inside out, she forced herself to leave the stall and wash her trembling hands. The face in the mirror was flushed with humiliation. Unshed tears were proof that what she heard was painfully close to the truth. *Worst of all, what will Jaxx think when he meets me for the first time?*

Chris jumped when Pookie burst through the door.

"Come on, Chrissy. We can't be late. That airhead won't know where to find the cue cards if we don't point her toward the camera."

After another successful Sunday morning edition of their program, Chris tried to stay busy. Crushed by the hurtful words of the two glamorous women she overheard in the ladies room, she waited for Jaxx to write to her. His loving words would soften the blow and make her feel loved and worthy again. Her heart ached with disappointment, each time she looked for a message from him and found nothing, but she knew when he wrote he would tell her how much he loved and adored his beautiful, colorful, little parakeet.

A chill had settled over Christine when she overheard the women, and not having heard from Jaxx for so long, her life felt meaningless and empty. Chris was worried, hurt, frustrated and upset, but she waited, because she knew he must be busy.

Just before bed, she logged on to the forum and found a message from Jaxx waiting for her.

Private Message from Frenchtoast to Witzend:

"*Christine, ma fille magnifique,*

Ma chérie. Mon amour. You must be so lovely and elegant. Please send your picture to Jaxx. I want to hold it next to my heart. I don't think I have ever met anyone like you before. You have given me hope and the strength to work hard. *Merci. Merci, beaucoup.* I know you work hard. You have revealed to Jaxx how hard you work. Your inner strength is so powerful. I want you. I want to hold you. Kiss you. Make love to you to feel your power and your strength. *Ma chérie. Ma bébé. Mon amour,* you, only you, make Jaxx feel this way. *J'amoureux de toi.*

Vous avez mon coeur,

Jaxx"

Jaxx will love me forever. And that night, like so many of his birds who were filled with lies from his cunning charade, she fell asleep clutching his empty, pretty words to her heart.

~18~

"Women and wine, game and deceit,
make the wealth small and the want great."
~Benjamin Franklin~

London, England
December 2004

Jaxx wrote to the three women on the forum he'd pulled from his JAXXPOT for the day to receive his vows of undying devotion. Christine was in that group. He sent a private message to her without having read a single word she wrote about her exciting New York adventure.

<u>Private Message from Frenchtoast to Witzend:</u>

"*Ah, ma belle chéri,*

I have been so very busy. My business is taking all my time. Taking orders. Ordering. Shipping. Tracking. Oui, je suis très occupé, so very busy from morning until night. I miss my colorful little parakeet that has stolen my heart and flown away with it to Cleveland in America. *Mon amour. Mon coeur.* I cannot wait until we meet. Jaxx' heart is yours and yours alone. Please take care of his tender, loving heart. Do not break it!

J'adore toujour,
Jaxx"

For Jaxx, it was all about the thrill of the chase. In the early days of their liaison, he was right on top of his responses to Chris, but Jaxx bored easily and the thrill was gone. Now, it might take several days before he drew her name from the birdcage again.

Of all the women whose heads were filled with flights of fancy by Jaxx' pretty words, Chris was the most gullible and ardent in her responses. Trusting and completely open to him, she wrote lovingly and shared her deepest feelings. However, for Jaxx, who wouldn't recognize true human emotion, it was all just an amusing game.

Jaxx had wooed most of the women on the board. He began by writing a get acquainted message, inventing something to write to each woman, and always asked a question. When they answered, he charmed them into his snare.

He whispered stories of his business success to the birds. He must be successful, they thought, doesn't his website prove it?

"Orders are pouring in for my wines and beers," he bragged, thinking himself amusing and clever.

They twittered and tittered; it wasn't what he said, as much as the way he said it.

The women flocked to him and he became Mr. Popularity. He captivated them with his alluring words and enthralling sensuality. He assured the plain and colorless women they were beautiful and sexy; he made the simple and uneducated feel brilliant and witty; and he made the older women feel young and desirable.

However, to Jaxx they were not women; they were his flock of tamed birds. While they swirled around him he gathered them to him and tied beguiling love notes onto them. He opened his palms releasing them into the air, to return to him with their own messages of love.

"*Mon amour, j'adore*," they wrote to Jaxx, the love of their lives.

Jaxx' ego could never be stroked long and hard enough to arouse the shriveled relic of his humanity. Having no conscience meant that Jaxx allowed himself to disregard social mores and taboos. Loaded with those shortcomings and a great deal of stamina and tenacity, he went pigeon hunting using his charm for bait to trap the needy and unwary.

He considered it a challenge to win over the resistant and flighty, he wanted their hearts to belong to him and he wrote to them until he persuaded them they were wonderful, gorgeous, thrilling, adored, and they were convinced he couldn't live without them. His brand of seeds addicted them like crack cocaine without the shame. It took place unseen in the anonymity of the internet.

Jaxx was clever at keeping them separate in his mind and at keeping them apart.

"*Ma chéri*, our love is our secret. No one must know."

"Of course it is, Jaxx. It is ours and ours alone. I'll never tell a soul! There can never be another love like ours. I love you so much, *mon cher amour*."

Each woman believed he meant his declarations of undying devotion to her alone, and she longed for him to make love with his pretty words. Sadly, what they would find in their future would not be the love Jaxx promised forever; they would find only disillusionment and heartbreak.

And so, Jaxx played his game -- his deceitful game of love. Jaxx was very good at this game, beguiling and ensnaring them in his trap, but in the end, like Christine, they were all just pigeons.

Day by day, from his birdcage Jaxx pulled out three brightly colored paper birds with the names of women he would write to that day. Symbolically, he had trapped and caged women with his lies and deceit, but in the days to come, Jaxx would find he'd trapped a bird of prey that would turn his narcissistic world inside out.

Zara registered a secret puppet account as another source to gather information about Peter and Hayley. The account was *Solitaire* and that source of information was Frenchtoast. Oddly enough, as soon as she logged on as Solitaire, Frenchtoast sent her a friendly private message welcoming her to the forum. She answered him with a message loaded with sensuality and sexual innuendo. It wasn't long before he responded to her messages with his usual loving words of undying devotion.

Zara had learned to play Jaxx' game better than he and knew Jaxx was an easy mark with no morals and a very big ego. He had taken the bait and Zara's campaign began. Anything he knew about Hayley and Peter that Chris revealed to him, she would know.

According to Hayley's messages to Peter, Jaxx was in love with Witzend and Witzend was a friend of Diva. "I know you are going to New York for the Getaway," she pouted. "How do I know you aren't meeting a lover?"

"How can Jaxx be in love with anyone else now that he has met his glorious, red-haired Solitaire? *Oh-la-la! Vous êtes une jolie fille!* Ah, no; I am only going to meet my friend, Witzend."

"How do I know you love me more than Witzend?" She sulked and begged him to copy Chris's messages and send them to her. "*Je suis très jalous, mon amour.*"

"*Oui, oui, vous êtes mon morceau savoureux,*" he soothed her. "Do not be jealous, ma Solitaire. You are Jaxx' tasty sweet and spicy morsel, and someday soon, you will spread yourself on top of Frenchtoast, *n'est-ce pas?* I will write today to tell Christine that Jaxx wants to know more about her life and I will send you all the messages I have received from her. Will that prove without a doubt that my love for my glorious Solitaire is beyond compare?"

Private Message from Frenchtoast to Witzend:

"*Ma Cheri Christine,*
Jaxx is so busy he cannot take time to write, but please write to Jaxx even though I do not have time to write to you. Tell me of your love, your life, and your plans. Tell Jaxx about *votre amie, Hayley et votre ami*, Peter, before I meet them. Oui, I want to know everything, every petit detail, because *vous ête mon coeur, mon sang, et mon vie.* You are my heart, the blood flowing through my veins nourishing my yearning body, and you are my life.
Bisous et amour ma coeur toujour,
Jaxx"

With her sensual words, Zara filled him with delight. *À Jaxx qu'elle est son idéale, elle est fascinant, this wonderful, glorious Solitaire.* She made Jaxx flush with her outrageous sexuality. What she wrote burned up his screen and he placed his hand over the words that filled him with desire.

It was a teasing game with Solitaire. She baited him; he baited her. His little cockatrice couldn't wait to have sex with him. She wanted rough sex. He wanted forbidden sex.

Her fire inflamed Jaxx. She was his fantasy, his colorful cockatrice, her hot colors blended and changed as they twisted, turned and swirled in his mind. He fantasized about her while he was alone at night, or while he lay in the arms of some other colorless bird in a cheap hotel room during a secret tryst.

No one from the forum knew whom he met and where he met these birds of his because Jaxx insisted on secrecy. What he couldn't know was that Solitaire wanted secrecy far more than he did, and she wanted far more than sex from him.

Jaxx knew nothing about his beautiful, red-haired Solitaire, except that she wanted him desperately and she promised to meet him someday. *Soon*. Enthralled by the ecstasy of his lust, Jaxx had no idea that the bird he ensnared was not like his pigeons --

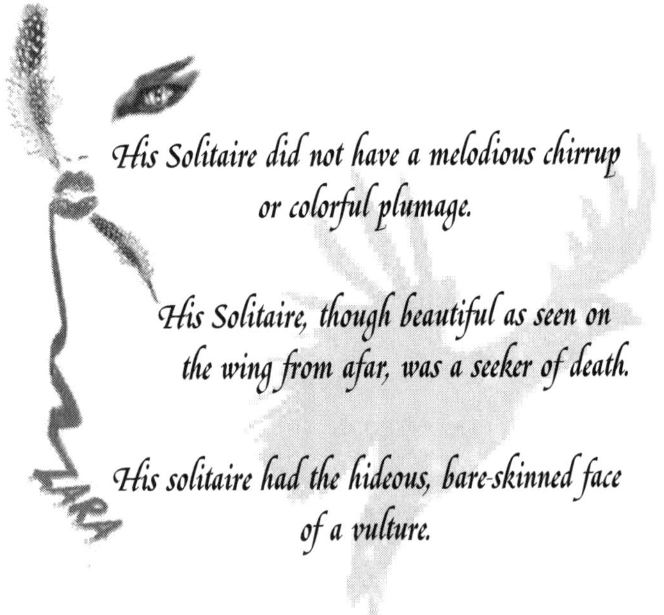
His Solitaire did not have a melodious chirrup
or colorful plumage.
His Solitaire, though beautiful as seen on
the wing from afar, was a seeker of death.
His solitaire had the hideous, bare-skinned face
of a vulture.
ZARA

~19~

"Anger and jealousy can no more bear to lose sight of their objects than love."
~ George Eliot~

Oxford University
Oxfordshire, England
December 2004

Zara's obsession with Peter and her hatred for Hayley had taken over her life. From day to day, she enticed Jaxx with tantalizing sexuality for information and scrutinized the flow of messages between Peter and Hayley.

While they assumed they were sharing their thoughts only with each other, during the summer and fall months the parasite attached to Peter's computers hung onto and recording every keystroke, every word, and every thought that passed between them.

She did little else but work at her job and come home to spy on Peter. She sat at her desk, smoking cigarettes, drinking countless tumblers of scotch, and waiting for messages between them. When she wasn't monitoring their emails, she sat crouched in her car under blankets in the cold winter weather. She waited and watched, spying through the bug in the wall, recording everything she saw.

Through her spying and through Jaxx' forwarded messages from Chris, Zara learned much more about Peter than she had been able to glean in person. He had allowed Zara to see only a stuffy and serious professional man. Surprised by his wit, depth and tenderness, she read his words in agony; she wanted the attention and affection he showered on Hayley. Reading his words made Zara's insides curdle with jealousy and rage.

Privy now to Hayley's daily life, Zara knew about the penthouse and her surrogate family, Uncle Arthur, Marisol, and Miguel. Hayley shared with Peter how her parents' death had destroyed her world and how much his friendship was helping her to enter the outside world again.

Hayley confided to Peter that Chris and Jaxx were in love. Zara knew how ludicrous that was. Through her online affair with Jaxx, she knew he was far lustier with her than the over-the-top, insincere twaddle in his messages to Chris.

Wherever Peter went, she skulked on the edges, or hid amongst the crowd. Whether Peter ran a marathon, or played with the Oxford Chamber Orchestra, spoke at conferences, or lunched with associates, she hid in disguise, watching him, taking clandestine pictures. Having complete access to Peter's computer and desk calendars meant she constantly knew where to find him.

Peter and Hayley communicated almost exclusively by telephone by early December and what they said in those calls, Zara couldn't know. He convinced Hayley to accompany him to the New York Philharmonic's December 18 concert. He'd already purchased concert and airline tickets, but Zara didn't know that Peter and Hayley had secret plans they hadn't mentioned to anyone. Chris didn't know, therefore Jaxx couldn't know. Zara couldn't know that all their waking thoughts were of each other. The brightest moments of Peter and Hayley's days were spent on the telephone talking to each other. They laughed together and shared their private thoughts.

The late-night phone calls Peter made to Hayley that Zara wasn't privy to gnawed around the edges of her consciousness. She would repair that broken link. Hacking his computer, she knew when he'd be gone from home or the office. Late one night she used a master key she'd copied to enter his office and checked his desk calendar. She read that his mother planned a celebration before

Christmas and Peter would be spending a weekend in London with his family.

Then she spotted it. He'd planned a trip to New York.

Pounding his desk and livid with rage, she screamed, "He wants to go to New York! To see *her!* To be with *her!* The bloody bitch! If it's not the mother in my way, it's the daughter!"

While at work, Zara behaved normally. She saw Peter at the office when she had business meetings with Sean to discuss the expense of software changes for the graduate research projects. To be with Zara, to talk to her, one would never know that alongside her brilliance was a twisted demon buried deep within her mind, driven by a dangerous obsession.

Zara saw an opportunity to sidetrack and derail him from taking his trip to New York. She was sure he'd invite her to the family's London festivities if she were on hand. It would take a bit of work, but she thought she could pull it off and began working her scheme early in December.

On the pretext of needing to discuss some details about software requirements, she asked Peter and Sean to join her for a business lunch and suggested Oxford's charming Duke of York Pub. Zara interspersed their conversation with small talk about Christmas, starting with the fact that she hadn't made any plans.

"How about you, Peter, have you sorted your Christmas plans?" she asked casually.

"Yes, Zara, my plans for Christmas are fixed."

"Really? What *are* your plans, Peter?"

"The family is taking the children to the Prince Edward Theatre in London to see the musical, *Mary Poppins*, although Matthew will not be able to join us."

"Oh, how clever!" exclaimed Zara. "So, you've an extra ticket, then, Peter. I'd love to see the play. I'm sure you wouldn't mind if I tagged along."

"I don't supposed you'd enjoy what we've planned, Zara. No, it will be a family weekend. We're celebrating Christmas early this year. This is strictly for the family."

"Oh, but that's brilliant! Yes, I would enjoy...I would *adore* it, Peter! Yes, I want to see the play with your family. I'll arrange my schedule!"

Zara could feel the pulse throbbing in her temples. She was breathless trying to manipulate Peter to inveigle an invitation to the family's celebration.

"No, Zara, that's not a good idea, actually. You'd be with people you don't know and I don't see how a children's musical would be of any interest to you."

"Oh, but of course it would. Count me in! Where are we staying?"

"The family has booked at the London Ritton. Yes, I do happen to have an extra ticket for the play, so you might as well make use of it. We would see you at the theatre."

"Of course I'll stay at the Ritton. This is wonderful, Peter. I'm so excited about the weekend with your family!"

"Let me make this completely crystal clear for you, Zara, so there's absolutely no misunderstanding. This is not an invitation to join my *family* for the theatre. I will merely give you my extra ticket. You can use it that night, or exchange it for some other more convenient performance. Understand this; the family's celebration is private. Under no circumstance, are you welcome to join us."

"Oh, well... not a problem; I'll be there. You can count on it."

However, as it turned out, during the holiday season the London Ritton hadn't a single room available on such short notice. Zara made a reservation at the Park Lane in Mayfair, but it kept her from being in close proximity to Peter. She knew she couldn't join their celebration on Saturday, but certainly, they would invite her to be with them on Sunday. It might take time, but she would see to it.

Pleased with own cleverness and her patience, she planned to be so captivating that he couldn't resist.

~20~

"The happiest moments of my life have been the few which I have passed at home in the bosom of my family."
~Thomas Jefferson~

The London Ritton Hotel
18 December 2005

Barbara Gabriel-Johns gathered her family together for the weekend in the King Edward Suite overlooking Piccadilly Park at the London Ritton Hotel before the play for a Christmas celebration. It was the first time her entire family wouldn't be together on holiday at Seven Valleys for Christmas and Boxing Day. Peter would be in New York and Matthew had told her not to count on him. She was painfully aware that her sons were growing away from her. *I suppose it happens to all mothers eventually*, she sighed, *but today, my family will be together.*

The décor of the Ritton's King Edward Suite was elegant with its marble-floored lobby, spacious sitting room and carved marble fireplace, two bedrooms, and two baths. Barbara arrived early to check out the accommodation and the hotel staff was placing poinsettias and holiday floral arrangements throughout the suite. They had decorated a huge Christmas tree with antique ornaments and twinkling lights. She walked through the suite thinking that it would be perfection to Lady Elizabeth's eye. The original antique furnishings and the blending of other periods with the Edwardian style would win her seal of approval.

After the whole family arrived, butlers served tea in the suite, with plates of delectable little sandwiches -- watercress, cucumber and cream cheese; curried chicken; smoked salmon; asparagus, ham, and herbed boursin; and all were decorated with edible flourishes. On the tray were scones with Devonshire cream, lemon curd, and an assortment of Ritton's spicy fruit jams. There were mouthwatering desserts of chocolate truffles, lemon tarts, and fairy cakes and while they enjoyed their tea, Peter took out his violin and they sang along while he played the family's favorite carol, *The Angel Gabriel*.

The angel Gabriel from heaven came,
His wings as drifted snow, his eyes aflame;
"All hail," said he, "though lowly maiden Mary,
Most highly favored lady," Gloria!

'For now a blessed mother thou shalt be,
All generations laud and honor thee,
They Son shall be Emmanuel, by seers foretold,
Most highly favored lady, Gloria"

Then gently Mary meekly bowed her head,
"To me be as it pleases God," she said,
'My soul shall laud and magnify his holy Name,"
Most highly favored lady, Gloria"

Of her, Emmanuel, the Christ, was born
In Bethlehem all on a Christmas morn,
And Christian fold throughout the world will ever say:
'Most highly favored lady," Gloria!"

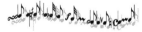

Tea now over, Barbara brought out summer landscape paintings of the manor house and gardens at Seven Valleys to give to her sons.

"I painted them for my spring exhibit at NobleArtists Gallery, but I especially liked them and wanted you to have them. I'll have time to paint others before the exhibit."

"Thank you, Mum. I'm sure Matthew will treasure his painting as much as William and I. This is my favorite view of the wolds from the estate. It will have a special place in my home."

"Now, Jess, this is for you." Barbara placed a small box in her daughter-in-law's hand.

Jessica opened her gift; nestled in the cotton was a classical blue moonstone and diamond pendant on a gold chain from Barbara's own personal collection. It was the something blue she wore when she married Edward.

"I'm so touched, Barbara; I cannot find the words to thank you," Jessica hugged her mother-in-law and held the brooch tightly in her hand, looking fondly at Barbara.

"I wanted you to have this brooch, Jessica," and she added with a snigger, "after all, you are my favorite daughter-in-law."

"Barbara, thank you for that sentiment, however, might I remind you, I'm your only daughter-in-law," Jessica chuckled.

"That may be, Jess, but I hope to live until the day Peter and Matthew marry so that I may have more daughters-in-law. My greatest wish is that they are as lovely and charming as you, dear."

Her mother-in-law was not finished bestowing personal pieces of jewelry. Peter received a small polished gold box, as did William. She gave each of them cuff links belonging to her father. Peter's were emerald cut diamonds surrounded by tanzanites and William's were a cluster of diamonds with large rubies in the center.

"Mother, does your giving me these diamonds mean that we are officially engaged?" He was kidding, but Peter's emotion wasn't lost on Barbara. She knew the sentimental gift pleased him.

Sarah read her new Disney book, Mary Poppins, to her little brother and they played with their Christmas gifts and toys.

The doorbell rang and the suite's butler entered with several carts of food for their Christmas dinner. As the butler's staff set the table and served the meal, the youngsters "*oohed,*" and "*aahed,*" at the lavish and bountiful feast. Barbara chose the menu and it was as festive as meals prepared and served by the kitchen staff at the Manor House on past Christmases. There was caramelized onion-glazed roast prime rib of beef au jus and Yorkshire pudding. There was sliced roast turkey, a nod to Barbara's American heritage. There were seasoned roast potatoes and a mélange of cauliflower, broccoli, carrots, peas, and sprouts. Stilton and cheddar cheese were combined with leek and pear tartlets. There was a traditional plum pudding for the adults; and for the little ones, a non-alcoholic trifle heaping with whipped cream. They served Bristol Cream Sherry with dessert.

The family joined hands around the table and Edward asked the blessing –

> *"Dear Heavenly Father, this family is grateful to be together today and we never forget how fortunate we are for your blessings. May we always share our love and good fortune within our growing family and may we never forget the needs of others. May you always assist us in our mission to improve the lives of those who are not so fortunate. Bless this bounty today and bless those whose hands prepared this feast. We ask in His name, a-men."*

After they toasted Christmas and Matthew, who couldn't be with them, William stood and raised his glass.

"And finally, a toast to my namesake. Here's to William Shakespeare, we thank him for imbibing tons of grapes in juicy form, which no doubt primed and pumped the master's own creative juices. We cannot be sure the bard didn't actually write Mary Poppins, now can we, James and Sarah?"

"Dad, don't you know anything?" Sarah held up her book. "Look; Mary Poppins was written by Mr. Walt Disney!"

"To Shakespeare," they raised their glasses to the bard, "Cheers!"

Jessica hugged her daughter and added, "And three cheers to Mr. Walt Disney!"

"Just a small reminder, William," Edward said with a crooked smile, "You are actually named after me, Edward William Andrew, but I won't quibble."

"Ah, I have news about Shakespeare," Barbara took the opportunity to discuss festival plans.

"There can be *news* about Shakespeare?" Edward teased; a twinkle in his eye.

"Yes, indeed. I have talked to Sir Adrian Howard and I'm pleased to tell you that he has agreed to bring his entire Shakespeare troupe to Seven Valleys for the Wolds-on-Thames Festival again. He plans to present *The Tempest* and it's definite that they'll present *Romeo and Juliet,* because Matthew will play Romeo again this year. It's fixed."

"That's wonderful," said Jessica. "I suspect the productions are dress rehearsals for the summer playhouse in the state of Utah-pi-ah, but it doesn't matter one whit. I shall have to ask Matthew to bring back a cowboy hat for William. Maybe that will encourage him to exercise his horses."

"*Pffft*; please don't do me any favors, Jess," he scoffed, "Unlike my toff brother, I don't need to dress up in any special Yankee Doodle Dandy attire to ride."

"Well, then, William," Barbara said, "I suggest you come to Seven Valley's more often and pay attention to your horses. Right now, they think they belong to Matthew. He races them across the pasture every weekend."

Finally, Barbara and Edward opened their gifts. Barbara received a set of her favorite oil paints and some high quality sable brushes she wanted. Edward received gift certificates for new varieties of David Austin English roses he'd selected for this year's planting.

"What, no tie!" Edward pouted. "Not even one?"

William reached behind his back and produced a box.

"From Matthew," he announced with a wink, passing the gift to Sarah, who took it across the room to Edward. Giggling, she handed the box to her grandfather and curtseyed, her waist-length blonde hair falling over her shoulders. She kissed him on the cheek and snuggled up to him while he opened the box.

"Oh good Lord, I spoke too soon. Oh, my yes, I bloody well needed *this* one," he laughed.

Edward held up a wide shocking pink and turquoise tie with large white and red roses outlined in broad strokes of black.

"Grampie, I like all the bees and spiders on it!" Sarah took the tie and held it under his chin. She tickled all over his face with her fingers while she sang --

"I once knew a lady who swallowed a fly,
I don't know why she swallowed the fly...
she swallowed a spider that wriggled
and tickled and jiggled inside 'er..."

Edward chuckled and tweaked her nose. "It's the perfect tie for the Constant Rose Gardener, isn't it, Sarah? Do you remember last year's tie? It looked like a huge pink tongue. Matthew, you are tricky devil, and I thank you *en absentia*."

Evening fell and it was nearly time to dress for the theatre. While they freshened up and prepared to leave, William started winding up Peter.

"This is all Peter's fault, you know. If it weren't for him we wouldn't be in this godforsaken hell hole of a hotel, eating this miserable food," he grinned.

William held his palm up and circled the luxurious suite in the most prestigious hotel in London.

"What makes you say that, William?" Barbara was fully aware that it was Peter's turn in the pillory.

"Well yes," William snorted, "Peter's in a New York state of mind. If he weren't going to the colonies in pursuit of the apple of his eye, he'd be having Christmas at the manor, as usual."

"Peter, ignore William," Edward chimed in. "You have every right to fly off to the colonies to pay your respects to *New York*. We'll stay here and look after *Old York* whilst you are gone."

"Now, now," laughed Peter, "Matthew is missing this weekend because he's having it off with his lady-of-the-hou-...minute in Harrogate. I hope he doesn't freeze up there in the far north of Yorkshire, or he'll never be able to father children. Mum won't like that. Why on earth didn't he ship her here instead?"

Before Barbara tackled Peter's question, she reflected on a heated argument she'd had with Matthew earlier in the day.

"Forget it, Mum. I'm not changing my plans to suit your beloved Peter's whims," he snarled.

"Matthew, occasionally you must sacrifice," she admonished. "This is one of those occasions. Your *duty* is to your family."

"Sod Peter; tell the wanker to go and jump off a cliff."

However, to Peter she said, "He didn't ship her here, because you failed to ask him if he needed an extra theatre ticket." There was no hint in her voice of the pain Matthew caused her. "Now you have an extra ticket, Peter. What shall we do? Stand outside the theatre and pretend we're scalpers?"

Peter chuckled at the thought.

"Oddly enough, Mum, I no longer have an extra ticket. I gave it to Zara Chandler, a computer consultant who works for the university."

"Oh, Peter!" exclaimed Barbara. "You've been holding out on us, Darling. Is this another lady love?"

Smirking, William jumped all over this news, while James and Sarah stood close by, enjoying their father and uncle teasing each other.

"So, Peter, please tell us how many lady loves are needed in your life; one in the old country and one in the new country? Ah, too bad

Matthew couldn't be here to witness this revelation. I'd enjoy it so. Maybe you're not as boring and unlovable as old Matt claims," he laughed at Peter's discomfort.

Peter groaned, "This is not what it seems."

"That's what they all say," Jessica said wryly. "How disappointing, Peter; I thought you were a cut above. Now I see you are cut just like the rest of them."

"Stop it, all of you," Barbara pretended to be cross. "You are going to make poor Peter weepy. See there, he's chewing his lower lip."

"Peter is a legend in his own mind, make no mistake about that," William sniggered, "but there's no doubt in anyone's mind that he's a cut above."

~21~

"Oh, that way madness lies; let me shun that."
~ William Shakespeare

Prince Edward Theatre
London, England
December 2004

During the ride to the theatre, Peter decried his lapse of good judgment and damned himself for giving the ticket to Zara. He obsessed over his weakness that day at lunch, because he didn't say what he thought -- *Yes, I do mind, Zara; sod off, stay away from me, get a life, and stay out of mine.* He knew now that he couldn't deal with her like a normal, reasonable person and vowed never to allow her to manipulate him again.

When they arrived, he found her seat still empty. He lifted his eyes to heaven, praying she'd changed her plans. *Knowing Zara, it isn't bloody likely.*

The theatre was dim, hot, and musty from the smell of old wood and crowded warm bodies. Peter was sweating, but more so from anxiety than from the heat. James was hot and restless waiting for the curtain to go up. He sat tucked between Barbara and Peter and they were entertaining him with word games.

The orchestra began playing the overture and the curtain was about to rise. Murmurs drifted through the crowd like a wave. Peter heard quiet gasps as heads turned toward the aisle. He followed the direction of their eyes and beheld Zara. He caught her scent then; that strong, musky perfume she always wore mixed with booze and stale cigarette smoke.

Zara held everyone's attention. If her aim was to stage an entrance and bathe in the spotlight, she had hit her mark. She stood at the end of the row, dangling a black feathered cape on her hip. The slim cut and deep décolleté of the short black dress accentuated her broad shoulders, narrow hips, and long legs. She wore a triangular black hat decorated with long whimsical black feathers perched on her head.

Peter groaned, lowered his head, and covered his eyes with his hands. *I wonder if she has any idea how bizarre she looks.*

She had slicked back her spiky, bright red hair and the angled theatre sidelights made scimitars of the sharp planes of her face. The gash of red on her lips, circles of rouge on her high cheekbones, and the thick, black makeup around her eyes were striking against the whiteness of her gaunt face. The clownish makeup against the bright red hair and the black of the dress reminded Peter of the Joker from a Batman movie. He expected that any minute she would break into a maniacal laugh.

Peter's loathing for Zara slammed him in the gut. By the time he could bring himself to look at her again, she was still at the end of the row, posing arrogantly with her chin held high. Staring at her standing there, he realized that he found her so repugnant that looking at her made him feel physically ill.

All around him sniggering rippled through the crowd. When she waved to Peter, a man sitting in the seat behind them mumbled, "*A-hah.* I see an old crow has flown in. I hope it doesn't perch in front of me."

Zara slithered down the aisle to Peter's seat, she bent over James, and simpered, "Little boy, be a dear and move to the empty seat at the end of the row beside that woman." Her arm fully extended, her red nails flashed as though brushing away a pesky fly. "There's a good lad. *Move to her. Now. Love.*"

With a haughty gaze, she pointed at Jessica who was beckoning to him, giving the appalling woman a scathing look.

James looked terrified having this black feathery creature standing above him. He scrambled onto his grandmother's lap, Barbara gathered him in her arms, and whispered in his ear. He crawled over his father toward the empty seat and Jessica pulled him onto her lap.

With her chin raised in a regal tilt, Zara slowly lowered her body into James' vacated seat. Apparently convinced she appeared elegant, Peter assumed it was as graceful a move as she could manage considering she'd probably sat at her hotel bar drinking wine all afternoon and into the early evening. Her entrance and outlandish trappings humiliated him and he was angry that he had allowed his family to be drawn into her fiasco, but above all, her treatment of his young nephew infuriated him and left a curdled taste in his mouth.

William leaned toward his mother and whispered in her ear, "Well, we were *expecting* her, but not expecting *her*. Thank heaven you and Jess have enough social grace to dress appropriately." With a finger, he traced the black embroidered design over the shoulders of his mother's light gray suit that she'd worn with casual silver jewelry. "The show was supposed to be on the stage, Mum. That woman is creating a production of her own. Obviously, she was confused and dressed for Ascot. What in bloody hell was Peter thinking? Oh, good Lord, how I wish Matthew were here." He snickered, "Mere words cannot describe this woman."

Peter could hear tittering amongst the ladies. He was embarrassed for the family, but made the best of a damnable situation. His jaw muscle working, Peter muttered under his breath, "Damn it, I bloody well *knew* better."

With a toothy grin, Zara aggressively extended her hand toward Barbara.

"*Oh, Mrs. Gabriel-Johns*! I've been waiting to meet you. My dear friend Peter's been neglecting to get us together."

Barbara nodded politely, without touching Zara's outstretched hand. She leaned forward and caught Peter's eye, noticing his embarrassment.

"Peter's your *dear friend*, you say?" *Not bloody likely, I'd say.*

During the production, Zara's whispering in Barbara's ear finally irritated her enough to put a stop to it and Peter was increasingly annoyed when she continually touched him and stroked his arm. His patience at an end, he roughly removed her hand and whispered in her ear.

"Don't lay a hand on me again, Zara. You are creating a disturbance and I shall have the usher remove you. Not that you haven't already made a drunken spectacle of yourself."

She giggled and slowly ran a long, red fingernail down his sleeve.

After the play, they all stood outside the theatre waiting for the car Peter hired to take them back to the Ritton. A chill wind swirled a light dusting of snow around their feet. Peter hiked his coat collar above his chin wishing he were a turtle and could disappear inside.

Zara gazed inquisitively from one to the other, and chirped, "Where are we off to now, everyone?"

William snorted and rolled his eyes. He was keeping his distance from her, carrying James, and holding Sarah's hand. Jessica and Edward disassociated themselves from Zara by walking arm in arm close to the theatre and pretending to review the posters.

"We are going back to the Ritton, Zara. We're all done in from our festivities today and in need of a good night's sleep."

Zara pouted. "*Oh, pooh*, I was hoping we could go somewhere for a nightcap, Peter. Don't you fancy a toast to Christmas? We could go to the Park Lane…"

Peter interrupted, "*No!* Thank you, Zara; I've already toasted Christmas and frankly, I'm the one who is all done in."

"Well, then. I'll just join you all for breakfast at the Ritton," she tittered, oblivious that she'd surpassed the end of her luck.

Barbara interrupted, "Oh no, I'm sorry; that won't be possible. We're having a family-only breakfast served in our suite and then we're leaving for home." She added in her most dignified way, "But it certainly was...*uh*...an *experience* meeting you, Zara."

William hailed a taxi and his family returned home to Mayfair for the night. Peter's hired car arrived just as he hailed a taxi for Zara. He paid the driver and sent her on her way. Pulling away from the theatre, Barbara took Peter's hand in hers and gave him a gentle squeeze.

"My apologies to the family for that unfortunate spectacle, Mum."

"Well, she certainly was entertaining, Peter. On the other hand, darling, you'd do well to keep your distance. It's obvious there's something not quite right about her."

He draped his mother's wool shawl over her and put his arm around her shoulders to keep the chill night air away.

"Yes, Mum; don't I bloody well know it."

My mother is a master of understatement.

"Zara held everyone's attention. The slim cut and deep décolleté of the short black dress accentuated her broad shoulders, narrow hips, and long legs.

She wore a triangular black hat decorated with long whimsical black feathers perched on her head."

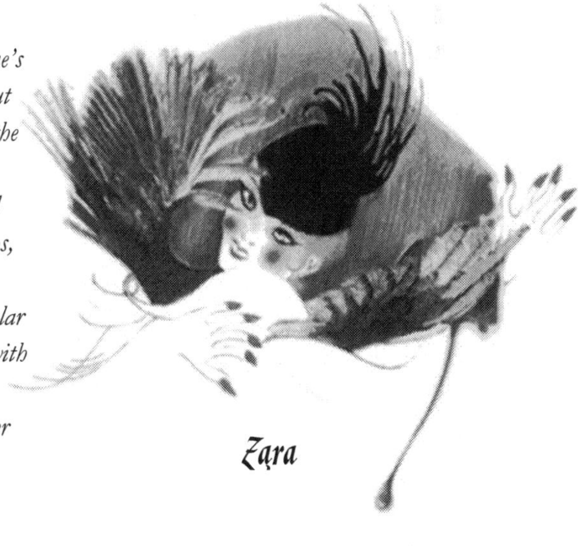

Zara

~22~

"The keenest sorrow is to recognize ourselves
as the sole cause of all our adversities."
~ Sophocles~

Hackney Wick
London, England
December 2004

Zara spent the night drinking alone in her Park Lane hotel room instead of as she'd planned -- in bed wrapped around Peter in the throes of passionate sex.

The next day at check out time, the maid service called reception.

"Room 204's flat out, pissed out of her head, bottles flung everywhere, and lying stark naked. Any ideas?"

"Try to wake her and get rid of her."

Again, the service called reception.

"*Nope*. Got her up, but she rolled over. Called me a sad cow and fell over into the pillow. Then she told us to piss off. She's out cold again and you don't pay me enough to sort out drunk rich bitches."

There was no alternative but to allow her to sleep it off and charge her for another night. Thus, Zara slept until Monday morning and after two nights lost in her dark dreams, her waking thoughts were of Peter.

After a lazy breakfast from room service, she paid her bill and set out carrying her overnight bag. She left Park Lane with a plan in mind. Having grown up in London, Zara knew her way around the city and roamed aimlessly for an hour.

The day was grey and dreary with a cold mist in the air. She ambled up Piccadilly to the London Ritton, sauntered through the lobby, down the long, wide, French Aubusson carpeted hallway, and past the lavish Georgian Colonnade Court. She gazed into the beautiful gold and white Edwardian dining room.

Chilled to the bone, she stopped at the Ritton's Londres Bailey and Bar to warm up with chai tea and cognac and bathe in Peter's aura that he'd left behind.

Peter, who continues to elude me.

When she left the hotel, her mood reflected the dreary weather. It was a long way from the Ritton to Marble Arch, but Zara wanted to kill time and walked to Euston Station to catch the number 30 bus to Hackney Wick. Arriving at her stop, she got off the bus and sauntered around Victoria Park before heading to her mother's house on Kenworthy Road. Brooding, she sat on a stone bench thinking about Peter, oblivious to the chilling mist in the air. She knew she was living for the future. *It had better be soon; I'm not getting any younger.*

Still brooding, Zara left the park and wandered through the neighborhood deep in thought. She was surprised when she found herself across the street from her mother's shabby Victorian house. She stood there for a moment in the drizzling rain, staring at the broken pavement, worn steps, and peeling paint before approaching the door and ringing the bell. In short order, her mother peeked through a tatty lace window curtain.

The door flew open and Norah Twigg rushed to her daughter with flailing arms, shouting, "Blimey, Kedzara, me darlin'!" Her face lit up at the sight of her daughter. "I was just thinking about you and here you are." Her whole body shook as she chortled at the irony of it. Fat jiggled on her double chins, wobbled on her huge arms, and rippled down to the bloated ankles that nearly covered her tiny feet. She grabbed Zara and hugged her to her ample bosom. "So what brings you here, Love? Couldn't stay away from yer old mum, is that it?" Her coarse, phlegmy laugh assaulted Zara's ears.

Zara extracted herself from the smell of stale cigarette smoke and unwashed clothes, while her mother grinned, showing her few remaining teeth, yellowed and brown from smoking and neglect.

"I was in London and thought I'd pay a visit. It's great to see you, Mum, it really is," but even as she spoke, Zara fought to suppress a shudder of disbelief that this woman was indeed, 'Mum'.

"Crikey, Kedzara, darlin'! Well, ain't this luvvly-jubbly? Come on in and tell me what yer been doin'." Norah dragged Zara into the living room by her wrist and shoved her into a chair.

"You must 'ave a cuppa cha and a bicky wiv me darlin'. I'll put the kettle on. Sit there and rest yer bones. Are you a bit weary, Love? I hope you ain't been workin' too hard, sweet'eart," she yelled to Zara over her shoulder.

Norah wrapped herself in an immense, threadbare wool blanket to stave off the chill in the house and scuffled to the kitchen in her worn men's slippers. Her tiny head wobbled on top of her great bulk as she swayed from side to side like a freighter caught in a rough sea.

Zara sank into the overstuffed chair; a puff of dust exploded from the cushion and rose like a miniature cloud to join the threads of cobwebs lining the ceiling. Dog-ears hung from the corners of the faded original Victorian wallpaper. Immense ancient furniture filled the dingy living room. The hanging coiled springs made deep wells in the tops of the threadbare cushions. The furniture was colorless, but the smell of cigarette smoke and gas from the fireplace clung to the grimy fabric and infused the stale air.

Quaint German knick-knacks and religious statuary cluttered small tables. There were cracking black and white photographs of young Zara and covering the walls were pictures of Jesus that had hung there since Zara's youth. There was a large picture with yellowed glass over the fireplace of Jesus with children gathered around him. Norah had always pointed to the picture and assured Zara that Jesus took care of the little children. Zara murmured, "Jesus never took care of me, Mum; I took care of myself, I did, and I got what I wanted, when I wanted it."

Over the years, nicotine painted the inside of the house yellow. Years of neglect had settled in and even if Norah attempted to clean the room, ground in dust and dirt wouldn't have come out of the crevices of the cracked, dry wood. When Zara sneezed, grey kittens of dust skittered across every surface. Filled with disgust, she muttered, "This is why I don't come home."

In the kitchen, Norah spiked her own tea with whiskey. Convinced that Zara looked knackered because she wasn't sleeping well, she laced her daughter's tea with a touch of chloral hydrate that she'd pick-pocketed from a bloke at the pub who knocks out tourists, and nicks their money and Rolex watches.

"Here we go, Ducks," she whispered to herself. "And that's the good stuff we both been needin'."

When Norah returned to the living room carrying a tray with two cups of steaming milky tea and a plate of biscuits, she wriggled into her favorite chair. The sagging springs squealed in complaint about the effort they were making to hold up this great weight. Her head nestled into the billowy cushion and her springy metallic halo of brassy hair pushed forward toward her face. She stared at Zara with watery blue eyes squinting in her stark face; her nose a red plum on a mountain of whipped cream.

"Ta, Mum. I could do with a cuppa."

"Now, me darlin', tell yer mum what yer been up to. And don't be tellin' me no porkies, now. The moment I clapped me eyes on yer, Kedzara, I said to meself, she's peakie. I hope they ain't workin' yer too 'ard at that bleedin' university. After all, yer a consultant and can set your own hours, right?" She peered at Zara waiting for her to verify what she said and poured a bit of tea from the steaming cup into her stained saucer. She blew on it and slurped up the cooled tea.

"Nah, Mum, it's all *tickety-boo*. I'm not working too hard; I've been playing too hard." Zara sniggered.

"That's a load of buggery-bollocks, Kedzara. Yer too peakie to've only played too hard."

"No, it's true, Mum." Zara bragged about Peter to her mother, embellishing his family's aristocratic heritage.

She described their estate and revealed to Norah how much she wanted him and that she intended…no, *would* marry him.

"I was invited to see the play, Mary Poppins, with Peter's family on Saturday night," Zara boasted to her mother.

Norah spat out a sip of milky tea and guffawed. "That's the funniest thing I ever 'eard; Kedzara goin' to see *Mary Poppins!*" She snorted and coughed until her face went from white to bright red. "*Awwww*, Kedzara. You've gone and got yerself a sense of humor, y'little cheeky-bugger," Norah slapped her knee and laughed until she was breathless. "Kedzara seein' Mary Poppins; that's the best joke I've 'eard in a long time, it is." she snorted and wheezed, thinking it was a good story to tell the blokes at the pub tomorrow.

Zara didn't tell her mum the true reason for her exhaustion was that she'd stayed in London until today because she drank herself into a stupor and slept through the weekend. She neglected to tell her mother she stalked Peter night and day, hacked his computers, and stole his privacy.

The two women chatted while the dusky winter light filtered through rain-spattered windows. The smoke from their cigarettes circled in plumes and settled in hazy layers in the airless, dingy room. It had become increasingly chilly in the house, so Norah turned on the gas logs in the fireplace.

Drugged by the mickey, in a short time Zara's head bobbed and she began to snore softly. Norah lifted Zara's feet up on a footstool and covered her with a scruffy blanket. She sat back in her chair and smoked another cigarette. Her thoughts returned to Zara's childhood. *My gel was a clever one she was, but sneaky though; always nickin' and hidin' stuff. She threw a wobbler when Chauncey laughed at her goin' ta Oxford. Always wantin' ter get above her station, he said.*

Norah never saw Kedzara without thinking about the death of her husband, Chauncey Twigg. His sudden death happened shortly after he stubbornly refused to listen when Zara voiced her desire to be educated at Oxford. He took a drunken fall down the steep, winding flight of stairs; his head bashed in and his neck broken. All she heard was the thudding of his body falling on the steps. He never screamed, or for that matter, never uttered a sound. Norah rushed to him seconds after he fell and she thought she glimpsed Kedzara at the top of the stairs, standing in the shadows smugly looking down at them. Then…she was gone. Had she really seen her daughter?

"Never sure," she mumbled, "but I never want to get on Kedzara's bad side...or 'ave 'er at my back."

After Chauncey's death, Norah made ends meet from her widow's pension. Then Zara won a place at Oxford. She left home and moved into her aunt's house in Burford, the same house Zara inherited when her aunt passed away. *It was what she wanted. Kedzara always gets what she wants.* Norah took one last drag on her cigarette and she stubbed it out in her teacup. It sizzled in the tea left in the bottom of the cup.

Norah waited until she was sure Zara was fast asleep and rocked her great bulk back and forth. With one final heave, she pitched forward out of the chair. She gathered her daughter's purse and overnight bag and took them upstairs to the bedroom to go through them.

"*Awww,* Lawd above, not a tuppence worth of anything I can use in this 'ere bag," she mumbled, pulling out the black dress, the hat, and shaking out the feathers on the cape. She felt around inside the bag and tugged at an object caught in the frayed lining at the bottom.

Gor blimey, wot's this?"

She pulled out a mud-covered bracelet. Wiping off the dirt, she saw the initials H.E.H. between double rows of diamonds on the wide gold band. She tried to hook the bracelet around her wrist, but the clasp was broken and there was a two-inch gap between the ends. Having no concept of the bracelet's worth, she pocketed it and went through her daughter's purse.

"Blimey, quite the haul of dosh, I'd say." She pulled out a few huge wads of pounds with rubber bands around them. "Kedzara won't miss a few quid," she sniggered, peeling off some twenty-pound notes, and shoving them in her pocket.

While Zara slept off the mickey, Norah busied herself in the cluttered, greasy kitchen, cooking for the two of them. She shook Zara and woke her.

"Kedzara, me darlin', I got the dinner ready. Do yer fancy bangers and mash and a kip?"

"Yes, Mum," Zara stretched and yawned. She'd already planned on a meal and a bed for the night. She had work to do on Tuesday in London.

Zara woke up in the morning with a pounding headache, took four analgesics, and dressed inconspicuously in black wool slacks and a grey jumper. She ate tea and toast whilst Norah lumbered round the kitchen, blethering about the sorry state of her life.

"Kedzara, just wait till yer get old, like yer Mum. I got such aches and pains and me feet hurt so bad, I can't hardly walk to the pub anymore. Can't afford a taxi...you'd think at least one of them blokes would pick up an old gel now and then, or at least treat 'er to a pint. I got me a bar bill long as yer arm. Crikey, Kedzara, how hard life is for a poor ol' pensioner and me always by meself, too. You never call yer poor old mum...and would it hurt yer to offer a few quid now and again?"

Norah continued her rambling monologue sharing with her daughter her plans for the day, which included shopping for groceries to replace in the pantry what she'd cooked, a clear bid to squeeze a few more quid from Kedzara to help out. Zara was nodding and smiling, but far from listening or caring. She was lost in her thoughts and making her own plans for the day.

After breakfast, Zara asked to use the phone. She didn't want to use her mobile to make the call. She knew the number from memory; it was a number she couldn't write down. The phone connected at the other end in Finsbury Park.

"Speak," a deep male voice commanded.

"I want to speak to Ra'id."

He dropped the receiver with a clatter and Zara waited. A few minutes later, Ra'id picked up the phone.

"This is Ra'id. Who is this?"

"A friend, Ra'id. We have to talk. I need to get in touch with the Rad brothers."

"Ah, I know who this is. Very well, my friend; I'll meet you today at the usual time and place. *Uh*, do you have what I need?"

"Yes, and I'll be waiting, Ra'id."

"Her head nestled into the billowy cushion and her springy metallic halo of brassy hair pushed forward toward her face. She stared at Zara with watery blue eyes squinting in her stark face; her nose a red plum on a mountain of whipped cream."

Norah Twigg

~23~

"It is difficult to say what is impossible, for the dream of yesterday is the hope of today and the reality of tomorrow"
~ Robert H. Goddard~

New York City, New York
December 2004

On Board the Great Escape's forum members were buzzing with excitement as the time for the New York City Getaway approached. The forum was alive with greetings from other members who could not get away, all wishing the travelers *bon voyage*.

Chris organized the venue for the members and kept them apprised of the activities. Hayley worked with her diligently researching options and they became even closer friends. She realized Hayley was not able to face a large crowd of strangers, but at least they would be together when she met Jaxx at the Plaza Hotel on Saturday afternoon. The Plaza was not far from the Top of the Turret, so it was a convenient place for everyone to meet.

Peter arranged to stay at the Plaza; Jaxx at the Courtyard Midtown; and Chris at the penthouse with Hayley.

Hayley and Peter felt the past five years melt away while they became closer friends. During the flight from London Heathrow to New York City on British Air, Peter couldn't keep his thoughts from drifting to Hayley. There was no one to whom he felt more connected. He could almost feel his arms around her. He wanted so much to be with her, but most of all, he wanted nothing more than to make her happy during this time together.

Peter landed in New York on Friday morning, December 17. After checking in at the Plaza, he called Hayley from his room to assure her he'd arrived safely and that he would meet her for high tea at the Palm Court on Saturday.

"Hayley, I wish we hadn't delayed getting together until tomorrow."

"Yes, what were we thinking, Peter." she chuckled. "Now we have to wait another whole day. But, I know you have an appointment and you are probably jet-lagged, so let's just go with our plan."

"All right, Hayley. I'll be waiting in the lobby when you arrive at the Plaza."

"That's Wonderful, Peter. Christine, Miguel, Marisol, and Jaxx will be with me. We'll see you then."

His next call went to Sydney Lawton. He confirmed his appointment to see her that afternoon. They would discuss current trauma theories and Peter was interested in her opinion on an Oxford graduate students' study that showed promising recovery results. They both planned to attend a two-day conference in the city before Christmas. Peter, the keynote speaker, spoke with expertise, sincerity, eloquence, and with a great deal of presence in front of a group. Suave and handsome as well, he'd become a much sought-after conference speaker.

The day was overcast when Peter arrived in New York with temperatures hovering close to freezing, but the weather was windless and dry. Peter needed to stretch after the long flight and dressed for a run. He sprinted a mile and then slowed to catch his breath.

He walked past a woman sitting on a bench alongside the path. She was colorfully dressed with a red sweatshirt over bulky clothing and wore reindeer antlers on top of a dirty, smashed hat. She grinned and nodded, jabbing her finger at him.

He stretched and began running again and went some distance before he came upon the Park East Café where he stopped to rest.

The Café posted a delectable menu and Peter chose a dilled chicken salad sandwich on thick slices of homemade wheat bread served with a cup of creamed cauliflower and carrot soup. The desserts were fetching, so he finished lunch with lemon custard pie and a cup of English breakfast tea. The café's cozy atmosphere and the appetizing food cheered Peter. It changed his mood from lonesome and gloomy back to relaxed anticipation.

Seeing Hayley under these circumstances would be far different from the first time he met her. She was a shell of a young woman then; grieving over her terrible loss and filled with fear. When he left her at Stony Point, he struggled with a strong desire to pack her up and take her with him. He knew his mother would approve, but felt he'd be getting in over his head. And the timing was all wrong. Just all wrong. Worst of all, he realized he'd developed feelings for her that he simply couldn't cope with at the time. Now, the timing was right and they needed to explore where their relationship was going.

Hayley occupied much of Peter's waking moments. There were times when he would sit in a therapy session lost in thoughts of Hayley. For minutes at a time he had no idea what his patients talked about and had to play back the tape.

Peter emerged from his deep reflection and realized that even though it had been a long-distance relationship, they came to know each other so well over the past few months. The question was...how would they feel when they actually met?

As their friendship grew, Peter found that night after night, he went to bed weary from the day, but as soon as he tried to close his eyes, his mind traveled to Hayley. He imagined what she was doing, wearing, thinking. His vision of her kept his sleepless eyes open staring off into the darkness. She appeared like a bright star in his mind's eye. She was his Lorelei, calling him from the depths of his yearning. She distracted him with the beautiful melody of her siren song, shipwrecking his sleep on the rocky coves of his consciousness. He longed to hold her, to be with her. He wondered if she thought about him and if she lay awake at night staring into the darkness, too.

By the time he left the café, he became more aware than ever that truly, his thoughts were never far away from Hayley.

Hayley could think only that Peter was within walking distance from the penthouse. She sat in her living room gazing out the window at the lake in Central Park, sipping tea while she twirled a lock of hair around a finger. Peter sat in the nearby Café dawdling over his cup of tea. Both were lost in thoughts of each other.

Hayley had met with Lippy that week and several times called him Peter. Her financial advisor thought she seemed spacey and wondered if she hadn't been sleeping well. Her accountant noticed her staring off with a dazed smile while going over household figures, and while walking Diva that morning, she arrived at home with no conscious memory of how they got there.

She tried to occupy her mind by admiring the outfits she'd selected from a few dozen dresses, gowns, shoes and purses that Lydia brought to her. What she chose were from the last of her mother's exclusive handmade vintage-style collection, and she was dismayed when Lydia told her Buddinghill's might close the shop.

Lydia approved of her selections and was pleased to see Hayley taking an interest in her life again. Hayley was satisfied with her choices and realized these were the first new clothes she'd bought since...with a long sigh, she willed herself to stop thinking about the past and focused on what the next day would bring. She was excited but nervous about seeing Peter again and realized she was happily looking forward to seeing Chris. *Happy! That's what I am*, she beamed. *I'm feeling happy, after feeling sad, lonely, and afraid for such a long time.*

Christine and Pookie got together late on Friday afternoon in Cleveland, while Peter and Hayley nervously anticipated their meeting the next day. Chris packed her clothes in a small duffle bag. Her outfit for the meeting was classic couture and she was satisfied that it would work. She went to some trouble to assure her clothes were fashionable and attractive, but her long, straggly hair was still unkempt and woefully lacking in style.

Pookie arrived at Chris's tiny apartment with Chinese takeout of Wonton soup, egg rolls, vegetable fried rice, and shrimp chow mien, so they could spend the evening together. Sitting on the sofa while they ate in front of the small television set, they discussed the details of Pookie's assignment. She would have the whole burden of getting their Sunday morning news program on the air.

"No problem. I've watched you manage those pinheads for three years now, and I know what to do."

Chris chuckled, and said with a lisp, "Your *perthonal perthpicacity ith particularly pleasing, McPookerth."*

"And you've *thurpassed your allowable allocation of alliteration, Crithy*."

Business taken care of, they relaxed and stretched out on the sofa giving each other a foot massage. Pookie enjoyed their casual conversation until Chris's chatter about meeting Jaxx grew to a fevered pitch.

"Chrissy...*please*...give it a rest. I'm weary of Jaxx-talk," she grumbled, "and I'm going to barf if you don't cut it out," she pointed her finger in her mouth.

"*Shut up!* You're particularly disagreeable tonight."

"Thank you for noticing."

"You're welcome."

"Honestly, Chrissy, are you trying to convince me or yourself that he is what you think he is? I think we need to do an innervention."

"Oh, really, *Pook-a-lator*? You and what army?"

"I'll call your mother and father."

Chris scoffed, "Right; they'll say, '*Christine, who?'* And by the way, that's *intervention*...if you're going to *do* something, at least know how to pronounce it." Christine sighed heavily. "Come on, Pookie. Be happy for me. He's as anxious to meet me as I am to meet him. We're looking forward to finally being together."

"Hark! What is that I hear?" Pookie cupped her hand around her ear. "Oh, yes! *Mmm-hmm*, it's a loud and clear *booty* call. You *do* know what that is, don't you, Chrissy?"

"Yes, I do, Pookie, and I made the call." Chris chuckled, and tickled the bottom of Pookie's foot. "I decided it wasn't worth protecting my virginity at the ripe old age of twenty-four."

Pookie breathed a long, exasperated sigh and slowly shook her head. "I wish I could be happy for you, but I just can't see how this can turn out well." She dropped her voice and tweaked Chris's toes. "I can't believe this flim-flam sham-man could bamboozle a woman as intelligent as you, Chris."

Pookie wondered if Chris even thought about the pitfalls of moving to the next level in what she thought was an utter charade. *She's going to get hurt; I just know it.*

"Chris, do you know if the police ever found out who blew up the Hamilton's plane?"

"No, they didn't, Pookie. Why do you ask?"

"Because I'm not sure Hayley should be putting herself out there until they find the killer."

"Well, she'll be surrounded by a circle of friends protecting her. Moreover, it's been five years, Pookie. How long should she wait?"

"Whose idea is it for her to come out to play?"

"I guess it's her own idea, but she did tell me that Peter has encouraged her. She's tired of living in a cloister. Why do you ask?"

"*Hmmm...*Well, I've been working in the news long enough to know that if they want to get her, they will. Chrissy, you and this man, Peter; are you prepared to wield swords in front of her? You know, don't you, that you might get hurt."

Christine took a red eye flight from Akron to New York City. She arrived at the Plaza Hotel before eight o'clock armed with all the paperwork she needed to meet with the tour guide. Assured that everything was in order, she jumped in to help register the arriving members.

Excitement spread as the group gathered in the lobby at nine o'clock for tours and activities. After breakfast, the participants chose the option of either going with the guide, or off on their own until dinner at seven o'clock when they would meet at the Tavern on the Green. Everything now set in motion, Chris was free to meet Hayley at the penthouse.

View of the Plaza Hotel
From Snowy Central Park

~24~

"She walks in beauty like the night
Of cloudless climes and starry skies;
And all that's best of dark and bright
Meet in her aspect and her eyes:
Thus mellowed to that tender light
Which heaven to gaudy day denies."
~ George Gordon, Lord Byron~

New York City, New York
December 2004

Symington opened the taxi door and offered his hand to Chris when she stepped out at the Top of the Turret. He wore his formal uniform in full-dress regalia, placed a sprig of holly in his cap, and wore a cheery red plaid bow tie clipped to his shirt. When he greeted Chris as she stepped onto the curb, he thought there was no comparison between this young lady and the disheveled Halloween costumed woman he met one evening in early October.

"Hullo, Ms. Horowitz! I hope you are having a grand holiday season. It's a pleasure to see you. May I add that you are looking especially well?"

"Hi, Mr. Symington; It's great to see you, too. Happy Holiday and please call me Chris. Love your classy threads! All the shiny buttons and gold braid – is...well...*spiffy*! May I borrow your red jacket for this evening? It's much prettier than mine," she teased.

Symington chuckled at her comments and replied, "Only if you intend to open doors tonight. Besides, there's nothing unattractive about your turquoise jacket. I like the western style."

"This jacket is charmed and has a surprising history, Mr. Symington," she spoke softly, but that's not what I'm wearing tonight."

"Please call me Symington, Chris." He reached out and touched her arm. "I understand you are Hayley's overnight guest. I'm delighted that you two have become good friends."

Thank you, Symington. Whether you know it or not, your blessing means a lot to me. You are important to Hayley; she loves you very much."

Symington smiled at Chris' words while the homeless woman crept up on them. Chris had her back turned to the slatted entrance; she was unaware that the little old derelict had crouched on her haunches behind her, until she cupped her hands around her mouth hissing like a snake. Startled, Chris jumped; Symington grasped her hand to steady her.

"Here, here!" Symington frowned, scolding the old woman. "We'll have no more of that! Behave yourself; you're more annoying than usual today," he shook his finger at her.

"She's the snake," she retorted, flattening her palms together while undulating her arms. The old vagrant was dressed in a huge, tattered red sweatshirt appliquéd with a green satin Christmas tree decorated in colored metallic balls and jingling silver bells. She wore large felt reindeer antlers on her Aussie hat. She covered all eighty-five pounds of her with Christmas tinsel as though she'd thrown it into the air and a silver shower rained over her.

"Well, Merry Christmas, *Dream-Girl*. What are you doing out of your hovel?"

She wheedled, "I came to tell you that I need coffee...*and money*. Tell the swan that boy didn't bring my coffee this morning...and don't call me *that*," she grumbled.

"So, she's the swan. How come *she's* the swan and I get to be the *snake*?"

"Because she is; I dreamed it. 'Can't help what I dream, snake," she whined, while she stamped her foot, pounded her fist in her hand making all the bells on her shirt bounce and tingle, and her reindeer headdress jingle and ring.

She started to run back to the doorway and suddenly spun around, her knotty bowed legs twisting together like ropes on a swing.

"Tell the boy I want coffee. *Go now!*" she demanded, pounding her fist in her hand.

She scrambled under the loose boards. They could hear her singing Jingle Bells while she jumped up and down making the bells on the sweatshirt tingle and the big bells on the antlers ring.

"Well, someone is full of the Christmas spirit," Chris said wryly, shaking her head. "I wonder if she ever heard the word, *manners*, or even *please* or *thank you*?"

Symington chuckled while nodding in agreement. He opened the lobby door when Miguel appeared.

Miguel nodded pleasantly. "*Feliz Navidad*, Miss Horowitz. Is this your only bag?"

"Yes, it is. *Feliz Navidad.* Merry Christmas, Miguel."

Entering the elevator, she watched intently as Miguel tapped the wall. The elevator rose without noticeable motion. The doors glided apart when they reached the twentieth floor.

Chris stepped from the elevator into the luxurious pink marble foyer. She felt as if the elevator had catapulted her through a time warp into the past, or she woke up to find herself alive in a book of beautifully illustrated fairy tales. Marisol had replaced the roses in the foyer with a bouquet of light red, white and green poinsettia, mixed with sprigs of holly, spruce, and white berries. Miguel tapped the wall to open the penthouse door that Marisol had decorated with a large holiday wreath. Hayley heard their voices and rushed to the door to hug Chris.

"Welcome, Chris, Merry Christmas!" Hayley's voice was full of excitement and her enthusiasm was contagious, as was her Christmas spirit. Diva leapt around Chris's feet, spinning and yapping as though greeting an old friend.

"Come here, you darling little dust mop." Chris picked up the tiny dog, hugged her, and straightened the cock-eyed candy-striped bow on Diva's topknot. Diva flicked kisses at Chris and nuzzled into her shoulder.

To Chris, Hayley was the essence of the season in a red cashmere turtleneck sweater and Hunting Tartan plaid slacks of navy, green and red. She wore a long matching plaid scarf draped around her neck and shoulders, pinned in place by a large gold enameled brooch that Chris recognized as the same Hamilton coat of arms that they'd inlaid in the foyer floor. Heavy gold chains set off the red sweater; she had pulled her hair off her face in a loose chignon and the twisted gold earrings she wore were different from anything Chris had ever seen before. Hayley's boots were black suede just like her own.

"I love your clothes, Hayley. May I borrow them when...*if*...I grow up?"

"Please don't grow up Chris; you're my playmate; you'll leave me all alone!"

Chris hugged her, "Don't worry; I'll never leave you, Hayley." She stepped back slowly, and turned in a circle. "Notice anything?"

"*The jacket*! Yes, I gave the jacket to you when we met! I can't believe you still have it." She lifted Chris's hand over her head and twirled her around. "That's remarkable!"

"Of *course* I still have it and it's been ten years, Hayley. We made a pact to meet at the Plaza when we were twenty-four, do you remember? I promised I'd wear the jacket."

"You're incredible, Christine. Of course, I remember. We did it, didn't we? We're going to the Plaza exactly ten years after we met, just as we agreed."

"But our lives are nothing like I thought they'd be, are they? Remember I said we'd be old women, all grown up and have babies and diaper bags." She shook her head and hugged Hayley again.

"I don't feel old, Christine, or grown up, for that matter!"

"Yeah, maybe we'll never grow up, Hayley. We might be like Peter Pan."

"Only if we're lucky, Christine!"

"Or stuck in an episode of the Twilight Zone. What do you think?"

"Where do you think I've been stuck for the last five years, Chris?" She laughed. "Let's go inside. First, I want to know if you ate breakfast at the Plaza with the group, or would you enjoy coffee and Marisol's delicious treats that she made for us?"

"No, I haven't eaten anything since I left Cleveland and yes, coffee and treats would be wonderful. That reminds me, there's a scrawny little *Jingle-Beggar* downstairs urgently *requesting* a handout."

"Oh, yes, I know *exactly* how she makes requests," Hayley nodded. "Miguel tended to her earlier. She's hungry again, I suppose. I noticed she's losing weight, which concerns me, so we've been making sure she gets more than coffee and sweet rolls. I hope that she's eating the nourishing food Miguel takes down to her." Hayley chuckled at Chris's expression.

"Hayley, you're such a softie!"

Hayley took Chris's hand to show her to her room.

"You were my first guest in the penthouse, Christine, now you have the distinction of being my first overnight guest as well."

Hayley beamed at Chris while showing her the luxurious bedroom with its stunning views of Central Park.

"This is where you'll sleep. Through your room is a private bath. I hope you'll enjoy being here with me tonight, Christine."

"How could I not? I feel like a princess when I come to this penthouse, Hayley. If the Plaza were rated a five-star hotel, then *Chez Hayley* rates a ten. You even have entertainment posted at the entrance. She's priceless. I called her Dream-Girl. I'm not sure she liked the name, but it fits!" They were both amused as Chris described the actions of the little imp and the image of her prancing in her Christmas outfit, hissing, and making her usual demands. "So, it sounds like you and Symington have adopted her," she laughed.

"She thinks we have, Christine." Hayley rolled her eyes. "She's become a family pet, you see."

"I do see," Chris nodded snickering. "What's this on the bed, Hayley?"

"It's a small Christmas gift for you, Chris. I thought it would be something you could use today. I asked Lydia to select some makeup for you. This is what she thought would flatter your skin. I hope you like them and it wasn't too forward of me," she lowered her eyes. "I wanted to have my esthetician come in to give us facials, but there wasn't enough time today."

Chris opened the package and inside was a complete collection of mineral-based makeup and several glamorous hair ornaments.

"Thanks, Hayley, it's very thoughtful of you. I'll certainly give it a go."

They walked to the kitchen, where Chris and Marisol greeted each other warmly.

"*Feliz Navidad, Marisol*," Christine hugged her and Marisol, blushing, timidly hugged her back.

"Marisol, Chris hasn't eaten today, so will you please serve brunch? Miguel, will you take some treats to Symington and the little old woman? It's close to lunch time and they're probably getting hungry."

Marisol had prepared a tray for them. On it was a pot of coffee; fresh citrus fruit cup; sandwiches of sliced chicken breast with marinated roasted red-pepper strips; melted mozzarella cheese with pesto rolled on thinly sliced focaccia bread; cranberry-nut bread with whipped cream cheese; lemon-iced almond biscotti; and freshly baked Christmas sugar cookies. She placed the coffee and treats on the table in the living room.

They sat together chatting and enjoying their lunch in front of the warm fire. After awhile, both were lost in thought. Chris was first to bring up what was foremost on their minds.

"Hayley, how are you feeling about seeing Peter again after so long? You haven't mentioned him today. Are you nervous, or…"

"Let me say this; no way, no how, does nervous cover it. I couldn't be more terrified if I were standing naked at midnight in a cemetery, when all the graves open up, and a host of ghouls and zombies of the undead come shuffling toward me. Does that tell you anything?"

Chris snorted with laughter. Hayley's humor took her by surprise.

"Yeah, well…*okay, then*; and I couldn't be more terrified if someone just – *oh, yeah*, I like that *naked* thing – strapped me naked to a chair, taped my eyelids open, made me watch Ann Coulter and Bill O'Reilly, and made a tax deductible charitable donation in my name to the Heritage Foundation."

"Oh, that's *good*, Chris! *Let's see...*"

Marisol interrupted Hayley. "*Perdón*, *Señorita* Hayley, you may want to start..."

"Oh, good grief, Chris, look at the time! We have to get ready."

Christine dressed hurriedly and sat in front of the fireplace in the festive living room drinking coffee with little Diva on her lap. She listened to the instrumental Christmas music played softly throughout the penthouse and breathed in the fresh, pine scent of live evergreen. She sighed and swallowed nervously.

Why am I sitting here looking happy and mellow surrounded by the beautiful sights and sounds of the holiday, when I'm wishing I were a million miles away. If I weren't frozen to the spot, I'd make a break for it.

"Oy, vey, I'm a bundle of nerves. What am I doing?" She smacked her forehead with her hand.

Oh, God...I'm going to meet Jaxx. This is where the rubber meets the road. I've played this scene over and over in my head. Once we meet, it changes everything. We can never go back to what we had. What if he thinks I'm not pretty enough...not skinny enough...not sexy enough? What if he's expecting someone with all the things I'm not? A woman with regular features and classic beauty? Chris swallowed hard. *Maybe with my hair tamed and this make up, I might look all right. Oh, God...I wish I could die on the spot and then I wouldn't have to do this. Descending into Hell wouldn't be this scary.*

With her eyes closed, Chris stroked Diva and willed her heart to stop racing. She took a deep breath. Turning her thoughts to Hayley, she imagined Peter's reaction when he saw her again.

Hayley is everything a brilliant young Don from Oxford could want. For that matter, Hayley is everything any man could want; intelligent, dignified, talented, kind, witty, and wealthy. Above all, she's so very beautiful. When he sees her, how could he not want to run over, pick her up, and swirl around the room with her in his arms?

"I'm ready, Christine," Hayley said quietly, gently breaking into Chris's reverie.

Chris opened her eyes. Hayley looked very much like the antique cameo she had pinned to her collar. She casually piled up her hair and long tendrils curled around her face. She had dressed in a pale ivory crocheted blouse with a fringed turtleneck, a belted suede jacket with a tuxedo collar and matching skirt and boots, all in the color of bisque terra cotta. Her clothes fit superbly on her enviable figure.

"Hayley, Lydia brought you exactly the right clothes; you look *très exquisite et beaucoup chic*. In other words, you look awesome!"

Marisol and Miguel accompanied Hayley to the Plaza. She told them it was for the pleasure of their company as much as for her protection. Miguel called for Hayley's towncar and driver shortly before they were ready to leave. It was a chilly overcast day and the streets were alive with Christmas shoppers. The lightly falling snow dropped a sheer white veil over the city and traffic was moving at a snail's pace. No one spoke; they were mesmerized by the slow bump-bump-bump of the windshield wipers.

Hayley sensed Chris's dread about the moment Jaxx saw her for the first time. The weight loss wonderfully improved her figure. Hayley thought she looked trim in her outfit of a black turtleneck sweater and slim black pants, classic white wool jacket with black piping, and black suede high heeled boots. Her chunky gold jewelry saved the look from being too businesslike and added a bright touch. She looked smart and chic.

"Christine, you look smashing! I'm glad you used the makeup and pulled your hair back in a braided chignon." From Chris's surprised expression, Hayley could see she was not used to receiving compliments. "Stop worrying; Jaxx came a long way just to meet you. I can't wait to see how pleased he is when he finally sees the woman with whom he's fallen so deeply in love!"

The towncar stopped directly in front of the Plaza's entrance.

"We're here, Hayley." Chris's throat was tight and she swallowed hard. "Take a deep breath; it's now or never."

Peter waited anxiously in the lobby with a clear view of the entrance. His mouth was dry and his chest felt so tight it was hard to breathe. He saw Hayley searching for him when they came through the door and her face brightened when she spotted him. They walked toward each other across the lobby, embraced, and kissed each other's cheeks. Peter looked into Hayley's eyes and saw the love and trust she felt for him.

While Peter and Hayley greeted each other, Christine nodded at Marisol and Miguel. "They look like two kids who just found a pony under the Christmas tree." She chuckled. "*El muchacho de oro encuentra a la muchacha de oro*; Golden boy meets golden girl. Clearly, they are made for each other, *¿Eso correcto*?"

"*¡Claro que si!*" Marisol smiled and nodded. "Yes, that's right. It is like love at first sight, but I think they fell in love a long time ago."

Hayley introduced Chris, Marisol, and Miguel to Peter. They chatted for a few moments and Christine noted that Jaxx was late. They stood watching the door waiting for him to arrive, until Peter checked the time.

"Will you excuse me for a moment? I'll go to the Palm Court and change the arrival time to give us fifteen minutes more to wait for Jaxx."

"I know where to find the hostess desk, Peter. I'll go with you." Chris fell into step with him. "Maybe Jaxx will have arrived when we get back and I can hide behind a potted plant and get the drop on him." She chuckled and peered at him from under her heavy eyelids.

Peter laughed. "I like your cheeky humor, Christine. I believe you're a good influence on Hayley."

At the Palm Court desk, Peter approached the tearoom hostess and smiled.

"If it would be possible, I'd like to request a few more minutes for everyone in our party to arrive. The reservation was made under the name, Gabriel-Johns."

Chris watched the hostess' reaction and mumbled to Peter, "That poor thing is going to swoon."

He could have just stepped out of Brooks Brothers; he's so veddy British, so veddy proppa and uppa-crust. She snickered. *All he needs is his bowler and brolly*. She watched the young woman sweep over Peter with her eyes. She missed nothing; his blonde good looks, the buttoned down white collar on his blue tattersal shirt, the navy double-breasted blazer, and paisley tie, grey flannel pants and fringed loafers.

"Of course, of course," the woman babbled looking at him. She spoke rapidly, flustered, tripping over her words. *"D-Do I know you?"* She looked back and forth from Peter to the register, trying to associate the name with the man. *Um*...A-Aren't you an actor? I know you are British from your accent, so you aren't an American actor. Wait a minute... Are you Simon Baker? That's who you are, right?"

"Simon Baker is Australian, dear." Chris laughed, "But, I'll have you know that Dr. Gabriel-Johns is the Posh Poster Boy for British-Button-Down Magazine."

"No, no, I'm just ordinary folk." A crooked grin curved Peter's mouth and he touched the woman's sleeve as they walked away.

"Yeah, right, Peter, you're ordinary folk, as much a commoner as the Prince of Wales. I wonder if Jaxx is here yet."

Walk slowly, Sir Long Legs; I've gotta get the drop.

Jacques Bonnier had arrived in New York early Saturday morning and checked into the Courtyard Midtown, where he settled into his room. A thrill of anticipation rushed through him as he murmured, "Jaxx will finally meet his beautiful little parakeet, the *charmant, elegante, petite* Christine*; ma cheri amour*."

Arriving at the Plaza, he swaggered into the lobby; a man full of confidence; a man used to walking into a room, getting attention, and expecting flattery. Jaxx believed he was a sexy, handsome, elegant Frenchman, but in reality, he was a man one could only describe as *medium*. His build was medium, he was medium height and his medium brown hair was thinning, a fact that he hid by cleanly shaving his head. Jaxx was lacking in many ways, but he used his accomplished pretentions and the allure of *savoir-faire français* to his advantage.

Hayley saw a man with a shaved head, dressed in safari clothes and a leather bomber jacket coming through the door.

"Oh, I think he's arrived." She had the impression of an arrogant man who appeared tan from head to toe. She took an instant dislike to him while watching his beady rat's eyes dart around the crowd through small wire-rimmed glasses. Then, with a flash of recognition, he opened his arms wide, and rushed toward her.

"Christine, m*a cherie! Mon ange! Joli perroquet*." His eyes and smile were wide. He covered the distance from the entrance to where they stood, calling out, "Jaxx is *soooo* in love. He knew when you first wrote that you would be *très, très elegante et très magnifique*.

Vous êtes la belle femme de mes rêves! Non, non; beyond Jaxx' wildest dreams*!*"

Standing before Hayley, Jaxx bowed from the waist and reached out to take her hand. She gasped and shrunk back. Before his fingertips could touch her, Miguel slid his tall, muscular body between them and grabbed Jaxx' shirt collar, roughly pushing him across the lobby. He held onto Jaxx by the front of his shirt and with his fist under his chin, he fiercely admonished Jaxx, his deep voice a harsh whisper.

"*Señor, no moverse! Idiota absurdo,* stay away from *Señorita* Hamilton. You will never try to touch her again. *¿Tengo entendido, hombre feo?*"

"*Se que? Señorita Hamilton*? I do not understand. She is not Christine? *Mon dieu! Jaxx est très, très embarrassé.*"

Turning his head to look at Hayley, his brow wrinkled, one hand over his heart, he extended the open palm of the other toward her in a show of regret.

"Please forgive Jaxx for his mistaken identity. *Jaxx est désolé!* He is so, so sorry! But where is my glorious Christine?"

Peter and Chris had walked toward them and watched the whole incident. Peter rushed to Hayley's side and put his arms around her.

Standing behind Jaxx, Chris spoke in a quavering voice, "*Bonjour, mon ami; Je suis Christine.*"

Jaxx spun around to face her. His expression hadn't changed and his hands and face held the same show of regret.

"*Vous êtes Christine*?" he blinked repeatedly. Convulsed in confusion, he jumped, almost falling over backward. Looking at Chris's face, he couldn't fathom what was happening. Jaxx went from his emotional high, thinking gorgeous *Mademoiselle* Hamilton was his Christine; a magnificent and rare bird, who could be the love of his life, to a pit of disillusion. The reality of the situation tumbled in chaos through his mind.

"Christine, *ma cherie!*" He closed his eyes and slowly bent over, kissing her hand. Then, in an exaggerated show of happiness, he hugged her, rocking from side to side, using the moment to regain his emotional equilibrium.

Oh, non, non! Mon dieu, Jaxx now understands this hideous witch dressed in black, this spooky and ugly Baba Yaga with her big lumpy nose, gummy smile, bulgy eyes and frazzled hair is Christine! Non, non, non...my incredible Christine has turned into a hobgoblin. What is Jaxx to do? Jaxx will just have to make the best of this until something changes. Jaxx will make it change. Ah, oui, there will be many colorful chirping, twittering birds at the meeting and Jaxx knows they all love him. One will love him enough to keep him warm in his hotel bed tonight.

No one spoke. Stunned into silence, no one knew what to say.

"Well, then. All right." Peter cleared his throat and placed Hayley's arm in his. "High Tea at the Plaza awaits us straightaway," he announced to break the awkward silence. "We're off."

"And we're leaving," Chris mumbled.

Despite the dreadful start, the three couples had their high tea as planned. Sitting beside Christine, Jaxx was gushing in his praise and extravagant in his gestures, hugging her repeatedly, taking her face in his hands and kissing her forehead. With his skillful pretensions, he made Chris ignore the ominous beginning.

She looked vibrant with happiness while he fed bits of sandwich to her and pecked her lips with tiny kisses. He took her hand and kissed the palm, folding his kisses inside. She flushed with pleasure while he murmured sensual words in her ear in French. She whispered lovingly back to him. The others watched him operate with head-shaking disbelief, aware that Hayley's beauty held him spellbound.

"*Je dois l'avoir. Elle doit être la mienne,*" his eyes and mind were transfixed on Hayley, he murmured and sighed, *mon dieu - Oh, I want her. She must be mine!*

Christine heard his murmuring and whispered in French that she belonged to him, "*Je suis à vous, mon amour, je t'adore.*" She gazed lovingly into his eyes, while Jaxx shuddered inside.

Peter, Hayley, Marisol, and Miguel instinctively knew what Jacques Bonnier was.

"He's a low-class, lecherous lothario," Peter whispered into Hayley's ear.

Hayley whispered back, "He's a philandering gigolo and not good enough for Christine."

"El es un burro estúpido," Miguel mumbled to Marisol.

"Si, Miguelito, y el es un rata sucio, whispered Marisol into her handsome husband's ear, trying to hide her look of distaste for this dirty rat.

Christine and Jaxx spent Saturday evening with the group from On Board the Great Escape. They had booked the Crystal Room and it was gratifying for Christine to be involved so thoroughly with the group she came to know in writing. She spent the evening visiting each table, making sure everyone was having a good time.

Jaxx, on the other hand, was busy working the room intent on finding a bird to twitter and coo in his ear all night and warble sweetly as he made love to her. He knew, for sure, who it definitely wouldn't be.

"*Mon dieu*," he muttered, shaking his head and visibly shuddering as he peered at Chris across the room, "*anyone but the hideous Baba Yaga.*"

~25~

At Last

"Oh, yeah, when you smile, you smile
Oh, and then the spell was cast
And here we are in heaven
For you are mine
At last"

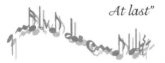

Mack Gordon and Harry Warren
as made famous by Etta James

New York City, New York
December 2004

Peter returned to his room after sending Hayley, Marisol and Miguel safely on their way to the penthouse in Hayley's towncar. Back in his room, he prepared to take a shower and thought about Hayley. During those five years, she'd changed from a frail and terrified teenager to an exquisitely beautiful woman. *She's tall and elegant, slender and graceful, with delicate classic features and coloring so much like my own.*

He found himself humming and whistling love songs and singing words he had not been aware he knew. He felt young and raffish and as he changed into black tie attire, he hummed and sang –

"At last, my love has come along, my lonely days are over and life is like a song...hmmm...hmmm...hmmm...la-la-la-

la.....Oh, oh, oh, yeah, yeah, yeah, when you smiled and then the spell was cast and here we are in heaven, for you are mine, at l-a-a-a-a-s-t...."

When he'd put his arms around her at the Plaza, the magnitude of his feelings overwhelmed him. Everyone in the room faded save Hayley. He could have been alone in the world with her. He'd held back his impulse to kiss her soft, full lips. *I want to make love to her; to protect her and worship her. The desire Hayley aroused in me took my breath away.* He could hear the words and music in his head. While he put in his cufflinks and tied his bow tie, he sang –

"Take my breath away...hmmm...hmmm...hmmm... oh-oh-oh...take my breath away...laaa-laaa-laaa...yeah-yeah-yeah...turning and returning to some secret place inside... watching in slow motion as you turn my waa-aay and take my breath away...la-la-la laaa...laaa... you take my breath away..."

Peter had a fleeting vision of sitting on the terrace at Seven Valleys, holding Hayley's hand like his father held his mother's hand. His search was over. He knew that she was the one he wanted to bear his children. *Our children;* he was filled with happiness and an overwhelming sense of peace. He knew without a doubt that she was the one, the only one. There could be no other. It wouldn't have mattered where they lived in the world; it had been their destiny to find each other and be together, forever.

At nearly seven o'clock, Hayley's driver picked him up at the hotel for the concert. Although the air had the weight and scent of snow, the evening was still clear when Peter arrived at the Top of the Turret. He asked the driver to wait and walked toward the doorman. He knew the man was Symington from Chris's description.

Just as Peter began to introduce himself, he felt a tug on the back of his coat. He grinned when he turned and saw the little old woman standing behind him dressed in her Christmas getup.

"You are the horse," she jabbed her finger toward him. Her reindeer antlers jingled as she nodded her head, looking him over. Satisfied, she repeated, "Yes, you are the horse."

Then she turned and ran back inside her doorway where she happily jumped, stamped her feet, and skipped around making her merry-bells tingle, jingle, and ring.

"Now you know," joked Symington. "You are the horse."

"I know who she is," he chuckled. "Hayley and Chris described her to me at tea this afternoon and told me about her dream. I saw her sitting on a bench yesterday in the park. And you must be Uncle Arthur. I'm so pleased to meet you, Sir," Peter shook his hand cordially and laid his hand on Symington's arm.

"And I as well." Symington inclined his head toward Peter.

Hayley appeared in the doorway and astounded him; she *literally* took his breath away. She had swept up her long hair and loose tendrils curled softly about the sides of her face and down her neck. Peter felt a rush of desire when he kissed her hand and touched her cheeks with his lips. His memory flashed back to Stony Point. *How sweet her frail hands felt in mine when I warmed them.* Now, the touch of her hand excited him and desire rose in him that he had never felt from any other woman's touch. *I'm undone; she's ruined me for any other woman.*

Peter swallowed hard and found his voice was thick with emotion, "Hayley, you look lovely tonight. Is your coat a fashion from your mother's collection?" He admired her long bittersweet-colored coat trimmed with mink around the caped collar and hem. The coat closed at the waist with an old-fashioned frog and mink tassels.

"Thank you, Peter. Hayley smiled, gazing into his eyes. Yes, I wanted her to be with me in spirit tonight."

"Both of you are regal," Symington bowed toward them; the gentlemen's gentleman smiled his approval of Peter's black tuxedo under his unbuttoned black wool coat, black bow tie, pin-tucked white shirt, satin cummerbund, and vest.

"Thank you, Arthur." Hayley smiled with affection and took his hand. She reached into her pocket and withdrew a small, wrapped gift. "You may enjoy having this before Christmas. In this box is a key and the first clue to our annual Christmas treasure hunt," she chuckled. "Merry Christmas, dearest Uncle Arthur."

"Thank you, Hayley. I'll open it tonight in front of the fire while I have my sherry and start my hunt," he smiled at her lovingly and Peter could see the depth of their fondness for each other.

Symington opened the door for them. "I hope both of you will have a wonderful evening." Hayley's demure smile and shy glances at Peter touched him.

When they entered the hall, Peter helped Hayley out of her coat. She wore a delicate vintage diamond choker and a form fitting, empire waist gown, made of the palest ivory peau d'soie. Crystal beads, pearls and rhinestones embellished the gathered bodice and cap sleeves.

"Hayley, Was your dress designed by Lady Elizabeth?"

"It was, Peter, it is one of my mother's creations. It's one of the last to have a signed certificate. It means a lot to me to own it."

Peter offered her his arm and linked with him, she looked lovely and delicate as she walked through the crowded theater with the same aura of tranquility that Chris had admired years ago.

"So elegant," a woman whispered to her friend pointing to Peter and Hayley. "Are they're celebrities or actors?"

"I don't recognize them," she craned her neck to see. "But, yes. Both of them are simply gorgeous!"

The concert was captivating to these two musicians. During intermission, while they were sipping wine and discussing nuances of the music, Peter glanced over Hayley's shoulder and interrupted himself.

"That's Tom Leighton, an Oxford graduate and inventor of the Leigh Web Link. His innovation provides worldwide web interconnection that transformed the internet. Let's talk to him."

Peter introduced Hayley and himself and told Tom that he also was an Oxford graduate. He explained his position at Simon Wessely and Tom told him the year he'd graduated. After a very short conversation about the university, Tom shocked Peter when he asked if he knew Kedzara Twigg.

"She graduated in my class and sometimes goes by Zara. I believe she's still hanging around the university as a computer consultant."

"I've never heard her called Kedzara Twigg, but I believe you're referring to Zara Chandler. Is she tall and slim, with red hair and early forty-ish?"

"That would be her, actually." Tom nodded with a smirk, taking another drag on his cigarette.

Zara was the last person Peter wanted to think about this evening and was astonished that the conversation had so quickly turned to her.

"I remember Kedzara Twigg."

Peter's jaw dropped. "You've met her, Hayley?"

"Yes, I remember because Kedzara Twigg was such a Dickensian name. It rather reminded me of 'Wackford Squeers.' She was consulting with the Rhodes scholarship office when I went to Oxford with my mother to visit her college. It was early in May of 1999, just before I graduated from Wellesley. We bumped into her in the Bodleian Library while we were touring the university. I had glimpsed her hovering around us, actually. I glanced at my mother when the woman greeted her and a look that I never saw before crossed my mother's face. It was utter revulsion, as though she uncovered decomposing carrion. It made me shudder.

Obviously, she disliked the woman immensely and preferred not to speak to her, but she would have appeared rude under the circumstances. She introduced her to me as Kedzara Twigg and said she was a former classmate at Oxford. The woman said her name was now Zara Chandler. My mother couldn't get away from her fast enough."

"Then the interview she gave to Airway News five years ago at the time of Elizabeth's death was mere twaddle." Peter shook his head with disgust. "Apparently she used it simply to aggrandize herself. She made up a story far removed from the truth about their supposed friendship and called her, Lizzy. She claimed that Lady Elizabeth visited her at Oxford when she and Hayley were there."

"Oh, no, Peter, no one *ever* called my mother, Lizzy," Hayley laughed and shook her head. "There was no visit, only a brief stumble upon, and I know for certain that she and my mother were never, ever friends."

"I saw that interview, too. *What utter tosh!*"

"How well did you know Zara, Tom?" asked Peter.

"I knew her too well for my own good," he snorted, blowing smoke through his nose. "Zara got me into some trouble at Oxford, if the truth were known. Is she still up to her old tricks?" he said wryly.

"*Her old tricks*?" Peter's eyes narrowed. He was curious about this information, but before he could ask Tom more about Zara's *tricks*, intermission was over. When they parted, the two men exchanged cards.

"I'll be in touch, Tom." Peter made a mental note to contact Tom soon.

Snow was swirling on the streets when Peter and Hayley returned to the penthouse for dinner. The dining room glowed in the soft candlelight and a backdrop of falling snow curtained the floor to ceiling windows. The table was festive with a white tablecloth and polished silver sparking in the light from the crystal chandelier. Marisol set the table with Elizabeth's holiday china, and in the center, she placed an arrangement of sprigs of holly, spruce, red berries, white roses, and sprays of tiny silver balls.

Marisol prepared a veal roulade, made with thin veal cutlet wrapped around a filling of prosciutto ham, spinach, artichoke hearts, and parmesan cheese. She topped the roulade with a sauce made from veal stock, sun-dried tomatoes, pine nuts, and sweet green bell peppers. For dessert, she made vanilla glazed brie and cranberry parcels. Symington had asked Marisol what she was serving and he brought up a bottle of *Nuits St. George.* She told him it was an excellent selection to go with the veal.

Marisol returned to the penthouse after her family's Christmas celebration. She treasured Hayley and she was as important to Marisol as her own family. She served their dinner and stood aside to watch them for a moment with a satisfied smile on her face.

Chris arrived while they were enjoying coffee and Miguel escorted her to the penthouse.

"Christine, please join us at the table! Tell us everything. How was the evening; did you have a wonderful time?"

"*Señorita* Horowitz, would you like dessert and coffee?"

Chris hugged Hayley and smiled at Marisol. "Honestly, I really would. I was having so much fun flitting from table to table and getting to know everyone that I didn't eat. And Marisol, *please* call me Chris."

"*Si, Señorita* Chris; I happen to have another dinner prepared," she pulled out a chair for Chris. *"Un momento, por favor!"*

"Did Jaxx have a good time?" Peter asked, trying to hide his disdain for the man.

"I think he did, but most of the time I only saw him from across the room. It appeared that he already knew many of the women. I heard gasps when we walked in and then there was a flurry of excitement in the crowd. Women sitting at tables all over the room popped up like weasels, or slithered out of the woodwork like creepy-crawlies. They skittered across the floor toward him all sparkly and shimmery as if they'd dressed for the red carpet. When they gathered around him in their low cut gowns of velvet or chiffon in pretty colors, I could see Jaxx' eyes bugging out and I thought I noticed a little drool at the corner of his mouth," she laughed. "I was totally miscast. My black and white outfit was *completely* out of character. I looked like a penguin or one of the waiters. I wonder if I'll ever learn to...*um...dress the part*."

"Chris, you looked smart and chic. After all, it was only meant to be dinner; who knew it would turn into the junior prom? However,

I'm surprised to see you so early. I didn't expect you until the wee hours."

Yeah...*yeah, well,* I'll admit that I'm a little confused. When Jaxx and I were leaving, we stood in front of the restaurant under their long canopy away from the falling snow. I assumed we were waiting for a taxi to take us somewhere together, but then, a white stretch limo full of young gals from the getaway dinner pulled up and inched along in front of us. A gorgeous, double D blonde babe popped out of the back door and shouted, 'Jaxx, come on, get in!' She didn't say, '*Chris* and Jaxx.' He *kinda* hugged me and air-kissed my cheeks. Then he ran after them, saying, '*Au revoir* until we meet again, *ma chérie*. You must always write to Jaxx *ma jolie perroquet, ma chérie, je t'adore,*'" Chris gestured dramatically and exaggerated a French accent, "And while he was jumping in the back of the limo, he shouted, '*Au revoir, au revoir, je vais vous reunit encore, ma petite perroquet!'* It sounded as if he expected to see me again."

Peter and Hayley glanced at each other while Chris talked. Peter frowned, "So, he just left you there? Not very gentlemanly, is he?"

"A taxi pulled up right away, but I'm a little hacked off that he didn't invite me to go with them. It *was* late, so maybe they were going to drop him at his hotel. In all honesty, I'm disappointed that I didn't have more time to spend alone with him. It was rather anti-climactic. The idea was for him to come to New York to meet *me*." She heaved a sigh. "So, how was the concert?"

They described the concert to Chris, told her they'd met Tom Leighton, and told her about their discussion.

"So this Zara person works with *you* now, Peter? It sounds like she's not exactly *kosher*."

"Yes, she is under contract as a technical consultant for the University and has a temporary office in our college, Chris, but I'm planning a necessary change."

Dinner now over, Chris yawned and excused herself, "I'm beat; I'll see you all in the morning."

Hayley and Peter stood at the living room windows sipping their wine. They looked out at the city for a few minutes and then went outside on the balcony. The air was moist and cold and without speaking, they stood close together under the halo of moonlight in the frosted sky, watching the glow of city lights through the falling snow and listening to the hushed melody of the night sounds below.

Peter draped Hayley's coat around her shoulders. Her fingertips lightly brushed his hand and she felt a tingle from the warm touch of his skin. She smiled up at him and sighed when he turned her around and gently pulled her against him inside his coat, wrapping his arms around her to use their body heat for warmth. She melted against him as he lovingly caressed her face with his fingers and brushed his lips across her forehead. Peter rested his cheek on Hayley's hair, breathing in her fresh scent of citrus and sandalwood. He slowly wound a long tendril around his finger and touched it to his lips.

The snowfall and their movements seemed in slow motion, but their hearts were racing. Hayley's awakened desire left her flushed and trembling. When Peter gazed into her face, their eyes met and neither could look away.

Hayley moaned softly while Peter tenderly kissed the pulse in her throat. Driven by their passion, he placed his hand on the back of her arched neck and slowly kissed her waiting lips.

Later, when they kissed goodnight at the door, it was obvious they both wanted more of each other. Hayley was dreamy and preoccupied while she prepared for bed.

She sat in a robe and wrote in her journal --

HEH

As long as I live, there will never be another day like this. It will live eternally in my memory.

When we came together and Peter took my hands, his touch and the way he smiled at me made my heart race. I looked into his eyes and I couldn't breathe from the heat rising in me. His kiss was sweet and tender, but then a spark went through me and I felt passion that I've never felt before.

I know I'll remember forever his touch and his clean, masculine scent at that moment. It was then I knew I have longed for him since he left my side at Stony Point.

I know now, without a doubt, that I have loved Peter from the moment he came into my room and told me Barbara sent him to me. He told me his mother said I'd love him. She was right; yes, Barbara was right.

I am in love with Peter.

~26~

"My interest is in the future because
I am going to spend the rest of my life there."
~ Charles F. Kettering~

New York City, New York
December 2004

New York City was bright and crisp the next morning, and the two friends took Hayley's towncar to the Plaza for Sunday breakfast with Peter. Afterward, Christine said a tearful goodbye to them and headed back to Cleveland.

The city's colorful Christmas decorations filled Peter and Hayley with holiday spirit and they used the towncar and driver to tour the city. Their first stop was Rockefeller Center where they dared each other to put on ice skates. They wobbled and slid around the rink, laughing and holding each other upright. Neither was aware of a dark figure stalking them and still shadowing when they went to the Guggenheim and the Modern Museum of Art.

On Tuesday, in a small room at the Metropolitan Museum, Hayley spotted that same dark figure wearing a black trench coat with the collar up, huge sunglasses, and a slouched hat that she had glimpsed earlier on the street, at other places on Sunday and Monday, and in other rooms at the museum. She whispered to Peter and they moved stealthily, zigzagging from room to room. Finally, they were positive that someone was stalking them.

"Shouldn't we tell the guard? I want to call Miguel, Peter."

Peter took Hayley's trembling hand, "Don't be afraid, Darling. I'll take care of it."

When they went through the exit, he pulled her against the building to wait. When the dark figure slithered through, Peter rammed him from behind with his shoulder and raised his fist to throw a punch.

"*Non...non! Mon dieu, s'il vous plait. C'est moi!* Don't hit me," he pleaded, covering his face with his arms.

Peter yelled, "Who are you and why...," He stopped in mid-sentence, for when he pulled off the man's hat and sunglasses, he found the stalker was Jacques Bonnier.

"*What in bloody hell...?*" Peter shouted.

Hayley gasped and stood behind Peter when she saw who he was. Peter knocked him down and stepped on him holding him on the ground with his foot.

"Somebody, please get the guard, quickly. He should be right inside the door."

Hayley ran inside and Peter grabbed Jaxx by the collar, lifting him to his feet.

"What the hell do you think you're doing, Bonnier, you bloody wanker?" Peter scowled, grabbed the front of his coat, and shook Jaxx.

Jaxx was visibly trembling; his face a mask of fear. Before he could answer, the guard appeared and asked Peter if he wanted to call the police.

"*Non. Non! S'il vous plait...s'il vous plait. Je dois l'avoir. Elle doit être la mienne. Je ne veux dire aucun mal. Je t'aime. Je t'adore.* I must have her. Jaxx must *have* Hayley!"

"Bonnier, you utter pratt. You're nothing but a prowling tomcat. Get out of here before I do something I'll regret. Go back to London straightaway," he growled low in his throat, "or we'll have you arrested for stalking."

"*Oui, oui.* Jaxx *ira à la maison maintenant.* No police, okay? I will leave New York City tonight...I will go now, *oui*? *Au revoir, ma chéri, mon amour sans parallèle. Je t'aime*!"

Jaxx threw kisses at Hayley while he turned and fled. There was a mixed reaction from the small crowd gathered around them. They clapped, laughed, or booed Peter for letting Jaxx go without throwing a punch.

Peter gathered Hayley in his arms. "Are you all right, Darling?" He kissed her forehead and held her tight against him.

"Yes, I think so," she exhaled deeply, "but let's go home now."

Peter hailed a taxi for the short ride back to the penthouse. He sniggered thinking about Bonnier's startled expression. Then Hayley giggled.

"Did you see his face? I heard Miguel muttering on Saturday that he's a stupid jackass and Marisol called him a dirty rat. He's a pathetic gigolo who isn't good enough for Christine."

"Yes, he was one scared little gigolo, Hayley. I think he's going back, though, and I'll check on him straightaway when I return to Oxford to make sure he's back in London. A sorry lot, isn't he? He may be a stalker, but I don't think he's dangerous - or the *one*. I fear we're going to have to protect Christine from him one of these days," he paused, "or perhaps it's more accurate to say that we'll need to protect Christine from herself. I've never seen anyone in such denial."

"I'm sorry for Christine. He's one of the most insincere men she could have possibly come across. Why can't she see him and the whole situation for what they are? I wish she could meet someone worthy of her."

They spent early Tuesday evening at the penthouse listening to music, comparing favorite wines, and reminiscing about their lives and their families. Peter began to drop hints about how he saw their future together. Each evening he left her was harder than before.

The city was hectic that week with last minute shoppers. Blowing snow and the bitter cold wind made battling their way around the city much worse. On Wednesday and Thursday, Peter went to his conference, glad to be off the streets and in a warm place. Afterward, he stopped at Tiffany's, where he'd found a pair of heart-shaped ruby and diamond earrings he wanted to give Hayley as a Christmas gift.

Later that evening, Peter rang home to chat with his parents. He told Barbara how powerful his feelings were for Hayley.

"Mother, is it possible there is a moment in time when you know you have met someone with whom you are destined to spend your life? Isn't it fair to say a life together with Hayley is my destiny? There were so many opportunities when we could have met and so many forces pulling us together. I can't help but believe this is true, even though ultimately, I believe in free will."

"Perhaps that says it all, Peter," she replied. "I know that's what happened when your father and I met. We seemed fated. Edward and I might never have met if I selfishly had gone off with Julie to Malibu, as I wanted, instead of going to England with Pat. The moment I saw your father, I knew with absolute certainty that he was the one with whom I would spend my life."

"That's exactly how I felt when I saw Hayley. My heart thumped in my chest when I saw her at Stony Point. Of course, I was distressed to see her doing so poorly, but it was more than that. I felt an inexplicable and undeniable connection to her, but she was in such a crisis, that I really couldn't focus on it until I was on my way home. It was as if I had prescience that I was destined to meet her. She responded to me because I think she felt that connection, too. At that moment, she desperately needed someone in whom to place her trust. I knew then you were right to send me to her. You knew, didn't you, Mum?"

"Yes, I knew you should go to New York for her, for Elizabeth - and for me. Of course, I don't believe in arranged marriages; love will find you, but I sensed that she was the right woman for you when I met her, Peter. Hayley brings something to you and to the family that you would have a hard time finding in many other women. And that's a very good way to describe that foreknowledge, Darling. I experienced a foresight when I saw Edward for the first time. It was revealed to me with such clarity of vision that I knew it was meant to happen."

"*Exactly,* Mum! I knew you'd understand. A vision came to me when I met Hayley at the Plaza. We were sitting on the terrace at the manor house and a feeling that she would be the mother of my children washed over me. I have often longed for someone to share my life in England, Mum, and if she'll have me, I want to share my life with Hayley.

Peter

"You are the horse," she jabbed her finger toward him.

Her reindeer antlers jingled as she nodded her head, looking him over.

Satisfied, she repeated, "Yes, you are the horse."

~27~

"No living man can send me to the shades before my time; No man or woman born, coward or brave, can shun his destiny."
~ Homer~

Top of the Turret Residence Tower
New York City, New York
December 24, 2004

The overcast sky on Christmas Eve looked ominous to Symington. When he went on duty in the morning, the weather was still cold and miserable, but the snow had all but disappeared from the ground. Dream-Girl hadn't come out to stretch her legs early in the morning, as was her habit. Maybe it's too cold or she knows Miguel hasn't arrived with her coffee yet, he thought, but he was especially busy and didn't take time to check on her.

Most of the building residents were at home and going in and out finishing their holiday chores and shopping. Many used this morning to give Symington Christmas greetings in the form of money gift cards and large gratuities. Throughout the year, the tower's generous residents gave him tips, season tickets to ball games, theatre tickets, and holiday gifts that amounted to much more than his annual salary. He was grateful for the gifts, and for many years, he lived frugally, saving his money for the future. Since Elizabeth's murder, he longed to return to England to live, but he would stay here until Hayley sorted out her life. *Now, that day may be closer. I can stop worrying; she has Peter to watch over her and her life is turning around. Elizabeth would have been very pleased.*

Across the street, a runner in grey sweats and a hooded jacket, panting hard, had paused to rest in a doorway. Symington noticed vapors swirling in front of the runner's face.

Two figures coming into view on the opposite side of the street appeared to attract the runner's attention. A tall, slender woman and a Hispanic man were returning from an early morning jaunt. Both were wearing heavy coats and hats, and the woman carried a cup of coffee from the Park East Café. Walking beside her on a leash was a sprightly little Yorkie. The man carried a cardboard tray of coffee and a paper bag.

Arthur noticed the runner was shivering when reaching into a pocket for a cell phone. *It's a cold, nasty morning for a run.*

Hanaz Rad answered his cell phone on the first ring.

"Speak."

The runner spat out the words into her cell, "It's time to move - and don't miss this time."

Hanaz Rad and his brother, Dawid, were sitting in their parked car around the corner from the Top of the Turret building waiting for the call.

"This is the second time this person paid us to do a job. The first time, five years ago, we hid in heavy brush for the Learjet to leave the Fitchburg airport."

That day in May, they had positioned themselves well beyond the airport. The weather was sunny and hot; sweat trickled down Dawid's body and he wiped his face with his sleeve. His nerves were on edge and the black shirt clung to his back.

Five years ago, with help from foreign sources, The Rad brothers smuggled a short-range shoulder-fired launcher into the country and they estimated that they would need only one rocket to take down the plane. The two men, experts at bomb making and at constructing explosive devices, were unaccustomed to building rockets.

Dawid picked up the launcher and looked through the site. He examined it and tried to assure himself that he would make it work.

They had carefully calculated height, speed and other factors, yet he worried, unsure of the timing and of his aim for a fast-moving target.

"Are our calculations correct, Hanaz? And what if I miss? You should have let me practice."

"Shut up, Dawid, stop moving, and stay low."

That time a call to Hanaz' cell phone came from the airport at exactly four o'clock, PM.

"Are you ready?" said a voice over the phone.

"Yes, we're ready," Hanaz hissed.

Tension and fear mounted in the brothers. They had only one chance to succeed. They heard the plane roar down the runway and waited for its ascent. It lifted to a perfect climbing angle.

Hanaz saw Dawid freeze and punched his brother's arm. "There it is," he scowled and slammed his fist into Dawid's back, shoving him forward. "Do it *now*, Dawid!"

With his teeth clenched, Dawid raised his shoulder and lifted the missile launcher, keeping pace with the Learjet.

Hanaz growled low in his throat, "Dawid, you're holding the launcher wrong. It's too close to your face." Dawid struggled with the heavy launcher trying to position it and Hanaz shouted over the roar of the plane. "Shoot now! You have a perfect shot. Aim for the… *NO! Wait!* Mark the fuel in the wing!"

Dawid let the rocket go on his brother's timing. He delivered the deadly missile, piercing the aircraft's wing, igniting the fuel, and exploding pieces of the burning wing into the fuselage.

"*Aaaaagh*!" Dawid screamed in agony as the heavy launcher rebounded from the force, shattering his eye socket and propelling splinters of bone into his eyeball.

"Let's go!" Hanaz grabbed Dawid's arm. "The smoke trail will give away our position. Hurry, you fool! I have the launcher. Get in the car."

Dawid stumbled through the dense brush, trailing screams of agony behind him. He threw himself into the car and Hanaz sped away from their hiding place.

"Close the door! Close it, or you'll fall out!"

"I can't see," moaned Dawid, doubled over, his arms pressed against his eyes, his voice hoarse from the excruciating pain.

"*Move!*" Hanaz growled, as he shoved Dawid back against the seat, leaned over him and slammed the door while the car careened over the road.

Hanaz quickly gained control of the car, stepped hard on the gas pedal and sped onto the highway. They were gone from the spot before the wreckage hit the ground.

"Too bad you couldn't see the explosion last time, Dawid. It spread across the sky before my eyes as beautiful as an Arabic Rose."

This time was easier. This time the brothers knew exactly what kind and size of bomb would do the job. Hanaz started the car. It was beginning.

The moment the car began moving, Arthur took the coffee offered to him, while Miguel sat a tray in front of the old woman's doorway. Mere seconds later, the nondescript car entered traffic coming in their direction. The runner was panting, and Symington noticed she had squeezed inside a cranny in the wall and hunkered down, flat against the wall, much like a homeless person.

At that moment, Miguel walked from the doorway where he'd placed the coffee and sweet rolls, picked up Diva, and retreated inside the building.

The car stopped in front of the Top of the Turret and held up traffic. Drivers behind it began impatiently honking their horns. Symington touched the arm of the woman and began walking toward the car. The passenger rolled down the window, touched the black patch over his eye, tossed the bomb at Symington's feet, and the driver sped away.

The bomb exploded into a fiery ball, throwing them up against the wall in flames. The force of the explosion blew away chunks and pitted the front of the building, laying bare the rebar and setting the paint of the wood framing on fire. The bomb blasted the doors, hurling shrapnel, ball bearings, nails, and glass fragments into the lobby, propelling Miguel and Diva against the marble wall and onto the floor.

Deadly quiet ensued. Smoke and steam rose from the broken bodies; their skin charred from the intense flames. The smell of burning flesh fouled the cold air and stung the nostrils of the runner, who stood staring at the harrowing scene in lurid fascination.

Dream-Girl missed nothing from her hideaway. She saw the runner across the street staring at the broken, charred bodies and burning façade of the building. She watched while the runner pushed back the hood and saw a slow smile spread across her face.

In a flash of recognition, the old woman whispered, "The panther. It's the panther." She threw her hands over her face to block this vision of evil. "Where is the horse?" she wailed.

Creeping along and dressed in her Christmas finery, her whole body racked with sobs, the old woman moaned in horror and grief while onlookers heard the distant wail of a fire engine. She fell on her knees when she saw a vision of ravens circling the bright auras rising from their bodies. Rocking back and forth, she clasped her bony hands together and raised them to the sky, just as Miguel regained consciousness, and dialed 9-1-1.

~28~

"Accept the things to which fate binds you, and love the people with whom fate brings you together, but do so with all your heart."
~ Marcus Arelius~

Hayle House
Southampton, New York
Christmas Eve, 2004

Wolcott and Abigail Pettigrew were delighted with their Christmas decorations. Holiday music filled the air in Hayle House while they went about putting up the tree and decorating it with old-fashioned trimmings they'd retrieved from storage.

"Wolcott, look at these darling *papier mache* ornaments of musical instruments and tiny dolls dressed in old-fashioned costumes. I believe Hayley made these when she was a child. I can't wait for her to see this tree. She will be so pleased."

Abigail made a pitcher of sparkling cranberry and pomegranate punch to sip while they worked. The sturdy couple decorated throughout the house, with lavish garlands of fresh spruce greens mixed with holly and held together with generous red plaid bows. The garlands spiraled up the staircase banister and trimmed the massive stone fireplace.

Around the house and on the porches they placed huge copper pots filled with poinsettias and red and white amaryllis. Large fresh greenery wreaths decorated the outside doors. When they were finished, they were pleased with the traditional holiday effect.

"This is the first time Hayle House will be used by family at Christmas since Mr. and Mrs. Hamilton died. Hayley hasn't set foot in this house in all those years."

Abigail and Wolcott came to Hayle House when Wolcott retired from a career as a Maine fishing boat builder. They were paid a salary and provided with living quarters in the house as part-payment for their jobs as housekeeper and caretaker. For many years, the Hamiltons turned over the main house to returning summer renters, who sometimes left disorder in their wake. Abigail and Wolcott took their job seriously. They corrected all the breakage, and cleaned up the mess they left before the next group of renters arrived. If Hayley were to have come at anytime, she would have found the house in perfect order and in fine condition.

"Wolcott, have you lit the gas logs in the fireplace in the two bedrooms that Hayley requested? You asked me to remind you."

"Yes, Abby, I have. The rooms are comfy, now."

There were four bedrooms in the house each with a gas fireplace and private bath, not counting the Pettigrew's own two-bedroom wing; another entire house in itself.

The main house, a two-story construction of clapboard and stone built on a high dune, was a storybook architectural masterpiece following the designs of Grosvenor Atterbury. The house sat within a few steps of the beach below.

"Abby, have you got breakfast ready? I expect they'll be hungry when they get here."

"Yes, everything's ready, Wolcott. I'm excited to see Hayley and delighted that she's bringing a friend. This may be a boyfriend, don't you think? She sounded happy when she called this morning."

Hayley requested that Abigail serve a traditional British and American dinner on Christmas Day of oven roast turkey, gravy, and stuffing, sweet potatoes and mashed potatoes, Brussels sprouts, cranberries, plum pudding and brandy butter, but left all other meals up to her. She'd asked Abigail to prepare a Christmas Eve breakfast and surprise her. It was ready and waiting with freshly brewed hazelnut coffee and tea water simmering on the stove in anticipation of their arrival.

"They should be here soon, Wolcott. They're a little late." Abigail checked her appearance in a mirror next to the door. She was dressed in old-fashioned oxford shoes and serviceable hose. It was Abigail's tradition to wear gray and with her tidy graying hair, she reminded Hayley of a cuddly, grey kitten.

"Best change your clothes, Wolcott. You don't want her to see you in those baggy old jeans and mukluks, dear."

"Aye, I will. I've been watching that couple walking along the water's edge."

"Yes, I see them. They look so much in love, Wolcott. He has his arms around her. Look, he's kissing her and has folded her inside his coat!"

"That they do, Abby, look so much in love." He put his arms around his wife and pulled her close to kiss her. Unbeknownst to Abigail, the skirt of her gray print dress was lopsided, as the belt caught some of the skirt above the waist on one side. "I'll be back after I've changed. Let me fix your dress there, Abby."

On this cold, misty morning, the inland wind picked up, but the sea was calm with only hints of whitecaps on the waves. The tide was out leaving a vast stretch along the water's edge dotted with shells and seaweed. The young couple had dressed in warm clothes and covered their heads with hats and scarves to protect them from the icy wind. They walked up the beach and back again. Now, they stood facing the house.

"I always loved spending summers here while I was growing up. When my parents built the house, my mother named it after Hayle in Cornwall because she thought the coastline with its inlets and the estuary looked much like the Cornish seacoast."

"Yes, it's delightful, Darling, and the coastline does remind me of Cornwall. In my village, Wolds-on-Thames, they constructed a dam during the fifteenth century and created the Apollo and Venus

Lake on which wild geese, ducks, and swans swim. The Cygnet Inn is located on a bluff overlooking an inlet that forms a lake. It's quite picturesque, actually, and people gather on the terrace of the Snuggery Pub adjacent to the Inn enjoying the wildlife and watching boat races on Sundays. It's Matthew's favorite pub and he's spent hours gazing at the water, drinking, soaking up the sun, and pouring over his literature." Peter laughed, "I've often teased Matthew about becoming a drunken sot because he spends too much time in the Snuggery. We three brothers are close, but Matthew and I are adversarial siblings. He thinks he has to engage me in rivalry to win our mother's affection."

Hayley chuckled. "Being a doted upon only child, I've never had the experience of rivalry with a sibling."

"The contest is all in Matthew's imagination, actually. My mother loves all three of us equally."

"We must take some pictures to show Matthew, then. This house could have posed as a model for Daphne Du Maurier or Rosamund Pilcher, I think, for some of their classic novels set in Cornwall."

"Matthew might say that Du Maurier has written classics, but Pilcher - I've heard him say she's got a long way to go."

Hayley winced. "I'm a low-brow, I guess. I've always enjoyed Pilcher's romantic characters and stories. Peter, I noticed Wolcott has painted the doors and window frames a silvery green. It's perfect against the grey stone and weathered clapboard. The house looks like a Christmas card with the smoke curling from the stone chimney and with the bright Christmas lights in the windows." She looked out at the ocean and then slowly looked up at Peter. "It's making me sad to see it now."

"I understand, but you have happy memories of Hayle House, don't you, Darling? Those memories will always be with you."

"Yes, I have happy memories of being here in the past, but your coming with me has made it possible for me to be here now, Peter."

"Please trust me, Hayley. I will always be here to love and protect you. There is no corner or dark place for you to fear."

"I know you will. I'll be happy and feel safe wherever you are." She stood for a moment enclosed in his arms, and then, she looked up at him with merriment in her eyes. "You know, Peter, my thoughts and feelings would surprise you."

"*Oh, really?* I'm happy to hear that. I know it's becoming increasingly difficult for me to keep a clear head when I'm near you. Don't even ask what happens when I touch you!"

"Peter, my goodness, I'm shocked," she said coyly, "Whatever can I say? Perhaps I should tell you that you make me feel all warm and mushy inside, and that I'd like you to grab me and throw me down right here on the sand."

"I think it's little chilly, Hayley, and there might be a better time and place, but if you're willing…"

They both laughed and Hayley said, "I suppose we should go inside. It's getting late and Abigail is expecting us for breakfast."

Hayley took Peter's hand and started for the house. Then she dropped it and turned to him with a lopsided grin.

"Race you to the front door!"

He winked at her. "You'll never win. Remember, I'm a marathon runner. But, I'll give you a head start to even the playing field."

Hayley was fast, but Peter overtook her, scooped her up, and threw her over his shoulder. As they approached the front door, Wolcott opened it and he could see they were giggling and full of gaiety.

"What can I do for you folks?" Wolcott asked.

"Are you expecting a Miss Hamilton?" Peter said, balancing Hayley over his shoulder and working hard to keep his face expressionless.

"Yes, we are," Wolcott said, giving this tall, wholesome stranger a quizzical look. "You are the couple I saw walking on the beach, are you not?"

"Yes, Sir."

Peter slung Hayley off his shoulder and set her on her feet in front of him.

"Hi, Wolcott; It's me, Hayley," she said with a broad smile as she walked through the door, "and this is Dr. Peter Gabriel-Johns, my...*um*...friend from England. Don't mind the entrance; I wanted Peter to see how lovely the house looks from the beach before we came in."

Peter enjoyed listening while Hayley, Abigail, and Wolcott reacquainted throughout the morning. Abigail served a sumptuous breakfast of crusty Quiche Lorraine, spicy sausage rolls, scones with clotted cream and strawberry jam, and a fresh citrus fruit salad, all things Abigail knew were Hayley's favorites.

The dining room, with its French doors leading to a stone patio, had a wonderful full view of the ocean from the house. The day turned sunny and bright with billowy clouds all the way to the horizon. Tall trees, surrounding shrubs, and during the summer, immense flower gardens gave the house privacy from the beach.

Later, Peter toured the house with Hayley. It was tidy and pleasant, with polished hardwood floors, a gourmet kitchen, and comfortable English country furniture. A sweeping staircase from the foyer to the second story gave the house a feeling of spaciousness. He could hear the grandfather's clock in the entrance strike the time.

The second story bedrooms were large with gas logs in the fireplaces and a private marble bath in each. Wolcott had lighted the logs in the fireplaces making the rooms warm and cozy. Abigail had placed bouquets of fresh flowers around both bedrooms, and Hayley noticed she had stocked her mother's *Rhapsody* scented soap and body lotion in the bathrooms.

When Hayley showed Peter her bedroom, with its soft colors, the warm muted tones of the antique Persian carpet, the king-size canopy bed and table beside a cozy upholstered wing chair, he thought it reflected her perfectly. Then he noticed a large oil painting hanging above the fireplace.

"That's my mother's painting of the Walled Ladies Rose Garden at Seven Valleys! That's why Lady Elizabeth kept the painting. She wanted it for you, Hayley. My mother and father will be so pleased to know that."

"My mother could have sold that painting a hundred times, Peter. Nearly every guest who has stayed in this room wanted to own it."

Peter was pleasantly surprised by dinner that evening. Abigail started with a glass of spicy Gewurztraminer wine. She'd prepared lobster bites with drawn butter, double-creamed brie cheese, and black olive and tomato tapenade to spread on herbed toast points. At the table, they started with sour cream baked potato and chive soup with a glass of Bordeaux. She had prepared a Beef Wellington, Brussels sprouts sautéed with pancetta and onion and drizzled with lemon juice. After the entrée, she served a mixed green salad sprinkled with chopped hazelnuts, dried cranberries, goat cheese and raspberry balsamic vinaigrette dressing.

"Abigail, the meal was exceptional. Where did you learn to make a perfect Beef Wellington?"

"Oh, perhaps Miss Hamilton didn't tell you. Before Wolcott retired, I was the master chef at a popular floating restaurant in Portland, Maine, called, the Tattershall Schooner. Since we've been here, I cook for the merry making Southampton summer guests, but we close to weekly guests for the winter every November and I hold a cooking school here at the house. Would you like a glass of port, Dr. Gabriel-Johns? I'll serve Stilton with dessert and coffee now. Can I entice you with an English sticky toffee pudding and warm vanilla cream sauce? I've prepared it in your honor."

After the sumptuous meal, they settled cozily in front of the living room's stone fireplace with a bottle of wine. Hayley relaxed against Peter and rested her head against his chest. He stroked her hair, tracing the silky waves that caught the firelight. He gently rubbed the inside of her wrists with his thumbs and couldn't remember a time when he'd felt more at peace.

Hayley finally spoke what was on her mind.

"Peter, when I reflect on the future, I can't help thinking about the difference in our ages. I've just turned twenty-five and you'll be thirty-six, I'm inexp..."

Peter interrupted her, "Wait, please, Darling. I've thought about all of that, too. Granted, there are eleven years between us, but I believe our age difference is meaningless compared to our feelings for each other. In the end, Hayley, everything else simply doesn't matter. I need you, Hayley...I want you and I need you.

When they went upstairs to retire, Hayley opened the door and the glow of her happiness appeared to illuminate the bedroom.

Peter embraced Hayley and tilted her face up to his. "Hayley, I yearn to wake up every morning to hear the sound of your breathing, feel the warmth of your skin, your soft lips on mine, to breathe in your scent, and be able to touch your lovely body with my fingertips."

"Oh, Peter," she sighed. "I love you. I have longed to be with you," her voice was soft and breathless.

"And I love you, Hayley; it makes me happy to see love and trust in your eyes. I can't imagine ever finding anyone else who would make me feel the way I do about you."

Having opened their hearts, the spiritual essence of their tender love swept through them. All his instincts told him that, until this moment, their lives had been suspended in time.

Peter looked into her lovely face and brushed her forehead with his lips. They stood clinging to each other while they kissed long and deep.

"You are the one I want to cherish and care for; the one whose beauty, softness and fragrance fill my heart and whose body I want to worship."

He sought her breasts; she gasped as a wave of desire spread through her. With her neck arched, she breathed a low moan and whispered, "*Oh, don't stop...*"

Weak with passion, Hayley held onto Peter, their hearts beating wildly, they breathlessly removed all obstacles to their mounting desire and stood before each other with no inhibitions, their beautiful bodies exposed and vulnerable, consumed by their desire for each other.

On the edge of intimacy, they reached out, aching to cross the final threshold to their deepest longings; they entwined their bodies and their lives and found ecstasy in each other's arms.

Hayley & Peter

~29~

"Even in the deepest sinking
there is the hidden purpose of an ultimate rising.
Thus, it is for all men, from none is the source of light
withheld unless he himself withdraws from it.
Therefore, the most important thing is not to despair."
~Hasidic saying~

Hayle House
Southampton, New York
Christmas Day, 2004

Hayley awoke, smiled sleepily, and stretched. She saw that Peter was already awake.

"*Mmmm...* Merry Christmas, Peter."

"Good morning, Sweetheart, Merry Christmas."

Propped up with his cheek on his hand, Peter was gazing at her. She stroked his hand and he took her into his arms.

"I'll never forget our first Christmas together. I'm looking forward to giving your gifts to you."

"I suppose we should get up and start the day, Hayley, but I don't want to think about anything else but being here with you and holding you in my arms. You are my treasure, Darling. Your love is the greatest gift I could have ever hoped for."

"Oh, Peter, being with you is more than I dreamed it would be."

"Darling, after I met you, I realized that I couldn't be satisfied with any other woman. This week with you has been the best part of my life, Hayley." Peter took her face in his hands, "Please believe me; my life was empty until you came back into it. You entered my soul when you entered my life five years ago. We bring so much joy and happiness to each other. I want us to be together and someday, whether we are sitting as one reading books, or in the midst of passionate lovemaking, you will still be the best part of my life."

"Oh, Peter; you make me so happy. The gift of your love has changed my life."

"Hayley, I have a gift to give you later that I think will please you. However, first things first..."

"Whatever you say, Peter."

He pulled her willing body against him and his kisses were soft on her lips. Hayley had longed to be in Peter's arms; to hear his breathing; to feel his touch. She could no longer live without this joy; without his love.

Later, they roused themselves, bundled up, and set out to walk the beach. Hayley was glad that she brought heavy clothes. She needed the warmth against the cold wind coming off the ocean and had dressed in a white cable knit turtleneck with a long black and white plaid skirt and warm boots.

They sat on the rocks watching the sea while warming each other with their embraces and murmured words of love. Hayley turned facing Peter with her legs straddled over his lap, protected inside his jacket, her head resting on his chest.

"You know, Sweetheart, the wind is picking up and making your cheeks awfully red." Peter kissed her forehead. "We should go in now. Have you told Miguel where we are, Hayley? I've confided in no one, but I'm going to call my family now and wish them a Merry Christmas. Although I have my patients covered by an associate, my family should know where I am in case there is some emergency."

"Yes, Uncle Arthur, Miguel, and Marisol are the only ones who know. Let's go back to the house. You can call home and I'll get us some hot coffee."

Peter went to the fireplace to warm his hands while Hayley brought coffee and the telephone to him. He made his call and they both chatted with Barbara, Edward, and the family, except for

Matthew, who was skiing in Switzerland and meeting friends later in Amsterdam.

They settled in front of the fire to open their gifts.

"This is something I wish I'd have given to you the night of the Philharmonic concert to wear with your tuxedo."

Peter opened a small black velvet box containing a pair of diamond and onyx cufflinks and a matching tie tack set in platinum.

"Hayley, they are exquisite."

"They were my father's, Peter. He would have wanted you to have them."

"I'm touched, Hayley, thank you; I'll treasure them. Now, I have something for you, Darling. I chose this as a symbol of our love. I think you'll understand when you see them."

Hayley opened the Tiffany box with the ruby heart and diamond earrings. She was speechless for a moment and then put her arms around him.

"Peter, thank you so much. This holds such significance for us. I'll put them on now, and we must dress for dinner tonight so we can both wear our beautiful jewelry. I've brought a long, red wool dress and the ruby and diamond earrings will look perfect with it."

"You know from last night and this morning how I desire you and how much you mean to me, Hayley. I adore you. You are my happiness." He kissed her tenderly and after years of fear and loneliness, she'd found contentment and peace.

"Now, please open your other gift. Hayley smiled broadly while she went behind the tree and picked up a large, gaily wrapped box.

Peter opened his gift and astonished, he exclaimed, "Darling, I'm speechless. How? How did you know I have always coveted a hand-made David Gusset violin?"

"It was a lucky guess."

He took the magnificent instrument out of the case, fondled it, stroked the gleaming wood, plucked the strings, and tuned it while Hayley watched, pleased by his delight and appreciation.

Placing his handsome new violin under his chin, Peter walked across the floor, stood in front of the piano, and began to play "The Angel Gabriel," his family's favorite carol. The rich, mellow tones of the classic violin pleased him. Hayley seated herself at the piano and accompanied him.

"How do you know that piece?" he asked with surprise.

"You forget, Peter, my mother was British and I was born in London!"

"Yes, I do tend to forget that, don't I?" He grinned and Hayley laughed when he said, "It's because you are *so - very - American!*"

Abigail came into the room while they were playing duets of Christmas carols. Before she even spoke, they could tell something was wrong from the bleak expression on her face.

"I'm so sorry to interrupt, but there's a Miguel Alvero calling. He wants to speak to you, Miss Hamilton; says it's urgent."

A chill of foreboding went through Hayley.

"*Hola*, Miguel. *Feliz Navidad. Que pasa*? What is it? Is everything all right?"

"*Hola, Señorita* Hayley. I must bring something to you. Please believe me; I would not do this if it were not important."

"Miguel, can't it wait? This isn't the time. Miguel, is Diva all right? Please tell me your family...*everyone*... is all right and Diva is fine."

"Yes, yes. Diva is...all right. We will bring Diva with us. It is not that. Please let me...please wait until I can tell you in person. We will be there in a couple of hours."

"Very well, then. I'll see you about two o'clock for tea." A sense of dread went through Hayley. She glanced at Peter, her heart hammering in her chest. "I think there may be some bad news ahead," she spoke calmly, her lack of expression masking her fear.

Miguel and Marisol retrieved Hayley's town car from the Tower's underground garage and the bereaved couple drove to Southampton in silence.

Neither of them wanted to get out of the car when they arrived. Miguel's heart ached so much he could hardly breathe. Marisol rang the doorbell, while Miguel stood behind her protecting Diva inside his coat. His hat covered the bandages on his head, and heavy clothing covered the injuries to his body. Not so with Diva; the little dog was cut by glass, pellets, and nails, then sewn and bandaged by the vet. Diva's injuries were impossible to hide.

They were welcomed into the house by Wolcott. Miguel refused to take off his coat and hat. When Wolcott saw Miguel's dire expression and Diva's bandages, he shook his head sadly.

The instant Hayley saw Diva, her hand went to her throat. Miguel carefully placed Diva in Hayley's arms and the little dog whimpered and cried out in pain. Hayley held Diva, kissing and murmuring to her while she looked over the trembling dog, and placed her on a soft pillow.

"How did this happen to Diva, Miguel?" *Can I never leave her out of my sight?* Hayley was distraught and Peter wrapped his arms around her to comfort her.

"Please sit, *Señorita* Hayley and *Señor* Doctor Peter, and I will tell you what happened yesterday after you left."

Although Miguel attempted to soften the blow as much as possible, his tears began to flow with his first words. Marisol wept quietly with her head bowed while she twisted her hands in her lap.

"Please believe me," he sobbed, "I would rather cut out my tongue than to tell you," Miguel words came out ragged through his tears, "*tu Tio Arturo…*"

"What...what is--it?" Hayley interrupted, fear squeezing her throat and choking off her words. "Is Arthur hurt, too? Is he all right? Miguel! *Please*! Tell me!"

"*Arturo, mi amigo, mi amigo mejor*, he has … he is … *Tu Tio Arturo es muerto, y Clarissa... ella es muerta, también.* They have…been…murdered." His body racked with sobs, Miguel covered his face with a large handkerchief.

Hayley gasped in disbelief. "*No! No! No*! Please tell me this isn't true. *Oh, my God. Not my dearest Uncle Arthur!*" She dropped to her knees and sobbed uncontrollably, her slender body shaking in agonized grief. Peter cradled her in his arms. She rose then and paced, wringing her hands, her face a mask of pain while Miguel described the bombing.

"They thought Clarissa was me, didn't they? *Oh, my God...oh, my God...*I was never sure before, but now it's obvious...it's me they're after. This is my fault. I will never forgive myself. Now Uncle Arthur is gone. Uncle Arthur, who never hurt anyone. And Clarissa; poor Clarissa, all she was doing was walking Diva. *She was so young and innocent*. She was just beginning to live. *Why?* Whatever could I have done to be the cause of these tragedies? How could someone commit such heinous acts on innocent people? Why is everyone I love taken from me?"

Hayley crumbled into Peter's arms, but after a moment, she pushed him away. "No. Don't touch me. Stay away. I must be alone. Just leave me alone, all of you," she demanded. "All I can handle is my grief. Leave Diva and please go. All of you."

Marisol pleaded, "Please let us stay here with you, *Señorita* Hayley. We do not want to leave you."

"No. Please leave. Everyone leave, please."

"Hayley, I won't leave you alone. You are too fragile..." Peter attempted to take her into his arms.

"No, don't touch me." She pushed him away. "*No. No.* Please go, all of you. Go away. *Now. Oh, God. Oh, God. Please…no.*" She held her head in her hands.

Then, her strength gone, Peter carried her to her bed and sat by her through the night. She slept sometimes fitfully, sometimes quietly and then startled, she bolted upright, staring but unseeing, then falling back and sleeping again. Toward morning, she lay quietly, her normally fair skin, now ashen.

Fully awake, she arose and paced the room.

"Peter, you must go. This is my fault and I cannot allow anyone I love to be near me. You wouldn't be safe. It's too dangerous for you to stay."

"I can't leave you. I won't. Please don't ask that of me. This is not your fault, Hayley. You can't blame yourself."

"Please; you *must* leave, Peter. I cannot rest while you're here. Miguel and Marisol will drive you to the airport. Abigail and Wolcott are here if I need anything."

"I can't stand for you to suffer so; please, Hayley, you are being unreasonable."

She was unbending and rebuffed every advance he made toward her. Her rejection was complete and total. She left Peter no alternative, but to leave and drive back to the city with Miguel and Marisol. He took the first flight out of JFK.

Alone, Hayley cried until she could no longer speak for the ache in her throat. When evening came, Wolcott and Abigail sat with her, until she rose to walk upstairs and collapsed into their strong and caring arms.

~30~

"Murphy's Law:
If something can go wrong, it will."

Cranmer Close
Oxford, England
December 26, 2004

Peter arrived at London Heathrow and Edward picked him up in the farm's Range Rover. Exhausted and depressed, filled with regret for not standing his ground with Hayley, Peter was expressionless while driving home to Seven Valleys. The sharp planes of his face had the firmness of ice.

"It's like we were standing on the deck of the Titanic and went down with the ship. All my warm emotions have all gone cold, Dad. How long will it take for this pain and emptiness to pass?"

"I don't know, son. However, I assure you it will pass for you and for Hayley, too. She's suffered another devastating shock, and Peter, you know that better than anyone does."

Peter was miserable. "This is my fault, Dad. After all these years without incident, there didn't seem to be any reason why it wouldn't be safe for Hayley. I convinced her to go out in the world again. This is a terrible setback and she's right to be frightened -- someone out there is intent on harming her. For God's sake, why? Of all people, why Hayley? And why Symington?"

"I don't know what to tell you, Peter. I'm at a loss."

"I was distraught watching her fall so fast from sheer joy and complete happiness to total devastation. I should be with her. I should've gone against her will and stayed, but she was unbending and adamant. I couldn't budge her. She needs me...she needs my love and solace. I feel guilty, Dad; so guilty."

"You must not take on someone else's guilt, Peter; you are not responsible. The authorities will have to sort out who this killer is. And as far as answers to affairs of the heart, you'd be better off talking to your mother. All I can offer to you is what I think Matthew might quote from Shakespeare, that '*the course of true love never did run smooth.*' She wasn't rejecting you; she simply cannot handle the world right now. Give her some time, Peter. That's what she needs."

Peter hugged his mother when he arrived at the manor to pick up the Bentley. He had talked to Barbara on the phone from the airport and the news distressed her terribly.

"My sense of finally belonging with someone, Mum...it's all gone wrong. I think Murphy's Law has caught up with me."

"Seems so, Peter." She sighed. "I have never before seen you look so crestfallen. You, who possess the strength to support so many others, will now have to find the strength to help yourself. Remember, your dad and I are here for you whenever you need us -- even if it's only for a sounding board -- we're here for you."

Exhausted, Peter shook his head, "I can't talk about this tonight, Mum."

Barbara patted his back. "I know, Darling; go home and try to get some rest. This has been an emotionally exhausting ordeal. We'll talk later when you're ready, but I know that when you've had time to think this through, you'll have the right answers."

"Yes, that's what I'll do. I'll see you tomorrow, Mum. Thanks, both of you, for your wisdom and condolences tonight."

It was dark and raining when Peter arrived at Cranmer Close. In his exhausted and emotional state, he couldn't remember the drive from Seven Valleys. He eased the Bentley onto the carpark in front of the house. He walked through the door and dropped his suitcase in the foyer. Even before he turned on the light, a faint disagreeable musky odor assaulted his nose. Cigarette smoke clung to the still air.

A shock went through him when he recognized the smell. *Jesus Christ! Bloody Zara's broken into my house.*

His face grew hot with anger. It was as if the house itself felt violated by Zara's presence. He stood still and listened. The air inside virtually quivered with tension. All was quiet, but he was certain she'd been there.

He cautiously walked through the house turning on lights as he went. After looking in every room downstairs, Peter found nothing disturbed. He started the hot water boiler and went to the kitchen to run water through the pipes. He went to his office, picked up his mobile phone, and then he picked up his suitcase and headed up the stairs, turning off the lights again.

Zara mumbled "*Shite*, he's back too soon."

She'd already bugged his phone, but his early return interrupted her embedding a wireless pin dot webcam upstairs in the wall facing his bed. She'd been there all day and slept in his bed the night she returned from New York. She finished embedding the webcam, and thought, *There; I was afraid I'd have to stop before it was done. He must be very lonely now that his precious Hayley is gone, the sad cow. Shame, isn't it? We'll see how long it takes him to turn to me for sympathy and consolation. I'll be ready and waiting.*

Hearing footfalls coming closer, Zara slipped from his bedroom and pressed her body against the wall in the shadow of a huge Chippendale highboy. Dressed in black, she pulled a skullcap over her hair, and was invisible in the dark hallway. She stuffed her small tools in her pocket and noiselessly curled up a ball under the highboy.

She watched his feet coming and going in the hallway, searching rooms, switching the lights on and off. He headed for the bathroom, dropping the heavy suitcase in front of the highboy. The thump startled her. The pulsing of her heartbeat throbbed in her ears and she breathed in silent, shallow pants.

She'd begun to crawl out when he turned on the shower tap, but he withdrew from the bathroom to move his suitcase into the bedroom. She recoiled when his shadow fell in the hallway in front of her and her tools moved slightly in her pocket.

Peter stopped short when he heard a faint click. Trembling with outrage, he shouted into the darkness.

"I don't know where you are Zara, God damn you, but I know you're here! Get the hell out of my house, you bloody psycho freak!"

The words echoed in the silent hallway. He slammed the bathroom door, locked it, and dialed 9-9-9 for police. He turned off the shower and waited while his mind hurled angry thoughts.

Damn, I'm knackered, but I'll have police go over the house to flush her out. If she's gone, I can't prove she broke in, but that scent leaves no doubt that she's been here and that click I heard told me she was still here when I got home. Her sickening smell permeates the rooms of this house. She's like a fox or some bloody feral animal. A fox cannot hide its tail and Zara Chandler can't hide her odor. First thing in the morning, I'll have the locks changed and secure the house. I can't stay here from now on. Her very presence contaminated my home and I'll always feel her lurking. I'll let out Cranmer Close and temporarily move back to Seven Valleys while I start the process to get rid of that evil bitch once and for all.

I really must learn not to procrastinate. It's my worst failing. The time is long past due to get that pariah, Zara Chandler, out of my life.

He stayed locked in the bathroom until he heard police at the front door and dashed down the stairs to let them in.

When she thought Peter was in the shower, Zara slipped out of hiding and crept down the staircase. She was attempting to lock the front door when she heard the wail of police car sirens turning into Cranmer Close. Panicked, she fumbled and dropped the key on the doorstep and ran through the woods.

~31~

"No medicine is more valuable, none more efficacious, none better suited to the cure of all our temporal ills than a friend to whom we may turn for consolation in time of trouble, and with whom we may share our happiness in time of joy."
~ Saint Alfred of Rievaulx~

Hayle House
Southampton, New York
December 2004 – January 2005

Powerful Park Avenue residents wanted the incident to go away saying it was too close to Christmas for this sort of news; that it must have been an accident; and it had no particular interest to the public.

NYPD quietly went about their investigation. There were two deaths and the damage was limited to the front of the building. Miraculously, no one sitting in cars behind the killers was hurt in the bombing. A description of the killers was impossible through the darkened windows and the car sped away from the scene so fast that no one got the license plate number, which in fact, had been mud-covered.

The local press mentioned the incident in a small item on their back pages calling it an accident, but other than printing obituaries, they downplayed the murders and damage to the building. Local radio and television news stations were relatively quiet on the matter. The incident never made the national news, the Associated Press, or Reuters. It escaped cable TV news channels, but Christine happened to read a New York news feed at the studio about an explosion at the Top of the Turret Residence Tower. She almost missed the item because it was a mere half-beat barely audible within low-keyed background noise.

Chris began making calls. She called the penthouse, but Miguel and Marisol didn't pick up. She left several voicemail messages asking Hayley to return her call. She thought it was useless to call Capshaw; he was never forthcoming before. She called Savvy News and the New York Police; neither would tell her anything, but the Times obituary columnist sent her an E-mail with a web link. The obituary told her nothing of the circumstances, only that Symington had died.

Frustrated by her inability to obtain information, she called the University to find out when Peter would return. Her call came in on Sean's line and he gave Peter the message.

Peter returned her call on his mobile phone while driving home to Seven Valleys. He got her voicemail and left his mobile number.

That evening, she called his mobile number from home.

"Chris, I'm glad you called. I wanted to talk to you as soon as possible after receiving your message. I want to brief you about what they're calling an accident at the Top of the Turret and assure you that Hayley has escaped any harm. We were in Southampton when it happened. But, believe me; it's taking all my courage to tell you what's happened to Symington."

Christine was silent for a moment after Peter finished talking. Then she raged, "*God damn it all to hell, Peter.* Who could have done this? Hayley loved Symington," she sobbed. "Hasn't she suffered enough? How could something like this happen?"

After she hung up the phone, seething with anger and railing at God, Chris decided that this time she wouldn't ask anyone's permission to see Hayley. She didn't care if she was welcome or not, she was going to Southampton and that's all there was to it. She called Pookie to tell her that she and their staff assistants would have to manage production by themselves for about a week.

Less than twenty-four hours later, Abigail found a disheveled, windblown young woman standing before her.

"Is this Hayley Hamilton's address?" Chris said to the grim woman answering the door.

"Yes, it is, but she's not receiving callers."

"But I *must* see her."

"I'm sorry, miss, she isn't seeing anybody."

Abigail was abrupt, but when she attempted to shut the door, Chris pushed past her and strode into the house.

"I'm sorry, too, but I'm not just anybody. I'm Christine Horowitz and I want to see her *now*. Where is she? Take me to her," she demanded.

Abigail made only a mild show of protest. She was afraid Wolcott would disapprove, but Hayley was doing poorly and they weren't having any success getting her to eat, or even bathe. She wouldn't leave the bedroom, or for that matter, the bed, After Chris explained who she was to Wolcott, she gave her driver's license to him and he called Miguel's number to verify her story. Miguel was relieved to hear that Chris was there. With his approval, they led her to Hayley.

Shocked, Chris stared at Hayley sleeping on tearstained pillows. Chris never before saw such pallor. The delicate bones of her face seemed robbed of their flesh. Her lips were bloodless and her hair lay moist and tangled. Hayley was always thin and fragile, but now she was unrecognizable as the enchanting woman at the Manhattan penthouse wearing a glamorous silk gown merely a few weeks ago.

Diva woke and a low growl rumbled in her throat. She jumped off the bed barking and snarling and went for Chris's ankles.

"*No, no,* Diva, baby, *shhhh*, it's me; it's only Chrissy," she whispered to the trembling dog. Carefully picking her up, Chris held Diva so that she could see her face and gave her puckered kisses. When Diva recognized Chris, she began whimpering and allowed Chris to cuddle her and murmur lovingly.

Hayley stirred when she heard Diva's commotion. Startled to find someone in the room, her vision cleared and through a voice thick with sleep, she stuttered, "*Christine*...*w*-what are you doing here...*h*-how did you get in?"

"Never mind that, Hayley; answer *my* questions. Have you looked at yourself lately? You have the worst bed-head I've ever seen. When was the last time you ate anything? Or bathed? *Ugh,* Hayley, you smell like the *Jingle-Beggar*. Good grief, now *that's* atrocious.

I know what happened, but Hayles, you simply cannot give up living; that's not the answer. And you can't close yourself off from the people who love you and need you. Peter is miserable and beside himself with worry. Marisol and Miguel are overwrought and grieving. Why did you send everyone away the moment you needed them most? You must let them come here to be with you."

"Go away, Christine. Leave me alone," she whined. Frowning, she dropped her head into the pillow. "Go home; you're not safe here. No one I love is safe with me."

"All right, Hayley. I'll leave you alone...for a few minutes, but you can expect me back here with some food and hot tea."

Leaving the bedroom, she found Abigail and Wolcott listening outside the door.

"Oh!" Startled when she saw them, Chris nearly collided with Wolcott. She composed herself and touched Abigail's arm.

"Abigail please make some tea and toast and a pot of chicken soup, and will you turn on the gas logs in the fireplace, please," she said to Wolcott, "its damn near freezing in that room. I'll make her eat and then I'll get her up to bathe. This has gone on far too long. I'll call Miguel and Marisol and tell them to come here in a couple of days, but I want some time alone with her first to get her back on her feet. Peter's distraught. I'll call him now and tell him what's going on here."

No longer able to hold back her tears, Chris put her hand over her face and wept; with ragged sobs, she cried for Symington, for

Hayley, and for Peter. She cried for little Diva, still cradled in her arms.

"What the hell kind of world do we live in," she murmured to Diva. "There must be special places in the hereafter for people like Hayley, because Heaven just isn't good enough. And for you, too, baby," she said, kissing the top of Diva's head. The tiny dog looked into her face and licked her tears away.

Chris carried her backpack next door to Hayley's bedroom and went to the kitchen. She saw mail from Peter lying on the counter. She took the mail and a tray with tea and toast to Hayley's room and sat on the edge of the bed.

"Eat this toast and drink this tea, *now,* and don't even think about telling me *no*. After you're finished, you're going to get out of those grungy pajamas, take a shower, wash your hair, and put on some clothes. Then you're going to eat some soup, we're going to get a few minutes of fresh air, and then we'll warm up by the fireplace and talk."

Somehow, Chris knew the right approach to get through to Hayley. It wasn't long before she got up in the morning without coaxing, and began to eat regularly. Choked with tears, Hayley read Peter's letters that arrived daily. She had long talks with Chris contemplating all that had happened.

After Chris had been with her for a few days, they walked on the beach with Diva and sat on some high rocks to rest. Hayley fell quiet and had a faraway look.

"Are you still with me, Hayles?"

"Why me, Christine? I don't understand. Why *my* family? They were caring, solid people, who lived good lives."

"Hayley, I didn't have a religious upbringing. Neither of my parents pushed their religion on me, but I started thinking about the existence of God after your parents died. Since then, I've wondered about destiny, mortality, morality, and how the forces of good and evil affect us...all of us. It's always in the back of my mind, you know. I'm always mulling it over."

"My family wasn't religious either, Chris, but it's so clear to me that they taught me by example. They were kind and good people. Morality is goodness and kindness and it's the obvious right choice. I suppose it would be naïve to believe only in the force of good, that humans should choose to be altruistic, virtuous, and compassionate."

"Yes, it would be naïve. Human beings can be equally as violent as they are virtuous...and that's not something my parents taught me. I learned that by observing human nature. Inside us, we have the ability to be good, kind and righteous, or we can choose to be selfish, cruel, and vindictive. There are those who haven't the moral rectitude or the ability to choose goodness. Evil is their moral order. Hayley, someone has brought evil into your life, but you can't stop living because you fear this human force of evil. You have to fight your fear and look this being squarely in the face. Think about who it could possibly be, so you can recognize *who* brought this evil into your life."

"How can I fight it? Is it my fate to die at the evil hands of this...*this devil*?"

"Hayley, please...don't be afraid to let those you love and trust into your life. Peter and I are not afraid, and we are here for you, to help you find and fight this evil. We'll stand with you, to protect you. Let us help...be your guardian angels."

"Yes, but Christine, it's *me* they're after. You and Peter have nothing to fear if you stay away from me."

"Hayley, I know that, but allow us to help you."

"I don't understand *why* this evil has come into my life. This evil has strength and tenacity. It doesn't give up; I don't have the strength to fight it and I'd sooner protect myself by shutting myself away."

"That's no way to live your life, Hayley. Goodness has strength, too, and you must push this evil back with greater force. There's strength in numbers, so let us stand with you. If you give up without a struggle, that evil force will crush you and it will win. Why give in without a fight? Be strong, Hayley. You *can* be strong. Peter and I will be by your side defending you with broadswords in our hands."

Hayley woke during the night shortly after the visit from Chris. While she lay in bed, she saw a flickering shadow overhead as if the light were coming through the bars of a prison cell. She traced the shadow to a slatted bed tray leaning near the firelight that created the illusion.

I might as well be in a prison, locked away from Peter. He's so kind, good and devoted to me. Why did I send him away and why can't I free myself from these chains of fear? She longed to be free. She was so close and then...and then... Hayley breathed deeply and sighed.

Remembering Arthur, Clarissa, and her parents, she wept again. The chains of fear and hopelessness cut deep into her senses. She searched her mind to find answers, some reassurance, something within that would strengthen her and give her hope again. She struggled to conquer her turbulent emotions and feelings of guilt for whatever she did to deserve this.

"It's not my fault," she cried aloud, "I'm not the guilty one."

The guilty one has created this and I will leave this prison. Peter and Chris have unlocked the door for me. It's up to me to step outside, because if I don't, I'll never find my way back to him and that's where I want to be.

By morning, Hayley realized what she'd given up and that she'd already wasted years being afraid. She held Diva and stood by the window looking eastward toward the wide ocean that separated her from Peter.

Later in the day, Hayley wrapped Diva in the pink Pashmina and carried her to keep her warm. While she walked on the beach, she held her little dog close, protected in her arms while cold gusts of wind whipped her hair against her face.

Thinking about her future, she climbed high on the rocks above the wind-driven waves crashing beneath her while powerful riptides swept them back to sea.

Even though the tide is powerful, it is helpless to resist the greater power of the sun, moon, and stars in their eternal waltz across the sky.

No matter how fiercely the wind and ocean resists the pull of these heavenly bodies, it's the tide's fate to be swept along in their never-ending journey.

Whether I live in the world outside with Peter, or alone, sequestered in a world apart, am I like the tides, powerless to control my destiny?

Is the fate Peter and I share already written in the stars? Is it as unstoppable as the earth and moon in their never-ending journey around the sun? I cannot know what fate holds for me, but I do know that I am afraid.

"Courage, Diva," Hayley sighed deeply and whispered to the little dog, "I must find courage. If I can't do it for myself, then I will do it for Peter."

With that, Hayley placed her future in the hands of a long-known truth… courage to benefit another is sometimes more readily found than courage to benefit oneself.

She trembled when she envisioned becoming engaged in life again and was terrified of the danger she might have to face. She pushed these thoughts aside and prayed for strength and courage to follow the only course her love would allow.

~32~

"All truths are easy to understand once they are discovered; the point is to discover them."
~ Galileo Galilei~

Seven Valleys Estate
Wolds-on-Thames
Oxfordshire, England
February 2005

Miguel and Marisol talked to Peter every day and assured him that Hayley was beginning to recover. When Chris called and told them she was ready to return to Cleveland, they drove to Southampton to stay with Hayley. They were relieved to be useful to her again. They would stay in Southampton until the building repairs were complete and they would drive back to New York together.

Peter begged her to let him help her through this ordeal. He wrote letters to Hayley telling her that she meant the world to him; that he wanted her in his life forever; and that he would wait however long it took her to recover from the shock and trauma she suffered.

"... Darling, say the word and I will abandon my whole world to be at your side, to protect you and keep you safe. Let me come to you now. I love you with all my heart..."

Hayley replied --

"...I will return to the penthouse next week, but it will not be the same world I left. Once again, I must make a new world for myself.

Miguel, Lippy, and I will work with the police to try to find whoever did this. They have been working quietly, but persistently.

I love you, Peter, and I want to be with you. I couldn't bear the thought of living my life without you. I hope we'll be together soon, but please, give me more time to sort things out."

Peter let the Cranmer Close house to students and moved permanently to Seven Valleys. He kept his mind from dwelling on Hayley by helping his father plant new rosebushes, prune grape vines, and crate his mother's large paintings for shipping. During this time, he was able to discuss Christmas Day with Barbara and reaffirmed his deep love for Hayley.

"I want to marry Hayley and be with her, Mum, so that I am better able to protect her. She has an innocence that demands my protection, and there is a goodness emanating from her that I have never known in anyone before. However, Hayley's cloistered there and I'm entrenched here. Even if I could bring her to England, I'm not sure Seven Valleys would be the right place for her. Maybe her home in Belgravia might be best. My house in Oxford was only a convenience and I'll never live there again. I have no emotional ties to it and I plan to sell it or keep it as an investment. I have found traveling to work from here quite agreeable really, and Seven Valleys is my life, too. This is my home and that may complicate things depending on how Hayley feels about permanently moving to England. Here she'll have a family again. Your life was uncomplicated when you met Dad and it was simpler for you to move here with him."

"That's true, Peter. However, I'm not saying there weren't feelings of homesickness or nagging regrets about leaving home. Being an ocean apart from my sister was especially hard for me, but I would have walked through fire to be with your father. Compared to this situation, it *was* simpler, except that Hayley has no family or social life to leave behind. I see no reason why she can't build her future with you. Frankly, at this point, I think it's all about real estate."

"Quite true; but still, we'll have a lot of adjustments to make. It won't be easy."

"It's never easy; marriage is a big adjustment, but you will make it work. It's the right thing for both of you. No matter where you live with Hayley, Seven Valleys is your home and it will always be here for you, Peter. Ultimately, for better or for worse, the estate is yours. Keep that in mind."

Later that week, Peter called his brothers in London and asked them to meet him for lunch. While they were eating, he told them what happened to Hayley and shared his dreams for their future together.

"I want to buy an engagement ring for Hayley today. Will you both help me pick it out?"

"Of course we will, won't we, Matthew?" William patted his brother on the back. Matthew grunted and shrugged.

"I suppose so, Peter, as long as it doesn't take all day for you to make up your mind. I'm off to my car club meeting this afternoon."

"Are you sure you want to go today, Peter? Have you talked to mother? She might have a suitable ring in her collection of diamonds."

"No, I haven't. I wanted to buy something for Hayley of my own choosing and yes, today. Shall we go now?" Peter felt enthusiasm for the first time since Christmas morning.

"I know the best place to go, William said. "I found earrings for Jessica at Gemstone Jewelry in Hatton Garden."

When they arrived, the jeweler showed the men a tray of traditional diamond engagement rings.

"They're beautiful; but sir, I favor something exquisite and unusual."

"I have some lovely rings from estates, actually. You might look at them. They are quite different, but I must warn you, they're pricey."

While Peter looked over the estate rings, he noticed an antique sapphire and diamond ring in a case off to the side. The beauty of the stones and the platinum openwork frame of the design intrigued him. The ring was from a private collection. The jeweler was friends with the last owner who placed it for sale, but knew only a little history of the ring.

"Hayley is an extraordinary woman with classic beauty. This ring would be right for her. The sapphire will look beautiful on her hand."

The brothers all agreed on the ring and the price was negotiable. Peter would have paid any amount for it, but the jeweler didn't haggle and agreed to his offer. Afterward, the two brothers waited by the door while Peter and the jeweler had a long conversation.

While Peter waited for the jeweler to ring up his purchase, he noticed a wide diamond bracelet lying among pieces in an unlighted case with a sign, *Pawned.* The initials, H.E.H., engraved between two rows of sizeable diamonds on the bracelet took him by surprise. His breath caught in his throat and he could hear his heartbeat pounding in his ears.

"Where did you get that bracelet?" He demanded from the jeweler.

"A man brought that bracelet in just before Christmas," he reached into the case. "It will be hard to sell as is, because the bracelet is quite dirty and the clasp is broken. If you want it, I can remake it for you using the stones. There are probably 20 carats of diamonds altogether and the stones are brilliant and unfractured."

"No...but, thank you, I want it as is. Wrap it up, please. Don't bother to clean it and try to touch it as little as possible. Peter thought there might be fingerprints on the wide band that could lead them to the thief. Can you give me the name of the gentleman who sold it to you? It's imperative that I..."

"No, I'm sorry. I didn't get his name, but I remember he owns a pub in Hackney Wick."

Peter left the shop shaken by finding a piece matching the description of the missing bracelet that Hayley wore when the plane went down.

"What in hell is going on here?" he muttered, rubbing his forehead as they left the shop. "There cannot be two bracelets like this. It would be too bloody much of a coincidence," he said panting. His chest tightened, leaving him gasping for air.

After the three men left the shop, the jeweler walked to the back where his wife was cataloguing new acquisitions. He sat down heavily and heaved a sigh. When she looked at him, she knew he was troubled.

"What is it, dear?"

"I just sold this sapphire and diamond ring from the estate of the couple in Amsterdam. The gentleman who purchased it, Dr. Gabriel-Johns, left it with me to be engraved."

He sat down and rubbed his eyes. His wife picked up the ring and held it under the light.

"It's very beautiful. I'm sure she'll fancy it." She placed it on a velvet pad.

"Yes, but frankly, I was sorry he saw this ring. I would hate to think that fine man was giving someone he loves so dearly an evil ring with a dodgy history."

"Darling, you're not serious!" his wife put down her pen and looked at him quizzically. "Who told you such a thing? An evil ring with a dodgy history? Please; it's laughable."

"Rutgers De Kooning brought the ring in from Amsterdam and he said so. Well, I hope the legend of the curse is merely a figment of his overactive imagination, but he's convinced it's malevolent and has evil powers. I promised Rutgers I would warn anyone who wanted the ring. When Dr. Gabriel-Johns chose this ring, I told him what De Kooning said about it."

"What did he say, dear?"

"He said he didn't believe in superstition and that an inanimate object couldn't cause disaster. He said, 'It's not dodgy rings that trouble me, it's the evil, dodgy humans I'm worried about.' But, what if he's wrong; what if this ring is evil and causes disaster to befall her?"

"Nothing's going to happen to her because of that ring; don't be daft. I think Rutgers has been smoking too much *wacky t'backy* in the Absinthe Coffee House!" she guffawed.

"I warned him, dear," he said shaking his head sadly. "I hope he's right and De Kooning is wrong."

~33~

"Let us follow our destiny, ebb and flow.
Whatever may happen,
we master fortune by accepting it."
~ Virgil~

Top of the Turret Residence Tower
Upper East Side
New York City, New York
March 2005

Hayley returned to New York from Southampton after being at her lowest ebb since her parents' death, but this time she wasn't alone; she had Peter and Chris to help her overcome the tragedy and it was her love for Peter that gave her courage to move on with her life.

At first, it was difficult not to go back to being a recluse. She had to move forward and resist the temptation to resume the life she had built for herself. It was frightening to walk Diva and painful to pass through the doors where Symington and Clarissa were killed. Hayley was ever mindful of the danger about her. She knew there was still someone out there and she was still at risk. She had to make a choice; live in a cloister forever, or face the danger in the world outside. Every instinct told her to choose seclusion. She knew by choosing the outside world, the reality was that she was setting herself up to draw out the killer.

She missed Symington terribly. He had been a part of her life forever. Now there was no one left. The other residents of the Top of the Turret quickly forgot Symington as soon as the new doorman, Studs MacMahon, replaced him. A tall, handsome younger version of Symington, MacMahon had recently arrived from Ireland with a green card looking for a job. When the hiring committee told him about the bombing, he didn't flinch.

"We'll see if lightening strikes twice in the same place or not."

He was charming, polite, competent, and good looking with a boyish grin, green eyes, and dark curly hair. In a short time, MacMahon endeared himself to everyone going in and out of the building.

Miguel found Studs entertaining, although he often had trouble understanding him. He told Hayley and Marisol that Studs confided what he did before he left Ireland.

"I worked on a draught horse stud farm in County Limerick, hence, my name, Studs. My given name is Strachan, but I rather prefer my nickname. How'd you like me to call you *Mickey*? Make Miguel into a little *Irisher*, then, *boyo?"* Studs laughed, and poked Miguel in the ribs with his elbow.

Miguel told them that Studs laughed at his confused expression.

Studs and Miguel assumed Symington's tradition of watching over the old woman. Hayley continued her habit of bringing morning coffee to Studs just as she had to Symington, and coffee and sweet rolls to Dream-Girl. Continuing these traditions helped ease the pain of his death for them.

An early morning phone call woke Hayley shortly after she returned to New York. She reached over Diva and the caller I.D. showed it was Christine's cell.

"*Mmmm*, Good morning, Chris," she yawned. "Aren't you the early bird?"

"*Hayley, Hayley*, I'm so excited, I don't know what to do first! I got a call last evening from Savvy News in New York asking me to interview for a job as an Assistant Producer. *Savvy News, Hayles!* They liked my résumé and I have to go there next week. They are going to pay my travel expenses and I'll be in New York overnight."

"*Oh, Christine*...how wonderful for you! You must stay with me again while you're here."

While Chris chattered, Hayley got out of bed and carried the phone to her desk to open her calendar.

"Chris, what are the dates?"

"I'm interviewing on April fourth, so I'll try to arrive on the third."

"We'll have a lot to do before your interview. Come a day early, Chris, and when you get here, I'll go with you to Buddinghill's, we'll book with Lydia, and she'll find exactly the right outfit to wear. Then, in the morning, I'll have my stylist work on your hair. Why not go a little shorter, perkier and blonder? We'll all work on your make up. Marisol and I will take you through a mock interview to help you get ready.

"You don't need to do that, Hayley."

"Listen to me Christine. I can never repay you for your kindness and encouragement in Southampton."

"No, Hayley, it's too much."

"I won't take no for an answer. It's my gift to you, Chris. I've been lonely without you and I'm selfish enough to want you here with me in New York."

"Hayles," *Sniff.* Chris's eyes filled with tears. "I cannot believe this. It's a dream come true. I thought you were a princess, but it turns out you are my fairy godmother." *Sniff.*

Chris's makeover was off to a good start. Lydia found an Armani pantsuit in black lamb's wool with a white chalk stripe, a wrap front, and bow tie closure at the side in a size three from his spring collection. It fit Chris's now slender and attractive figure perfectly. Lydia found a pair of Bruno Magli soft leather black and white spectator shoes with a pointed toe and a slim, black leather briefcase with a shoulder strap that doubled as a purse. In it, Chris could adequately carry a DVD of the Sunday Morning Program, writing samples, extra resumes, commendation and recommendation letters, and copies of her awards.

Lydia remarked, "You'll have a perfect ensemble for any business event, Ms. Horowitz."

"Me…I'll be wearing an actual ensemble for the first time in my life! Won't Pookie be surprised?"

They went to the BareMinerals counter and bought makeup in colors that blended well with Chris's skin.

"I don't know how to use all this stuff, Hayles, and I'm not sure I can do it. This takes *chutzpah.*"

"Don't worry, I have secret *chutzpah* weapons. You'll look smashing. Trust me."

Chris took it all seriously, because she now grasped how important that first impression would be. For Chris, who lived for her career and with her greatest ambition being to work for Savvy News, this would be the most important day of her life.

They walked to the same exit where Chris left Buddinghill's on her first New York City shopping trip. She returned to the mirror where she caught her reflection as she was leaving the store and thought she looked…well…like *Clumpy-Frumpy-Dumpy*. However, this time what she saw pleased her. A slender woman, dressed nicely, with an air of confidence. Yes, except for her hair...and of course, her nose, which she thought was beyond redemption. She smiled affectionately at Hayley and when they left the store, she was whistling, *With a little bit of luck.*

Together they created exactly the right look for the interview. Hayley's stylist greatly improved her hair by streaking it with blonde highlights and warm lowlights. Within a couple of hours, it was deep-conditioned, glossed, and shaped it into a flattering, updated style. Hayley's esthetician came in and gave Chris's skin a brightening facial. They all worked on her makeup and it was well done. The makeover gave Chris a classy new look and the confidence of a stunning and capable woman.

Marisol, Hayley, the esthetician, and the stylist were Christine's audience while she practiced her sale's spiel. When she was ready to go, Hayley told Chris to leave her nerves at the penthouse.

"Chris, if you leave your nerves here, then you'll be free from the jitters." Hayley winked at her. "When you return afterward you can tell us all about it and pick up your jitters then."

"Pookie told me to stand up straight, not to sniff or twitch, and to *break a leg.*"

"Let's have one final look at you, Chris, before you walk out the door." Hayley spun her around. "Wow, Christine, you sizzle! You're going to *knock 'em dead.*"

Chris looked sleek and polished when she left the penthouse. The Wednesday afternoon of the interview, she sat down with a hiring committee of Savvy News producers, a director, a reporter and Slick Slate, a talented and popular anchor.

Sitting with them was not Frumpy-Dumpy, the woman who slept in her old car on a parking lot all night, eating from a carton of cold, smashed McDonald's French fries because she was too cheap and stubborn to call a taxi. This was a slim woman, beautifully turned out, dressed in a classy suit with a chic, stylish haircut, and manicured nails. This was a woman on the threshold of beauty, whose only flaw was a childhood disfigurement, who was perfectly groomed, primped, and primed into self-assurance and confidence by Hayley Hamilton and her makeover crew.

That day, Chris sold herself to Savvy News with her professional demeanor, great ideas, ready answers, and right-on-the money experience, qualifications, education, and enthusiasm.

When she left the interview, the team agreed she possessed the right experience and the potential for additional assignments. She had the right stuff. How could they not offer her the job?

Two days after she returned to Cleveland, Chris was in the control room at CableCoNews when Pookie rushed in.

"There's a call from Savvy News in New York for a Christine Wyndham," Pookie looked at Chris wide-eyed with surprise. "Do we know a Christine Wyndham?"

"*Gangway!*" Chris yelled, rushing to the phone. After the call, with the receiver still in her hand, she dialed Hayley.

"Are you sitting down, Hayles?"

"Chris, you got the job!"

"Yes! I'm coming to New York City to work at Savvy News as an Assistant Producer. My dream has come true. Thank you, Hayley. You did it. I owe it all to you."

"No, Chris. You did it. You knew what to do and you did it."

"I have to give two weeks' notice. I'll have a lot to do."

"Call me when you get here, Christine, and we'll celebrate with champagne."

Pookie helped Chris pack and both women felt gloomy while they sorted through Chris's belongings.

"Pookie, I've packed my personal stuff, sentimental *tchotchkes,* and new clothes. They're too large, now, but they'll do until I've made time to buy new ones."

She gave her furniture and old clothes to Goodwill. Pookie would ship the packed boxes to Chris as soon as she called with an address.

"I'll miss you terribly, Chrissy." Pookie wrapped her arms around Chris, and held on for a long time. "My life is changing, too, and I'll have to take the bad with the good. Trust me; not having *you* in my life is really, really bad."

This was an unhappy time for Pookie. She felt sad and abandoned, but she knew this would happen someday, because she knew Chris's ambitions. Chris's friendship had always been important to her and she had been Pookie's mentor as well. It was a mixed blessing; now that Chris was leaving, CableCoNews hired Pookie as Production Manager for the Sunday morning program to replace her.

Chris bequeathed the Woodie station wagon to Pookie, who drove it to a classic car resale as soon as Chris was gone. Pookie had no idea of the value of the Woodie. She told them to give it a proper funeral if they couldn't find anyone to buy it, but before she left the property, it was sold and on a flatbed.

Chris had given the name, Christine Wyndham, to Savvy News, because she wanted a break from the past and in her mind, it was who she had become. *Christine Wyndham. I'm someone else now.* She sighed contentedly; *I'm starting an exciting new life, with a new job, in a new city, with a new name. I'm walking away from Dumpy Frumpy Chris Horowitz. I'm jumping the Dumpster and leaving it behind in Cleveland.*

She knew the hardest task she'd have to tackle would be the call to her parents in Laurel Canyon. She decided to get it over with, and picked up the phone.

"I have news. Are you ready for this?"

They put her on the speakerphone in their office, and Diane said, "All right, Christine, we're ready for it."

She gave them an account of all that had happened throughout the past few months, saving her new job for last.

"Christine, darling, I'm so sorry to hear about Hayley, but I'm delighted for you. You've worked hard to achieve your goals and we're so proud of you."

"Mom, you sound like your pants are on fire. What's the rush?"

"Oh, well, Christine; you always manage to call at a bad time. I'm running late for a meeting, so talk to your dad. He'll fill me in later. *Kiss. Kiss. Hug. Hug. Bye, sweetie.*"

Ben picked up the receiver. "*Mazal Tov*, my sweetheart. We always knew you have what it takes."

"Thanks, Dad, but in the process I've done something you may not like and that's really why I'm calling." Chris heaved a great sigh and went on nervously. "*I...I...um...* probably should've asked you first. I've switched my last and middle names and I'm using my mother's name, Wyndham. So, now I'm Christine Diane Horowitz Wyndham. Dad, will you tell mom? I really wanted to tell her myself. *I...uh...* hope you aren't too dismayed."

"Not at all, Christine, calm down. I think you do both your mothers honor by using their last name. *Who knows*? A handsome stranger will come along and marry you and you'll change your name again, *'eh*?"

"Yeah, sure, Dad," Chris snorted, "fat chance."

"And Savvy News; I'm surprised, I'll admit. I'd have thought they'd be too conservative for a lib like you. But, I'm impressed. I knew it, *Bubbalah*. You'll be famous one day all on your own, won't you? You know we've always been proud of you, Christine, despite your propensity for going against the grain."

Chris dropped her head in her hands and changed the subject, "What's your latest project, Dad?"

"*Ahhh*, I'm glad you asked. Your mother and I are working together on a complicated project that may result in several series connected by a common thread. We're talking to both comedy and police drama writers, because as well as crime substance and authenticity, I want action, some wry humor, casts who crossover back and forth from series to series, spectacular locations, blue-eyed, square jawed, flash and dash actors and gorgeous, skinny blonde actresses with big asses and lots of jiggle. I want to offer the viewers more than dark drama, car chases, and explosions. Although I want *that* good stuff, too. I'll know more about that when we talk again. In the meantime, a group of backers has asked Diane to think about selling one of her period comedy projects for a Broadway musical production before we pitch it as a big screen production. You know the one -- *Beautiful Dreamer*. The one you called smarmy...and corny...after which your mother wouldn't speak to you for a week." He cleared his throat to stifle a chuckle.

"Yeah, I remember. Leave it to me; Miss Subtlety...*not*."

"Anyway, we're in negotiations with former ABBA members to write original music, but they're involved with the movie version of *Mamma Mia* right now. We're hopeful, though. We have some great choreographers interested. Personally, I think it'll outdraw, outshine, and outlast *Phantom* and *Cats*."

"That's great, Dad; so exciting! Yes, I know I said that, but it's a love story. Love stories are icky, but if you remember, I always said Beautiful Dreamer had lots of potential for a musical, too. Look, please tell Mom I love both of you very much. I'll call soon and we can entertain each other by tooting our Oompahs."

"Keep that Oompah polished, kiddo!" Ben chuckled, trying to hide his emotions. "Break a leg, *Bubbalah.*" Chris heard tears in Ben's voice, "You know who loves ya, baby."

"Same back 'atcha, Daddy," she chuckled at all the clichés.

Ben signed off with puckered kissing sounds that made Christine tearful...and feeling a little homesick. When she hung up, she walked away from the phone humming, *With a Little Bit of Luck. Yeah, I'll have to start reading Variety when I get to the city.*

Christine arrived in New York City, grabbed a rental listing, and found a fifth-floor furnished walk-up in Greenwich Village. It reminded her of the apartment in *Barefoot in the Park*, so she took it. She thought with a month-to-month lease, she could move quickly when she could afford a better place.

The night before she started her job, Hayley invited Chris to the penthouse. Marisol and Miguel sat with them to toast Chris's new life and her new name.

The next morning, Chris was swimming in all the details of her new job assisting Slick Slate's producer. She loved Savvy's fast pace. A variety of assignments gave her the opportunity to talk to most of the staff and on-air talent. For days, she didn't think about the one thing that constantly occupied her mind. She didn't think about Jaxx.

~34~

"What we anticipate seldom occurs,
what we least expected generally happens."
~ Benjamin Disraeli~

Oxford University
Oxford, England
April 2005

At the top of Peter's list of priorities was getting Zara out of the Wessely building and out of his life. He'd been preoccupied and had let getting rid of her slide too long. He'd made the decision in December and it was already April. It took that long to wade through the miasma of bureaucratic paperwork. To help move it along, he had issued paperwork to upgrade Sean as their sole technician.

Zara was busy elsewhere and not in the office while they waited to make it official.

"I hope she'll stay away until we can get this accomplished," he told Sean, "I don't want to be reminded of her again."

Then, they had a surprise visitor who stood in front of Sean's desk looking down her bulbous red nose at him. Sean stared at her with his mouth dropped open.

"*Uh...Can I help you?* Are you lost?" Sean blinked repeatedly.

"*Blimey*, how does a gel get to see his highness, Lord Gabriel? I mean to see him now," her gravelly voice demanded, followed by a loud *thwack*.

Sean flinched when her umbrella hit his desk, "*D-do y-you* have an appointment?" Sean stuttered, appalled by this cockney caricature standing before him.

"I don't need no appointment; I'm his future mother-in-law, I'll have you know, and I come all the way from Hackney to visit his highness."

"What's all the fuss out there?" Peter rose from his desk and walked to the doorway of Sean's office. He stared, unable to grasp who this woman was. "I'm Dr. Gabriel-Johns, Director of the College. Who are you looking for?"

"I'm *lookin'* for *you*, yer Lordship. I'm Kedzara Twigg Chandler's mum, Norah Twigg here, and I'm meanin' ta meet me future son-in-law."

She spoke with a wide grin, exposing a few lonely teeth that were conspicuously yellow and brown against the whiteness of her puffy face. Peter thought that her grinning was inadvisable considering the sorry state of her mouth.

What in God's name? Flying through Peter's mind were all kinds of possible set-ups; was this another of Matthew's bad jokes? It wouldn't have been the first time. Was she put up to this by some undergrad students who thought it would be humorous to stuff the old boy?

The woman shuffled her huge body toward him on tiny feet. She greeted Peter holding out a hand that looked like a limp white rat. When she lifted her hand and shook his, the fat on her huge arm rippled and jiggled, bringing to Peter's mind Sarah's song about the old lady who swallowed a spider...*that wriggled and wiggled and tickled inside her...*

"How do you do, yer Highness." She greeted him with bowed head and lips pursed into a subservient smile.

Puzzled, he inclined his head toward her. "You're Zara's mum? I thought her mother was deceased and lived in Burford."

"Crikey, are you *deaf*...or just cheeky? I said I'm her mum, didn't I...well, didn't I? *I'm her mum!*"

She spat out her annoyance and directed it toward Sean, who sat round-eyed, overwhelmed by this behemoth in front of him.

Sean flushed and stuttered, "*Oh, y-yes ma'am*. Yes, you did. How do you do, Mrs. Twigg?"

"Zara isn't here at the moment. I assume you're here to see her?" Peter hoped he'd guessed right.

She threw her head back and her laugh was loud and coarse. They could smell the whiskey on her breath. She shook her head slowly and they watched fascinated when the triple chins that lay like raw squid circling her neck began to bounce, taking on life of their own.

"You're from Hackney, you say? How did you get here all the way from London?"

Peter was desperately trying to figure out what to do with her and hadn't even gotten to the business about the son-in-law yet.

"A bloke from the pub was comin' 'ere ta Oxford today fer a delivery and I hitched a ride. Where's me Kedzara? She works 'ere, that's right, *innit*?" She leaned into Peter's face, squinting narrowly through tiny, wire rimmed glasses.

"Yes, but she hasn't been in all week, I'm sorry to say.

"Strewth, I'll just bet you are sorry beings that you're goin' ter marry my gel," she gave him a wicked smile and patted his bum.

"Why do you say that, Mrs. Twigg?" Peter moved to the other side of Sean's desk, putting a barrier between himself and Norah. "Zara and I are not, I repeat, *not* getting married, there was never any mention of marriage, *ever*. I don't know how you got that idea. We aren't even friends."

"*Wot*? Wot's happened 'ere, then?" She spoke menacingly, her beady eyes stuffed inside a frown. Glaring, she pinned him with a stare, as though accusing him of lying, or of some kind of foul play. "My Kedzara says so," she scowled. "She says she went to the Poppins theatre with yer fancy family and she's goin' ter marry the *pasty* likes of you."

"I'll repeat myself; Mrs. Twigg, that is simply not the case. We did not go to the theatre together. I merely gave her an extra ticket so that it didn't' go to waste. Regardless of what you've been led to believe, your daughter and I are not friends," he spoke with sarcasm dripping from his voice, "unless you think that being someone's friend consists of wanting to hide behind high walls topped with sharp, pointed stakes when that person is nearby."

The foul odor from the old woman's body, whiskey on her breath, and stale cigarette smoke clinging to her dirty clothes was beginning to irritate both Peter and Sean. The whole conversation was setting Peter's teeth on edge, like scraping nails on a chalkboard. He was exercising great control to avoid being rude, but he wanted her out of there.

"Mrs. Twigg, I think you need to rush to Zara's house in Burford, straightaway. You'll have to ask her those questions. I really have no answers for you," he turned on his heel and walked back to his office.

"Oh...well...then. I'll just be off. Snooty, ain't he? Pasty toff," she said to Sean, jerking her thumb at Peter. "It was nice ter meet yer highness anyways," she yelled after him. She turned her enormous body around; her tiny head wobbling whilst she shuffled toward the exit using her umbrella as a cane.

"My God," Sean mumbled under his breath watching Norah as she trundled through the door with her back to him. "The woman has a body like a sack of doorknobs. Her bum looks like two huge boulders bouncing and colliding as she walks."

When she was gone, Peter walked back into Sean's office. He frowned and straightened his shoulders.

"Well, Sean. All right, then. That's it...*Zara's history*. Let's push that paperwork through the system. Get it signed, delivered, and get rid of that bloody trog."

Peter started to walk back to his office and turned to Sean with a quizzical look.

"A pasty toff? Am I pasty, then, Sean?"

~35~

"The greatest pain that comes from love
is loving someone you can never have."
~ Anonymous~

Burford Village,
Oxfordshire, England
May 2005

Shortly after his promotion, Sean approached Peter with a suggestion.

"Peter, let's save some money and use an old program for a new research project. The one I'm thinking of has exactly the same components we used successfully before. It was loaded onto a disk for safekeeping when Zara overhauled our computer network."

"That's an excellent, cost-effective idea, Sean."

"The program should be with our other disks; I've looked for it, but it's not here. I feel sure Zara has taken it home. I'll call her and see if I can get her to return it."

Zara didn't respond to Sean's messages. They called round and learned she had not been to work for nearly a week; that she was quite ill with a bad case of influenza. The gossip was that she had fallen ill after pub-crawling one extremely cold, wet, and windy Friday night. She took to her bed a few days later and tried to nurse herself back to health with fluids and antibiotics, but her fluids were in the form of scotch and the antibiotics were doing nothing to fight the flu virus.

Peter and Sean drove to her house in Burford to get the disk and to see if she took home any other workplace disks they might need before they officially cut her out. They wanted no loose ends.

When they approached the house, they saw her black Jaguar in the carpark. There was no answer to their knocks and no response to the doorbell. Peter found the door unlatched, so they entered calling her name and Sean slipped on mail scattered all over the floor. The house was in a mess and smelled foul.

Glancing at the top of the stairs, they saw her weaving as she padded about in her bare feet carrying a tumbler of scotch and wearing a thin robe. She was disheveled and blind drunk. The grey roots of her spiky red hair showed; her face was bloated and pale; and she looked ghastly thin.

"Zara, please take care; you're terribly shaky. Stand away from the top of the stairs," Peter warned her, not wanting the responsibility if she took a tumble.

"We're here to look for a disk. Do you object to a quick look for it?"

"*Bloody hell, I don't give a rat's ass what you do,*" she wheezed, her voice phlegmy, and her speech slurred. "Just leave me alone." She turned slowly and coughing hard, she staggered away.

"Sean, could you make out the disks if you saw them?"

"The disks are numbered and have labels that I designed specifically for our software and computers. Yes," he nodded, "I'll recognize them. Easy peasy."

"All right, then; let's give it a go. We'll hunt for her study and see if we can locate them. I'll leave a note reminding her we were here."

The two men looked around the disheveled house until they found the closed door in the kitchen that led to her windowless study. It was unlocked; they opened the door and turned on the light. They were thunderstruck by what they saw.

There were nearly a hundred candid shots of Peter hanging on the walls. Zara had stalked him while walking to his office and house, playing in concerts, running marathons, dining in restaurants, lunching with associates, on his weekend runs or rides, and driving his car through the gates at Seven Valleys.

There were pictures of him with Hayley in New York, at the concert in their seats and talking to Tom Leighton, ice-skating at Rockefeller Center, at restaurants, getting in and out of taxis at the entrance to the Top of the Turret, as well as with Chris and Jaxx at the Plaza. The most shocking was a shot of Peter with his foot on Jaxx chest in front of the Metropolitan Museum when they discovered Jaxx stalking them. She had gotten that close without detection.

"Good grief." Sean turned to Peter, "What does this all mean?"

"I'm gobsmacked, Sean. Obviously, it means she's a delusional stalker with a serious obsession, and has been for quite some time."

"Stalking's not all she's done. I'm sorry to tell you this, Peter, but look what's on her computer screen."

"Those are Hayley's emails! She's hacked my work computer, Sean. She's as dangerous and demented as I suspected. I'll have to report this to university administration. She cannot be allowed access to campus." Peter's expression was grim while he looked around the room taking it all in. "My gut instinct was correct. I suspected she did some dirty work when she broke into my house and now I know what to look for."

Sean shook his head slowly, "This is very creepy."

The two men made a sweep of Zara's office and found disks of his emails and private message to Hayley. They found DVDs she'd made while looking through the bug in his office. Sean found that she'd taken away all the program disks he needed.

Peter's lips were white with rage. He ripped the photos from the wall, slammed them into boxes with the disks, and loaded up the car. Ready to leave, they heard loud snorting, gurgling, and whistling sounds from her bedroom. They walked upstairs and found her fast asleep. Her arm dangled over the side of the bed. A glass of scotch had spilled out and puddled on the floor.

"Zara, wake up." Sean shook the bed until she woke and propped up on her elbow.

"*God damn it, stop that you bloody cretin*," she snarled at Sean, unable to comprehend what was happening.

His face flaming with indignation, Peter shouted, "Zara, from now on I don't want you anywhere near me; do you understand? Stay away from me!"

She sat on the edge of the bed, her mind cloudy and muddled, trying to lift out of a stupefying fog. Was Peter there, telling her he didn't want her?

"Oh, no, Love; we were meant to be together. Are you so bleedin' dense you can't see that?" She spoke smugly, "Mate, after you've been with me you won't want to bang anyone else. Blimey, I can make you explode with orga…."

"Christ, Zara!" Peter cut her off, "You revolt me. I don't know how you got the preposterous idea that we ever have, or ever could, mean anything to each other. I don't want you." He shouted, "I have *never* wanted you. Got it? I don't want you near me. In fact, I don't ever want to lay eyes you again."

"Oh, but Peter, look what you'd be missing," Zara pulled open her robe, exposing her gaunt body and cupping her breasts in her hands. "Touch me, go ahead," she lay on the bed arching her back. "Now. Do it now, Peter. You know you want me! You know you always have. Do it, Peter, I promise you that you'll never want anyone else ever again. You'll be mine, Peter, just as it should be."

"Stop, Zara! You're drunk...and demented. For God's sake, cover yourself," Peter's voice filled with revulsion.

Sean gasped, grabbed Peter's arm, and pulled him out of the room. The two men stood outside where they couldn't see her.

Peter shouted from the stairway, "You have deluded yourself. Listen to me, Zara, whilst I say it again; I do not want you and I never did. It's always been strictly business. *Please* listen to me. You *must* get help. *You've gone over the edge*. I'm serving you with a Court Injunction and you'll go to jail if you come near me. You'll hear from university administration shortly. *I'm warning you, Zara; stay away from me from now on!"*

Zara laughed at the idea that anyone would think she needed help. After they left she fell asleep on the bed again, nude and holding onto an empty bottle. She woke fully an hour after the two men drove away, but even in her groggy state, she remembered Peter had been there, talking to her. Peter here? At her home? *Cor blimey, I didn't want him to see me like this.* Then, she remembered Peter's words. *Why would he come into my bedroom and tell me...*

"No, Peter...No! No!"

She had made her best moves and lost. *But, this is only another move. Damn and blast; he left the Cranmer Close house after I planted all those bugs. I can't access his computer at Seven Valleys and now I can't log on to his office computer. This game isn't over, though; I still have moves. I will have Peter; make no mistake.*

Peter was astounded by the extent Zara stalked him. He arranged for a team to go thoroughly over the Cranmer Close house, his car, his office, and his computers. They found all the computer spyware, the phone, and camera bugs. He installed a security system in the house, in his car, and in his office. For good measure, he had his mobile number changed.

Upon receiving Peter's report, the university administration immediately sent Zara a letter terminating her contract. The staff packed up her personal belongings and sent them to her home through an independent delivery company. Peter obtained a Court Injunction. She could not be anywhere near him or she would wind up in jail. Thus, Oxford University severed Zara Chandler's employment.

~36~

"When the effects of female jealousy
do not appear openly in their proper colours of rage and
fury, we may suspect that mischievous passion
to be at work privately, and attempting to undermine
what it doth not attack above-ground."
~ Henry Fielding~

London, England
May 2005

Jaxx birdcage sat in a dusty corner untouched for days. The paper birds lay forgotten piled atop one another in a careless heap while he whined and moaned, writing message after message to his Solitaire telling her of his heartache, his undying love, and his commitment.

"You are my Helen of Troy...you have struck my Achilles heel. Why isn't Solitaire writing to her heartsick Jaxx? Where are you? Jaxx cannot live without his Solitaire."

Jaxx read mail from his birds, but he wasn't taking time to answer them. Any messages he'd received from Chris were forwarded unread to his glorious Solitaire.

For that matter, he no longer cared one whit about any of his bird's twittering; he was obsessed with his Solitaire. He waited for her to write to him every minute of every day. His business and his birds were an intrusion on his thoughts of her. He ached for her, longed for her, she was his fantasy and he could think of nothing but her.

Utterly enthralled by his beautiful Solitaire, Jaxx must have her even if for only one night, and so he continued begging her to meet him. When Zara felt well enough to write to Jaxx, he was overjoyed and begged her to meet him, any time, any place. She agreed and they arranged to meet about seven o'clock at the Old Thameside Inn. It was a pub close to his flat and close to a cheap hotel he favored.

Solitaire confidently strode toward him, flaunting her sexuality. She wore thigh-high, laced-up black leather boots with stiletto heels. She was tall, slender, and she possessed that extra eye-popping appeal. Jaxx caught his lower lip with his teeth and drew in his breath while he watched her sensuous movements in the short, skin-tight leopard dress with the low décolleté. He could see her nipples through the sheer fabric. *Mmm...très bon; très sexy... Solitaire is everything Jaxx' hoped she would be. She promised to please Jaxx with many treasures in her large, black pouch.*

They reached out to each other; Jaxx grabbed her and held her by the back of her neck. He kissed her hungrily with his hand pushing hard on her *derrière*, thrusting himself against her so that she could feel him rising. They found an outside table with a view of the river and ordered drinks, but neither was hungry for food or conversation. Their hunger was for each other. Jaxx husky voice breathed in Zara's ear that they must go, or he would take her right there on the table.

"*Ma chérie*, I am so in love with you, I cannot wait to explore your glorious body inside and out with my curious fingers."

Zara's lips were on his neck and her breathy voice was smooth and sultry.

"*Mmmm*…well then, let's go, Jaxx," she whispered, "and you can show me how men are meant to make love to a woman."

"We can go to a hotel nearby. I know one." He patted his pockets. "Oh, but Jaxx has forgotten his wallet." "*Je suis très embarrassé*. Jaxx cannot ask his beautiful Solitaire to pay for such a thing!"

"Oh, I'm so sorry, Jaxx, and I am embarrassed to tell you I cannot pay. *Aww*, Jaxx, that's too bad. In my large pouch, I have many things that will pleasure you, but money is not among them. It bloody well could've been such fun," she stood up to leave throwing the strap of her black pouch over her shoulder.

"No, Jaxx will not have this," he pouted. He'd waited too long for this night. He refused to give up the good time he planned and threw caution to the wind. "*Oh-la-la*, my beautiful Solitaire, we will go to Jaxx' flat. There we will take our time and make long, slow love to each other until tomorrow's light comes through the window."

"*Oh-la-la*, Jaxx, that's brilliant! We shall go."

They walked toward his flat in Shad Towers. On the way, Jaxx coated his fingers with a small amount of white powder hidden in his pocket. He sniffed it and offered it to Zara. It was the first time she'd used cocaine and the rush that burst into her senses made her feel alive, dynamic and energized. As they walked, their words brimmed with sexual innuendo and they began to pleasure each other with their hands and mouths.

In the darkness, they walked up the outside steps of the building unnoticed. The flat was the last door facing the river. As soon as Jaxx unlocked and pushed open the door, the fetid air made Zara gasp. She could smell the filth in the room. The light was dim, but she could see there was only a single bed without sheets or a pillowcase and only a seedy, stained blanket. She filled with revulsion at how he lived and was determined to touch as little as possible.

Jaxx drew a tattered old curtain over the window and in one swift motion grasped Zara by the throat, and ordered her to take off her clothes while he took off his pants. Throwing her on the bed, he began to thrill her with unbelievable foreplay. His angry sex was as rough as Zara liked it and she was pleased. He found every sensitive spot, making her pant with pleasure and groan with gratification. He took out his aggressions toward women on her and after she was completely satisfied, he asked what she planned to do for him.

Jaxx wanted forbidden sex and Zara was willing to do anything. She tied his arms to the heavy bedside tables, because there was no headboard on the bed. She used silk scarves and when she'd securely tied him, she took sexual toys from her pouch and used all of them pleasuring him in ways he'd never experienced before. When Jaxx couldn't take any more, she made him beg her to stop.

With his hands still tied, they lay satiated and Zara used more cocaine, while they amused each other talking and laughing at women on the forum.

"No matter how young or old the women, they all love Jaxx," he gloated. "They could be at death's door and they would make Saint Peter wait for Jaxx to write his sexy words to them. On each of Jaxx' birds he has written a dossier, so that he knows who they are and what they like. When he learns how old they are, he cannot believe their ages. Jaxx is thirty-four years old. I expect to live fifty more years and they will still want Jaxx' love."

He described Christine to Zara, and told her how he mistook Hayley for her in New York.

"I thought Christine was one of Jaxx' beautiful birds, his pretty little parakeet, but no, she's an ugly duckling, not fit to be with Jaxx or even in his JAXX-POT birdcage," he nodded toward a dark corner. "She's pathetically colorless and drab. I thought she would be exquisite and radiate feminine sensuality, but *non, non*, she's repugnant *Baba Yaga*, the witch, but I could adore Hayley; she is a glorious princess."

"Oh, yes, of course; Hayley." She sniggered. "You met Hayley."

"Ah, oui! *Oh-oh-oh-la-la-la!* Yes! When I met them at the Plaza Hotel, I mistook gorgeous Hayley for Christine. *Elle était si belle, si exquis. Elle a volé mon coeur.* So beautiful, so exquisite, I was transfixed. I lost my heart to this rarest of lovebirds the moment she first appeared before me. But she has gone from my life and Jaxx is desolate," he pouted.

Zara's green eyes darkened at his description of Hayley, and she grunted, "Too bad the buggery bitch is dead."

Jaxx looked at her quizzically. "I do not understand, Solitaire. I'm confused."

"The sad cow's dead, Jaxx. On Christmas Eve, she died along with her benighted Uncle Arthur when a bomb hit her building. I know they are dead. I saw them die."

"Solitaire, you will be happy to hear she's not dead. Jaxx knows this. Christine wrote to me yesterday and I have not sent this message to you yet. She told me they went shopping at Buddinghill's and Hayley gave her a makeover as a gift. No, Solitaire, you are mistaken. She's very much alive."

"*NO*!" Zara jumped off the bed, eyes wide, she shrieked, "*Impossible! Impossible!* That cannot be!" Zara completely snapped. She literally bounced off the walls, screaming, *"Hell, God damned bloody hell!"*

Aghast, with a quavering voice, Jaxx pleaded, "My precious cockatrice; my glorious Solitaire, please untie your pretty scarves and let Jaxx loose so he can hold you and stroke you, whatever is wrong."

She wasn't listening; she was muttering to herself and then started screaming at him, "How could she not be dead? I saw her die. I paid Ra'id ∑5,000 to have her killed." She bellowed, "I was there, watching her go up in flames while she burned to death. *I watched her die!*"

Zara was wild-eyed; her face was ugly, contorted, and scarlet with fury. She threw a chair at Jaxx, smashing his face. Blood oozed from his mouth while he screamed in pain and fear.

Jaxx could only take shallow breaths from the shock of learning what Solitaire was. "Solitaire is crazy," he whimpered, struggling with the ties. "She is a murderess. I must get loose!"

Jaxx yanked at the scarves, but in his panic, he only succeeded in knocking over the heavy bedside tables. The scarves wouldn't budge and now his arms stretched out painfully, pinning him across the bed.

"Beautiful Solitaire," Jaxx voice was barely a whisper through his throbbing agony and terror, "Please let Jaxx loose. I beg of you. I am in pain!"

Slowly, Zara took a switchblade from her purse. He prayed she'd cut the scarves and set him free, but trembling with terror, he feared for his life.

"Yes, cut the scarves, *ma petite*," his voice was husky and weak. "Set Jaxx free, *oui, s'il vous plait, ma Solitaire*."

Overcome with terror, He tried to appear calm, "That's right my fiery little cockatrice, please, please cut Jaxx loose now. Jaxx has money, lots of money. He will pay you twice what it cost you for Hayley."

Jaxx was panting when she came toward him with a face belonging to a mad woman. Still nude, she straddled his body, pinning his hips to the bed.

"Don't patronize me, you disgusting slug. Here, let me free you." Zara positioned the knife at his throat, "This is for being a bad boy and bringing me such disappointing news."

Eyes wide with terror, Jaxx was screaming and writhing when, with one slice, she took from him his next fifty years. She gazed at his unseeing eyes still wide in death from the horror that he knew was about to befall him.

"*Hmmm...* Look at that," she shrugged, lifting her leg over his body, "I have killed the messenger. Well, now...sorry...I couldn't let you live, could I? You knew too much."

Zara dressed leisurely, wiped the switchblade on the mattress, and threw it back into her bag. She turned on his computer to see if she could read his Private Messages.

"Oh, thank you, Jaxx; you're logged onto the forum."

She deciphered his password, wrote it down and then clicked on his messages. What she read astonished her. *I shouldn't be surprised considering what a toe-rag he was. Fifteen women declared their undying love to the wanker, including cher Christine.* Yes, there was Witzend's message about shopping with Hayley and news about her job. Fury welled in her again.

While Jaxx lay dead, his hands still tied to the furniture, Zara took her time exploring his studio flat. The air was stifling and musty. It smelled of decay, dirty clothes, and rotting garbage. The room was dim and confined, dominated by a wall-to-wall, floor-to-ceiling window overlooking the Thames. She pulled back a drape covering a small kitchen area. Roaches crawled over the dirty dishes piled high in the sink. There was a sofa strewn with dirty clothing and musty towels, and a filthy bathroom no bigger than a closet. Books, magazines, and trash littered the floor. A Tele and storage cabinets lined the walls.

She emptied his JAXX-POT birdcage and scattered the colored paper birds over his body. She picked up a few birds and unfolded the papers to read the writing inside. Crikey, is there nothing private they didn't tell him? He's written facts that amounted to a personal profile on every woman. I wonder if he planned to blackmail these women in the future. She found her own paper bird and stuffed it in the bag with the bloody knife.

Then, having gone through every drawer and moving every piece of furniture, she found an aluminum briefcase hidden in a carved out space behind a heavy cabinet. She pried it open with her knife and inside were thousands of British notes of all denominations. *There must be over £150,000 here.*

"That's a lot of dosh. I hit the *JAXX-POT!*" She tittered at her own macabre humor.

Under the cash in the bottom of the briefcase were several plastic bags of white powder. It was too much for only one person to be using, and then she realized Jaxx was a drug dealer.

"So you were holding out on everyone, weren't you Frenchtoast, *mon petit pigeon mort*, my little dead pigeon!"

She emptied the briefcase, threw the plastic bags of cocaine back inside, and stuffed the money into her large bag. When she ran out of space, she found several stained wine sacks and filled them with money.

The door silently locked behind her when she left his flat. She crept down the steps, furtively hiding in the shadows. She walked to a main street and hailed a taxi to take her to her mother's house in Hackney Wick. Letting herself in with the door key from under the mat and keeping on her coat, she curled up on the sofa with her pouch under her head and covered herself with the same tatty old blanket her mother used to cover her the last time she was there.

"At least my mother's good for something," she muttered to herself before she drifted into a dreamless sleep.

Solitaire

"This bird, though beautiful as seen on the wing from afar, was a seeker of death. His Solitaire had the hideous, bare-skinned face of a vulture."

~37~

"Sometimes our light goes out
but is blown into flame by another human being.
Each of us owes deepest thanks to those
who have rekindled this light."
~ Albert Schweitzer~

New York City, New York
May 2005

Chris wrote an email to Pookie:

"Hiya Pook-a-rific,

Things are going smoothly at Savvy. I'm super busy, but loving it. How are things at my ol' alma mater, CableCoNews? Is the team still fighting a good fight?

I just couldn't be happier. I know that Jaxx really does love me. I write to him and he writes back with questions about what fun things Hayley and I are doing. He's such a romantic that he particularly wants to know about Hayley and Peter. I'm busy, but I take time to answer every message and keep him abreast of what's going on with us.

Write to me! I need my Pookie McNews fix."

Jaxx now had a ghostwriter who was more beguiling to his birds than ever. With Zara writing on a daily basis, messages with ardent sensuality from Jaxx exploded over Christine completely enthralling and overwhelming her. Jaxx begged her to write whenever she could and tell Jaxx anything she and Hayley were doing. Jaxx wanted to know everything.

Savvy News was a fast-paced atmosphere. It took a motivated person to keep up the tempo. Chris worked well both independently and with a team. She was free to work any shift and was willing to travel extensively on short notice. Her ability to multi-task, her good judgment, upbeat attitude, and strong writing skills, all made her a valuable part of the production team. She was excellent in choosing sound bites for use on the air and conducting interviews in person and over the phone. Pleased with her work, the station manager assigned her to Slick Slate's Scoop-City when he promoted Slick's production assistant.

Chris was standing on the set holding copy for Slick when a rookie cameraman trying to adjust a shot swung a shoulder-held camera into Chris, landing the full weight of the lens on her nose. They rushed her to a hospital in icepacks, where she asked for a phone to call Hayley.

"Hayles, I cannot win," she whined. I now have the biggest schnozzle in TV Land. It was a rock pile already, now it's a mountain. They say it's broken again. My eyes are bruised and swollen and I'm going to need surgery. I'll be in the hospital for a couple of days. Could you come, or send Marisol to see me? I need a hand holder."

"Don't worry, Chris, I'm coming. I'm calling a wonderful surgeon who specializes in facial reconstruction. He's a true artist. You'll stay with me at the penthouse to recover and Marisol and I will look after you. Now, relax and let the painkillers do their job."

Hayley arranged for one of New York's finest plastic surgeons to work on Chris's face. She assured him she would pay for any enhancements he recommended or that Chris desired. Chris agreed that he could reduce her froglike upper eyelids and lower her upper lip to cover her gums when she smiled.

"Just a few minor refinements will make a major change," the surgeon assured them.

Marisol was with Chris when her bandages came off a week after surgery. They both held their breath.

"Ah, I think you'll be pleased, Miss Wyndham. The swelling will subside, but already your nose is small and classic in shape," the surgeon assured her before he held up a mirror.

"I don't look half-bad, Doc," Chris started breathing again, "as compared to looking all-the-way-bad before. I like the way you raised the tip of my nose. It's cute and girly. And my eyes don't look froggy anymore. Thanks, Doc. Oh, and look at that; my gums don't show when I smile. Good job. I'm impressed. And I'm rambling. *Mazal Tov, Doctor!"* She took a deep breath and exhaled with a *whoosh. Yeah, Mazal Tov to you and to me.*

"Christina, tú es tan Hermosa. Si! Si! Si! Su nariz es bonita y dulce." Marisol bubbled with praise and hugged Chris. *Claro que si! Tú es muy bonita, méjita; muy, muy bonita!*"

"If I'd have known it would make such a difference, I would've bashed my nose into a camera lens a long time ago. Although, the real change is that I can finally breathe through my nose," she said, taking a deep breath. "I should have taken care of the problem years ago, but I was too pigheaded. Just ask my father," she laughed.

Hayley wanted Chris to have the best and to be her best. She was pleased with the results and she wanted to pay for the surgery as a gift to Chris. Although she appreciated the offer, Chris explained to Hayley that Savvy News covered the expense since it was a workplace accident, and that her parents insisted on picking up the tab for whatever extras she wanted.

Ben and Diane received an e-mailed picture of the new Chris. They were delighted with the results and pleased that she was taking an interest in her appearance.

Diane whistled through her teeth. "Finally; I thought she'd never get past the '*I like being the beast among the beauties*' phase. That baseball did a lot of damage to her face. Her eyes, nose, and upper lip were never the same after that. Benjy, did you notice that she looks somewhat like my sister? I always thought Christine was pretty and delicate; she was quite lovely to look at. Actually, she was the prettiest starlet of her day and a natural beauty."

"They can't hold a candle to you, my sweet *shiksah*," Benjy looked at his wife with love. "Listen, while we're about it," Ben brought up her car, "You know she finally unloaded that travesty on wheels. We should order a car for her to keep here. I think a Ferrari, Diane. What about color? Red, white, silver, black?"

"Ferrari it is," Diane agreed. "Definitely a convertible, Benjy. Should we ask her what color she'd like?" She paused, "*Nah, dumb idea.* She'll balk. Let's just order a Spider and tell her it's for her birthday. I vote for red...black top," Diane decided.

Savvy News gave Christine extra sick leave and paid workmen's compensation while she recovered for a month with Hayley in the penthouse. When she returned to work, the anchors and production staff showered her with compliments. Chris overheard one of the anchors whisper behind her back.

"*Wow...man, she's hot!*"

The young cameraman came to her office and brought a huge bouquet of spring flowers. He apologized again and reiterated that he was very sorry he'd run into her.

Later, standing on the set, he whispered, "Chris, you rock! The surgery has transformed you into an exceptionally beautiful woman. None of the anchors are as slim and gorgeous as you."

"Thanks for the compliment," she whispered back, "but, the real beauty is that now I can smell those flowers you gave me."

Chris often traveled for stories and interviews and brought footage back to edit for sound bites. She was an excellent interviewer and could handle being on the site of tragedies. She learned how to block her feelings while interviewing victims with sensitivity and care. The producers noticed and appreciated her humane style.

Late in May, Chris was writing breaking news copy when a panicky director rushed in.

"Chris, it's an emergency," he was waving papers and talking fast and loud. "The reporter who was to read the news at the top of the hour got into it with Slick and left the station in a temperamental snit. For this one time, will you go on camera? I think you're ready. You can do it."

"*Now*? *Right now*?"

"Yes. Why not? Try it; it's a one shot deal, but I need to know now, and you'll need to go directly to Slick's set."

Oh, my God; what should I do?

"I'll take the risk if you will."

The segment went well – she did what she'd watched other newsreaders do a thousand times. Chris was calm and poised, did a great job without fumbling, and loved doing it. Slick and the director thought she was great on camera; a natural, they said. They showed her footage and she was amazed. It was as though she were looking at someone else; someone who, at one time, she would have envied for her poise and on-camera appeal. She sighed. *Who is this person? Great hair, great smile, pretty eyes, and look at that sweet, little nose. New name, new face. I'll have to become a new me inside as well as outside.*

Shortly after she filled in, the director came to see her again.

"Chris, we have an on-camera spot on Sunday nights if you want it. Of course, I realize Sunday night is not the best time slot, but you should consider the experience you'll get and the exposure will give you an avenue for advancement."

Chris welcomed the opportunity. It was something she never in her wildest dreams thought she would do. *I have to remember I'm no longer Frumpy-Dumpy Blubster, Chris Horowitz, floating in a Yellow Submarine. I'm attractive and classy Christine Wyndham... thanks to Hayley Elizabeth Hamilton, the Snake Charmer.*

Monday after her first Sunday night on-camera, Hayley invited Chris to the penthouse for a congratulatory champagne brunch. When she arrived at the Top of the Turret, Chris got out of a taxi carrying a large open box, waved at Studs, and walked toward the boarded up doorway. Dream Girl watched Chris through the slats. "The snake...it's the snake," she said quietly, and crawled deeper inside to a dark corner where she slept on a pile of clothes and rugs.

"I know you're in there, Dream-Girl. Come out so I can see you. I want to talk to you and I have something for you. She waited for a minute and finally heard a small voice.

"Why? What do you want, *snake*? Go away and leave me alone."

"Come out where I can see you. I want to talk to you, Dreamy. Come out; I have something for you."

"*No.* Is it a cup of coffee from the Park East Café? A sweet roll? The Swan doesn't bring them to me on the weekend," she sniveled. "Put the box on the ground and go away."

"Yes, she does. I know she does, you old faker. This morning I have a huge cup of coffee and lemon, cherry, and cheese sweet rolls, but I have something else for you, too. Please come out; we've rarely seen you since Christmastime and I want to know that you're all right."

"No, I'm all right. I miss Uncle Arthur, is all. That Studs person scares me and he talks funny. He said to me, '*Yer a fair pox bottle, ya ol' fiend.*'"

Chris stifled a giggle, "Dreamy, I want to ask you how you knew I'm the snake and I have another question."

She paused…"I just knew. Don't ask dumb questions. I dreamed it, that's all. What else do you want? *Leave me alone*," she snapped.

"Thank you for telling us, Dream-Girl. I don't know if it was a self-fulfilling prophesy, or if you are prescient, or it's our karma, or if it was flat-out supposed to happen… Whatever it was, I'm grateful."

"I don't know what you're talking about. If you are so grateful, give me my coffee and sweet rolls and don't forget money."

"*Yeah, yeah...*in a minute. First, I have another question. I want to know where you came from and why you are choosing to live here in this doorway."

"That's two questions and I'm not going to answer either one of them."

"Why?"

"Because it's none of your business, *snake*. Now leave me alone."

Chris sat the coffee, a bag of lemon, cherry, and cheese Danish from the Park East Café, and a new Aussie hat with a five-dollar bill tucked in the band in front of the doorway. The scrawny hands darted out and snatched the box from the ground.

"Do you like it? The hat, I mean," Chris asked.

"Yes. Now go away."

"Bye, Dream-Girl."

When Chris walked away, she heard Dream-Girl's voice from inside the doorway.

"Stop calling me that...*snake*."

~38~

"Happiness is time spent with a friend and looking forward to sharing time with them again."
~ Lee Wilkinson~

New York City
June 2005

Early on a sultry June morning, Hayley answered her phone and Chris bubbled, "*Hayley, a news flash! I have a surprise that you won't believe. I don't believe it myself hardly...I mean, holy crap! I can hardly believe it myself.*"

Chris's excitement was so high she was talking fast and stumbling over her words.

"Chris, stay calm. You know I hate surprises. What don't you believe?"

"Don't worry; it's a good thing. The station is sending me to London to do a piece on...now wait for this... Witches Opposing Warming. I can't resist saying this Hayley, *oh, W-O-W!* The Broomstick Brig-A-Dears will be in Hyde Park on Wednesday, July 6, having a sit in to protest Global Warming and marching for a War on War right before the G-8 Summit in Perthshire, Scotland. Not only the witches, but on July 7, a Clown Cavalcade will be in the tube protesting the G-8 Summit.

Hayles, they've assigned me to go, not as the assistant producer, but as an on-air correspondent. I'll be doing the interviews on camera for broadcast live on Breakfast in Britain with Cal Chaser for Airway News, and then it will be rebroadcast on Slick Slate's Scoop City, during his morning program."

"Christine, I hardly know what to say. I think it's wonderful and you can have so much fun with those stories. Wow! I want to go with you just to Watch Our Witches," she laughed.

"Hayles, that's a wonderful idea. I don't mean the watching part; I mean the part about going with me. Peter would love it and so would I."

"Oh, *please*, Chris. Me? Fly? I hardly think so," she scoffed.

"You'll be flying with *me*, Hayley. Oh, I have a great idea! What if we ask Peter to come over and travel back with us?"

"I don't think so. Of all the things I'm afraid of, flying tops the list."

"Oh, I get it, Hayley; it's okay. You stay there, safe and warm in your little cocoon while life passes you by, and while your friends, who want to protect you, go off on a great England adventure. Peter will understand, too. Maybe by this time, he will have gotten the message that it's too much for you and he's just not worth it. It's a shame, but I'll call Peter and maybe he'll show me around London. Maybe he'll invite me to Seven Valley's to meet his family and show me around the estate. It's my birthday on July 4, so..."

"*Stop it, Chris!* I know what you're doing and it won't work. You don't understand...you can't *possibly* imagine..."

"Come on, Hayley, be brave. Take a deep breath and a leap of faith. Trust us. You'll have to fly again sometime. It might as well be now. I'll ask for time off before and after the protest and we can do stuff. It's not as if you'll be alone. We'll be together."

"Let me think it over, Chris."

"Awesome! I'll take that as a yes, Hayley. I'm so excited. Call Peter and tell him. I'm sure he'll be pleased."

"But Chris, I haven't…"

"No buts. We're going. *Call Peter*. Now, please."

"You're pushy, Christine. All right; I'll call Peter and..."

"*YES! Outstanding*! I'm going to buy new clothes. *Geez*, I'm a virtual clothes horse since I came to New York." Chris snickered. "Maybe I should pack a witches hat and a black dress."

"Silly woman; you'd make a *terrible* witch. Okay, I'll think it over."

"Seriously, Hayley, you're going. *Uh-oh*, Slick's paging me; gotta run. Call Peter. Bye."

Hayley shocked Peter with this news. She was amazed that she would ever consider flying. Peter would have done anything to have Hayley come to England and immediately suggested that he come to New York and escort them back to England. The dates were set and Hayley wondered if she'd completely lost her sanity.

"Hayley, this is wonderful and the timing is perfect. I want you to visit with my family. Every Fourth of July, we get together at Seven Valleys to celebrate American Independence Day for my mother. It's rather a joke, but we all enjoy it. Everyone in the family calls it, 'The Day the colonies celebrate sticking it to King George III.' He laughed. You must be there, especially to keep my mother company on the Fourth of July. Two Americans will thicken the plot against all of us Brits."

Hayley chuckled. "I'm not sure I can help her there, Peter. You forget I was born in London."

"Oh, right," he laughed. "I keep forgetting."

Hayley paused for a moment and sighed. "Very well, Peter. How can I refuse? With you and Chris ganging up on me, I can't say no. She'll be so happy and I long to see you and meet your family. Now I'm excited. And Peter, would it be possible for Chris to be part of the plans to celebrate her July fourth birthday?"

"Yes, of course. I'll invite Chris myself, or my mother will call her and ask her to join us."

"That's it, then, Peter. *Whoo;* I'm overwhelmed."

"Oh, Hayley, I'm so pleased for both of us. This is wonderful progress and I'll be at your side all the way. I've missed you so, and I love you more than I can say. I'll literally be counting the hours until I can hold you in my arms again."

Hayley worked with Chris to plan their trip and they arranged to leave for London on June 28 and return to New York on July 8. She booked a suite at the London Ritton for two weeks and asked for a single room next to the suite for Chris. She put the trip out of her mind until the date was almost upon them. For Hayley the trip was about being with Peter again and meeting Peter's family. It's what pushed her to overcome her fear of flying. That, and to return to England, was a dream come true.

Barbara called both Hayley and Chris and extended her invitation to them. She was thrilled by this wonderful turn of events.

Peter cleared his calendar for the week before and after 4 July. He booked first class flights on British Air for all three of them.

Chris had her feet in both camps -- on Sunday nights she went on-air reading the late night news and during the day, she still worked in production on Slick Slate's Scoop-City. She was as excited as a little girl at Christmas over her first foreign assignment as bizarre as it was to interview a coven of witches calling themselves the Broomstick Brig-A-Dears. She would be working with the producers at Airway News, the Savvy News' affiliate in London. It was a good learning experience to see how other national newsroom's pace as they produce the news. She expected Airway would be every bit as frantic as Savvy.

Pookie was Christine's only close friend for a long time, and she missed her. She wondered if Pookie would go with them to London. *All it will take is a phone call to find out.* She dialed Pookie's cell and she answered on the first ring.

"Hey, Pook-a-licious! How the heck are you?"

"Geez, is this Christine Wyndham? To what do I owe the honor of a call from a honcho at Savvy News in New York City?"

"Pookie, you are not going to believe this, but I have an assignment to cover a Coven of Witches' sit-in at London's Hyde Park on July sixth. I was wondering if you'd like to go with me just for the hell of it. Besides, I miss someone calling me Chrissy."

"Let me see -- you want me to go all the way to London with you to stare at a bunch of bloomin' Brits with pointy hats, striped sox, and broomsticks? Do you think I lost my marbles after you left? I can stay right here and stare at a witch. Just before you left, we hired one to anchor the local Sunday morning news if you remember correctly."

"Come on Pookie, It'll be fun. Not only the witches, but on July seventh, a Clown Cavalcade will be in the tube protesting the G-8 Summit. And that's not all. Get this; Peter's mother, Barbara Gabriel-Johns, invited me to spend the Fourth of July weekend at their estate called Seven Valleys and I'll stay in an actual Manor House. I feel certain that Mrs. Gabriel-Johns would invite you. It's a huge annual festival for charity and a family celebration: Besides, July Fourth is my twenty-fifth birthday."

"Seven Valleys, huh? So, what are they? *The Valley of the Dolls, the Valley of Death, the Valley of the Sun, the Valley of the Shadow...*"

"Come *on*, Pookie, this is the part where you say you'll go."

"Okay, Chris, I'll trade war stories with you then, and I don't mean Afghanistan or Iraq; I mean the CableCoNews Affiliate in Cleveland. Besides, you shouldn't be wandering around in a strange country without adult supervision."

"Pookie, that's wonderful! I miss you and can't wait to see you. Do you want to meet in London, or do you want to come to New York first?"

"I'll come to New York, Chris. You can show me the Savvy News studio. Where are we staying in London?"

"The London Ritton."

Chris waited for a response, but there was dead air.

"*Pookie...Pookie*?"

Pookie snickered, "Chris, I thought you said the London Ritton."

"I did Pooks. I know it's the most exclusive hotel in London, but you can share my room if you want, or I'll treat you to your own room, how would that be? Oh and Pookie, remember when I broke my nose and I was out of work for a month? Well, that was when I bought Symington's apartment from Hayley, so I've moved from that icky Greenwich Village walkup to the Top of the Turret. The apartment is small and has room for only one bed. Unfortunately, they've closed the Plaza, so I'll put you up at the Pierre à Taj Hotel. This is just for the pleasure of your company; we'll take care of all your expenses."

"Who are you and what've you done with my friend Chrissy Horowitz? You know the one I mean; the one who slept overnight in her broken down yellow submarine because she was too cheap to pay for a taxi?"

Chris snorted, "*Bite me,* Pookie. Yeah, I was; but since then, I've learned to value money differently and I know now what it takes to make money. Now that I've moved to the Top of the Turret, I pay Hayley's esthetician to give me facials; I have my hair done by her stylist; and I pay a personal trainer who comes in to work with Hayley, Marisol, and me. We do it as a group and afterward we use the gym equipment, sauna, and Jacuzzi. We take bets on who lasts longest on her treadmill. Hayley usually wins," she laughed. So, anyway, come on, Pooks...are you in?"

"Okay, I'll go along only to play devil's advocate. If nothing else, it will be worth the trip to see where the path to Hell really leads. Besides, nobody calls me Pookie anymore and... Oh, what the hell; I miss you."

Chris laughed, "You won't be sorry Pookie, I promise. I'm anxious to see you. I'll let Peter and Hayley know you're coming with me. Oh, wow, Pookie, this is so great. I can't wait for you to meet Jaxx."

"Oh wow, Chrissy; I can't wait to tell you how much that doesn't thrill me."

As soon as Chris hung up the phone, she called Hayley to tell her about Pookie. Hayley was so pleased that she called Peter. He was delighted and called Barbara. She was thrilled to have another American guest and called Pookie to invite her to Seven Valleys. Peter bought Pookie first class tickets for the flights. Now they were booked for the entire row, Peter emailed everyone and told them he felt that would help Hayley to feel secure.

After all their plans were firm, Chris wrote to Jaxx --

Private message to Frenchtoast from Witzend:

"Mon amour,

I will see you in London! Yes! I will be interviewing in Hyde Park on July 6. Peter is flying to New York to accompany Hayley, Pookie, and me. We'll stay at the London Ritton and we'll go to the Gabriel-Johns family's estate, for a festival. I'll fill in details later. You can show me where you live and work. I have a new look that I think you'll like. I love you so much and I can't wait to feel your arms around me.

Bisous forever,

Chris"

~39~

"What has puzzled us before seems less mysterious, and the crooked paths look straighter as we approach the end."
~ Jean Paul Richter~

New York City, New York
June 2005

London Heathrow to New York's La Guardia Airport is a seven and one-half hour flight. It was uneventful and, for Peter, the time passed slowly. Arriving mid-morning, Peter called Hayley on his mobile to assure her that he'd landed safely.

Peter found Miguel waiting at the terminal with Hayley's towncar and driver. He greeted Peter cordially and took him to the penthouse where Hayley was waiting. Miguel told him that Marisol prepared a Puerto Rican lunch especially for him.

Arriving at the Top of the Turret, Peter stood for a moment in front of the building while Miguel waited by the door with McMahon. He saw that all vestiges of the bombing were gone and the building was back to normal...except that Symington wasn't at the door to greet him. The senseless waste of his death made Peter melancholy.

He glanced to the right and saw a small figure emerging from the entrance to the next residence tower.

"Ah-hah, the furtive oracle appears right on cue," he said to Miguel, chuckling.

Hesitantly, she crept closer, patting her new Aussie hat. She'd decked herself out in a child's bright pink stretch pants, a purple tee shirt, and a pink and green flowered vest. Somewhere she found large turquoise and gold hoop earrings that dangled from her enormous earlobes. She was wearing her round black glasses frames and the long, unlit cigar dangled from her flaccid lips.

Squinting, as smoke was rising from the cigar, she peered askance at Peter. "I know you. You are the horse in my dream." She paused; "I told you that before, didn't I?"

"Yes, I'm the horse, but why? What makes me the horse?"

She ignored his questions and studied his face, as if to read his character.

"What's your name?" asked Peter. "Trust me; you can tell me."

"I don't remember." She glanced away and frowning, she pulled the corners of her mouth into a pout. "I don't *want* a name. I'm nobody. *Leave me alone!*" She huffed, her face scrunched, her features almost disappearing into all the deep lines and creases, yet she still held the cigar in her teeth.

"Come on now, Dreamy; play nice. Is that a new hat, then?"

With a grunt and a quick, hard movement, she pulled her new Aussie hat down to her eyebrows. Then, just as quickly, she leaned a shoulder toward Peter, squinted, and spoke in a wheedling voice.

"Do you have a sweet roll and coffee? Do you have five dollars? The swan does. That boy does." She pointed her long, bony finger at Miguel.

"No, I don't," he grinned at her. "I have no money. Horses don't carry money; they use credit cards instead. Miguel, can we bring her money and some food?"

Miguel nodded and glanced at Studs, who was looking at the ground. Studs shook his head slowly and muttered, "The knacker's daft as a box of frogs."

The old woman whispered to Peter, "I know a secret. Even the dumb police don't know what I know. They didn't ask and I didn't tell, because I hid." She began a ragged coughing spell.

"What is your secret? Don't you want to tell me?" Peter whispered.

She took a long raspy breath and nodded. "The panther killed Uncle Arthur. She did it. She was across the street, over there." She pointed to the doorway opposite the building. "There was a *boom* and fire and the raven flew away with Uncle Arthur and the dog-girl. *Boom*! Then, the panther ran away. *Boom*!" She made a wide arch with her hands.

"Thank you for trusting me and telling me that secret." Peter frowned and asked, "But, Dream-Girl, how do you know the panther did it? Did the panther throw the bomb?"

"No, but I saw her hide. She *told* them to throw the bomb."

"What did she look like, Dreamy?"

"Leave me alone, Horse!"

"Tell, me, won't you?" Peter reached out to her.

She pulled away, and squinting at him, she said, "Put the swan on your back, horse, and fly her to a safe place, or she will see the panther. The swan must not see the panther and the ravens. Be careful. Be very careful," she warned harshly, jabbing her finger at him.

"Yes, I agree. I must go now to see the swan and I'll protect her with all my might. Goodbye, Dream-Girl; you must take care of yourself and let others take care of you, too."

"Don't call me that!"

The little old derelict turned and scampered toward her hovel. After she slid through the opening, she poked her head out, stared at Miguel, and scowled.

"Boy! Don't forget my sweet roll and coffee. *No! Wait!* I want Coca Cola. And a sandwich. Corned beef and Swiss cheese on rye. With sauerkraut. And mustard. And money," she scatter shot her demands at them punctuating every word by stabbing the air with her bony finger. She disappeared into the doorway. "Don't forget the money," they heard her yell from inside.

The three men smiled at each other. Studs tapped Miguel's shoulder and laughed, "Sweet Lamb a-Jaysus, any odds ye kin double that order, mate?"

"What will become of her when they finish that building?" Peter asked Miguel while they walked to the elevator. "Will she be all right?"

"*Claro que si, Doctor Peter*; *Señorita* Hamilton has arranged for her care, and *Señorita* Chris says we adopt her like a scratchy kitten." Miguel entered the code for the penthouse. "But for now she's happy where she is. We provide for her food and drinks just like *mi amigo, Tio Arturo*. The crew knows she's there and they have sealed off the hallway on the inside of the building to keep her safe until they finish. She has a working water fountain and a small lavatory. *Ella esta buena para ahora*."

Hayley flew into Peter's arms when he stepped off the elevator. He hugged her and only air-kissed her cheeks, because Miguel was standing there and he'd need much more privacy to kiss her the way he'd like. They walked into the penthouse and little Diva, wearing a festive pink rosette on her ponytail, pawed his leg asking him to hold her. He picked up the tiny dog and carried her into the penthouse in his arms.

"You have a special way with women, Peter," Hayley beamed at him. Even Diva is happy to see you. Marisol has made an extraordinary meal using her family's recipes and she's insisted on serving us."

"*Por aperitivos*, to serve *con una piña colada*," Marisol spoke shyly, "I have prepared sizzling-hot *empañadillas*. They are crescent-shaped turnovers filled with lobster and crab.

Then I will serve *carne guisada puertorriqueña*; a stew with chunks of beef, green peppers, sweet chile peppers, onions, garlic, cilantro, potatoes, and olives stuffed with pimientos."

When they were finished eating, Peter complimented Marisol on both courses.

"Marisol, you could open your own restaurant. That was a wonderful lunch. Thank you from the bottom of my taste buds," he bowed to her.

Marisol prepared a smooth custard *flan* to finish the meal. Hayley invited Marisol and Miguel to sit with them in the dining room for coffee and dessert. Smiling shyly, the young couple took seats at the table.

The conversation turned around to Symington.

"I miss Uncle Arthur so very much," Hayley's words caught in her throat. She took a deep breath, "I miss seeing him standing at the door when we return from our morning walks, and watching the news together in the evening. That part of the day feels lonely for both Miguel and me. And Dream-Girl hardly ever comes out now. We leave coffee and sweet rolls in the morning and she scoops them up, but never says a word. Studs checks on her every day, but she doesn't like Studs. She won't speak to him. It's as if she resents him for taking Uncle Arthur's job."

"Perhaps she's fearful of getting to close to Studs, the way she did with Symington," Peter suggested. "She doesn't want to suffer the agony of loss again."

"Maybe; but we don't understand Studs' talk. Dream-Girl says he doesn't speak English. Yes, she misses him and I miss *mi amigo, Tío Arturo.* Uncle Arthur, he help me learn to speak English better. *Dios mio. Pobre tio Arturo*," Miguel's voice cracked and his eyes filled with tears. "Why did this happen to him? I ask myself this every day."

Miguel was unable to contain his grief and hurriedly left the table. Marisol rose and followed closely behind him while making consoling sounds.

"*Ohhhh, Mejito mio. Dios mio, Miguelito...mi Pobrecito.*"

Peter took Hayley's hand in his when he saw how Miguel's sadness affected her. He embraced her and crooned against her ear while her tears fell. The grief they all felt at losing their friend had given them many moments of sadness. Arthur Symington's death changed their lives.

Peter asked Hayley to show him the sheet of paper on which the old woman wrote her dream.

They went to the computer, found the dream symbols on a website and copied the description for each animal from Dream-Girl's paper. Hayley and Chris already had found the description for snake. After they'd completed the list, Hayley printed it and read aloud –

"The dream Black Panther represents hidden secrets; a stalker that walks slowly, creeps very close to its prey and kills totally and completely.

The dream Horse represents strength, power, love, devotion, and loyalty. In mythology, the Horse sprouts wings and carries its loved ones out of harm's way.

The dream Raven represents an agent out of the land of darkness and death.

The dream Snake's shedding of the skin represents a feeling of being limited or having outgrown the present condition.

The dream Swan represents grace, balance, and innocence."

"Dream-Girl was right about you, Hayley. You do represent the swan; you have grace and innocence. I think she was right about Chris, too. She represents the snake, because she literally outgrew and shed unproductive attitudes that held her back in her career."

"And you, Peter, possess all the qualities of the dream horse. You are devoted, loving, loyal, and strong. But who are the Black Panther and the raven?"

"Your Dream-Girl saw the ravens take away Arthur and the dog walker. I believe it's symbolic for death. She saw the black panther hiding across the street from the entrance when the bomb was thrown."

"Peter, *my God*, you mean there was a witness? Dream-Girl actually might know who threw the bomb?"

"But Hayley, I don't know how credible Dream-Girl is as an eye-witness."

"Just the same, I'd like to talk to her. Maybe if we all talk to her we can learn who she thinks is the panther. Will you come with me?

I'll ask Marisol to pack up some sandwiches and cokes for Studs and her. Miguel will go with us."

They went to the doorway and called to her. "Dream-Girl, we have something for you," Hayley prompted. "Will you come out please?"

There was silence from inside. Then a sneeze and a racking cough.

Peter coaxed her, "Come out, Dream-Girl. We want to ask you about the Black Panther."

"We have food...sandwiches, some apples, Cokes, and a special treat from Marisol. Do you want them?" Hayley said.

"Leave them and go away. And don't call me that...*horse*," she grumbled.

Hayley cajoled her, "Not until you come out and tell us who you saw in the doorway across the street. We have money too. Come out and tell us, then we'll give you what we brought."

"You're bribing me. Leave it there and go away."

"Who was it, Dream-Girl? Why won't you tell us?" Peter asked. "You know it's very important to us."

"Go away and leave me alone, horse. I'll think about it later."

"All right, then," Hayley retorted curtly, "we're just pushovers for you and you know it. Here's your food and Cokes. Miguel has money for you. You're a spoiled brat, Dream-Girl! One of these days, maybe you'll say thank you. I don't think that's asking too much," she scolded.

They placed everything in front of the doorway and Hayley walked away frustrated and disappointed. Two skinny arms popped out and snatched up the packages. They heard a faint, *"Humph."* There was no sign of gratitude.

Later that afternoon, Peter and Hayley sat in the living room facing Central Park and the city skyline, sharing a bottle of wine, and listening to the beautiful strains of Mozart's piano concertos,

Meditation from the opera, Thais, by Massenet, and Pachelbel's canon in D.

After dinner, they relaxed and discussed plans and schedules for the next two weeks. Peter knew Hayley needed to have everything arranged to the last detail before she left home. A condition she insisted on when she agreed to the trip.

"There are to be no loose ends," she'd said, "and I want to know every detail about everything."

"Mother and Dad will meet us at Heathrow and will take Diva home with them. I'm pleased that you can entrust them with your most beloved possession, Hayley, while we stay overnight in London at the Ritton."

"Pookie will be going with Chris on July sixth to her witch-hunt," she laughed, "and to search for clowns in the tube on July seventh. Hopefully it wasn't a problem to invite her to the festival at Seven Valleys," she glanced at Peter for reassurance.

"Not at all, Darling, it's a wonderful idea. We have plenty of room and the more Americans who turn up to support mother against the bevy of Brits, the happier she'll be." He was joking, but he suspected this was very close to the truth. "There are times when my mother is homesick for the states and longs to hear American accents."

"There's only one sour note in this. Chris wants to invite Jaxx to dinner with us at the Ritton and to Seven Valleys for the festival. Maybe he'll have enough grace not to accept - or a little pressure from you might keep him away. I won't ever mention the Museum fiasco to Christine. What do you think, Peter?"

"I don't care to have him around, Hayley. I'll see to it that he knows he's not welcome. I think Chris is in for some hard times ahead when she discovers the truth about Jacques Bonnier."

"Yes, Peter, but she won't hear it from me. She'll find out soon enough on her own. When the time comes, though, we'll need to circle the wagons to protect her from him and help her through the emotional downslide she's bound to suffer."

Later in the evening, after too long away from each other, they found comfort, passion, and fulfillment again in each other's arms.

Pookie arrived in New York City on Tuesday, June 28, the day before their flight to London. Hayley sent Miguel to the airport in her towncar. Miguel sat in the front with the driver and Pookie sat alone in the back. Not being used to this kind of thoughtful service, Pookie was quieter than usual on the drive to midtown. Peeking into every nook and cranny, she found the bar, bottled water, the phone, and took the flowers out of the vase by the window to smell them before she realized they were a deodorizer.

Miguel took Pookie to the nearby Pierre à Taj Hotel to check in and take her suitcase to her room. They left the hotel and dropped her off at the Savvy News studio. In the lobby, she asked the receptionist to announce her.

"Hi, I'm Poo- *um*...Kalia-Malika McKee. I have an appointment with Chrissy Horow-- *Wyndham*. Christine Wyndham."

Then, nervous and anxious, she sat and waited, checking out the furniture's upholstery, the walls, the carpet, the posters of the anchors, and the magazines. She stood up, stretched, and paced for a minute.

"Are you sure she heard you?" Pookie asked.

"She'll be along shortly, the receptionist assured her. "Slick Slate's Scoop-City afternoon show is just ending."

After a few minutes, Chris burst through the door into the lobby, saw Pookie, and squealed with delight.

"*Hey, Kalia-Malika! My little Pook-a-rama!* Come and give us a hug!"

Pookie saw a classy blonde woman with a beautiful face she didn't recognize, huge, sparkling blue eyes, a creamy complexion, fabulous Savvy News makeup and hairdo, wearing a tailored cornflower blue Armani suit and expensive spectator shoes, coming toward her as though she knew her.

Chris stopped in her tracks and dropped her arms when she saw Pookie's expression.

"Pookie, what's wrong?"

She sat there stunned. "My gosh, Chrissy." Pookie stared at Chris, wide eyed. "There isn't a hairsbreadth of resemblance between the woman standing before me pretending she was Chrissy Horowitz and the woman I knew in Cleveland."

"Come on, Pooks, give us a hug." Chris held out her arms and took a few steps forward.

Pookie's eyes brimmed and tears spilled down her face. She rose and went into Chris's outstretched arms.

"Geez, you gave your sniffling to me." *Sniff*

"Bite me."

"You clean up pretty good, girl."

"You're a laff-riot, Pookie."

"It was a second hand joke."

"It's an ancient cliché."

"But it's appropriate, Chrissy."

"It's old as the hills."

"I like it."

"It has whiskers, Pookie."

"I need new material."

"Yeah, come back when you get some, but for now, come on inside."

Chris opened the door to Savvy News studio's inner sanctum. Pookie eyed Chris's jewelry while she held the door.

"That necklace probably cost more than my entire wardrobe," she said, while the door closed behind her.

Studs carried Christine's bags to the lobby while she took the backstairs up to the penthouse to join Hayley and Peter for breakfast. Hayley was a jumble of anticipation, anxiety, and fear and she couldn't eat.

Miguel collected Peter and Hayley's suitcases, Diva's carrying case and took them to the lobby. Hayley planned to hold the little Yorkie until the last minute before boarding.

When Pookie arrived, Studs walked her to the elevator to wait for Miguel. He introduced himself and chatted until Miguel met her at the elevator. When Chris greeted her at the door to the penthouse, Pookie had a crooked smile and a devilish look in her eyes.

"What's with you, Pooks?"

"Chrissy, how come you never told me about Studley-McMuffin?"

"*Who?* Oh, you mean…Studs McMahon."

"Yeah, *no*, I meant *stud-muffin*. Wow, cute! Love his dark curly hair and big puppy eyes. Nice build, too! But, is he a big flirt. You know what he said to me? He said it was a beautiful day to meet a colleen and deas, too, and told me I'm the dog's bollocks. Then he asked me, 'What's the *jackanory?*' I haven't a clue what he said, but I knew from the look in his eyes *exactly* what he meant!"

"All right, Pookie, *behave…*" Chris giggled and while she handed Pookie a cup of coffee, she introduced her to Hayley, Marisol, and Peter by her given name, Kalia-Malika McKee.

"I'm so happy to finally meet you. Please call me Pookie. I'll think you're my mother if you call me 'Kalia-Malika'!"

Hayley hugged her. "It's wonderful to finally meet you, too. Any Pookie of Chris's is a Pookie of mine!"

Dream-Girl watched Peter and Studs help the driver load the suitcases into the towncar. Peter was standing at the curb when he felt Dream-Girl tug on his sleeve. She wore the same outrageous outfit and smelled like a wild goat. In the bright morning light, he could see dirt caked in her hands and under her nails. On top of her dirty, matted hair, she wore a silver New Year's Eve party tiara.

"Do you like my crown? I wore it for you. I am royalty now just like you and Uncle Arthur."

"Hullo, Queen Dreamy," he bowed to her. "Why, yes, I like it; you're looking quite elegant this morning."

"I want to tell you – but only *you*, horse - about the *boom-maker* who was hiding across the street. She's the Black Panther and her hair was like the red feathers on top of my beautiful crown."

She started coughing and couldn't stop. He gave her his handkerchief and told her to keep it.

"Queen Dreamy, please let Miguel call a doctor while the swan is gone.

"No!" she shouted and stamped her foot. "Did you or the boy bring me coffee? *No*. Did you bring me a sweet roll? *No*. Did you bring me money? *No*."

"The boy will do that when he returns from the airport this morning," Peter spoke softly.

Before Dream-Girl turned and disappeared through the doorway, she handed him a folded piece of a paper bag. He heard her coughing behind the wooden slats.

Peter got into the towncar and the driver pulled into traffic. *Queen Dreamy is ill; I must remember to ask Miguel to alert an agency for the homeless and call a doctor for her.*

He unfolded the paper she handed to him. It was a crayon drawing, so artfully rendered that there was no mistaking who it was. Dream-Girl's drawing of the Black Panther with the feathery red hair looked exactly like Zara Chandler.

She was here in New York in December. She hung pictures on her wall of us entering the residence building. Yes, she could have been there. She obviously didn't throw the bomb if she was standing across the street, but she could have arranged it.

Fear gripped him. A chill ran down his arms and spine that made his insides shiver. Peter felt colder than if he were up against an arctic wind.

And what about the plane? Was she responsible for the crash? Would Zara be psychotic enough to be at the bottom of all of this?

Why? What possible reason could she have to do this? Is putting the swan on the back of the horse, sprouting wings, and carrying the swan out of harm's way a warning to take Hayley to England ...or not? Are the wings a symbol for an airplane? Is it too late to turn back, just in case? Is there an outside chance that it isn't Zara? If it is Zara, I fear I'm taking Hayley straight into the lion's den.

Peter, an intelligent and considerate man, but also a chronic procrastinator, had to make a judgment call and a quick decision. In taking Hayley to England, he might gain what he so dearly wanted, but against his better judgment.

Do I tell them to turn the car around and return Hayley to the safety of the penthouse, or keep going to the airport and to England?

All he had to do was say it -- *turn the car around* -- but his decision was to keep this information to himself and not to reveal to anyone what he suspected. *I can keep her safe and I will deal with this myself.*

On this sweltering day in June, with these unspeakable thoughts in mind, panic grabbed him and he was drowning in fear. By the time they reached the airport, he felt light-headed as if he were smothering from lack of air.

"Do you like my crown? I wore it for you. I am royalty now just like you and Uncle Arthur."

Queen-Dreamy

~40~

"There is no den in the wide world to hide a rogue.
Commit a crime and the earth is made of glass.
Commit a crime and it seems as if a coat of snow
fell on the ground, Such as reveals in the woods
the track of every partridge, fox, and squirrel."
~ Ralph Waldo Emerson~

Ritton Hotel and Spa
London, England
July 2005

After the four friends boarded British Air and sat comfortably in First Class seats, Pookie pulled all the magazines onto her lap, played with the headset and television and pushed her seat back and forth.

Chris snickered, "*Having fun, Pook-a-snoopy?"*

After takeoff, she settled down and quietly enjoyed the flight. The attendant served cocktails and Pookie tapped Christine's shoulder.

"Chrissy, we get to do this again next week," she whispered, sipping through a straw a tall glass of sparkling water with a twist of lemon, lime, and several maraschino cherries.

"I know Pookie," Chris leaned toward her and murmured, "We need to kiss Peter's ring for all of this good stuff."

"I'll kiss anything he wants, Chrissy," she smirked, slowly shaking her head.

"*Shhh*, *Pookie!*" Chris giggled, "Behave yourself, or Peter will pull your passport."

"Hey, Chrissy; do you like my French braid? I went to a hairdressing school and a student taught me how to do it."

"I do, Pooks. Could you show me? Your hair is really long, so you have a lot to work with, but I think my hair is long enough, too."

"I'll show you tonight, Chrissy. What are you going to do first when we get to London?"

"Oh, yeah, speaking of French; first of all, I'm going to check my messages to see if Jaxx has accepted my invitations."

Pookie rolled her eyes and heaved a sigh. "Where's the door? I'd rather free fall from this plane than have to watch *that* disaster."

Peter overheard and caught Pookie's eye. He raised his eyebrows and nodded in agreement.

The flight was exceptionally smooth and Hayley slept through most of it with Peter holding her hand. Diva slept in the carrier at their feet. When they arrived at Heathrow, Hayley was relieved to be on the ground, although the pilot set the plane down as smoothly on the runway as if landing on a sheet of glass.

They presented Diva's paperwork, went through customs and baggage claim, picked up their luggage, and headed for the exit. As soon as they walked through the doors, Peter saw Barbara waving and bouncing excitedly. Edward smiled widely, while holding an armload of roses from his garden.

"Peter! Here we are, darling!" Barbara rushed through the crowd and hugged him. Then she hugged Hayley, Chris, and Pookie, not waiting for an introduction. "I'm so delighted to see you again, Hayley, and to meet Christine and Kalia," she beamed and babbled, grinning at them. "*Ah, what absolutely gorgeous American girls! Speak to me! Let me hear you... touch you!* Hayley, your pictures don't do you justice. You have grown up to be the most perfectly beautiful woman I have ever seen. No wonder Peter snatched you up as my new daugh-... *ummm...* we're excited that you are all visiting us for the Wolds-on-Thames and Seven Valleys' Arts Festival. And you two girls; you are absolutely breathtaking. Why haven't some fine young men swept you up already?"

Then with a lot of "*ohhs,*" and "*ahhhs,*" Barbara held out her hands to take Diva from Hayley. Diva went to her willingly and

Barbara enveloped the tiny dog in her arms, murmuring to her, while peppering the top of her head with kisses.

"I think she likes you, Barbara."

Hayley chuckled at Diva. She was shyly enjoying Barbara's fussing over her.

"Diva will have a wonderful time playing with Lizzie and Maggie, our very spoilt King Charles spaniels. Don't worry about her for a minute, Darling." She clasped Hayley's hand, "I plan to overindulge her with treats and attention just like I do my children."

Edward presented a bouquet of pink roses to each of the women and Peter hugged his dad. Already overwhelmed by everything, all Pookie could say was, "Thank you, Sir," and shook his hand.

Pookie whispered to Chris, "Are we supposed to call him, My Lord?"

"You're too funny, Pookie" she whispered. "Yeah, actually you pronounce that, *m'lord.* No, really; according to Peter, they aren't peerage. They don't have an inherited title, however, they are wealthy landed gentry. Mr. Gabriel-Johns will work, although in Hayley's case," she giggled, "I think '*Dad'* might be proper."

The travelers were weary, but after checking into the suite, Peter went back to the registration desk and asked them to look out for Zara Chandler. He showed them her picture and they said they would recognize her by her bright red hair.

"Understand, she's a dangerous woman and I have a Court Injunction against her."

Weary or not, the four friends met in the Ritton's Londres Bailey and Bar for a light evening meal and to go over their plans for the next day. They would meet in the suite and order breakfast from room service. Afterward, Chris and Pookie would have facials and massages at the Ritton's luxurious Roman Thermae Baths and Spa. Later, they would shop at Harrods and would return to the Ritton for high tea in the elegant gold and ivory Colonnade Room. They arranged for a casual dinner served in the suite.

Edward and Barbara took Diva home to Seven Valleys after delivering the four travelers to the Ritton. Early the next morning, Barbara met with the committee in Wolds-on-Thames to assure, as she told Edward, "that nothing goes higgledy-piggledy."

Then she met with Emily's housekeeping staff to discuss sleeping room arrangements, and with Emily to discuss meals, starters, and tea times, before their guests began arriving for the weekend. Edward did the rounds of the estate with his gardeners to assure they all understood their role in the festival.

Hayley enjoyed being at the Ritton. The renovation of the hotel was her mother's last project and she never considered staying anywhere else in London. The style of the hotel and furnishings were so similar to the penthouse that she was experiencing a high level of comfort that she hadn't expected. With Peter in the suite with her, she felt safe and secure.

Peter intended to drop in on a colleague to discuss a few new ideas for treatment of trauma victims from Iraq. He would call him in the morning to set up a visit and then join the three women for dinner. The next day, Friday, they would leave the Ritton and return after a few days at Seven Valleys. Peter hired a limo for the trip. He'd left the Bentley at home before he left for New York. His plans were fixed.

Pookie went to her room wondering what incredible planet they'd landed on. Having never traveled out of the country, working in the Midwest, growing up in a tiny village on Kauai, she had lived a life of simplicity, sun, and ocean. In the morning, Pookie felt blissfully relaxed and pampered by an early morning massage at the spa. She enjoyed every minute of this luxury, but her thoughts about Chrissy were constantly troubling.

The changes in Chrissy are amazing. She's as gorgeous as a model, or any starlet. Who would have thought? Her newfound confidence is refreshing, too. Now if she could just realize that Jaxx is nothing but a phony player, she could pass go, get out of fantasyland, find someone who'd fully appreciate her, and enjoy the realities of her new life. I fear Chris had allowed herself to fall into a bad thing and in the end, there will be nothing but disappointment and heartbreak.

Chris was anxious to see Jaxx and invited him to the festival weekend at Seven Valleys. It was six months since the Great Escape's New York Getaway. She wanted to see his face when he saw her for the first time since the reconstructive surgery. She wasn't the same woman he'd met in New York.

The last thing Chris did before she went to bed was to turn on her laptop and check email messages. There were a few from staff at Savvy News telling her to have a great time playing with her witches and clowns and to get some fabulous footage.

Then, she logged onto the forum to check her Private Messages. She found nothing from Jaxx.

Dispirited, she wrote to him, hoping he'd respond:

Private Message from Witzend to Frenchtoast:

"*Mon cher amour,*

I haven't heard from you and now we are in England. Can we meet tomorrow night? Can you come to the Ritton to join us for dinner? Let me know when you arrive. You can go to the registration desk at the hotel and they will call the room. I'll check for a private message from you the minute I get back from Harrods.

Tout mon coeur,
Christine"

Zara read and wrote Private Messages to all of Jaxx' birds, but there was only one she waited for every day. Chris never failed to respond to the loving words from Frenchtoast. *No need to write from now on. Witzend has given me all the information I need to trail these sad cows. Aww...that is wonderful news. It's an open invitation for me to prove two old sayings, 'Three's a charm,' and 'If you want something done right, you'll do it yourself.'*

Aww, poor Jaxx; the bloke's tied up and can't come to dinner. Aww, poor Froggy's missing a free meal and a chance to see his glorious princess again. Strewth, I wonder if they've found him yet. Maybe I need to start reading the newspaper or watching news on the Tele.

Zara was sure she knew all of Peter's colleagues in London and she would be waiting when he left the hotel in the morning. Later, she thought, I'll follow the sad cows to Harrods, where there might be an opportunity too good to miss.

Thrilled by what this would mean for her, she laughed manically, turned off her computer, picked up her bottle of scotch, and trotted off to bed.

Friday morning found London's normally foggy weather clear and mild. *Its good weather to leave the hotel and enjoy shopping at Harrods,* Chris thought. She was delighted to be in London. Being with Hayley, Peter, and Pookie; having her first foreign assignment as a correspondent for Savvy News; anticipating some shopping at Harrods; and best of all, she was going to see Jaxx. Life couldn't get any better.

Everyone's plans for the day changed the moment Peter called Chris's room after breakfast.

"May I come to your room for a few minutes? There is a matter I'd like to discuss with you."

Peter sat with Chris and confided the troubling thoughts on his mind. "First off, Chris, I think Dream-Girl is ill. She has a terrible cough. We need Miguel to arrange to have her taken to a doctor, or at least be sure she gets something for that cough. The renovation is almost complete and she will have to leave her sanctuary quite soon anyway. I'll pay for whatever extra care she needs."

Taken aback, Chris realized she hadn't thought about Dream-Girl leaving her doorway. *Some changes happen whether you're ready for them or not.*

Her voice fell to a whisper, "Hopefully we can find good accommodations for Dream-Girl." She took a deep breath and let it out a *whoosh*.

"Can you have your friends at Savvy contact Miguel? I could have Hayley call him, but I'd rather we'd handle this ourselves."

"Yes, I can, Peter. When I return to New York, I'll keep a close eye on what's happening. What else is on your mind?"

"Even more disturbing than that, Chris, I have to tell you what's been going on here," and he explained Zara Chandler's stalking and repeated what Dream-Girl told him about the red-haired panther.

"I've just got off the phone from a long conversation with Tom Leighton. You might remember Hayley and I met him at the New York Philharmonic concert. He was a classmate of Elizabeth and Zara Chandler's at Oxford. I decided to call him because he mentioned something about Zara's 'tricks' when we met the night of the concert. It was on my mind to call him and I regret waiting this long, because what he said was alarming."

"Oh, God, Peter, you're scaring me."

"This won't be word for word, but it's what he related to me. He said that Zara had a gift for computer science, as did he. Whilst an undergraduate student at Oxford, she experimented with the technology, taught herself computer languages, and knew just enough about hacking to get into trouble.

He confided to me that while they were freshmen, they were briefly involved in a steamy affair, and late one night Zara talked him into helping her hack into the university computer to change one of her grades.

Elizabeth was a graduate student at the time. She happened to be passing by and saw him sneaking into the building. Curious, she followed him and saw what he was doing. She reported him to the dean. The incident caused the university to place a black mark on his record and they forbade him the use of any university computers from then on.

She didn't report Zara, only Tom, but somehow she learned Zara was involved. She thought Tom should tell them about Zara, but he never revealed her complicity in the scheme to the university. Soon after the incident, he realized Zara wasn't a woman he wanted in his life. She stalked him for months to the point of harassing him in her effort to get back together. He finally warned her that he'd go to the police if she didn't stop."

"Based on all of this, it sounds like her *modus operandi*. But what does any of this have to do with Hayley...or Lady Elizabeth, for that matter?"

"Now, this is where it gets really frightening, Chris. According to Tom, Zara blamed Elizabeth for breaking them up. He said he regrets he didn't realize sooner that he should have taken her threats more seriously. She told Tom it was all Elizabeth's fault and she would get even if it took her forever. Her exact words were, '*I'll see her burn in hell'*."

Chris was stunned and felt bile rising in her throat.

"My God, who would ever have suspected?"

"You know, when we were with Tom at the Symphony, Hayley related a chance meeting with Zara at Oxford when she and Lady Elizabeth were visiting just before the crash. She told us it was obvious that her mother found Zara so repulsive that it made her skin crawl. She hated Lady Elizabeth so much that it must have pushed Zara over the edge to have her daughter at Oxford as a student."

"Yes, it's the answer, Peter, the two missing pieces of the puzzle. Now we have the answer to *who* and *why*. Who knew she was that insane. We need to tell Hayley...to *warn* her."

"No, I think not. Not yet."

"She needs to know. She's not a garden gnome, Peter. I want to tell her now."

"I can protect her, so let's deal with this without alarming her needlessly."

"You'd better tell her now, Peter. If you don't, she's gonna be *pissed off* at us when she finds out."

"I'll handle it, Christine."

"But, Peter, *she...I...we...*"

"I'm afraid there's more, Chris.

"There's more?"

"Yes, another piece that might fit into this puzzle. I recently went to a jewelry shop in London and there I discovered this bracelet. It's exactly like the one her parents gave to Hayley and it just cannot be a coincidence. It has to be the very same bracelet. A pub owner in Hackney Wick pawned it. Would you want to go to Hackney this afternoon to see if we can locate the pub and find out where he got it? I suspect we can trace all of this back to Zara Chandler. Based on what I've learned so far, where this woman is concerned, we should proceed on the notion that *anything and everything* is within the realm of possibility."

"Of course, Peter. I would be honored to do anything I can."

"Wonderful. I'd like your help, Chris. Before we left New York, I thought I'd send Hayley to Harrods in a car with a private bodyguard to protect her, but under the circumstances, I don't feel even that's safe. Pookie must stay with her. I don't want them to leave the hotel. You and I will go to Scotland Yard and have them look into Zara Chandler. I'm convinced she's at the bottom of the murders. You already know how to manage these things."

"All right, Peter. What specifically do you want them to investigate?"

"I want to know when and where she was in the states during the past five years. I want them to investigate her phone records, or anything that can give us a clue. I want to know if she bears responsibility for the deaths of these innocent people. Apparently, she hated Elizabeth and I'm sure she didn't want Hayley at Oxford as a reminder, so she planned to destroy them all. We must do whatever it takes to protect Hayley."

"So, this woman is looney tunes, Peter?

"Probably not clinically correct, Chris, but yes, that's one way to put it. I'd say she's absolutely barking mad. Are you still in?"

"Yes, I am and always will be ready to protect Hayley. You can count on me. Let's go to the police this morning, Peter. Maybe we can get them started right away. There's no time to lose. Oh, God, this is all my fault. I cajoled her into coming with me. If anything happens to Hayley while we're here, I'll never forgive myself." Chris covered her face with her hands and sighed deeply.

"We'll see to it that nothing does," Peter reassured her.

"Peter, another thing; I don't understand why Jaxx isn't answering my emails or Private Messages. So, while we're about it, I want to find Jaxx' address and, if you wouldn't mind, take a minute to drop by there today. Will you do that with me to find out why he hasn't responded to my invitations? Perhaps I should try calling him first, though."

"Yes, Chris, Jaxx *is* listed in the book. I do happen to know that."

She called information to get his phone number. "Success, Peter! There is a Jacques Bonnier listed at Shad Towers, London." She called the number they gave her and got a message that the voicemail box was full.

"Let's try the phone book, Chris. Addresses are often listed." Peter quickly thumbed through the book. "Ah, here it is. All right, then. Let's check on Jaxx, then we'll head to the police station."

"I remember his reaction when I met him at the Plaza. I would be more honest to say that I'm anxious for Jaxx to see me."

Peter explained to Hayley that they were going to find Jaxx.

"He isn't answering her messages and she can't reach him by phone. We'll take the tube and return in time for tea. But, I really want you to stay in the suite with Pookie, darling. You have my mobile number. Please call me if you think there is any reason to be concerned and you know emergency is 9-9-9, right?"

Zara tailed them and changed her plan once she saw they were going toward Shad Towers. Alarmed, she turned around muttering, "*Blimey, I don't want to be around when they find Froggy, then.*"

Jaxx' flat was around a few turns on the outside of the building. The flat faced the river and the doorway was off to itself. They found the door and quickly became aware of a noxious odor coming from inside. They couldn't imagine what could smell that vile. Chris knocked on the door and rang the bell. Dread overcame her and she couldn't catch her breath. After a minute or two, there was still no movement from inside.

"Chris, I'm going to find the super to unlock the door."

"Yes, Peter, please hurry!"

They opened the door and a swarm of flies buzzed around their heads. The odor in the room was horrific, but the grisly scene inside the torn up flat with Jacques Bonnier's bloated, decaying, and maggot-infested body lying on the mattress gagged Peter and made Christine faint. Peter dialed 9-9-9 emergency and asked them to send in Scotland Yard.

After they revived Chris, the super helped Peter walk her to his flat and they waited for police to arrive.

Chris was shaking, wringing her hands, and sobbing, "Oh, Peter, how could anyone do such a heinous thing? *Poor Jaxx; oh, my God, poor Jaxx.*"

Peter gently rocked Chris in his arms.

"Why don't I get a taxi for you and send you to the hotel to rest, Chris? I'll go pub hunting and to Scotland Yard about Zara. You're not up to this today."

"No, Peter. I'll go with you. I don't want to be alone," she replied sadly, "and I would have to explain to Hayley and Pookie why I'm back early., I'd have to steel myself for the *Pook-a-nialator's* zingers and I'm not ready for that. Actually, I rather rip out my tongue than have to tell Pookie."

They hailed a taxi and told the driver they needed to make a few stops. He agreed to drive them and headed for Hackney Wick. They met with success in the third pub they visited. Peter showed the bracelet to the owner and saw a faint flicker of recognition on his face.

"Oi, I remember that bracelet. Ya, I pawned it in Hatton Garden."

"How did you come by the bracelet?"

"Well, I'm not sure I remember that," he smirked.

Peter took out a twenty-pound note. "Will this jog your memory?

"Well, maybe. Let me think. No, sorry, mate, I'm still not remembering."

"All right, then. Does another twenty pound note help?"

The owner took the note and held it to his forehead. "Oh, yes. I remember. It was a woman, actually; name's a bit foggy, though."

"Who was it? Come on, man. *Tell me!"* Peter tossed three more twenties at him.

"Oh, right. It was Norah Twigg. Yes, that's who it was. Yes, I remember now," he sniggered, stacking up the twenties. "Used it to pay up her bar bill."

"Where does she live? Oh, never mind. I'll find out for myself," Peter muttered.

"Thanks...*mate*. Uh...it's been *charming*," Chris tossed the words over her shoulder as she walked out the door.

They left the darkened pub and in the broad daylight, Chris saw the color had drained from Peter's face. He leaned against the side of the building.

"What is it, Peter? What's wrong? Are you ill?"

"No, Chris, I'm not ill." Peter swallowed hard, "It's just that this is exactly what I feared. Norah Twigg is Zara Chandler's mother."

London's New Scotland Yard metropolitan police's modern American looking steel and glass building surprised Chris, but once inside, it was all British again. When they approached the desk, she asked to speak to a detective.

They sat across the wide desk of Detective Chief Inspector Bob Bowkler who introduced himself. Peter told him the whole story of what happened to the Hamilton's and why they suspected Zara Chandler was at the bottom of these crimes.

"This is her photograph, Detective, and I have this drawing by an eyewitness." Peter unfolded Dream-Girl's crayon drawing and handed it to Bowkler.

"Why was this not given to the New York City detectives at the time of the murders?"

"The eyewitness...is a homeless woman. I believe she was afraid she would have been dismissed as unreliable or harassed by the police, so she gave it to me."

Bowkler listened sympathetically, but shook his head, "There's precious little we can do. All you lot have is hearsay, circumstantial evidence, and an eyewitness who, by her own admission, would not be taken seriously. Furthermore, these crimes were committed in the states. New York police would have to act upon this information."

"But, the stalking, Inspector; perhaps you can investigate her for that? Ask the New York police to interview Tom Leighton; she stalked him too."

"But, Dr. Gabriel-Johns, she's no longer stalking either of you. I don't see how..."

"Detective, let's try coming at this through a different door," Chris said. "How did her mother gain possession of the bracelet? It's obvious that someone found it at the crash site. You must admit it's not too much of a stretch to believe Zara Chandler gave the bracelet to her mother."

"Yes, can't you interview Norah Twigg?" Peter asked. "It's a logical place to start."

"Very well, we'll start there, although we have no actual grounds. Just be advised, she can refuse an interview. We'll photograph the bracelet, copy her photograph and the drawing, and alert the New York City investigators about the information you've uncovered. You'll probably hear from them and I'll be in touch. Ring me if you think of anything else."

Peter hurried back to their suite when he arrived at the Ritton. He wouldn't let Hayley out of his sight again until this whole mess was finished. He decided he wouldn't tell her about Jaxx. He thought it best if Chris brought the news to the two women, but when he arrived at their suite, he found they already knew.

"Turn on the Tele, Peter," Hayley said, jumping up when he came into the room. "Pookie and I were sitting here watching Airway News when there was a News Flash about Jaxx being murdered. It was utterly ghastly. We saw both of you standing there with the police. Are you all right? Is Christine all right?"

"Not really, Darling, it was gruesome for Chris. She's devastated, but she's tougher than we thought. I'll turn on the news now."

A News Flash on Airway News in graphic detail about the murder of one Jacques Bonnier came on the screen. The Airway News reporter, the same handsome young man who interviewed Zara Chandler about her friendship with Elizabeth, stood in front of the building with shots of the Thames River included in the footage.

"Late this morning, two friends, who requested their names be withheld, discovered the badly decomposed body of Jacques Bonnier, a thirty-four year-old expatriate Frenchman in a small flat in Shad Towers. Someone had slashed his throat approximately six weeks ago, according to London Scotland Yard's medical examiner.

Investigators say the motive for the murder is unclear. Apparently, the killer was someone he knew. On the surface, it appeared to be an assignation gone badly but police determined it also could have been a drug-related case or a robbery because of a strong box that contained several liters of cocaine.

Mr. Bonnier, who goes by the name, Jaxx, worked alone, conducting an on-line business from this tiny flat, but apparently he was involved in other unlawful activities. Forensic investigators have just arrived on the scene to begin their search for clues.

This is Cal Chaser, reporting Thameside for Airway News from Shad Towers in London."

The report included footage inside the flat and outside the building showing the coroner removing the body. Peter and Chris stood in the crowd of onlookers, but they refused an on-air interview.

Chris declined dinner, threw herself on her bed and shed bitter tears. She lay there and thought about all the loving words she and Jaxx poured into their Private Messages.

Pookie joined Peter and Hayley for dinner, and while they were eating, Chris tapped on the door. She had mulled the circumstances surrounding Jaxx' death and she needed to discuss a sequence of events that didn't fit. She asked Peter to step out in the hall for a moment.

"Peter, it just doesn't add up. I've been receiving Private Messages from Jaxx for the past six weeks and if he lay there dead, then who's been writing them? And to make matters worse, for weeks I've been telling all of our plans to whomever it is," she said with a stricken expression.

"I think we both know who it was, Chris. It was someone who knew how to hack into a computer; who knew how to crack passwords; and who knew her way around the Great Escape forum. It's all right; don't blame yourself. I don't. How could you possibly have known? Can you email me the information you've passed on to her? Then I'll know exactly what Zara knows. I'm glad you told me. We'll deal with this," he laid his hand on her bowed head.

Later, when Peter and Hayley slipped into bed, he made love to her and afterward, held her close to him while he slowly stroked her hair. His mind was whirling. *Perhaps Chris is right;*

Hayley needs to know about Zara. Is it wrong to withhold this information from her?

Sleepy, Hayley sighed and said, “Peter, do you remember when we met, I called you Peter Rabbit, and you gave me the little book when you left Stony Point?"

"How could I forget?" Peter replied, chuckling softly, “Such a wistful memory, Hayley. I was surprised when you teased me; you were so deep in depression. It was then I realized you had an irrepressible sense of humor.”

Closing her eyes and breathing slowly, she nestled closer into his arms, finding the best position for soft comfort.

“I was sinking deeper into despair every day. Rescued by a rabbit,” she chuckled quietly. “I never thought it would be Peter Rabbit who would rescue me from my isolation and grief.”

Peter heard Hayley sigh and her body relaxed against him. He kissed her forehead and stroked her cheek. *Every day, I deal with people who have survived traumatic events, but Hayley's Peter Rabbit must protect her before that bloody psychopath does her worst. Maybe Christine is right. It might be better for her to know.*

He waited, summoning the courage to tell her what he knew. He swallowed hard and finally dove in.

“Darling, I believe I know now who the criminal is and I will protect you and keep you safe. It’s a little late, but I feel I must tell you. Chris wanted to tell you this morning, but I waited...”

Peter looked down at Hayley and realized she had fallen asleep. Lying beside Hayley, he thought miserably, *My God, what am I doing? What have I done?*

Christine curled up on the bed with the pillow over her head. She lost all interest in the forum now that Jaxx was gone. She didn’t log on to read board messages that night, but, if she had, she would have seen that the forum was alive with news about Jaxx.

The furor began as a rumor that Jaxx was not faithful. It blew up after a one woman, heartsick from the loss of her Jaxx, wrote a eulogy and posted his declarations of love for her. After that, the women copied their Private Messages from Jaxx to the open forum. When they learned he'd written the same meaningless words to all of them and they were crushed, irate and bewildered.

If he's been dead for six weeks, then who wrote all those erotic messages?

JAXX

"In Jaxx' London studio flat, there was a battered and rusty birdcage that he'd found in a junkyard. Inside the cage were dozens of colorful origami birds with all the forum women's names, including Chris,' written on them. Each day, he shook up the cage, reached in the door, and pulled out three brightly colored birds."

Jacques Bonnier

~41~

"(A mother) discovers with great delight that one does not love one's children just because they are one's children, but because of the friendship formed while raising them."
~ Gabriel Garcia Marquez~

Seven Valleys Estate
Wolds-on-Thames Village
Oxfordshire, England
July 2005

Just before guests were to arrive for the weekend, Emily Thirtle set out a dinner buffet on the terrace. William's family arrived, and while their parents were settling in and chatting with Edward in the drawing room, the youngsters headed for a swim before carpenters laid a thick wooden floor over the pool.

Barbara cuddled Diva while she sat on the terrace overseeing James and Sarah splashing in the pool. It wasn't long before Matthew sped up the tree-lined gravel road in his vintage silver Aston Martin DB5 and parked haphazardly near his space inside the garage. His arrival alerted Maggie and Lizzie who left their poolside vigil to welcome him.

"Hullo, my girls," he stopped to greet the dogs, lifting and stroking each of them. The dogs trotted at his heels up the footpath, positioning themselves between Matthew and the buffet table. They knew he'd slip them a treat from his plate.

Matthew crossed the shady terrace and tossed his cowboy hat into a chair. Behaving as though no one else was there, he helped himself to the buffet and threw tidbits to the dogs. Finally, he acknowledged his mother's presence.

"So, Peter's here?" Matthew turned from the table munching a sandwich while he sauntered toward his mother. "I noticed his stodgy old Bentley's parked in the garage. Where is he? I saw the horses being ridden in the pasture. Is it Peter and Company?"

"Hullo to you, too, Matthew. You're being especially rude today." Barbara couldn't force a smile, her blue eyes were frosty, and her voice had a hard edge. "But, come and give me a hug. It's the price you'll pay to get information about Peter."

"Hullo, Mum. It's always a pleasure to hug my favorite girl. Whose cute little Yorkie is that?"

"This is Diva, Hayley's pet. I know you aren't the least bit interested in hearing about Peter. I'm assuming someone else has aroused your curiosity."

"*Well, hell, yes,"* Matthew smirked. "So, where are they? Riding? I can't wait to see the hermetically sealed, ugly American heiress Peter's trying to snag. Tell me, Mum, is she as dour and humorless as my brother? I hope she's got enough dosh to float this family once we come up short." He sniggered at the grim expression on his mother's face.

"Heaven's Matthew, that's crass!" Barbara frowned and spoke sharply, "Why would you say something like that? You always get your generous handouts, don't you?

"Well, I..."

"Look, I'm not going to mince words, Matthew. I do hope you'll behave this weekend and do not create a row. Try not to *prove* you're the black sheep of this family, won't you?"

Matthew's shortcomings were increasingly irritating to Barbara and she feared that eventually he'd regret his demeaning attitude toward his oldest brother. She planned to have a serious talk with her husband about their youngest son's arrogance, his appalling attitude toward his family, his dalliances with women, and his lack of initiative.

"To answer your question, Peter is not here, but will be along shortly. He's been staying in London and has organized a car and driver. He's bringing his Hayley with him."

"Oh, right. That bit makes sense. I suppose they're stopping overnight in London to shop at Harrods. Tell me though, Mum, will Peter fancy sporting his hair shirt this weekend? Will they both fit into Peter's shirt, or was he clever enough to have Harrods knit one for his meal-ticket's very own?"

"I'm warning you, Matthew," she cautioned, "don't cause any problems this weekend. Hayley is bringing two friends to visit with us for a few days and I don't want any incidents because of your nonsense."

"*What*? This woman travels with wingmen? *Brilliant!* Peter has pets! You've really piqued my interest, Mum."

Matthew enjoyed verbal fencing with his mother. She was often good at parrying, but rarely a good sport when it came to her favorite son.

"Do behave yourself, Matthew, and don't be flippant with me. Your rudeness and fiendish humor are not appreciated."

"Oh, but Mum, I've been so looking forward to this weekend," Matthew's charming smile didn't hide the sarcasm in his voice. "I'll especially enjoy Peter's new cats and dogs. Does he keep them kenneled, or does he have them on leashes? Oh, but I do suppose when they get here, he can just let them run wild with Maggie and Lizzy. And little Diva, too. Are they trained to understand commands, or when I meet them, do I just go...*Woof-Woof...meowwww?"*

Barbara chuckled to herself. *You're in for a big surprise, bucko.*

"We both know you're here because you didn't have a choice, *Romeo*. This is a command performance. Your father would skin you alive if you missed my Fourth of July celebration."

"Too true, Mum," Matthew turned away from his mother and muttered, "*Too damned, bloody-well true*."

The limo meant to drive them to Oxfordshire arrived at the Ritton on time. It was a leisurely hour's journey from London to Wolds-on-Thames and the smooth road wound through the picturesque rolling green hills and vales of Oxfordshire. The women enjoyed the purple and yellow wildflowers in the meadowlands along the countryside and watching the sheep and dairy cows grazing in the pastures.

While they traveled, Hayley asked Peter to tell the history of Seven Valleys to Christine and Pookie. "I know this is a huge event, Peter, what is planned?"

"Oh, right, Hayley, I'll tell you lot about it whilst we ride."

He recounted the estate's history beginning with Simon de Valle and ending with the festival. "My mother and sister-in-law, Jessica, manage the planning committee for the annual Wolds-on-Thames and Seven Valleys Arts Festival. They have help from dozens of workers from the town and volunteers from charities that will benefit from the event. They put up the Shakespeare troupe in village bed and breakfasts, but my parents entertain Sir Adrian at the manor. This little nicety assures my mother that Matthew has a role in at least one of his plays when they get to the summer playhouse in Utah.

The local Oxxette Youth Orchestra and choir will arrive from Oxford on Sunday afternoon to give their concert. These are high school students whose talent qualified them to be taught by members of the Oxford Chamber Orchestra."

"Tell us more about the estate, Peter. How does it work holding the festival there?" Chris leaned forward and took a bottle of water from the ice chest.

"I'm guessing that you all know this estate is a working farm as well as a parkland and manor. The gardeners will take people on walking tours of the rose gardens. This year my mother took a design from a jokey tie Matthew gave my dad at Christmas for vests. The outlandish whimsical print is bright pink and turquoise with red and white roses outlined in black and the design has spiders and bees all over it," he laughed. "She had the vests sewn for everyone to wear, including my dad and my nephew, James, who will assist dad taking guests for a ride on the farm's train through the estate's pastures and vineyards.

"I'd like one as a memento," Pookie spoke softly. "Would that be possible?"

"Of course, Pookie, the gardeners will sell them at a booth. I'll see to it that you each have one to wear if you'd like. You may be interested in collecting a few things to take back with you. Local artists and craftspeople will set up white marquées and sell their creations. The theme this year is angels and fairies and they must use those images for anything they've created to sell at the festival. Local restaurants and pubs bring in food and serve all weekend. It will be fun to see how creative the food vendors can be with the theme."

"I'd imagine angel food and fairy cakes will be a given," Hayley said, chuckling.

"No doubt," Peter grinned, "and finally, after all costs are paid, the money from ticket sales this year will go to charities to benefit children cancer victims and women's breast cancer research."

Pookie asked, "Does the family allow the festival to be held on the estate as their involvement with the community?"

"Yes, Pookie, we do; the family's been involved for nearly one hundred years. The festival is over Saturday and Sunday for the public, but the family will gather for a long visit from Friday to Tuesday.

Well, we're almost there. Mum and Dad are delighted that you're here and are looking forward to spending time with all three of you." He beamed at Hayley and gently squeezed her hand. "I'm looking forward to you meeting the rest of the family."

Peter used his remote to open the gates and the long black limo eased into the driveway. As they approached the manor house, Pookie took a deep breath and slowly whistled through her teeth.

"I thought Chrissy was leading me down the road to Hell on this trip, but I was wrong," she murmured to Peter. "I've landed smack in the middle of an episode of the Lifestyles of the Rich and Famous. Peter, it wouldn't surprise me if your family fills potholes in this road with Simon de Valle's gold doubloons."

Peter laughed, "Not that I'm aware, Pookie, but you can dig around if you'd like. I think all you'll find will be Churchill, Maggie, and Lizzy's buried dog bones and some pieces of centuries old broken wagon wheels."

The family had gathered on the terrace at the rear of the house for afternoon tea, when the limo driver wound his way up the road to the front door. The dogs heard car doors slamming and jumped up, yapping, and racing full bore through the house. The entire family followed closely behind.

Chris took off her oversized sunglasses and stood staring up at the enormous honey-colored stone edifice. It was striking and so immense it made the house in Laurel Canyon seem puny by comparison, but the *Power House* was spacious by anyone's standards. Peter had explained that the limestone of Oxfordshire used to build the house was quite like that of the Cotswold's, and in England, gardens are an extension of the house, with the style of one complimenting the other. *Yes, I see exactly what he means.*

A figure moved in front of Chris, invading her space. Her view of the house disappeared and in its place stood Matthew Gabriel-Johns. He stood too close and stared down at her. Chris smiled faintly, nodded, and backed away.

Moving to the other side of the group, Chris hid her eyes behind sunglasses while she looked furtively at this golden boy. *He's a younger, slimmer, more laid-back version of Peter, dressed in tennis shoes, a pale blue tee and tight jeans that outlined every muscle in his body. This man exudes charisma and tremendous sex appeal. I've never seen a more seductive face outside Hollywood. His virility would appeal to all women. Peter mentioned he's nearly thirty, but he looks far younger. He has freshness, youthfulness, a healthy outdoors quality, and that masculine magnetism that is so irresistible to women.*

Matthew moved toward Chris and there was a warning within her; like a bell pealing, forewarning her that for her own well-being, this man was *off limits*.

"Hullo, there; I'm Matthew Gabriel-Johns." He smiled casually, but she heard seduction in his voice. "And you are...?"

"Hello, Matthew. I'm Christine Wyndham," she shook his proffered hand and looked into eyes the color of a bright, cloudless sky. "I'm a friend of Hayley and Peter's, and I'm very pleased to meet you." Chris smiled widely revealing perfect teeth.

"Not nearly as pleased as I," Matthew crooned. They pulled their eyes away from each other when William's family gathered around Chris for introductions.

Pookie, who was nobody's fool, caught the way Matthew was eyeballing Chrissy. She often wondered why Chris was so naïve. She settled on the assumption that it was simply a lack of experience with men and wondered if she was even aware that Matthew was coming on to her. *Oh, this can't be good; I'm going to warn Peter.*

Peter, who watched his brother slithering over to Chris, knew Matthew's reputation as a blackguard and rake with women. *I see trouble ahead; I'm going to warn Hayley.*

Hayley, although preoccupied with hugging Barbara and Edward, happily reclaiming Diva, and being introduced to the rest of the family, felt the heat from the spark between Matthew and Chris. She exchanged glances with Peter as if to say, I see t*rouble brewing; I'm going to warn Pookie.*

Matthew was smitten by Christine's long graceful neck and tousled blonde hair, her dreamy blue eyes and winning smile. Her sweet doll's face captivated the romantic in him. An artist at heart, he missed nothing about a woman. He was aware that she was a tad shorter than her friends, but appeared tall and slender dressed in a white pantsuit and a pink straw hat. He preferred his women fragile and petite, and imagined how her whole body would feel against him in a long embrace. The touch of her skin aroused him when he held her hand.

Handsome and suave, Matthew Gabriel-Johns possessed many irresistible charms but his virtues were few. Those very charms made shallowness and utter insincerity with women easy for him.

Sir Adrian Howard's car dropped him at the door. He approached the women with his usual flair for drama, tossing his long silk neck-scarf over his shoulder, bowing, and kissing hands. Peter had to rescue Hayley; Sir Adrian was so in awe of her beauty that he clung to her far too long, kissing her fingers, her cheeks, and locks of her hair. Sir Adrian appeared effeminate and was often mistakenly identified him as gay. The truth was that as an artistic soul, he simply admired and enjoyed classic feminine beauty.

Julie Quinlan and Barbara's sister, Patricia Van Der Piel, arrived with much less ceremony. Patricia, now known as Sister Angelica, flew with Julie to Heathrow on the same flight from New York. Barbara was excited to see her sister and her best friend from Vassar again after an entire year.

"Peter, will you show the girls to their rooms, please? Edward darling, will you help Julie and Patricia with their bags?"

Matthew turned to Chris, "I'll help you with your bags and I'll show you to your room. Which room is Christine's, Mum?"

"Oh, Matthew, dear; a moment, if you please." Barbara walked over to Matthew's side and whispered in his ear, "*How about Peter's dogs and cats, Matthew? Woof-Woof...Meow?*"

Patricia settled into her customary bedroom and after a short rest, went to the chapel to meditate and pray. The site for the new chapel was not far from the family's ancestral burial ground. Graves dated back to the seventeenth century. The family held William and Jessica's wedding and the children's baptisms in the new chapel. They gathered there to meditate and pray together in good times and bad, but Patricia was solely responsible for the chapel.

The two sisters remained very close and Patricia transferred her trust fund to Barbara when she began teaching mathematics in a Catholic girls' school. After spending a few years teaching, she went into a convent and took a vow of poverty.

Patricia made only two provisions for the gift. Most important to her was that Barbara and Edward would build a new chapel on the estate to replace the crumbling stone chapel allowing her to make all the major design decisions. Only four people -- Patricia, Barbara, Edward, and Peter -- knew the second provision.

Patricia invited Barbara to join her for a few minutes of respite and the two sisters whispered together in an intense and highly charged conversation. Barbara was solemn when she left the chapel. Patricia's past had caught up with her. Her life was about to change and Barbara wondered if it would be for the better or for the worst.

Guests went their separate ways throughout the evening. Over several glasses of an excellent Bacchus wine produced from the estate's vineyards, the two celebrities, Sir Adrian and Julie, shared increasingly dramatic accounts of the highlights of their long and fabulous careers, and the lowlights of their many short and turbulent marriages.

Little Sarah attached herself to Hayley and took possession of Diva. The tiny Yorkie was enjoying the time of her life with all of Sarah's attention and cuddling.

James curled up on Peter's lap entranced by wild, new stories of Simon de Valle's derring-do on the high seas until his mother collected him at bedtime.

Matthew drove off to have a pint or two with his mates at the Snuggery Pub in Wolds-on-Thames.

Peter joined William and Edward who were walking the grounds discussing Edward's new winery venture, the sorry state of Britain's politics, and the state of the family's diverse financial interests. They could talk freely, without Matthew present, about their involvement in a covert venture with a British consortium of investors.

Barbara sat with Christine and Pookie on the terrace enjoying a glass of sherry.

"I'm interested in your careers and how you met. I should think working in a newsroom is fun and exciting. It's so different from my work. Besides my charity work, I'm self-absorbed as an artist, expressing what I alone see and feel. I work in quiet and solitude, but you are in the midst of chaos every day, confronted and bombarded every second by world issues and dire circumstances. However do you do it without becoming frazzled?"

"This is how frazzled looks, Barbara." Chris laughed. "Well, Pookie and I worked together for several years in Cleveland producing a news program. Of course, you already know how Peter met Hayley. The seeds that you planted after the tragedy really blossomed when she wrote to him on his website. He suggested a cyber-meeting on an internet forum that he was moderating and that's where Hayley and I rekindled our friendship. We met in high school, but joining the forum reintroduced us and we've become close friends since then. If it weren't for the forum, we might not ever have gotten together again."

Barbara looked thoughtful for a moment and sighed.

"My dear, I often find that how things come together is one of life's greatest mysteries."

Chris looked into Barbara's eyes to see if she could read meaning behind her thought.

"Someday we'll have to discuss that comment, Barbara."

"I really wasn't keen on Chrissy joining the forum, but I confess, I feel fortunate to have met Peter and Hayley. Frankly, my fear about forums is the predators," Pookie looked directly at Chris. "There are a lot of them out there and many young girls and unsuspecting women are terribly vulnerable. I worry about Chrissy; I think she's naïve. She wouldn't recognize a predator if he jumped up and waved a sign in her face." With her nose inches away from Chris, Pookie waggled her fingers and spoke in a deep, scary voice, "*I am Pook-a-pred-a-tor'.*"

"Well, maybe so," Chris chuckled at Pookie's antics, "but seriously, I'm aware that predators are everywhere, men and women alike. We are their prey and their victims no matter who or where we are."

Chris wondered if Scotland Yard had made any progress on its investigation into Zara Chandler. She made a mental note to follow up with a call to Detective Chief Inspector Bob Bowkler in the morning.

Seven Valleys ~ Wolds-On-Thames ~Arts Festival~

Barbara arose at dawn Saturday morning before the festival began. She sat on the terrace alone watching the sun come up and thanking God for the dry weather. She balanced on the wide stone balustrade to enjoy the peaceful vistas of the estate before the festivities changed the landscape for the next two days. There were times when she wondered about the wisdom of doing this. The first day of the festival was one of them. If this weren't an already long established tradition, she would have never committed to it. She detested having masses of people violating the estate. *Oh, well, noblesse oblige, then*, she sighed, while she enjoyed a cup of coffee in the cool morning air.

By six o'clock, vendors and volunteers appeared and began to erect huge white marquées over the tennis courts and set up dining tables and chairs. Restaurants and pubs delivered their serving and warming tables for food and beverages.

The festival was underway. At ten o'clock, the first busload of visitors arrived at the gate. The estate's uniformed security guards took tickets and stamped hands. Stone steps and walkways that separated three manicured grass terraces were crowded with people. Tents and tables where artists and artisans sold their creations cluttered the lawns. The gardeners roped off the sloping banks of floral parterres close to the manor house and the stone terrace along the back of the house that served as a stage. The audience watched productions from rows of chairs set up on the floor over the pool. Others stretched out or sat on blankets and low lawn chairs on the grassy terraces.

Seven year-old Sarah's dancing in the Saturday afternoon Morris was the highlight of the weekend for the family.

"Sarah, you must relinquish Diva to get ready," Jessica reminded her daughter, who had taken ownership of the tiny dog. "That is, unless you're going to tie her to your apron strings."

Sarah reluctantly handed the dog to Hayley, jumped up and down and danced while all the women helped dress her in the Molly Dancing costume. Her mother buttoned up her long pink flowered dress with the ruffle around the skirt and tied a big bow in the crisp white apron. Her doting group of ladies-in-waiting admired how sweet and fresh she looked.

Pookie never before heard of Morris dancing and she whispered to Chris, "Do you know what they're talking about?"

"I just asked Hayley," Chris whispered. "Briefly, the Cotswold Morris is a traditional folk dance in villages around Oxford in the spring. It's an exhibition or pageant for the entertainment of the villagers. The dancers wear dozens of bells on their legs, wield sticks or handkerchiefs, and dance to lively folk tunes."

"Oh, yeah; is that where the poem came from, *Rings on her fingers and bells on her toes, she shall have music wherever she goes?"* She giggled, "I'm willing to put bells on my fingers and toes!"

"Pookie, I can see you don't know your nursery rhymes," Barbara overheard Pookie and laughed. "That is a poem about Lady Godiva. So...can we expect to see you ride a cock-horse in the nude?"

Then, Barbara confessed to Sarah that she had a secret.

"A secret, grandmum, can you tell me, now?"

"Yes, it's time to tell you and I don't think anyone but your mother and I know this. Your father will play his lute and your Uncle Peter will play his violin with the band. Your Uncle Matthew will play the fool."

Pretending to faint, Sarah fell over backward on the bed.

"Uncle Matt will play the fool?" She giggled. "You're joking! That's rather in character, then, according to what my dad says."

Barbara's cheerful expression darkened. "I admit I'm a bit put off by Matthew at the moment. He should play the part well."

At two o'clock, they took Sarah to the dance floor constructed over the pool. The men dancers were dressed in the usual Morris costume of white trousers and shirts, decorated with red and yellow ribbons, sashes and bells. The women were dressed much like Sarah in long dresses of pastel colors and white aprons.

"Sarah is a beautiful dancer," Hayley commented to Barbara and Jessica. "All the girls are darling, but she's graceful and is more confident about the steps than the others."

"I agree with Hayley. She has – *you know* -- the natural presence of an entertainer."

Jessica rolled her eyes. "Oh, *please* don't tell her that. She already entertains us with songs and dances that she makes up and practices in front of a mirror when she thinks no one is watching."

After a reel, the dancers invited those who thought they could keep up to join them for the last set.

"Come on, Chris and Pookie," Hayley pulled them onto the dance floor. They were all wearing blue jeans, white tee shirts, and Barbara's bright pink and turquoise gardeners' vests. Sarah showed them the steps and they danced jigs, polkas and reels, but their feet tangled in each other's as they tried to swivel and swing their ankles and legs. Pookie broke into a hula when they realized they were on display.

"The crowd is watching us, Chris, waiting for us to make fools of ourselves." Hayley laughed. "I don't care, do you?" Christine smirked and followed Pookie's hula steps.

Peter and William knew the music and kept up with the band. Matthew, playing the fool, beat a colorful toy drum in time with the music. He had streaked his face with ash and wore an old red checked shirt, a huge pair of yellow clogs, and an old derby, the hatband stuffed with flowers and weeds

Matthew's job was to collect money from the audience. Chris, Pookie, and Hayley threw pound coins at him. When he bent over to pick up the coins from the ground and put them in his pouch, they pelted his upturned bottom with water-filled balloons that Jessica had slipped to them.

Peter was relaxing and listening to the loud calliope music piped all over the grounds. He was standing close to the entrance when he noticed a woman sneaking past the ticket takers. Something about the way she moved alarmed him and raised prickles on the back of his neck. She was a blonde-haired woman with huge sunglasses and a flowing dress that covered her figure. She carried a large pouch. By the time he'd alerted the police parked outside the gate, the trespasser had disappeared into the crowd.

The police came onto the grounds and he described the woman and told them what she was wearing.

"Don't just go by the hair color. It looked like a wig."

Terror overtook Peter. He ran toward the vendors searching for Hayley and found Chris.

"Peter, what's wrong. You're all out of breath."

"Chris; where is Hayley?"

"She was right here with me a moment ago," Chris said, looking around. "She might have gone back to the terrace to sit with Barbara. I'll go with you."

They hurried to the terrace where Barbara and Edward were sitting with the dogs. Swallowing hard, Peter said, "Mother, where is Hayley? If she isn't with you, I must find her." He couldn't breathe and his heart felt like it would burst through his chest.

"Peter, she went down to a vendor to buy an angel that she saw earlier. She left the terrace with Chris about fifteen minutes ago. I'm surprised she hasn't come back yet. What's wrong? You're both so pale you look like you've seen a ghost."

"No, Mum; I've seen something far more frightening. Hurry, let's all go look for her. We have to find her fast, or..." Peter's mobile rang and he answered while he was running toward the vendor tables. "You have her? Oh, thank God. He stopped, closed his eyes, took a deep breath, and exhaled slowly. Hold her for me, sir. I'll be right there."

"Each time we spotted her, she was wearing a wig of a different color. She ran us through the crowds, amongst trees, around fountains, and statuary. We caught up with her hiding under a table drinking a bottle of ale, but she slid out the other side and ran off. We finally caught her in front of a vendor's table standing very close behind a blonde-haired woman in one of your bright, flowered vests. This is her I.D."

"I *knew* it was Zara Chandler," Peter said, his hand trembling while he held the I.D.

"We searched through her pouch for weapons, but found only her wallet, keys, some silk scarves, several wigs, and her festival ticket. Our officers hauled her off the estate and put her in a police car that will take her down to the village."

They walked to the entrance and an officer grabbed Zara's arm and pulled her out of the police car.

"Can you give a positive identification that this woman is Zara Chandler?"

Zara was looking directly at him with a smirk on her face.

"Yes, that's Zara Chandler," he said, glancing away from her, his stomach churning.

"Do you want to press charges for trespass, Dr. Gabriel-Johns?" asked a police officer who pulled her from the squad car.

Peter's voice was tight, "Yes, I do want to press charges, but not only for trespass. She has disobeyed this court order." He reached into his back pocket, produced the Court Injunction, and showed it to the officer. "How long can you hold her?"

"I don't know, sir. You'll have to call London Scotland Yard and ask what you need to do. In the meantime, we'll hold her at the village station."

"No, I would like *you* to call Detective Chief Inspector Bob Bowkler at London Scotland Yard. He's aware of this case and will give you instructions on what to do."

The officer nodded and then Peter watched the police car drive away toward Wolds-on-Thames.

If only I could prove Zara Chandler was responsible for these tragedies. Bowkler was right; all the evidence was circumstantial or hearsay. I'll take what I know to the police when I return next week to New York City with Hayley, but for now, we know where she is. Locked up where she should be.

The family, guests, and staff were exhausted by the time the festival was over, but at least, for Emily, meals would be simple and easy for a few days. Restaurants and pubs delivered copious amounts of leftover prepared food to thank them for hosting the festival; enough to stock the freezer for a while.

Julie, Patricia, Chris, and Pookie were leaving Seven Valleys on Tuesday after the Fourth of July celebration. Sir Adrian was so enamored with the ladies that he decided to make it his pleasure to stay on and leave with them.

Jessica confided to William while getting ready for bed that she had searched for flaws in Hayley. "Simply because I'm a catty woman," she laughed, "but I couldn't have found a better match for Peter if I'd ordered her custom made. Your mother's anxious for Peter to ask Hayley to marry him. I told her that her son can fanny around with the best of them."

Yes, earlier in the day I spoke to her about Peter, too. She said she doesn't know what he's waiting for and that if he doesn't ask her soon, she'll be forced to propose for him."

"Matthew was aware that she was a tad shorter than her friends, but appeared tall and slender dressed in a white pantsuit and a pink straw hat."

Christine

~42~

"Whatever is in any way beautiful hath its source of beauty in itself, and is complete in itself;
praise forms no part of it.
So it is none the worse nor the better for being praised."
~ Marcus Aurelius Antoninus~

Seven Valleys Estate
Wolds-on-Thames Village
Oxfordshire, England
4 July 2005

The Gabriel-Johns family and guests gathered together on the Fourth of July to celebrate, "Barbara Day," and she never let her children forget they were half-American. They hauled out and dusted off traditional in-jokes about being half-breeds and half-wits. The wit and good breeding halves, they said, belonged to the British. They chose to ignore the American half.

Barbara chuckled and with raised eyebrows she said, "I find your remarks taxing and if you half-Brits want to start another war, *this* American will win...*again*!"

Each member of the family played a patriotic American song on his or her instrument. They gathered in the formal living room and Hayley joined them to play *Give My Regards to Broadway and Proud to be an American* on the grand piano.

Afterward, they'd taken walks around the estate, through the vineyards to the new winery. Emily served afternoon tea after which they all excused themselves to rest before dressing for a formal dinner, the culmination of the long weekend's events.

American and British flags stood proudly on each side of the fireplace in the gracious drawing room. The gardeners placed hundreds of red and white roses along with bluebells in vases on nearly every surface in the room. The roses scented the air with their sweet perfume and the room glowed with soft candlelight.

Edward invited the men to gather early to choose wine and champagne for the evening. Emily Thirtle waited just outside the drawing room and they brought their selections to her.

She'd grudgingly allowed caterers into her kitchen to prepare the starters and the evening meal and handed over the wines. The caterers prepared bite-sized phyllo wrapped asparagus with hollandaise flavored cheese spread; small sandwiches with prosciutto, sun-dried tomatoes, garlic and basil; and an assortment of spicy savories, all topped with delicate edible decorations.

This is the last time I'll permit those sad cows to come in, use my equipment, and make a mess in my kitchen. I'll just not have it, I won't.

At six o'clock, this elegant group of people began to gather for the evening's festivities. The men were handsome in their formal white dinner jackets and white bow ties. They laughed and chatted congenially while Emily walked amongst them carrying a tray of wine and delicious starters.

"Ah, this is lovely food, Emily."

"Delicious starters, Emily; thank you."

They helped themselves while she nodded and smiled at compliments, taking credit for the food that was beautifully prepared by other, more expert, hands.

Emily relished appreciation and praise for the food more than she would have if they told her she was the most beautiful woman in the country. Unwarranted praise for skill in the beauty of food preparation she could happily accept, whereas, honest praise given to a woman for her beauty, she could not.

Emily disappeared into a secluded corner to watch once the women appeared, dazzling in elegant *haute couture*. One by one, the women scattered amongst the men, adorning the room like a breathtaking collection of sparkling jewels.

Before Emily left her dark, secluded roost and returned to the kitchen to refill her tray, she passed judgment on the women dressed in their beautiful gowns. *Beauty begets pride and vanity; like this house full of women. These false women, prideful and vain, all bear my contempt.*

When Barbara arrived, she smiled at her husband from across the room. Her pale blue lamé gown that flowed down her slim body and pooled at her feet was dramatic with her honey-colored hair and blue eyes. She wore her mother's earrings with smaller diamonds surrounding a center tanzanite. Edward brought a glass of champagne to his wife and encircled her waist.

"Darling, you truly are a stunning woman...even if you are American." They both smiled and Barbara kissed his forehead.

"Edward, you have always been the most handsome man in any room."

"Thank you, dearest, a toast to the most beautiful and delicate of my flowers."

He lifted his glass and looking lovingly into her eyes.

Jessica's dark beauty shined in a turquoise chiffon gown and William was handsome in his dinner jacket. They sat holding hands and their faces held the expression of young lovers. Watching them, one could tell that after nearly ten years of marriage, they still enjoyed each other's company.

A nanny entertained their children in another part of the house. She fed them; they played with the dogs; played Zingo; and watched the movie, Nanny McPhee, until bedtime, when she read Mary Poppins, and tucked them into bed.

Hayley dressed modestly in a two-piece vintage white chiffon dress. Silver embroidery adorned the high collar, yolk, and long sleeves in a white floral design embellished with crystal beads, pearls, and sparkling iridescent sequins. A sapphire blue satin cummerbund accented her narrow waist and fastened above a ruffled peplum. The flowing skirt fell over her slim hips and softly flared at her feet. She'd casually swept her hair into an up-do held in place with diamond clips that allowed long tendrils to curl about her face and neck.

Sister Angelica dressed simply in an unadorned onyx chiffon frock and wore her childhood gold cross around her neck. She went to Hayley's side and took her hands.

"My dear, the elegance of your attire becomes you. You look so graceful and serene, a glorious vision from the past as though you might rightly belong among Edwardian society."

"Thank you, Sister Angelica." Hayley reached for Patricia's hands. "This dress was one of my mother's last vintage designs for sale at her *atelier, Antiqué de Classiquite*. I was ecstatic to find it. The dressmakers pay careful attention to detail and each dress from the shop has a parchment certificate signed by my mother with a handwritten note about the construction and historic period of the dress. I'm saddened that Buddinghill's may close the shop. When I return to New York, I must act quickly to save it."

Sister Angelica squeezed Hayley's hands and then looked toward the center of the room. She glanced at Chris and Pookie, and observed the contrast between one's fair, blonde loveliness and the glow of the other young woman's mellow beauty.

Pookie's waist-length black hair was lustrous and wavy. Earlier in the day, Edward presented her with a crown of peach and white rosebuds, tiny bluebells, and delicate sprigs of fern he'd fashioned for her to wear. It was perfect with her floor-length, silk Hawaiian print dress of bright sea and coral colors and patterns.

"Aloha, Pook-a-luscious!" Hugging her friend and admiring her beauty, Chris said, "Kalia-Malika, tonight you look like a Hawaiian princess and as charming as your name."

"Chrissy, you are my own personal glitterati. Your taste in clothes has blossomed along with everything else about you. You've recreated yourself as a full-bloomed fashionista!"

Pookie twirled Chris around to see the back of her dress and drew her breath in when she noticed the sexy low back. She hoped Chrissy was aware that she would certainly have Matthew's attention tonight.

Christine felt radiant in a rosy pink gown with sparkling rhinestone and silver sequined straps that criss-crossed the bodice and the low back. The empire waist hugged her slender figure. She wore diamond earrings and the effect was dazzling. She had studied herself in the mirror after she dressed and was satisfied that all her hard work was well worth the effort.

Julie appeared on the scene in an off the shoulder gauzy copper-colored dress, which she accented with elegant topaz jewelry that was lovely with her auburn hair. It wasn't long before Sir Adrian sidled up to her carrying two glasses of champagne.

"My dear, I'd like to toast a magnificent woman and an impressive actor, who has traveled across a wide continent and spanned an ocean to grace this celebration."

"Thank you, Sir Adrian," Julie lowered her eyes and nodded toward him with a pert smile. "I must say, it's been lovely meeting you. We'll meet again; I'm sure. I plan to attend your Summer Playwrights in the Park. Utah isn't so very far for me to travel and I promised Barbara I will keep an eye on Matthew while he's in the states."

She laughed at the thought of baby-sitting thirty year-old Matthew, Barbara's worrisome youngest child, her Godson.

"H*mm*...Julia, this reminds me of Love's Labor Lost. A little applied Shakespeare here. Perhaps I should watch the watcher watching good King Berowne, or in this case, the handsome and virile Matthew Gabriel-Johns."

Matthew approached Julie after Sir Adrian left to fetch more champagne and hors d'oeuvres from Emily's tray.

"You look smashing, Julie," Matthew kissed her on both cheeks. "The amber color of your gown is perfect with your hair. You still look as young as when my mother met you, actually. Hard to believe you're old enough to be my Godmother."

"*Ah, Romeo, Romeo...* 'What's in a name? That which we call a rose by any other name would smell as sweet,'" Julie said, reacting to the Godmother comment while Matthew kissed her hand.

"*Oh, lovely, youthful Juliet!* 'She doth teach the torches to burn bright. It seems she hangs upon the cheek of night like a rich jewel in an Ethiop's ear.'"

While he spoke to her, his azure eyes gazed across the room at Chris in her backless silver and rose gown. Her delicate femininity made him yearn to touch her. Tonight she was a woman about whom men wrote love songs. He thought everything about her whispered romance.

Julie followed the direction of Matthew's eyes, but Sir Adrian's appearance at her elbow blocked her view. Matthew excused himself, poured two flutes of sparkling wine, placed them on a small silver tray, and drifted toward Christine. Matthew took her hand and murmured in her ear. Chris nodded and Julie watched them glide across the room, through the atrium, and onto the terrace.

Christine and Matthew stood at the balustrade overlooking the estate's westerly parkland. The waning sun cast long streaks of light through the gathering clouds in the evening sky. Soft light filtered through the curved atrium windows, bounced off the chandelier's crystal prisms, and scattered rainbows across Chris's dress. Matthew took the liberty of allowing his hand to drift slowly down her bare back and her smooth skin pleasurably aroused him. She was so lovely, fragile, and petite, he mused...and then he said without thinking, "I've been admiring your lovely gown. The color so suits you and I thought to myself, Christine is as lovely as an English Rose."

Christine felt completely out of her depth, but decided to play along. "Matthew, you must remember that I can't be an English Rose; I'm American, just like your mother," a slight smile teased him from the corners of her lips. *Sheesh, I wish I'd have paid more attention to how girls were supposed to do this goofy, flirting stuff.*

"That's true, Christine. I stand corrected." There was twinkle of amusement in his eyes. "Then, may I say instead that you are as lovely as an American Beauty Rose? Yes, you're lovely tonight, Chris, there's nothing more I can say, but to add I am in love with the way you look."

Chris blushed, "Oh, thank you, Matthew; I'm delighted that you like my gown."

Matthew sounds as if he were quoting words from an old Fred Astaire movie. 'Someday, when I'm awfully low...I will feel a glow...just the way you look tonight...'Okay, now is he going to call me Ginger and ask me to dance? She giggled, wondering if girls really fell for his line, forgetting how easily she had fallen for Jacques Bonnier's charade.

Matthew stood so close she could breathe in his spicy masculine cologne. It was the first time she realized a man's scent could be terribly arousing. She supposed it depended on who was wearing it.

"You really must try my dad's new varietal, Christine. He allows me to name our blended wines and I wish I'd have known *you* before I named this one." He picked up one of the flutes of wine from the silver tray. "This wine, a sparking rosé, is a blend of lovely colors and exquisitely fine flavors of strawberry and summer fruit with a note of red berry." He held it up to catch the light from the chandelier's prisms. "It's a delicious, heady mixture, Christine, just like you. I named it *Blushing Angelica.*" He placed the glass back on the tray. "Here, you must taste it; I think you'll agree that it's heavenly."

Matthew stood with the length of his body against hers, his hand on her back, while he held her eyes with his. He dipped his finger in the glass of wine, slowly traced a drop around her full, soft lips, and then touched it to the tip of his tongue.

Matthew was irresistible; handsome and sensual, the powerful desire he aroused threw her off-guard. When he touched her, she tingled and felt breathless. Her quivering response to his sensuality took her by surprise. *Oh, good grief, don't let me fumble and ruin this moment even if we are both pretending and he doesn't mean a word of it.*

"Oh, Matthew," she glanced at him demurely, "the wine is delightful and the name is perfection." *Oh, good grief, I'm truly inept in a clinch. Oh, my God; I think he's going to...*

"Ah, Christine, I could get lost in your remarkable blue eyes," Matthew murmured, sliding his hand down her back to hold her firmly against him as he moved to kiss her.

"There you are, you two!" Sir Adrian barged through the atrium doors and onto the terrace interrupting the moment. "Our hosts have requested everyone's presence in the drawing room to toast America's Independence. May I escort you, Christine? You look so lovely, my dear."

Chris backed away from Matthew and patted his hand. *Saved by the queen.* She turned, took Sir Adrian's arm, blew out a silent *whoosh* of relief, and glided away from Matthew.

Hayley, Peter, and Pookie had a clear view of the atrium terrace from the drawing room windows. With their eyes transfixed on Matthew and Chris, they remained there until the couple came back into the drawing room. Peter had brought a sampling of the starters and a flute of champagne to each of the women. They unsuccessfully tried to distract one another by talking about the Walled Ladies Rose Garden.

"Most of the roses in the drawing room came from the garden my father created to honor his bride when they were married. It's in the center of the parkland surrounding the manor and it's one of the largest gardens on the estate. Doubtless, it's the most beautiful. The gardeners have planted over two-hundred of Dad's favorite David Austin roses and accented the design with tall, groomed topiaries and stone statuary. Have you walked through the parkland yet, Darling?"

"No, Peter, I wanted to see the garden with you, actually. Will you walk there with me later?"

"Of course, Darling, I planned to do that before dinner. You know, many who visit the rose garden say it's enchanted."

"Chrissy and I have been there, Peter. The willow trees hanging over the pool make the garden a peaceful glade. When we sat there today to rest and chat, Chrissy said to me, 'I heard this somewhere and I don't know who said it, but I wonder…when Edward brought Barbara here for the first time, did he say to her, 'Come into my garden, dearest; I want my roses to gaze upon you'?"

They all went their own way before dinner and Peter took Hayley to the rose garden's gazebo. Seated beside her on a white iron bench, he asked her to be his wife.

"Hayley, if I dreamed of a woman to search for, to find for myself, I could not have come close to a vision of you. You are a woman beyond my wildest dreams. I've loved you from the first moment I saw you. Then, after holding you in my heart and mind for so long, you stood in front of me at the Plaza and I thought you were so lovely and delicate. When I touched you, I knew I could no longer be satisfied only holding you in my thoughts; I needed to have you in my arms."

Hayley placed her hands in his, her eyes misty with tears. "It's because of my love and trust in you that I have been able to find courage, or I wouldn't be here with you today."

"I am so pleased that you have found the courage within yourself to begin to live your life to the fullest. Hayley, I don't want to live my life without you, so I am asking you to live your life with me. I know we'd have logistics to work out, but will you accept me as your husband with my promise to protect you and make you happy as my wife for the rest of our lives?"

"Yes, Peter, I will. I love you so very much."

He took a ring box from his pocket and opened it. "My darling, please accept this ring as an outward expression and symbol of my devotion to you. I chose this ring because sapphires have long symbolized truth, sincerity and faithfulness. The crown jewels abound with sapphires, the symbol of purity and wisdom."

Peter lovingly placed the exquisite antique sapphire and diamond ring on Hayley's finger.

"You, Darling, are the purist of all; you are *my* crown jewel."

Peter announced their engagement when they returned to the house and joined everyone waiting in front of the dining room for dinner.

"Hayley has honored me by accepting my proposal of marriage." Peter was unable to move his eyes away from his betrothed.

"Ah, Peter and Hayley; I've waited so long for this day." Barbara wrapped her arms around them. "I'm thrilled; it seems so right to have Hayley in the family."

"Peter suggested that we marry in the Sister Angelica Chapel on Christmas Day. He said that would be a perfect time and place and we hope you will all attend the ceremony."

The family and guests celebrated the engagement by toasting with a new variety of wine Edward produced on the estate and then went on to toast Chris's birthday.

Everyone gathered around them, kissing, hugging, and offering congratulations, except for Matthew. Peter watched his brother out of the corner of his eye. Matthew stood with his back to the group, poured another glass of wine, and gazed out a window.

Emily stood over the catering staff's preparation like a master sergeant shouting orders, dos and don'ts, telling them what they could and couldn't do in her kitchen. Never again would she allow strangers to invade her territory. She would see to it. She impeded their efforts at every turn and criticized their creation of savory roast leg of lamb and gravy flavored with rosemary and thyme, baked onion stuffed with nuts and cheese, and a colorful creamed carrot and cauliflower terrine.

Barbara requested a Banbury apple pie with hot vanilla sauce. She told Emily it was in Pookie's honor, to see if she would guess the name 'Banbury' was from the nursery rhyme they discussed earlier. It was the only part of the meal in which Emily had no interest.

When the meal was ready, she came into the drawing room and with the air of a major domo, announced that dinner was served.

Christine studied the incredibly attractive group sitting around an enormous candle lit dining table. She pictured herself in a romantic British period drama, set in the 1900s. *This could be Mansfield Park*, she giggled to herself.

The table was set with antique silver and dinnerware that the family acquired generations ago. After the staff served the entrées, Barbara pressed a small polished gold metal box into Chris's hand.

"Happy Birthday, bonnie lass," she said, and asked her to open it.

"Barbara, there is no need to give me a gift. Just being here with your family and friends is gift enough for me."

"But, Christine, I want you to have this. Go ahead; open it." Barbara touched her cheek.

Opening the box, she found a gold angel on a chain with its wings spread holding a brilliant diamond in its outstretched hands. Pookie took the necklace and clasped it around Chris's neck.

"So, it's official? Did I just make the team? Am I a Gabriel's Angel?" Chris joked to control her emotions. "It's beautiful and I will always treasure it. Thank you, Barbara, so very much. Thank you all; this certainly has been the most special birthday of my life."

Earlier in the day, she'd received an email greeting from Diane telling her there was a birthday gift waiting for her in Laurel Canyon. She added that they would see her in New York next week while wrapping up negotiations for Beautiful Dreamer.

They never forget my birthday. Why do I struggle with this? I suppose it's because as an adopted child, I've never felt as though I fully belonged to anyone. Maybe I resent my mother dying while I was being born as if it's my fault she died. And Ben and Diane's relationship is impenetrable. Their closeness made everyone else outsiders...even me. Oh, yes, they tell me they love me and I love them very much, but this family is different. This...this is a close-knit family, not a close-knit couple who happen to have children.

Christine felt as though she belonged somewhere, maybe for the first time in her life. Filled with emotion, she wished never to remove this symbol of the Gabriel-Johns family from around her neck.

This family has room in their hearts to care about others and take them into their lives. They have cleaned out the cobwebs and moved into that big space within me where I have always rambled about alone. I have yearned to fill this cold, empty place with warmth and tenderness. Hayley moved in bag and baggage the first time I met her. From the day I met Pookie, she set up a tent in there, too. Then there's Matthew. He's there, standing on the step, trying to push the door open. It's a little scary and I'd hate to admit it, but he makes me feel things I've never felt before...do I dare open the door a crack? After what happened with Jaxx, I don't trust my judgment about men and whoa, Nellie... Matthew's a whole 'nother set of problems.

Edward stood to make a toast, breaking into Chris's internal soliloquy and bringing her back to them. "Here's to Christine; our new Gabriel-Johns' team mate," he chuckled.

"Pookie, I'd like you to have this gold ring and little silver bell." Barbara waited until they served dessert. "It's a gift from me to you."

"*Oh, Barbara,*" Pookie exclaimed and shook her head. "I wasn't expecting a gift. It's not my birthday and I didn't know there would be a gift-giving today. I don't know what to say."

"There's nothing to say, dear girl. It has a significance that you will have to figure out on your own," Barbara's smile was impish when she placed the ring on Pookie's finger. "The ring is based on a Celtic Claddagh design."

"It has two angels facing each other holding a crown with a heart in the middle. It's beautiful, Barbara, but a bell and a gold ring? I'll have to think about it."

There was never a lull in the conversation during the festive dinner and toward the end of the meal, Sir Adrian began to quiz Christine about where she grew up and asked about her family. She decided it was now or never and told them about her mother's death, the adoption, and about Ben and Diane.

"Actually three of the blockbuster screen plays my mother wrote and Ben and Diane produced were written with Julie in mind and she starred in them. *'The Cream's on Top;' 'The Second Half;' and 'Regardless of the Rumor.'* Diane won an Oscar for the screenplay, *'Remove all Doubt.'* Lucky Julie; she got to act with leading men Robert Redford, Rock Hudson, Jim Garner, and Dustin Hoffman."

A silence fell over the table and then Matthew cleared his throat. "Wow," he murmured, slowly shaking his head.

"I had no idea," remarked Julie, "that we had such a formidable celebrity among us."

"*Au contraire*, Julie, I'm just a lowly reporter for Savvy News. Plain ol' Christine Diane Horowitz Wyndham, a.k.a. Christine Diane Wyndham Horowitz, Ben Horowitz and Diane Wyndham's adopted kid."

"Chris, of course Peter and I knew, because we've been friends for so long." Hayley noticed Chris spoke of herself as their *adopted* kid. She knows we love her; I wonder why she doesn't believe her parents love her and want her.

"Okay, Chrissy, confession time. I snooped and peeked at your employment file a long time ago. Surely, you realize your employers knew who your parents are. To their credit, they never told anyone, though.

Chrissy's far too modest, so I'll have to tell you that she improved CableCoNews' Sunday program so much that it became number one in Cleveland after they used her ideas."

Sir Adrian, always up for new bankable opportunities, filed this information away for future reference.

"My dear, you are lovely and I'm delighted that I have met you whoever you are." Smiling, he rose and kissed her wrist.

Edward patted her hand when he rose to leave the table. Barbara rose, kissed Chris's cheek, and whispered in her ear, "*Ta-da*!" And on that note, dinner was over.

Peter took Hayley to the chapel to explore the magical place where they would hold their wedding. When they arrived, Hayley saw a stone plaque on the outside wall at the entrance, *Sister Angelica Chapel*, placed there by her three nephews.

"Hayley, although this is a small chapel, I've always thought it was the most beautiful edifice on the estate. My Aunt Patricia designed it as a rotunda so that it could have this beautiful fresco ceiling with its skylight. I especially like its classic Palladian architecture. She dedicated it to the Archangel Gabriel, the Messenger of God. Look at the stained glass window behind the alter depicting the Archangel Gabriel blowing a golden horn."

They moved closer to the window and Hayley read the ribbon flowing under the angel Gabriel.

Lead Us to Paradise.

Hand in hand, they walked around the chapel reading the carving on the walls between the windows. Around the entire rotunda directly below the ceiling Hayley read:

"A lover is he who is chill in hell fire...
A knower is he who is dry in the sea...
Nothing can befall us but what God
has destined for us...
Peace will be upon him who follows the right path...
We each are angels with only one wing;
we can only fly by embracing one another...
Walk through the Seven Valleys to reach
Seventh Heaven."

Carved on the back wall over the doorway to the chapel she read

"The Seven Valleys,"

And to the left alongside the door, she read --

"The Valley of Search
The Valley of Love
The Valley of Knowledge
The Valley of Unity
The Valley of Contentment
The Valley of Wonderment
The Valley of True Poverty"

Carved to the right of the exit, she read --

"True Faith in God;
Eternal in the Past, Eternal in the Future."

"All of the writings come from the Baha'i faith, Hayley. After a great deal of research into religious writings, I believed nothing could be more fitting for this family and the Seven Valleys Estate than these words and ideals."

When they left the chapel, Peter said, "Hayley, I'll take you back to the house, now. I have a problem to sort out. Matthew's obvious infatuation with Chris is of concern to all of us. He's followed her all weekend, sniffing her trail like a hound dog. I don't trust him; he's a dissolute user of women and I'm going to put a stop to it."

Matthew had changed from his dinner jacket to casual clothes when Peter found him in the garage dusting off his Aston Martin.

"Matthew, what do you think you are doing with Christine?"

"Bugger off, Peter. It's none of your business." Matthew scowled, not meeting Peter's eyes as he flicked imaginary dust off the boot with a chamois.

"It *is* my business, Matthew. I brought Christine here and I don't want to see her hurt. You know I'm not happy with your reputation. Not only do I disapprove of your dealings with women…"

Matthew interrupted, "She's just fine, Peter. If she's not happy with my attention, let *her* tell me." He cocked the cowboy hat back from his forehead.

"Matthew, I'm nipping this in the bud. I'm telling you to stay away from her. She's a vulnerable, naïve young woman and not someone I'd want a smarmy git like you to trifle with. She won't understand when you dump her the way you dump all the others. I'm surprised you don't have little Matthews crawling all over the kingdom. If I were a woman, I'm not sure I'd trust you to use precaution."

"*Sod you, Peter, you bloody prat*. Go and meddle in someone else's business. Isn't that what you do for a living?"

Scoffing, Matthew turned his back. Peter forcefully turned his brother around to face him, slammed his back against the car and went nose to nose.

"Maybe so, Matthew, I may be all the things you accuse me of, but you're not solid," he growled. "In fact, Matthew, you're so transparent, I can see right through to your bones of contention. You're making *me* the problem with *you*. When are you going to grow up and get over it? What are you afraid of…*failure?* Or maybe not; maybe it's because success comes with too much responsibility."

Matthew rebuked him in a scathing tone of voice, "Again, this is none of your business, Peter, and how I live my life is none of your business either. Now, *back off!"*

He shoved Peter out of his way and stomped off in a huff.

While Peter talked to Matthew, Pookie and Hayley knocked on Chris's bedroom door. She invited them in and they asked her to sit down.

"What's going on?" Chris looked at them suspiciously.

"Chrissy, we noticed you're spending a lot of time with Matthew. According to Peter, he has a reputation as a womanizer. We're concerned, that's all."

"We don't want to see you hurt, Chris," Hayley said.

"I can take care of myself, ladies. Please - and I mean this in the nicest way possible -- mind your own business. I'm fine."

"Yeah, right, Chrissy. You've been sighing and moping around for days over Jaxx. Take our advice and stay away from Matthew. I agree with Hayley; we don't want you to get hurt again."

"Who says I'm going to get hurt? Yes, it's true, I've been mourning Jaxx, but that's perfectly natural. He loved me and I loved him. End of story."

"Oy vey." Pookie slapped her forehead in frustration, "You have to be the densest woman I've ever met." She grabbed Hayley's hand and stomped out of the room.

After they left, Christine sat in a chair by the bedroom window. Feeling lonely and bereft, she finally admitted to herself what she wouldn't admit to Pookie and Hayley. When she met Jaxx in New York, his actions insulted her. The way he'd avoided her at the dinner and left her standing in front of the Tavern on the Green made her feel wretched. She knew then what he was.

Her bravado tonight was a cover-up for the truth; that she knew all his loving words had been just that – merely pretty words, written without truth or sincerity. She breathed a long sigh.

Touchdown; I have landed back on earth. I accept there never was a romance; the whole relationship was a farce. If I were honest with Pookie, I'd have to admit that we never loved each other in any true sense of the word. Jacques Bonnier was a man completely devoid of truth, morals, and character. I was in love with his attention and with someone saying he loved me.

The reality had been creeping up on her for a long time, but now that she fully accepted it, she felt stronger and free from emotional pain. Chris got up from the chair and went to the mirror to study her face.

She murmured, "I thought I'd look different. Same blue eyes, blonde hair, pretty face. I guess there's no outward sign of an epiphany, but yes, it's there; I can see it and feel it when I look deep inside myself."

Matthew tapped on Christine's door.

"Christine, would you fancy joining me in the Walled Ladies Rose Garden? It's peaceful and serene at this time of day."

It was dusk and fairy lights twinkled around the walls and on trees giving the garden an ethereal beauty in the fading light. Chris thought it a glorious illusion of paradise with the fragrance of thousands of roses scenting the air. The serenity of the peaceful garden soothed her wounded spirit.

When Edward created this lovely retreat for his bride it was not just for contemplation; it was the embodiment of his everlasting love for her.

She noticed that Matthew wore his cowboy hat and had changed into cowboy boots, tight jeans, and a Cambridge tee shirt, but she hadn't taken the time to change from her pink and silver gown. Matthew took her hand to help her up the stone steps to the gazebo. They sat in the very same spot where, not three hours before, Peter embraced Hayley and asked her to marry him. Now, Matthew placed his hands on Chris's face.

"Christine, dear; you are an exceptional and beautiful woman. I love everything about you. Peter is needlessly concerned about us, though. You know that women are after me all the time because of my station, my social position, and my family's wealth. I'm not ready or willing to settle into a relationship. I hope I didn't mislead you with my attention. You're not terribly disappointed, are you?

Stunned, Chris brushed his hands away from her face.

"Matthew, please don't flatter yourself. You're assuming an awful lot. Forgive me for pointing out the *obvious* to you, but regardless of what your brother thinks, there is no *us*. Clearly, you are a charming man to level with me this way." *Actually, you schlemiel, you're anything but charming*. "I've just been given a talking to by Hayley and Pookie, who were needlessly concerned. I was already aware of your lecherous reputation. Don't worry, Matthew, you're safe from me; you'd be the *last* person I'd choose. Believe me; your cornball wine-tasting performance outside the atrium this evening did nothing to turn my head. I find you totally underwhelming. Frankly, from what I've heard about you, I'd sooner be in a relationship with the Marquis de Sade."

Matthew flinched, as though stung by her words. Blinking, he said, "Oh, I see now how little regard you have for me. So, you were leading *me* on then, is that it?"

"Excuse me?" Chris abruptly rose to her feet, trembling inside from anger and humiliation, "Good heavens, no! I certainly was doing no such thing! I've only just met you, Matthew. Neither have I been leading you on, nor do I have any romantic inclination toward you. Frankly, I resent your saying such things."

Matthew stood with his thumbs hanging from his belt. "Well, you wouldn't be the first, so I assumed…" He looked away, his jaw muscle working and his voice trailing off.

Chris snapped angrily, "So you assumed *what,* Matthew? It's obviously not for your money," She smirked at the irony. "You live on handouts from your mother. *You pretentious putz.* Oh, maybe you think I'd want some connection with you for your social standing or station in life. What *social* standing is that, Matthew? You act in amateur productions. And what *station*?" She chuckled harshly, "Now, if you were descended from an Earl -- and wealthy -- like Hayley, well, *that* would be considerable station in life. No, you are anything but a good catch and I hope the unfortunate woman who *does* catch you will have enough good sense to throw you back." Her words were harsh and her expression supercilious while she glared directly into his eyes, "You haven't enough stability, fortune, or physical appeal to interest me. You are a lazy underachiever and you have not lived up to your brothers in any way. And the truth is Matthew; I don't know how other women *tolerate* you, because while we've been here, you have been nothing but a damned nuisance."

Matthew was staring at her. "I'm gobsmacked. What in bloody hell happened here?"

"What happened, *schmuck*, is that your gianormous ego led you to false assumptions and unrealistic expectations. Oh, one more thing, Matthew; you are far too long in the tooth to play Romeo. Unlike you, Romeo was a young and handsome man."

Chris walked off in a huff and went directly to Pookie's room, plopped on the bed pouting, and railed at her.

"How dare Matthew say such things to me? Who does he think he is? I've put up with him chasing after me since we got here! I wish we could leave this instant, but we're locked in until tomorrow," Chris grumbled, crossing her arms across her chest.

"Make the best of it, Chrissy. Ignore Mr. Egotistical."

"Pookie, she sighed, "Why me? Maybe I was better off scaring men away with my big, honking, rock pile of a nose. I went from one extreme to the other. Is this what women have to put up with from men? You were right, Pookie...about...everything."

"I'm sorry, I couldn't hear you. What did you say, again?"

"I said, you were right, okay? If you make me say it once more, I'll choke on it."

Well, well! I can see the tabloid headlines now; *Shocker! Bolt from the blue! Popular Savvy News reporter Christine Wyndham finally GETS it!"* Pookie tapped Chris's arm with her fist punctuating her words. "I could point out the obvious, Chrissy, but you've been roughed-up enough for one day."

"Thanks for the lovin,' Pooks. You're a big help."

"I'm sorry, Chrissy. I wish I knew how to comfort you. Look, Jessica and I promised to play Zingo with Sarah and James until bedtime. I have to go and find them."

Chris sighed. "Oh, yeah, when I came back to the house from the rose garden, I stopped to say hello to Peter and Hayley. They're with the kids and the dogs down by the pool playing Simon de Valle with swords and boats. The kids have Peter tied to a lounge chair extorting pound coins."

Back in her room, Chris changed from her beautiful gown into jeans and her *I see dumb people* tee shirt. She logged on to her laptop and contacted Savvy News and Airway News by email to verify the logistics and finalize the details of her assignment. They fixed everything for the morning of 6 July, when she would interview the witches and 7 July, to interview the Clown Cavalcade in the tube. She would meet Airway News' live action reporter, Calvin Chaser, at the station. Ironically, both days the same staff from Airway News who reported the death of Jacques Bonnier would be with Chris and

Pookie. She hoped for a miracle that they'd avoid bringing up the subject.

She flipped open her cell phone and called London Scotland Yard to check on progress.

"I'm sorry, Ms. Wyndham, Detective Chief Inspector Bowkler is not available at the moment. I can have him return your call in the morning."

"Yes, well, can you at least tell me how long they will hold Zara Chandler in Wolds-on-Thames until Dr. Gabriel-Johns can get to the station?"

"*Uh…um…*well, they let her go."

"*WHAT?*" Chris was appalled. "*Why?* Dr. Gabriel-Johns told them it was important to hold her until they talked to Detective Chief Inspector Bowkler. Why was she let go?"

"*Um...uh...*well, when they called DCI Bowkler, they told him they had no grounds to hold her. Dr. Gabriel-Johns never came to the station to file a complaint. She purchased a ticket, so she wasn't trespassing. She carried no weapons and wasn't within 100 feet of Dr. Gabriel-Johns, so they didn't feel she could be held under his court injunction. Besides, they said she was such a nice lady and…"

"Oh my God," Chris covered her eyes. "I know he told them to call Chief Inspector Bob Bowkler for directions on this matter. I distinctly heard him myself." She took a deep breath. "Please have Inspector Bowkler call Dr. Gabriel-Johns mobile as soon as possible. He has the number. Please make sure he gets my message, will you?"

"Oh, right. Sure, Miss Wyndham," he barely stifled a yawn, "*first thing*."

Chris found Peter, took him aside, and relayed the bad news. He pounded the wall with his fist, turned on his heel, and went back to Hayley.

Matthew had upset and offended Chris and visions of the way Jaxx died were tying her stomach in knots. *Now this; I'll have to learn fast how to handle everything that's thrown my way if I want to go out to play with the big kids.*

Chris turned off her cell phone and the computer and went to the terrace to sip a glass of sherry in solitude. She was enjoying the tranquility of the evening when she heard the grinding of a car engine in the distance. Curious, she walked toward the garage and found Matthew trying to start the Aston.

She went to the driver's side and knocked on the window.

"Hey! You're going to kill the battery."

He cocked his eyebrow at her and got out of the car.

"That's *naff*, Christine; how would *you* know about *that*?"

She heard the sarcasm in his voice and replied, "Believe it or not, Matthew, some women are more than arm pieces, or just standing around waiting for your booty call. Turn on the overhead light and put up the hood, or whatever you Brit's call it. You know -- the thing that covers the thing that makes the car go?" She said, as though talking to an idiot. "Do you have some rags?"

"It's the bonnet, you bleedin' American."

"Oh, that's so cute. A *bon-net*," she mocked him.

Scowling, he did as she asked. She reached into the engine, moved some wires, jiggled a few parts, twisted and tightened something, and slammed down the bonnet.

"Your distributor cap was loose, *Mis-ter Bond.*" She pursed her lips, looked down her nose, and wiped her hands. "You're good to go, *Meshuganeh*," she shrugged, tossed the dirty cloth to him and moved out of the way.

Smirking, Matthew got behind the wheel and turned the key in the ignition as though fully expecting the car to continue grinding. The car started right up. She laughed at his surprised expression. He left the motor running and got out to face her.

"*Strewth*! *How did you*...You're bloody *cheeky*, Christine," he muttered, while they stood eyeball to eyeball.

"Oh...well, *yes;* I am cheeky, Matthew. Mockery is one of my free services. You're welcome to it. You deserve it."

"*Sod you*," he said rudely, his chin jutting out.

"*Pfft...Dipstick*," she said, shaking her head.

"*Twit*," he said, scowling into her face.

"*Play-baby*," she said, glaring at him.

"*Hack*, he said, hanging his thumbs from his waistband.

"*Schlimazel*," she said, planting her fists on her hips.

"*Bugger off*," he said, turning away and jumping into the car.

"*Oh, go and get a real life, Romeo*," she said, flipping her hand dismissively.

"If anyone asks, then," Matthew shouted at her, "I'm going to drown myself in ale at the Snuggery Pub."

"Nobody *cares*, putz," she shouted back, waving goodbye.

Chris went directly to the chapel. She'd never felt more abandoned and forlorn. She'd been bouncing emotionally from high to low all day. She sat with her head bent and hands clasped in her lap.

"Why?" she whispered, thinking aloud and heaving a deep sigh. "I know that we live in a society with a system of laws, but surely, they are there to protect innocents like Hayley from predators like Zara Chandler. The *morons* let her go," she said miserably. "We don't know where she is and Hayley is at risk again. Shouldn't we *tell* her; *warn* her? Please, God, give us the wisdom to do everything possible to take care of her until they can legally put Zara Chandler away. If there is a God and you are here in this chapel, tell me... *why did you let us bring her here? Please, grant us the wisdom to know what to do and give us the advantage we need to protect her.*"

Edward had come into the chapel for a few moments of meditation. He heard Christine's murmuring and quietly sat alongside her gently taking her hand in his.

"Christine, my dear, I'm so very glad you came here to us. I know you are grieving for the loss of your loved one and I know you are worried about Hayley. We all are. You have come to this place to feel closer to God. Sometimes we blame Him for our troubles and all the ills of the world. We cannot blame God as though he's responsible for what has happened, but we can take him into our hearts and our lives to let him guide and comfort us.

I hope you have found solace in this place; that's what it's all about, Christine. And, before you leave the chapel, I want to read something to you that is written on the wall –

'We each are angels with only one wing;
We can only fly by embracing one another.'"

Edward looked directly into her eyes and lifted the gold angel around her neck. There was something about Edward that made Chris feel as if he could see into her soul. It was as if he wanted to take away her pain. *Could this man be more perfect?* She thought.

"Our door is always open to you, Christine. Come here to be with us whenever you feel the need for another wing. This family has wings to spare."

"Thank you, Edward, for your kindness."

Chris brushed his hand with her lips and left before he could see the tears overflowing her eyes. She went to her room, but what she really wanted to do was climb upon Edward's lap to be comforted and cry in his arms like a child until she ran out of tears and emotions.

Seven Valleys had given Chris a remarkable sense of being lost in time and space. She felt as though the family had not only opened their hearts to her, she'd gathered them into her heart and wanted to carry their comforting goodness and gentility away with her when she left.

Having endured enough highs and lows for anyone's Fourth of July birthday, she took a shower, and took a sleeping pill to escape her desolation. She crawled under a downy comforter, and when Hayley and Pookie looked in on her, she was fast asleep and snoring softly.

~43~

"Honest criticism is hard to take, particularly from a relative, a friend, an acquaintance, or a stranger."
~ Franklin P. Jones~

Seven Valleys Estate
Wolds-on-Thames Village
Oxfordshire, England
Fifth July 2005

Seven Valleys' festivities were over on Tuesday, but Hayley and Peter planned to stay another day to visit with Barbara and Edward. They would return to London on the night of the sixth and fly back to New York with Chris and Pookie on the eighth.

William's family had packed and were ready to return home, but Sarah was reluctant to leave tiny Diva. She climbed on her grandmother lap to kiss her goodbye and whispered in her ear.

"Grandmum, I love you and Grampie, and I love Diva and Hayley." Her grandmother encircled Sarah in her arms and hugged her while Sarah's long hair fell over her shoulders. She peeked up at her grandmother. "I wish I could take Diva home with me and have her forever. She's supercalifragilistic-expialidocious!"

"I love you, too, and couldn't agree with you more, Darling." Barbara kissed her granddaughter all over her face. "You'll be seeing more of Diva now that Peter is marrying Hayley, don't you think? Where is James? Can you find him and remind him that his grandmum is waiting to see him before he leaves? Tell him she wants a supercalifragilistic-expialidocious kiss goodbye."

"He's with Uncle Peter down at the pool playing Privateer. They're racing remote controlled boats. I'll go and get him."

Sir Adrian offered Patricia and Julie a ride to Heathrow. Barbara was driving to London and couldn't fit everything into her Rolls.

"We'll all fit into the farm's Range Rover. I have several new paintings to deliver to NobleArtists Gallery. Chris and Pookie, I'll drop you and your luggage at the London Ritton. My goodness, I'll miss having you here. I've enjoyed your visit so much! I'll be anxiously waiting for you to return at Christmas for the wedding."

Edward spent the day outdoors with Hayley and Peter. At the end of their tour, Edward took them through the greenhouse. It was there he came alive. With great animation, he described the process of rose generation.

"And," Edward said, smiling, "I am pleased to tell you that I have been chosen as a consultant to the Royal National Rose Society, an organization that is working hard to refurbish its gardens. We are planning a public opening in June of 2007. They are planting my new variety of a blush hybrid tea rose and showing it for the first time. I have yet to name the rose, but I'm quite sure I'll choose Angelica Gabriella to honor my sister-in-law and my wife. I have another lovely rose that I'm working on, but it isn't quite ready yet. It's a fragrant peach colored hybrid rose, similar to one called, 'Just Joey'."

"Edward, I'm so pleased for you." Hayley went to him and hugged him. "I think it's a wonderful gesture to honor both sisters, and Edward, I'm familiar with Just Joey. It was my mother's favorite rose, you see. She loved the clear apricot color, its large bloom, lovely fragrance, and frilly petals.

I knew Just Joey was her favorite and I always cut a bloom to put by her dinner plate. I renamed it, Lady-Beth. I'm not sure she liked my cutting the roses," Hayley chuckled, "but she never reprimanded me. Just Joey won a gold medal from the Royal National Rose Society, isn't that right, Edward?"

"Yes, my dear, it is."

"Edward, one of these days we must sit down and I'll tell you about my family history. My grandfather, Lord Weston Hayles

Townsend-Brandley, Earl of Circencester's ancestral home, Brandlebury Hall, is in Cornwall, near Hayle. My mother gave it over to the National Trust after he died. I have leased my London home in Belgravia for the time being to a diplomat. Actually, she planted a Just Joey bush in the garden and was amazed that such a beautiful rose took ten years to get over to the states.

If Hayley hadn't won Edward over before, she surely had now. His first thought was that when he passed away, the estate would continue in the best hands imaginable with his oldest son and soon to be daughter-in-law.

Barbara returned from London and joined Edward, Peter, and Hayley on the terrace. Resting and playing with the dogs while Emily served tea, they were enjoying the peaceful estate now that festival hubbub was over.

Gravel splattered against trees when Matthew sped up the winding road returning from Wolds-on-Thames. He barely missed the Range Rover that Barbara left parked outside the garage on her return from London. He swerved and came to a screeching halt in the garage, stopping within an inch of ramming the Bentley. Their peaceful teatime was over as Matthew had been carousing all night with his mates and drinking heavily all day at the Pub. He staggered across the terrace, reeking of smoke and booze.

Matthew was loud and laughed nastily, "Well, hullo, Peter, how's *tricks*?"

"Hullo, Matthew," Peter said coldly, "please join us and lose the stage voice, won't you?" *Matthew's tanked and he's spoiling for a fight with his uncouth attitude and crude reference to Hayley.*

"*Yeah*...yeah, okay, mate," Matthew stumbled backward and tipped over a chair. "But, are you sure? I am, after all, *persona non grata,*" he tossed the words with a scornful expression. "Aren't you afraid your hermetically-sealed heiress might be contaminated by the likes of me now that you've...*uh... uncorked* her?"

Barbara gasped and her hand went to her throat. Hayley flushed with embarrassment. Edward rose abruptly and beat Peter to Matthew's side. He grabbed Matthew's ear and pulled him along the terrace while Peter grabbed him from behind and shoved him through the atrium to the drawing room.

"Matthew, your behavior is *un-for-givable*!" Edward shouted when they got inside the room. "What ails you, man?"

Peter grabbed Matthew's shirt under his chin and shoved him. "*Damned you, you blighter!* If you think you can come in here..."

"*Piss off, tosser,*" Matthew yelled, knocking Peter's hand away and pinning him with a steely gaze. He held up his palm to silence Peter and said scathingly, "Don't think you can tell me what I can and cannot do in this house, Peter. It doesn't belong to you yet."

"Matthew, listen to me, you..."

"You can say nothing of interest to me, you *pillock*. I find you an unbearable, crashing bore. When you open your mouth, you suck the oxygen out of a room leaving everyone gasping for air. Save your dull *bon mots* for your patients and that includes your little wooden dolly out there."

"Why you insufferable swine," Peter swung at his brother, landing a hard punch on his chin and knocking him to the floor.

Edward's voice boomed, "*Matthew!* You are intolerable. Your years of dallying and appalling, tasteless displays of miserable behavior have seriously undermined your upbringing. I expected more from you than you've delivered. Your family has watched you fritter away years during which you were meant to choose a career and achieve stability. However, you have not. You have a fine education and you have not yet proven yourself. Why, Matthew? For God's sake man, what is your problem? And let me tell you this before you answer, if you blame Peter or your mother, or even me, I will ask you to leave and not return until you *have* proven yourself to our satisfaction."

Matthew lay on the floor looking from his father to his brother. He had the overwhelming urge to laugh. To him they looked ridiculous with their angry red faces glaring down at him.

Laughing while he struggled to rise to his feet, he said, "Well, Father, it's very simple. Peter gets the mansion, the estate, and now the heiress –a luscious, *doable* one at that - and what do I get? *Nothing.*"

"*Jesus, Matthew...you are freaking depraved,*" Peter lashed out, winding up to land another blow. "Nothing is all you deserve."

"Ah, I see," Edward replied, grabbing Peter's arm. "I'm not the psychiatrist here, but it appears to me that you simply have a terminal case of plain, old-fashioned jealousy and resentment. So that's what's been holding you back? Too bad, you're wasting the best years of your life mired in self-pity and bitterness. Maybe what they say is true, Matthew," Edward inhaled slowly, "*we get what we deserve.*"

"Matthew, we need to talk!" Peter shook his head in disgust, but Matthew cut him off.

"You have nothing of any value to say to me, Peter. Go back to your precious heiress and cuddle her on your lap, little baby that she is." Matthew glared at Peter and scoffed, "You'll have it all, won't you, brother?"

Peter's laugh was hollow, but he couldn't resist gloating, "Your envy's showing, Matthew. *Hmmm...*All those nasty barbs about my luck with women. Little did you know..."

"*Leave now, Matthew,*" his son's attitude disgusted Edward and the words virtually growled out of his throat.

"I insist you apologize to Hayley on your way out, Matthew. She's done nothing to deserve your malicious and insulting comments toward her."

"*Bugger off, wanker.*" Matthew stood white-knuckled, glaring at Peter through narrowed eyes while his chest heaved with rage.

Edward sighed. "I'll call you when it's safe to return, son. Your mother and I have a lot to say to you, but for now, leave here this *instant* or..."

"Or what, Father," Matthew interrupted, "you'll disinherit me?" Sneering, he added bitterly, "Oh, wait. You can't. Your precious Peter already gets it all."

He lobbed this volley over his shoulder while he darted from the room, his feet pounding angrily on the stone floor. He left through the front of the house.

Peter and Edward returned to the terrace and both men dropped heavily into their chairs. Edward inhaled deeply and slowly exhaled a weary sigh.

"I apologize to you, Hayley, for my son's uncouth behavior. I suspect I know what you're thinking, Babs, that I could have handled it better, but Matthew was way out of line and he's more out of control than ever."

"No, Edward, I've had the very same thoughts for quite a while," Barbara reassured her husband. "To be honest, I was sitting here applauding you." She handed her husband a cup of tea.

They heard Matthew speed away, his tires squealing and gravel spewing against the trees as the Aston slid and zigzagged along the winding road.

"I was about to explain the terms of Aunt Pat's trust to Matthew, but unfortunately, he decided I had nothing of value to say. However, we should explain the terms to Hayley."

"All right, Peter, as your future bride, I think she should know. Edward, why don't you start?"

"Hayley, as you are aware, because of primogeniture, a landowner can pass on his estate to the oldest son and that is what I have chosen to do. However, before Patricia went into the convent, she knew she'd take a vow of poverty. Because everything she owned would go to the church, several years before she became a nun, she officially gave the bulk of her trust fund to her sister. When she did that, she stipulated very specific terms that Barbara and I have honored."

"Yes, we honored her wishes to the letter." Barbara sat forward in her chair. "The Sister Angelica Chapel was built with a specified percentage of the funds. I have invested the balance in a trust for William, Matthew, and eventually their progeny. She did this to even the playing field for them when Peter, as first born, inherited the Gabriel-Johns estate. Peter is designated as manager of the trust."

"However," Peter rubbed his chin, "I have the discretion to give my brothers' trust to them at a time of my choosing, based on my opinion of whether or not they can handle the funds. I can bypass them and bequeath it directly to their progeny, or to anyone else I so choose."

Edward cleared his throat, "I've never been sure it was wise, but they were not to know about this trust, because Pat wanted them to make men of themselves and be everything they could on their own. There is no question that William has -- no question whatsoever. William is now a talented and successful surgeon, but Matthew…well, Matthew hasn't found himself yet."

"And now we have learned why." Barbara sighed and lowered her head. "I am ashamed and embarrassed for my youngest son." Her voice sounded sad and tired.

At home in London, Matthew slept off his inebriation, floating amongst the ghosts that speak to him in his dreams. These same ghosts float in the mists that often cloud the vision in his mind's eye. When he woke, his head throbbed, although his mind was clearing and he was beginning to sober up.

Slumped in a chair in front of the Tele, Matthew watched an Airway News Flash describing Chris's segment on the Breakfast in Britain program about the witches' demonstration in Hyde Park. He regretted his actions with Chris and wished he'd handled her differently.

He knew he'd have to do something big to win back his mother because of the way he'd behaved earlier at Seven Valleys. Surely, by doing that he'd raised her ire. She resented his asking for handouts and if she cut him off, she'd throw him into a financial tailspin. He knew she was already irked because of his lifestyle and his attitude toward his oldest brother.

Peter is a bloody smug and self-righteous wanker. He doesn't deserve to inherit the estate. What if he didn't have a bleedin' heiress descended from British upper class in his future? Suppose I want her for myself? What I want they consider frivolous. I love acting and it's what I want to do. Dad doesn't or won't accept that choice. He snorted; *my father, with his bourgeois mentality, thinks it's beneath them to have an actor in the family. The old man's nothing but a damned dirt farmer, piddling with his fruit and flowers. And my pernickety mother runs around hawking her calendar art and always smells like oil paint and turpentine. Who do they think they are? They're nobodies who live in a fusty old stone house on a dirt farm. They're nothing. No title and nothing to pass down to me. Why can't they just accept me for who I am?*

"What is wrong with them?" he whispered to the ghosts lingering in the room. "Why don't they appreciate me?"

Bone weary, he snapped off the lamp and the Tele, his ghosts scattering under his feet while he stumbled through the darkened room.

Falling into bed, he whispered to them --

"Come join me in my bed, ghostly Ariel and magical Prospero. Calm my turbulent waters and promise that you'll come between my nightmares and me. Amuse me in my dreams and soothe my troubled brow whilst I slumber.

For I am afraid...that I have created my own tempest."

~44~

"Going to the fortune teller's was just as good as going to the opera and the cost scarcely a trifle more – ergo, I will disguise myself and go again, one of these days, when other amusements fail."
~ Mark Twain~

Hyde Park
London, England
Sixth July 2005

"We took a taxi," Chris said to the Airway News executive producer. "We had no idea where we were going and it seemed the most expedient way to get here." *Because you didn't have the courtesy to pick us up and I'll be damned if it isn't going on my expense report.*

Cal Chaser breezed in extending his hand to Chris and Pookie.

"Well, you're right on time. Cheers! Good to meet you! I'm Calvin Chaser," he said shaking hands. "These rude blokes call me "Calamity," because…well, clearly, it's obvious from the dreadful nature of the stories I cover," he sniggered. Then, squinting at Chris, "I've seen you somewhere before, haven't I?"

Chris ignored his question and introduced Pookie.

"This is my associate from CableCoNews in Cleveland, Ohio, Kalia-Malika McKee. I was wondering if she could ride along with us for the witch hunt."

"Sure. She can untangle the cables for the tekkies."

Pookie giggled, "Call me Pookie. Calamity Chaser...that's a hoot."

The five news people got into the station's well-equipped satellite truck and drove to Hyde Park. Passing Marble Arch, they saw Speaker's Corner was already lively with the witches' activities. The witches had begun their Pointy Hats Parade and were marching in an ever-increasing circle as more and more witches arrived and joined the others. Many were carrying signs and adding their voices to the chanting and singing.

Camera rolling, Chris and Cal marched with the witches and began their interviews. She questioned them with ease and poise.

"Will you tell our viewers your name and why you are marching today?"

"I'm called Moonrise and we're marching to draw attention to the way the earth is being torn asunder. We are Pagan, one of the oldest religions on earth. As caretakers of the firmament, we resent how the earth is being mistreated for the sake of progress."

Another witch, who asked Chris to call her Hellcat, added, "We teach the basic skills of magic and ritual, working with the elements, movement, sound, and the mythology of the Goddess tradition."

Three witches resting on a huge tree stump were dressed in black and purple, two wore pointy hats; one wore flowers in her hair and they all wore long stockings of purple and orange stripes, or green and purple stripes. They carried brooms of different kinds; one a push broom, one a straw broom, and one was yellow plastic. Chris asked them if they were part of the *Broomstick Brig-A-Dears*. She got them talking on live feed; their names were Cackle and Evergreen. The third witch, Crow-Bat, was holding the leash of a small white dog dressed in a black cat costume.

"We are here," Evergreen nodded unsmiling, "to express our concern about global warming and we are part of the Paganfest called, *Witches Opposing Warming*. We are also against war...any war. So, I guess we're Witches Opposing War, too. It's important for everyone, no matter what their beliefs, to have free speech and assembly without fear."

The scene was frantic with new activity popping up everywhere. Unfortunately, Airway brought only one cameraman, who ran from Christine to Calamity, trying to cover both of them and get as much footage as possible. Chris talked fast and ran from group to group to cover as much ground as she could. The team had one-half hour to tape and then they would go back to the studio to cut for sound bites. However, the half-hour was live feed on Airway. It meant Cal and Chris were live on Airway's Breakfast in Britain morning program. This assignment was a coup for Chris because they fed it to Savvy for Slick Slate's Scoop-City and it was the first time she'd be on camera as a correspondent during a morning program.

When they shut down the camera and the interviews were over, Chris used her digital camera to capture more sights and scenes as they unfolded. The marching witches split apart and circled structures and altars at the north, south, east, and west designating the far points of Speaker's Corner. Chris quickly comprehended the structures were labyrinths and represented Spirit, Fire, Water, Air, and Earth. The witches were reading palms and tarot cards in the labyrinth of Spirit. The colorful event fascinated her and she didn't want to miss anything.

Walking backward, Chris was taking a telephoto shot of a black and orange striped spider riding an old-fashioned bicycle with a huge front wheel. She stepped on someone's foot and turned to apologize.

"*Oh, not again! Oh, for Ch-...Go away!*"

"Chris, let me talk to you. I'm here to apologize. I knew you'd be here, but please understand; I'm not stalking you."

"Good grief, Matthew," she huffed, "Can't you take *no* for an answer?" Her frown showed her annoyance and she strode away from him. He caught up with her and grabbed her arm.

"*Let go of me, Meshuganeh!*" She scowled and tried to pull away, but his grasp was firm. "Let me go, or I call police for help."

"*Please*, Chris. I need to talk to you."

She saw how miserable he was, but snapped, "Matthew, leave me alone." She yanked her arm from his grasp, "*And don't touch me again!*"

"All right, but please hear me out. Let's sit for a few minutes at a table in the Labyrinth of the Spirit and have a witches' brew. They're actually quite good." He prevailed upon her, putting his hand on her shoulder, and quickly moved it away. "Please...just listen?"

"All right, Matthew, I'll listen, but make it fast. I don't have much time and I'm warning you, it had better not have anything to do with my parents or acting jobs."

Matthew was relieved. "*Oh, no*, nothing like that at all, Christine! I promise you it doesn't," he assured her hurriedly. "Please, I have a few things to get off my chest. I won't take long."

Chris saw the crew loading up the truck. she saw that Pookie was standing with Calamity Chaser. Pookie had spotted her, grimaced, and hit her head with her palm.

"You'll have to hurry, Matthew; the Airway News' crew is waiting for me."

Matthew's eyes swept over Christine. *She's so fetching in her apple green peasant dress,* he thought, steering her to a table under a marquée. Chris sat down on a wooden bench while he paid for two cups of a cold drink. She accepted the cup and sipped it.

"*Mmmm*, this is surprisingly delicious. It tastes like bubbly cinnamon spiced cider."

He apologized again for his conduct, "I assure you, I have the utmost respect for you, Christine. I'm begging you to forgive me." Words tumbled out as he explained what happened the day before at Seven Valleys.

"Yeah, Matthew, I already know. Hayley called me on my cell last night and told me what happened. You understand, don't you, that Hayley is my best friend and I would go to the ends of the earth to protect her."

Matthew shook his head, "It has nothing to do with Hayley, Christine; it's my brother. We just don't see eye to eye."

Yeah, you don't see eye to eye, because you're a little putz and Peter towers over you in every way. "I'm not getting in the middle of this, Matthew. You seem sincere, but actors can be awfully convincing and I hope this is not an act. All right, let's forget about what happened between us and move on. I don't want to have any misunderstands or hard feelings between a member of Hayley's future family and me."

"I didn't want you to go home thinking badly of me."

"Matthew, what I think doesn't matter. What you think of yourself does, but I must tell you, I love Hayley and the disrespectful way you treated her pains me. She doesn't deserve that from anyone. Man up, Matthew; talk to Peter and Edward. You must be straight with them. Your mother isn't too happy with you either, but I think you already know that. I hope you all can smooth this out without difficulty. I'm sure they want that as much as you. Just forge ahead with honesty and sincerity."

While they talked, a witch sitting nearby turned over tarot cards. She leaned toward them and smiled first at Matthew and then at Chris. "Would you like to know what the cards say about you?" she asked.

"Not really," Chris grimaced. "I get enough of that spooky stuff back in New York. Some little impish Dream-Girl told me I'm a snake!"

Matthew feigned shock and then smirked, "Whatever that means." He put his arm around Chris's shoulder.

The witch nodded at Chris, "Oh, yes, whoever said that was right, but there are more chapters to come. There will be another cycle of change involving people close to you. You will react in a way that will surprise you."

Chris mumbled, "Nothing I do surprises me," she said, and shrugged off Matthew's arm.

"All right, then. Please, can you tell me what the cards say about me?" Matthew sighed.

Your initials are M-G or M-J and your sign is 'Scorpio'. I have turned over the *Death* card for you. Don't be alarmed," she reassured him, seeing Matthew's startled expression. "The Death card means the beginning of *new* life. You have come to the end of a phase in life, which you now realize has not served you well. There will be an abrupt transformation and your way of life and patterns of behavior will go through a change."

"*Hmmm...a* good change or a bad change?"

"That will depend on what *you* make of the opportunity."

"That sounds right on the money, Matthew," Chris chuckled. "All right, I'll take a chance. What do my cards say?"

"The cards say your initials are C-H or C-W. Your sign is Gemini and the card I have turned over for you is the *World*. It means that you have accomplished a goal and you have achieved fulfillment from that goal. You have completed a personal cycle, a project, a series of events, or a chapter in your life. You will now go on to experience much success after a culmination of events and experience a sense of fulfillment."

"Thank you," Chris said softly, and smiled. "That sounds much better than being called a *snake*."

"Wait one moment. I have just turned over the *Tower* card for someone very close to you. Could this be a friend? It means disruption of well-worn routines, conflict, and major change. It means sudden loss, overthrow of an existing way of life, and dramatic upheaval. Change of residence or job; perhaps both at once. Widespread repercussions of an action not taken…"

"Wait! Please don't say anymore. You're scaring me!"

Alarmed by the witches' prophesy, Chris arose, tossed money on the table and walked away. Matthew fell in step with her.

"They're all standing by the sound truck waiting to leave, Matthew. I have to say goodbye. Take care of yourself and try not to spin the world out of control."

Calamity Chaser asked Pookie to do London after Dark after he'd gotten sound bites ready for other programs to use. Chris's responsibility was to have production ready for the Clown Cavalcade the next day, then she was free to go back to the Ritton.

The crew saw Chris coming and climbed into the truck. She jumped in. They started up and sped back to the studio.

Chris crossed her legs and shook her foot nervously. She was anxious to return to the Ritton and be there when Peter and Hayley returned. She wanted to warn them, but of what? *Something a witch told me? Peter told me that everything is within the realm of possibility. I don't care what Peter wants; I'm telling Hayley about Zara when I get back to the hotel.*

Matthew swallowed hard while he watched her walk away. He brushed his hair back from his forehead and adjusted his cowboy hat. He drew in a deep breath and exhaled slowly.

She was visibly upset. That last card really disturbed her, but at least we parted on a friendly note. That's all I care about. She's leaving soon and I shall miss that cheeky bit of skirt. I'll make sure I see her again.

A strange feeling had washed over Matthew while he sat with Christine. He shook his head, becoming aware that his keenness for her ran deeper than he was willing to admit.

The Witch followed the couple with her eyes. She sighed and piled up the cards, wishing the woman had allowed her to finish the reading.. *I could have warned them that I clearly saw there is much to fear; that their friend...possibly a brother...or someone around him, is facing grave danger in the immediate future. And there is tumult, deception, and upheaval in his near future, too.*

~45~

"Hell is empty and all the devils are here."
~William Shakespeare~
The Tempest

Ritton Hotel
London, England
Sixth July 2005

Peter and Hayley returned to the London Ritton and planned to leave from there with Chris and Pookie. Barbara and Edward would bring Diva and say goodbye at Heathrow.

While they rode from Seven Valleys to London, they discussed Matthew. He was splendid in Romeo and Juliet and with his talent, they understood why he wanted a career in the theatre.

Peter gathered their small suitcases and Hayley walked to the balcony on the second level. When she held her hand over the balustrade to look at him, her engagement ring fell from her finger and landed at Peter's feet. He ran up the stairs and placed the ring back on her finger.

"We'll have time tomorrow to have your ring sized, but for tonight, come along, darling, it's time to go to be-...get some sleep," he chuckled. Peter escorted Hayley to the suite, placed the luggage inside the door, and threw his jacket on top of the suitcases. He took her in his arms and kissed her. "I was just thinking, for a house as large as the manor, there isn't much privacy, is there? I wanted so much to come to your room, but someone or other haunted the hallways," he laughed.

Hayley batted her eyelashes, and said, "*Now, now*, Peter. What would Barbara think of such an idea?"

"She would have exorcised the halls," he sniggered. "Oh, Hayley," he sighed, "I'm going to love sleeping with my arms around you tonight. We'll see what else develops," he said with a sly grin, twirling an imaginary moustache.

"Oh, my goodness, you rogue! I simply cannot wait to see what you have in mind."

Peter's mobile rang. The hallway was dim and the bright caller I.D. light showed it was Zara Chandler. His whole body felt like he'd been stung by a swarm of bees.

"What do you want? How did you get this mobile number?"

She whispered harshly, "*Aww...*now is that a nice way to greet a fellow Ritton Hotel guest? I'm waiting for you in the Londres Bailey and Bar. You must come now, because if you don't...well, you'll have to pay the consequences."

He gasped and she ended the call. His chest hurt and he trembled inside. Panicked, but not wanting to alarm Hayley, he said, "All right, then." He swallowed hard, "Lock up, Hayley; don't open the door to *anyone* until I've returned and you know for certain it's me. I'm going to registration for a moment and I'll return shortly. Remember...do not open this door to *anyone* but me. Do you understand? Not anyone!"

He hugged her, kissed the top of her head, and waited in the hallway until he heard the click of the lock.

Hayley picked up a small suitcase and pushed the rest against the wall. She became aware of a musky scent in the suite. *That's such an unpleasant odor.* She laid the suitcase on the bed and opened it. She took out the white crystal bead and pearl-adorned dress that she wore the night Peter asked her to marry him. She held it against her cheek, smiling at the memory.

Taking her cosmetics bag from the suitcase, she carried it to the bathroom to prepare for the night. Returning for her nightgown, she sat on the edge of the bed before she went back to the bathroom to take her shower. Dreamy eyed, she held up her left hand to admire

Peter's beautiful ring. She took it off and read the inscription on the inside. She chuckled, slid the ring back on her finger and thought about Chris's comment about being one of Gabriel's angels. *I'll call her room to see if she's back from Airway News to say goodnight.*

When Hayley walked to the phone to call Christine, a shadowy figure emerged from the closet and silently crossed the dark side of the room behind her. There was the muted click of a serrated switchblade flipped open inside a trench coat pocket.

When she started to dial, Zara grabbed Hayley's long hair. In one swift motion, she twisted it around her hand, and jerked Hayley's head back.

Her eyes wide in terror, Hayley screamed and swung the receiver over her shoulder, striking Zara hard on the forehead. The weight of the phone and the shortness of the cord pulled the receiver from her hand, and it fell clattering to the floor.

Hayley twisted her head round and saw that it was Zara. "*Oh, my God, no! Stop, Zara, don't do this! What do you want?*"

"What do I *want?* I want you dead...just like your mother. Your mother reported Tom and got him in trouble. It was her fault he dumped me. *Her fault!* I hated her with a passion. I swore I'd get even with her and I did. If only you kept your distance, but no, you had to come to Oxford, didn't you?" She sneered, "And worst of all, you went after Peter. Peter is mine!"

Zara's sinewy arm went around Hayley's neck in a chokehold, making Hayley's screams mere rasps from her throat. Off balance, leaning backward with her hands flailing, Hayley grabbed Zara's arm with one hand, her nails clawed at Zara's wrist tearing into flesh and muscle. With her other hand she plowed deep furrows in the skin on Zara's face.

Angered by the painful gouges, Zara grabbed both of Hayley's wrists and while they struggled, she whispered in Hayley's ear, her voice was hard and her red face twisted in fury.

Trembling with fear, Hayley gathered her strength while Zara held her mouth against her face and ear; her hot, stale breath reeking of scotch and cigarettes.

"You would have been a constant reminder of how much I loathed your mother," she snarled, "I paid some blokes to shoot down the plane. Yes, it was me. I tried to get the lot of you, but you bloody well survived. Then damn you; you came back into my life trying to take Peter from me. I paid again, but all I got was a doorman and a dog walker. Yes, your beloved Uncle Arthur, but you are *still* here, ruining my life! I loathe you just as much as I loathed your miserable, interfering mother."

Zara released her grip on Hayley's hair, twisted her around and sliced at Hayley's throat with her knife, but Hayley had freed her arm, defended herself and Zara missed her throat slashing the knife across her wrist. Hayley gasped and cried out in pain.

"Make no mistake," Zara said, panting, "I'll not allow you to take Peter away from me. Oh no, I'll see you dead first."

Hayley found surprising strength fueled by anger that had been building for years while sequestered from the world.

"Not without a fight, you won't," Hayley grunted, wedging her foot behind Zara, tripping her and throwing her off balance.

Zara fell backward pulling Hayley down with her. The knife skittered across the room and they scrambled on their hands and knees to reach it. Hayley got to it first, scooped it up, and kicked Zara forcefully in the groin. While Zara shrieked in pain, Hayley held the knife firmly, plunging the sharp blade deep into Zara's thigh and pulling it out, she pitched forward, slashing Zara's arm. Hayley rolled away from her and stumbled toward the door.

"Oh, my God! Peter...help me! Somebody...help me!"

~46~

"Being deeply loved by someone gives you strength, while loving someone deeply gives you courage."
~ Lao Tzu~

Ritton Hotel
London, England
Sixth July 2005

Peter grabbed a lobby security guard to go with him to the bar to seize Zara, but she wasn't there. Filled with mind-numbing dread, he ran to registration. *We were almost home, one more night...that's all I needed. Just one more night, God damn her.*

He abandoned all civility and barged ahead of incoming guests waiting at the registration desk.

"I've just received a call on my mobile from Zara Chandler. She says she's a guest in this hotel. That woman is dangerous. She accosted us several days ago. Please check your guest records for her name."

The clerk calmly searched the computer registry. "I'm sorry sir; there isn't a registered guest by that name."

"Here's her picture. Do you at least recognize her?"

"No, sir; I haven't seen anyone of that description." He showed the picture to the other clerks and no one recognized her as a registered guest.

"Peter drew in a deep breath; his voice strident with fear and frustration, "I believe she's here somewhere in the hotel. She may be using the guest's door to the street. She might be wearing a wig. She wears wigs. Have someone monitor that door and if she comes through the lobby, please call police immediately. Let them apprehend her."

"We understand, Dr. Gabriel-Johns. We'll be on the lookout for her."

"I'd also appreciate having a security guard sitting outside the Piccadilly Park Suite during the night."

"Please rest assured we'll do that, Sir." The woman at the registration desk calmly nodded and keyed a message to security into the computer.

Peter dialed Hayley in the suite from the lobby. There was no answer. The automated system prompted him to leave a voicemail message. Concerned, but thinking she might be in the shower, he started to put the receiver back in the cradle.

"Oh, my God. That's it!"

Prickles ran up and down Peter's arms and back. His throat went dry. He dropped the receiver and rushed back to the Registration desk, shouting, "She may have used another name. Look and see if you have a guest named, Norah Twigg."

"Yes, sir, we do. Would you like us to ring her room?"

"No, listen to what I'm telling you. *That's her!* That's Zara Chandler. No, call the Piccadilly Park Suite."

"I'm sorry, sir, the receiver is off the hook."

Alarmed, Peter barked, "Send security to that suite. Something has gone wrong and..." *Oh, my God, I left my key in my jacket!*

"Certainly, Dr. Gabriel-Johns; we'll send a guard."

"And for Christ sake, call the police straightaway."

Christine was anxious to return to the hotel and frustrated when the planning meeting at Airway News ran later than expected. Entering the short hallway to their rooms, she heard screams and sounds of a horrific fight coming from Hayley's suite. She ran to the door, found it locked, and began pounding and ringing the bell while she searched her bag for her cell phone.

"Oh, my God, Hayley, who's in there? Can't you get to the door?"

"Chris! It's Zara...she has a knife and she's trying to kill me! Get Peter, *hurry*," Hayley screamed. "He went...call reception! Call the police!"

Fear punched Chris in the stomach.

"Zara, you crazy freak! Get away from her! Leave her alone. I'm calling the police. If you touch one hair on her head, I'll see *you* burn in hell!"

Her heart pounding, Chris ran down the hall toward the steps to the lobby, dialing 9-9-9 for emergency.

"I'm Christine Wyndham at the London Ritton. This is an emergency! A psychopath, Zara Chandler, is in the Piccadilly Park Suite on the second floor attacking my friend, Hayley Hamilton! Send the police here immediately! Notify Detective Chief Inspector Bob Bowkler, too! There's no time to lose. *For God's sake, hurry!"*

Rushing up the stairs and turning the corner, Peter saw Chris running toward him, shrieking, "Peter, hurry! Zara is in the suite attacking Hayley! She's screaming and crying for help! I've already called the police!"

When they reached the door, Peter realized his worst fear when he heard Zara's taunts, Hayley's screams, and the sound of furniture crashing as Hayley fought her off.

"*Oh, my God;* how in hell did she get in? Where's the bloody security? Chris, I forgot my key." He rattled the doorknob and pounded, damning himself for not taking the key with him.

"*Zara*! For *Christ sake*, don't hurt her! Open this door and let's talk! Zara? *Zara! Open the God damned door!* Zara, if you hurt her, I swear to God, I'll kill you!"

"Go away, lover boy," Zara crooned, "You're too late. You had your chance. You've already kissed the sad cow goodbye."

"Zara -- *don't do this*. Open the God damned door!" he pounded and rang. "Chris, quick -- call security again."

"I'll call security again and I'll run down to the desk and get another key."

Hayley heard Peter's voice; she tried to circumvent Zara and make her way toward him, but Zara had wrestled the knife away and taunted Hayley, jabbing the knife at her, forcing her toward the bedroom closet.

"Don't do it, Zara. You can walk away now," Hayley was panting, her chest heaved, and blood dripped off her outstretched hand.

"Oh, no, you plonker, you tried to take Peter away from me. For that you die."

"No, Zara. You're dead wrong. I couldn't take someone from you that you never had and neither could my mother."

With those words, Hayley kicked Zara in the stomach with her last ounce of strength. Enraged, and with a lunge, Zara plunged the knife into Hayley's ribs. When she doubled over, Zara shoved her upright by her face and slammed her head against the doorframe. Stunned by the blow, Hayley fell to the floor, but she'd grabbed on to Zara's arm and the loose ring rolled on the floor. Zara swooped up the ring and dropped it into her pocket.

"You'll not be needing this where you're going, will you?" She laughed harshly and shoved Hayley into the closet, kicking her repeatedly before shutting the door.

Limping, Zara staggered toward the bed, grabbed Hayley's fragile beaded blouse, wrapped the bloodied knife in it, and shoved it into her trench coat pocket.

A lone hotel security guard cut Chris off when he turned the corner of the short hallway.

"What's all this commotion? You lot are causing a disturbance. Please move away from the door. The Ritton won't tolerate this kind of conduct. Come along now; you'll have to come with me."

"We don't have time to explain, Sir. For God's sake, unlock the door! *Hurry*! This is my room; my fiancé is inside and she's in trouble. *She's being attacked!* I forgot my key and I must get in!"

Listening at the door, the guard heard only silence from the room.

"This is Hotel Security." The guard lightly tapped on the door and rang the bell. "Hello, in there? Open the door, please." He paused, listening. "I think you must be mistaken. There's no one in there. All right...come along you lot; let's get moving."

Frantic, Peter shouted, "*God damn it, man! Open the bloody door! Open it or I'll take the key from you by force and open it myself!*"

The guard glared at Peter, but calmly tapped and said, "If someone's in there please don't be alarmed. I'm unlocking the door and we're coming in to check on you."

Zara's chest heaved while she positioned herself behind the door just as the key turned in the lock. In a split second, Peter ran into the room, with the guard and Chris behind him. As soon as Christine cleared the door, Zara shoved her with a foot in the middle of her back, propelling her into the guard. They tumbled over Peter's luggage and fell in a heap on the floor. Zara trampled them under her boots when she bolted from the room and hobbled down the hall toward the service exit.

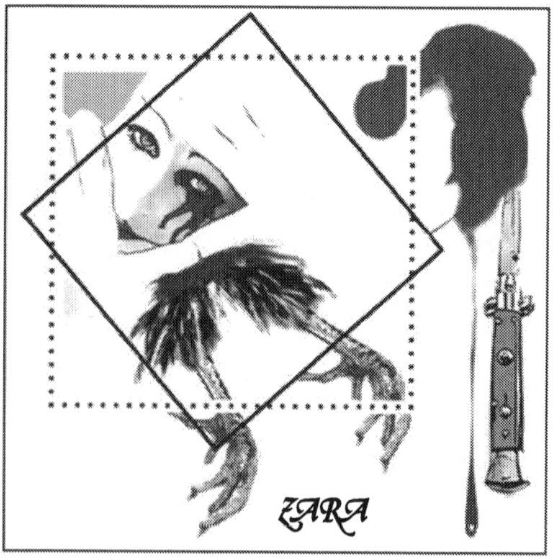

"She whispered harshly, 'Aww...now is that a nice way to greet a fellow Ritton Hotel guest? I'm waiting for you in the Londres Bailey and Bar. You must come now, because if you don't...well, you'll have to pay the consequences.'"

~47~

"Love is stronger than death even though
it can't stop death from happening, but
no matter how hard death tries to separate people
from love, it can't take away our memories either.
In the end, life is stronger than death."
~ Anonymous~

London, England
Seventh July 2005

Peter saw bloodstains everywhere when he ran into the bedroom. Terror stricken, he dashed around the jumbled suite in frenzy, but there was no sign of Hayley.

"*Zara, you freaking psycho-bitch, where is she? What in hell have you done! Hayley? Hayley!*"

Silence...all Peter heard was the sound of his own raspy breathing. Then, there was a low moan from the bedroom closet. Rushing to open the door, he found Hayley lying on the floor. Blood was dripping from gashes, seeping from stab wounds, and blood covered her face from a gaping scalp wound where Zara bashed her head against the doorframe.

"Peter..." Hayley's voice was barely audible.

Oh my God, no. Oh, please God, no. *Hayley*. Not this. "Baby, baby, you'll be all right. I promise." His heart lurched; nausea rose in his throat. Knots of fear tied up his stomach and lungs making it hard to breathe.

"She killed my parents, Peter. She caused the plane crash. She hated my mother. And Peter, Zara admitted killing Uncle Arthur and Clarissa," she sobbed.

"*Shhh*, Hayley, Darling, don't try to talk. Save your strength. I'm here now and I'll be with you always."

"Peter...she took...my ring," the words caught in her throat as she spoke between sobs.

"No, no, It's all right, Sweetheart. We'll find another one."

While he talked to her, Peter carefully moved Hayley from inside the closet to a larger space on the floor. He placed a pillow under her head, grabbed a sheet from the bed, tightly wrapped her wounds, and covered her with a blanket.

Chris had quickly scrambled to her feet and called 9-9-9 again.

"I called the police ten minutes ago, Hayley, but they aren't here yet!"

The phone connected to Scotland Yard and she bellowed, "This is the London Ritton again. *Get an ambulance and police up here, now!* Send Detective Bob Bowkler. Zara Chandler made an attempt on Miss Hamilton's life. She's been stabbed. *Hurry...please...hurry,"* she sobbed.

Peter was alarmed. "Hayley's going into shock. *Christ*, she's lost a lot of blood. *Quick, Chris!* Get another blanket from the closet and wrap her in it."

Peter lay beside Hayley stroking her hair and face and murmuring softly to her while he grabbed his mobile and speed dialed his brother William.

"William, meet us at Saint Bart's Hospital! Zara Chandler attacked Hayley… stabbed her… she's in shock and critically wounded. We need you. *I need you*. You are the best surgeon in London." Peter's voice broke.

"On my way, Peter; *both of you hang on*. I'll be waiting for you."

Peter called his parents and they insisted on rushing to the hospital. He promised he would ring again when they were on their way.

Hayley was unconscious when the paramedics arrived less than ten minutes later and began oxygen and an intravenous drip, but it seemed like hours to Peter and Chris.

The police arrived shortly thereafter and took the necessary measures to keep the crime scene from contamination. Hotel doormen and security kept the press and gawkers at bay outside the hotel and Chris reported the breaking news story exclusively for Savvy and Airway News.

Police talked to Peter and Chris to gather as much information as they could. Peter acknowledged it was Zara Chandler and gave them her description and address.

"Before she lost consciousness, Hayley told me that Chandler admitted to four other murders. Please contact Detective Chief Inspector Bob Bowkler. We recently requested that he have Scotland Yard investigate Chandler's activities; we believed she was behind several murders over the past five years.

One more thing; she has my fiancée's diamond and sapphire engagement ring in her possession. You can recognize it by the inscription on the inside, *Gabriel's #1 Angel*."

Peter called his parents and William again from the ambulance. When they arrived at the hospital, William was waiting in the operating room and they wasted no time taking Hayley through emergency and prepped her for surgery.

While Peter nervously paced the waiting room floor and Chris sat motionless, Barbara and Edward rushed through the door.

"Peter! Oh, my darling, I cannot believe this. That woman, that odious woman, to do this to Hayley is beyond the pale."

Barbara clung to her son in pain and horror. Edward sat down beside Chris and held her hand while Peter told them Zara revealed to Hayley she had the plane sabotaged and she arranged the bombing that killed Arthur Symington.

"That's not all; the police just confided to me that when they apprehend her, they'll charge her with killing Jacques Bonnier as well. Apparently she killed him during a sexual assignation."

"*What*? *What did you say*?" Chris jumped up and stared at Peter.

"*Oh, God,* I'm sorry you heard it this way, Chris." Peter felt miserable. "I know how much you loved Jaxx, but please believe me, he wasn't the man you thought he was and didn't deserve your devotion. There is more, Chris, but it can wait."

Barbara took the young woman in her arms and held her. With a quavering voice, Chris said, "Is there any hope for humanity with demons like Zara Chandler walking among us?"

Edward brought her a cup of water and Peter sat with her. She couldn't have been in gentler hands when she learned the truth about Jaxx' murder.

Chris sighed and said to Barbara, "I...I've made peace with what Jaxx was and was not. I know he was not what I believed him to be, or that we ever really had a relationship. It's over and I'm done with it."

At dawn, William came out of surgery to assure them that he expected Hayley to recover completely.

"At the moment, she's confined to Intensive Care and still not awake. She has a deep cut in her scalp and a serious bump on her head, but thankfully, no concussion. However, the knife grazed her rib and nicked the bottom lobe of her left lung, but fortunately, she has no other internal injuries. She has lacerations and abrasions all over her body, but I'm sure her injuries will heal well as she's young, healthy, and strong. Emotional scars are another matter. She's been through hell at the hands of that monster."

A few hours later, they moved Hayley to a private room with a police guard. Peter and Barbara sat at her bedside while she slept fitfully. In Hayley's dream, her mother appeared smiling at her and then, Dream-Girl was there, pointing at her, and telling her, "You're the swan; yes, you *are* the swan." Then, fading in and fading out, the dream went dark.

Mother...mother... I'm so afraid. Where are you, mother? Please don't leave me...

Hayley's eyelids fluttered while she dreamed. Her voice sounded hollow and echoed as if far away, but her murmured words were clear enough for Peter and Barbara to hear, if not fully understand.

"Mother's here, my darling," Barbara whispered to the sleeping young woman who she'd already come to love as her own. She held Hayley's hand against her lips, "You no longer have anything to fear."

With her hand in Barbara's, Hayley rested peacefully until she awoke, but seemed to drift away. Then, after a moment, she spoke again, her voice faint and wistful.

"Barbara, I was dreaming about my mother. I miss her so."

"I know you do, my dearest. I still miss my mother who I lost when I was very young, but I believe the spirit of our loved ones live on in us, Hayley. She will never truly be gone from you." Barbara pressed Hayley's hand against her cheek. "And she will continue to live on through your children."

There were now two police officers stationed outside Hayley's door and although Peter didn't want to go, exhaustion was clouding his mind. He felt it would be safe to leave her for a couple of hours. She would have around-the-clock protection until police apprehended Zara Chandler.

The nurse came in to check Hayley's vital signs and shone a light in her eyes to check her pupils' reaction. Satisfied with her progress, she told the family that William ordered a shot for her so she would sleep and a private nurse would sit by her bedside while they were gone. She suggested they all go home, get some rest, and come back later. They agreed and kissed her goodbye.

Chris went to Hayley's room before she left for her assignment. She was sleeping and Chris gently lifted Hayley's hand and held it to her lips.

"I'll be back as soon as the circus has left town," she whispered. At the sight of Hayley's pale face, she felt an overwhelming sense of outrage and injustice for what the Hamilton's suffered at the hands of that beast.

Although, calling the fiendish Zara Chandler a beast is an insult to beasts everywhere. I swear to God, the human beings on this planet must have done something terrible in another lifetime. This is really Hell where You have sent all your freaks and demons to torment us, isn't it?

Christine had handled the press outside the hospital and set up interviews with Detective Chief Inspector Bowkler and William, Hayley's surgeon. Forced to pull herself away because of her responsibilities, Chris called Pookie to tell her to join her at the Airway News studio, but her call went to voicemail. She planned to use the cameraman on the scene to go into the tube and interview clowns. How ironic, to go from this tragic situation caused by the dark face of evil to the zany painted faces of clowns.

After saying goodbye to William, Chris's cell phone rang and the caller ID showed it was Savvy News.

"This is Chris."

"*Where in hell are you, Wyndham*?" Slick Slade was shouting at her. "Terrorists have been bombing the London tubes! Get your ass to the Euston Station entrance. The Airway News crew and your friend, Pookie, are already at the site. *Hurry!*"

She listened in stunned silence to Slick.

'Right; I'm on it!"

I don't freaking believe this! She hung up, shook her head, and breathed a long sigh while she ran. *Actually, I don't know exactly where in hell I am, but it's definitely hell...*

"Hey, you! You on the motorcycle! There's been a terrorist bombing in the tube! Can you take me to Euston Station? I'll pay you. I need to get there fast. I'm a reporter for Airway News!"

The rider beckoned to her; she hopped on the back of the cycle and grabbed him around his waist. With her skirt flying in the air behind her, they sped through the crowded streets of London leaving one disaster behind and heading toward another.

~48~

...Revenge...

...is like a rolling stone,
which, when a man hath forced up a hill,
will return upon him with a greater violence
and break those bones whose sinews gave it motion."
~ Albert Schweitzer~

London, England
Seventh July 2005

Sweating and panting, Zara staggered down the hallway toward the hotel's backstairs service exit leaving a trail of blood drops from her wounds. Although she'd gotten a head start, the painful injuries slowed her down. She found the gate locked and began climbing.

"Damn and blast!" she screamed in frustration.

The guard had pulled himself to his feet and scrambled in pursuit following the blood spatters. He ran into the darkness and across the valet parking lot. He yanked her off the gate by the hood of her trench coat and grabbed her arm to hold her. Slowly, she turned to face him. Her chest heaved, she was gasping for air, as was the guard. Outwardly, she appeared calm, but her mind was racing and she was a mass of heightened awareness.

"You'd bloody well better hope that young lady lives."

The guard panted as he lifted his pager out of its holder to call for assistance. He glanced down, nervous and shaking, struggling to locate the buttons in the dark.

In a flash, Zara pulled the switchblade from her pocket and grunting, she lunged forward, stabbing him under his ribs.

The guard stared in horror and disbelief. Mortally wounded, he slid down Zara's body, falling at her feet in a heap. He'd barely touched the ground when she scaled the gate and jumped to the outside.

Zara limped up Piccadilly and crossed over to Hyde Park. Bleeding heavily from the deep stab wound, she entered the park and found a secluded area across from a water fountain. Like a furtive nocturnal animal under cover of darkness, she prepared a hiding place among the trees, pulling loose shrubs around her to create a thicket. There she would hide until daylight.

The deep wound in her thigh was throbbing and her pant leg was soaked with blood. She hadn't expected a struggle, or planned on injuries to herself. Even the heavy black hooded trench coat hadn't protected her from the sharp blade of the knife. Once settled, hidden by shrubs, she used the knife to cut the lining and made a tourniquet to stop the bleeding. The cut on her arm was not as deep and she used the lining to bind it.

Leaning back against a sheltering tree, she took Hayley's engagement ring from her coat pocket. She squeezed it in the palm of her hand. Finally, she placed it on her finger. It just fit.

"It was meant to be mine just as Peter was meant to be mine," she whispered, chuffed to bits with self-satisfaction.

Lying on the ground covered by her trench coat, Zara curled up in a fetal position, resting her head on the fragile blouse now stained with Hayley's blood. She fell asleep with the ring on a finger of her left hand.

At dawn, Zara was startled awake by a small animal or bird rustling in the underbrush. She awoke stiff, sore and in pain, but her leg wound had stopped bleeding. With effort, she raised her arm and saw that the time on her watch was 06:00. Her head throbbed where Hayley struck her with the telephone receiver and she couldn't think what day it was. Yes, it's Tuesday, seventh of July, she remembered.

Although it was midsummer, the early morning air was terribly raw. Her body was shivering from the dampness in the ground and her black wig and skin were wet from the chilling fog. She clutched at the trench coat and pulled the hood closer to her neck to keep off the cold air.

Seriously injured, weakened, and hungry, she was a wounded animal lying in the thicket. She knew they'd be hunting for her and she needed to decide her next move. *I have to wake up and gather my strength; the best thing to do is take a bus to my mother's house. She'll clean me up and get me proper bandages. All I have to do is get across Hyde Park to Marble Arch. At Edgeware Road, I'll get on the number 30 bus to Hackney Wick.*

She assumed no one would connect her with Norah, so her house would be a safe place to go. *We're never very far from the sanctuary of the womb. This is one of the few times I can remember being thankful for my mother.* Zara felt no love for her mother, but she needed a place to hide.

Light headed from lack of food, water, and loss of blood, Zara limped through the park dodging and weaving, creating a path to Marble Arch. She made her way across the very spot where Chris and Pookie spent an hour the day before interviewing the witches in their labyrinths. Zara was a fugitive trapped in a labyrinth of her own making.

She stumbled through the Park and in the distance, she saw two police officers on horseback emerging from the fog coming toward her on the footpath. Fear overtook her and she quickly diverted to the shrubbery on the side of the path. A thorny bush stabbed her forehead, catching the black wig, and tangling it in the thorns. She had to leave it and pulled the hood over her hair while blood from the sharp thorn's scrape trickled down her face. She wiped it away and her hand was sticky with blood.

Zara had no choice but to go the long way around. She continued toward Marble Arch hiding from view amongst the trees and shrubs. By 09:00, she was almost at the bus stop when she saw a number 30 pulling up. Sucking air through her teeth against the pain, she hobbled toward the bus. The driver began to close the doors and the bus started moving. She shouted to him and he stopped and opened the doors to let her on.

"Well, aren't you the lucky one. One more second and you would have had to wait for the next bus," he said, pulling into traffic.

Gasping from the effort, she used a young man with a large, heavy rucksack for cover by following closely behind him to the rear of the top deck. She sat across from him and he immediately took out his mobile phone. She felt sure he didn't recognize her and wasn't calling police. She exhaled and took deep breaths, trying to stay calm to control the pain.

Flooded with relief, Zara began to relax. She slumped down in the seat and closed her eyes. Drained from the effort, she began to doze. As the bus approached Euston Station, it crawled along and suddenly squealed to a stop. Lurched awake, she saw the pavements were crowded with hundreds of people, most waiting for buses.

Amongst the people milling about were people dressed as clowns. Some wore only red noses or colorful wigs, but many were dressed in complete costume. She thought she was hallucinating, but when she saw a slender blonde woman holding a microphone interviewing clowns and a tall mellow-skinned woman with a long black braid interviewing people in the crowd, she recognized Chris and Pookie. There were camera operators with them and the reporter, Cal Chaser. She saw a satellite uplink truck from Airway News. She assumed she wasn't delusional. In London, anything could happen.

Crowds of people poured out of the tubes onto the streets and boarded buses to get to their destinations. The driver opened the doors and the bus filled with clowns and young people on their way to their jobs and school, some chatting together, some talking on mobile phones. There was no laughter in their conversation. Shock and fear filled the air. Listening, she learned terrorist bombings in the tubes had caused evacuations.

The clean-shaven young man dressed in black across from her, moved his huge rucksack from a seat to the aisle between his legs. She studied him beneath lowered eyelids while he listened intently to people coming on the bus. Something about him made her flesh crawl, but she attributed it to exhaustion and her injuries.

Settling back into the seat and using her black trench coat as a blanket, she rested her head on the side of the bus using Hayley's bloodstained blouse as a pillow. The bus inched along, lulling Zara to sleep and she began to dream --

Thrashing in icy water rising and swirling around her, she began a long slide into a whirlpool and struggled against the vortex. Her head and body ached, her lungs felt ready to burst, but finally she dragged herself onto the rocky bank at the water's edge. Before her, the black barren trees were stark and lifeless, outlined against a fiery red sky alive with circling ravens.

Out of nowhere, a powerful black cat with red-rimmed eyes glowing like white-hot coals appeared in front of her. She could see its long, pointed fangs dripping with blood and she feared death had come to claim her. The black beast roared and she heard these rumbling words –

"Thou demon repent, for Azreal cometh."

The echoing words sounded like rolling thunder across the sky or crashing waves on a tempestuous sea.

"Noooo," she cried, but her voice carried no sound, there was only the great cat's roar echoing in her ears, filling her with fear so bitter cold her skin crawled and her insides shriveled. The huge cat was moving toward her with its mouth wide-open and its teeth bared; its fiery breath scorching everything in its path. The beast set her on fire in unbearable pain. She saw more blood dripping from its razor-sharp fangs and this time, she knew the blood was hers...

The bus jolted Zara awake. Police hailed the driver, who stopped the bus with a jounce. Panting and shaking from the gut-wrenching dream, fear took hold when she saw police boarding the bus, looking around and talking to the driver. *Why is this happening? Damn and blast; it should have been so simple.*

"I have a message from the officers," announced the driver. "We are being diverted from our route to Tavistock Square. The officers recommend that passengers walk to their destination. This would be a good time to disembark because walking will be faster than the bus can travel under these circumstances."

Many left the bus and began making their way on foot. The driver maneuvered slowly through the chaotic, crowded streets. Zara's mouth was dry and her throat closed with fear. Trapped at the rear of the bus, she knew there was no escape from where she was sitting. If only she could exit the bus, she could lose herself in the crowd, but there were police officers standing next to the driver and at the doors. After the driver made the announcement, he turned the corner to enter Tavistock Square.

Zara's wounds were causing her a lot of pain. She was lightheaded and panicky, nearly swooning from dizziness. It was 09:43 by her watch. Surely, they would be searching for her by now. She had to get off the bus!

At the next stop, three girls got on and walked upstairs to sit in empty seats on the side of the bus across from Zara. They were close enough for her to hear snatches of their conversation. One girl was holding the morning's Telegraph and read from the front page. Zara heard, "*British American heiress" - "knife wounds"- "hospital"- "expected to recover" - "Police looking for Kedzara Twigg Chandler" - "red hair, possibly dyed black or wig" - " black hooded raincoat."* Zara felt three pairs of eyes upon her. She withered; her heart pumping so hard she could hear it knocking in her ears and her head pounded so painfully, she could hardly think. She slid further down in her seat and pulled the hood of the coat over her red hair.

"*Not dead*," she muttered, "she's not dead? *No! No! It can't be...*"

Enraged and disoriented, her mind was in chaos when she saw the girl fold the article to the outside and carry the newspaper to the officer standing on the steps. She held it up, showed him a picture, and pointed to Zara. After she gave the newspaper to the officer, he beckoned to the other girls and all three left the bus.

Zara looked at her watch -- 09:46. Fear pumped adrenalin into her veins and heightened her desperation to get off the bus! Her eyes shot to the young man across from her; he leaned forward, opened his sack, and withdrew a bomb detonator. *Another terrorist;* she was twitching and frenzied. She stared at him wild-eyed.

On his face was a self-satisfied smirk. Zara knew he enjoyed her fear. She was familiar with that visage, that emotion. It was what she felt when she bashed in her father, Chauncey Twigg's, head in with a heavy metal statue of Jesus and shoved him down the staircase, killing him when he laughed at her ambition and forbid her to seek a position at Oxford. It was the satisfaction she felt when she smothered her sick aunt for her money and her house in Burford.

She saw on this twisted being's face what she felt when she watched from the Fitchburg airport when Elizabeth Hamilton burned to death in the fiery plane crash, and the gratification she felt when she'd watched Arthur Symington and Hayley Hamilton blown apart in front of the Top of the Turret.

She saw on his face the morbid satisfaction she felt when she sliced the knife across Jacques Bonnier's throat for telling her that Hayley was still alive.

It was the sheer pleasure she felt when she'd stabbed the security guard and saw his shocked expression just before he dropped at her feet, but most of all, she could see on this terrorist's demonic face the great power and satisfaction she felt when she thought she stabbed Hayley Hamilton to death at the Ritton.

"But, she's not dead," Zara mumbled, "*not dead.*" The police officer walked up the steps of the bus toward her and in front of him was Hayley Hamilton.

Laughing...she's laughing, and she has the knife...it's dripping with her blood. Zara fumbled in her pocket to the find the knife.

When she squeezed the knife in her pocket, it flipped open and the blade sliced her hand. *It's there. How can she have it?* .

The officer walked toward her and then Hayley...*laughing...* raised the knife above her head with both hands ready to plunge it into Zara's heart. Hayley had stopped laughing. Her red-rimmed eyes glowed like white-hot coals...*like the cat in my dream.* Hayley's face reflected back at Zara the lurid satisfaction she felt when she stabbed her.

Zara heard her throaty whisper, "Slowly, slowly catchee monkey."

When she's close enough, I'll kill her...I'll kill all of them...

"I'll kill all of you," she croaked, but she was too weak to do anything but slouch in her seat and face her imminent death sentence. Her eyes could not move away from the vision of Hayley standing in front of her with the knife poised to strike. A passage from Revelation that her mother read to her after they buried her father echoed in her mind –

"And I looked and behold a pale horse and
his name that sat on him was Death, and
Hell followed with him."

"She *knew*; my mother knew I killed him... I'll ride a pale horse into Hell..." she said, and looked at the terrorist with the detonator.

Split seconds later, at exactly 09:47, she watched in horror while the terrorist detonated the bomb.

The roar of the explosion was the last thing Kedzara Twigg Chandler ever heard and the flash of the explosion was the last thing she ever saw as her wretched world grayed into black. She met her death wearing the coveted sapphire and diamond ring of Peter's betrothed. A ring some say is cursed; the ring they claim possesses evil powers.

The bomb tore the roof off the bus at the junction of Woburn Square and Tavistock Place, spilling the blood of one hundred twenty-four people and splattering them over the frontage of the British Medical Association's front door.

Screaming bystanders saw the back end of the bus fly through the air. On the side of the bus were the remains of an advert for *The Descent*, a horror film released in theatres on 8 July. The advert proclaimed:

"OUTRIGHT TERROR! BOLD AND BRILLIANT."

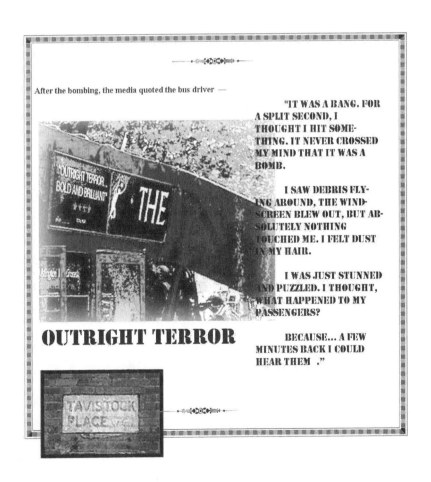

After the bombing, the media quoted the bus driver —

"IT WAS A BANG. FOR A SPLIT SECOND, I THOUGHT I HIT SOMETHING. IT NEVER CROSSED MY MIND THAT IT WAS A BOMB.

I SAW DEBRIS FLYING AROUND, THE WINDSCREEN BLEW OUT, BUT ABSOLUTELY NOTHING TOUCHED ME. I FELT DUST IN MY HAIR.

I WAS JUST STUNNED AND PUZZLED. I THOUGHT, WHAT HAPPENED TO MY PASSENGERS?

BECAUSE... A FEW MINUTES BACK I COULD HEAR THEM ."

OUTRIGHT TERROR

~49~

"I have always been delighted at the prospect
of a new day, a fresh try, one more start,
with perhaps a bit of magic waiting
somewhere behind the morning."
~ Joseph Priestly~

London, England
Eighth July 2005

Chris and Pookie visited Hayley at the hospital on the way to the airport to catch their flight to New York.

"No offense, Hayley, but for someone who rarely leaves home, you certainly know how to have an adventure." *Oh, God; did I just say that out loud?* Pookie thought.

"No offense taken, Pookie," Hayley's voice sounded weak and hoarse. "They say it's who you know, don't they?"

"Well, I told Chrissy that she shouldn't get involved in the forum, but she wouldn't listen."

"It has nothing to do with the forum, Pookie. If Hayley and I hadn't joined the forum, it's very likely we wouldn't have gotten together again. That would have been my great loss."

"But Chris, when I joined the forum, Peter and I exposed our relationship to Zara. Perhaps if I hadn't…"

"Hayley," Chris interrupted her, "This would have happened anyway, you know, whether or not you had gone on the forum. Barbara had tea with you and your mother just before your graduation. She invited both of you to Seven Valleys for the festival that year. You would have met Peter then. On the other hand, because of your mother and Barbara's friendship, you might have met him while you studied at Oxford if Zara hadn't... Well, you see what I mean?

Zara had it in for your mother, Hayley, and then you. It started all the way back at Oxford when Tom Leighton rejected her. She had to blame someone, so she blamed Elizabeth. When you showed up at Oxford, she couldn't allow that. She had to get rid of you. Anyway, you had already met Peter at Stony Point and you contacted him before you knew about the forum. It was Peter's suggestion to be there for his discussion. Zara would have known about you and Peter just by virtue of his interest in you. She was obsessed with Peter. It was Zara, Hayley, all Zara, but what I don't understand is why she killed Symington."

"Zara didn't know that Peter and I had already left New York for Southampton earlier that morning. She and the bomber mistook Clarissa for me, because she was dressed in a similar way and had Diva with her. What I don't understand is why she killed Jaxx. Although he was a womanizer, a player, and possibly into drugs, why kill him?"

Pookie scoffed, "Jaxx played it fast and loose with women, but he kept everything closely guarded so they knew nothing about each other. These internet predators operate that way. However, in terms of being a predator, Jacques Bonnier was chump-change compared to Zara Chandler. He was only a garden-variety narcissist; she was a flaming, psychotic nutcase. You were lonely and insecure, Chrissy, and he played you. He thought he played Zara, too, but, even though he made the rules and played his game well, he made his big mistake when he got involved with her. It became deadly when he met the master player. I think he lost the game to Zara because he knew too much."

"Pookie, sometimes I forget how smart you are."

"I started that rumor."

"Yeah, well, I figured that out for myself."

"Oh, I forgot to tell you that I figured out why Barbara gave me this ring and the bell. Do you know, Chrissy?"

"Yes, but I didn't want to ruin the fun of your own discovery, Pooks. Tell us what you think."

"Rings on her fingers and bells on her toes, she shall have music wherever she goes. Right?"

"Very good, grasshopper..."

They knuckle bumped, then lifted Hayley's hand and gently tapped her knuckle.

The three friends sat together until the nurse came in and asked them not to stay too long. She didn't want her patient tired out. Reluctant to say goodbye, the women hugged Hayley and kissed her.

"The next time I see you, Hayley, I want to see some color in those cheeks. What is it about you that touches me so and makes me want to cry?" Chris forced a smile. "Oh, God, I miss you already."

"Stop it, Chris. You're making me sad. I'll call you to let you know when Peter and I will return to New York."

"Let's go Chrissy, we'll miss our plane." Pookie took Chris's hand and pulled her toward the door. "Hayley, I hope we'll see each other again."

When they left her room, Pookie leaned backward in the doorway and whispered to her, "*Pssst, Hayley!*" When Hayley looked up, Pookie threw her a kiss with a big, "*muaah*."

"Well, it's almost time to go home, Chrissy," Pookie took a deep breath and exhaled a long sigh while they walked down the corridor to the exit.

"Pookie, I hate not being here to watch over Hayley."

"Pretty soon you won't have me to watch over you, Chrissy."

"Yeah, well, you're my own personal Greek chorus."

"Whatever will become of you with no grownups around?"

"Well, *hell*, Pookie, I only get into trouble when I'm with you!"

"Bite me, Buttercup."

"*Sheesh*, okay, yeah...I miss having you around, Pooks. *A lot*."

"If I were around, I'd borrow some of your clothes."

"Wait. You'll have to say that again. I think I was dreaming."

"OK, listen carefully, because I won't say this again." She whispered, "I'd like to borrow some of your clothes."

"Wait; you want to borrow my tee shirt that says, 'I See Dumb People,' don't you?"

Pookie snorted, "Noooo, how about what you wore yesterday? The emerald green peasant dress. And the shoes. And the jewelry, too."

"Oh, not the *emerald* dress! That's my favorite," Chris whined, smirking. "But listen; seriously, Pookie. About being around...we need to talk. You impressed the directors and station managers at both Savvy News and Airway News throughout this whole ordeal. Calamity Chaser asked a bunch of personal questions about you, too. What's with that, *Pook-a-rama, hmm?"*

"Okay, Buttercup, let's cover all that on the flight back to New York."

Chris held her knuckle up for a bump.

~ 50~

"Waste not fresh tears over old grief."
~Euripides~

Seven Valleys Estate
Wolds-on-Thames Village
Oxfordshire, England
August 2005

Barbara, Edward, and Peter moved Hayley to Seven Valleys when she was well enough for home care. Peter wasn't taking any risks with her health and employed a full-time nurse to be on the safe side. Local police guards sat at the entrance to the estate, Edward had surveillance cameras taping every day, 24-hours a day throughout the house and on the grounds. The estate's security guards patrolled the interior perimeter every hour.

Hayley was overjoyed to see Diva and the little dog kept vigil at her bedside. Her health improved rapidly during a few weeks of bed rest and loving care.

On a balmy summer morning, preoccupied by a matter that weighed heavily on her, Barbara joined Peter and Hayley whilst they chatted on the terrace.

"Mum, what is it? You look so serious. Is everything all right?"

"I'm not sure, Darling, but you can judge for yourself. I have already shared with Edward what I am about to confide to you. You both know, of course, that my sister Patricia plans to attend your wedding. I wanted you to know what I am about to tell you before she returns to Seven Valleys. Hayley, all of this involves some grievous family history that only Patricia, Edward, Peter, and I know."

"We thought this was buried long ago, Mum. Why has it surfaced again?"

"Patricia believed so, too, but hear me out, Peter, you'll understand in a minute. I have to start at the beginning so that Hayley will have the whole picture."

When she was a young girl, Patricia was fun loving, beautiful, and outgoing. However, she was always serious about her religion and actively engaged in our church parish helping the nuns with the sick and the poor. One day, when she was fourteen, she went directly to the church after school with an armload of altar flowers to arrange for weekend services. I wanted to go shopping with my girlfriends and threw a tantrum because I couldn't have the limo at my disposal. Pat told the chauffeur she would walk home. I was a spoiled, selfish girl and I'll carry that guilt to my dying day.

It was growing dark when Pat left the church and as she went past the bushes outside, a man accosted her. He dragged her into an awaiting car, severely beat her, and raped her." Barbara paused to control her tears. "Patricia fought her assailant hard, but she was no match for him. He threw her battered and brutalized from the car and left her on a wooded roadside to die."

Hayley felt a poignant ache in her chest, "Oh, Barbara, I feel so sad for Patricia. I'm very sorry."

Peter went to his mother's side and held her hand. "Mother, are you all right? You don't have to do this."

"Yes, I do, Peter. I have a good reason." She continued; "Patricia survived this horror, only to learn she was pregnant. In those days, an abortion was unthinkable for a good Catholic. She gave birth to a baby girl and gave her up for adoption. She has learned that her child, whose name is Chloé Rosenthal Meyers, had longed to know her birth mother. Now that her adoptive parents have passed on, she has found and contacted Patricia. Her baby is now fifty-two years old and a grandmother.

"Oh, I see where this is going. Does Chloé Rosenthal Meyers know about the money? Is that at the bottom of this meeting?"

"I don't know, Peter, but Patricia chose to make the trust irrevocable, so that's a moot point. Patricia told me about this on the day she arrived for the festival. After many hours of soul searching and prayer, Patricia decided to meet her. We sat in the chapel and I listened. I offered no advice and she asked for none. I have prayed it will go well for them and that this meeting will take place without complications. I hope there will be no strings attached. We will hear all about her daughter and the meeting when Patricia returns for your wedding."

"Mother, can we not find out what happens with the meeting before she comes here for the wedding? Surely she could use our support."

"Of course, Darling; I'll ask her to call us after the meeting with her daughter. Children, I had a reason for sharing this with you. Hayley, I particularly wanted you to know, because you of all people can understand the aftermath of such a tragedy and appreciate what she went through. Just like you, Patricia's life changed in an instant. You are going in one direction when your life is abruptly interrupted and the whole course of your life changes."

"It's as if you find yourself dropped in an unfamiliar place, with no roadmap, no signposts or symbols to follow, and you are blindly groping in the dark toward whatever your future now holds."

Peter entwined Hayley's fingers with his and said, "We wake up every morning not knowing what changes the day will bring, but we certainly don't expect the day to hold traumatic life changes to the extent you and my aunt had to face. Patricia had her family to support her; you had no one, Hayley. There was no one to guide you and you didn't know who to trust."

"Yes," Barbara replied, "it's true that Patricia's family was there for her, but I don't think she ever learned to trust again. She's still wary of men, but she believes what happened was a sign for her to place herself in God's hands and seek the safety and shelter of the convent. I think she also sees her daughter coming to her at this time as a sign as well."

Detective Chief Inspector Bowkler arrived midmorning at Seven Valleys from London to give them liberating news.

"London's Scotland Yard has confirmed Kedzara Twigg Chandler died in the terrorist's bus bombing on seventh July."

"Dead...she's dead? Oh, my God, Peter! I'm free; after all these years, I'm free!"

Overwhelmed, Hayley began to sob with relief. Peter took her into his arms and held her.

"Oh, Hayley, darling, it means you will never again have to live with the fear, loneliness, and emotional pain you suffered at the hands of Zara Chandler. Thank you, Detective Bowkler, for bringing us this astounding news."

The Inspector continued, "A young woman on the street told officers that she had just exited the bus before the bombing. While on the bus, she told a police officer that she recognized Chandler sitting in the back. I'm sorry to be so graphic, but we found the blood-covered knife in the pocket of her half-burned trench coat in a heap in the rubble. The explosion burned her body beyond recognition, but we discovered Ms. Hamilton's ring on her finger. We positively identified the body from your ring and from her DNA."

DCI Bowkler held out the ring and Peter took it.

"She'd hacked into the Ritton's registration logs and learnt that you were returning on sixth July and would reside in the same suite as your previous stay. The hotel staff didn't recognize her because she wore a black wig and her red hair was their prompt."

"Yes, that explains how she got past reservations, but I want to know how she got into our suite." Peter's voice had an edge to it. "The Ritton is supposedly a very safe hotel and I took great pains to assure Hayley's safety. When Hayley and I arrived at the room, Zara Chandler called me on my mobile and told me she was in the hotel. She said to meet her in the bar. Of course, she wasn't there. The call was a rouse meant to get me out of the room."

"The hotel manager believes she slipped in during the day while the service was refreshing the room. We discovered a tiny wireless webcam wedged in a crack in the wall across from Miss Hamilton's suite. We believe that she planted it for surveillance. They found her laptop and mobile, a pile of cigarette butts with her DNA, the ice bucket, water bottles, empty bottles of scotch from the bar, and an empty fruit plate in the back of Ms. Hamilton's closet.

We have solved several related cases and there will be a joint press conference tomorrow morning by Scotland Yard, the New York Police Department, and the Federal Bureau of Investigation. We wanted to bring the information to you before we release it to the public. After we go public, I think you can expect the press to hound you, so be prepared.

Of course, you already know that she murdered Jacques Bonnier. We removed the desktop computer from her house and learned she corresponded with him and arranged a liaison. Not only that, we found her fingerprints all over his flat and forensics found her hair on his mattress. We were able to rule out a drug-related murder after that."

"I think I already know the answer to this question, but what do you know about Jacques Bonnier, or Jaxx, responding on the forum for the six weeks he lay dead?"

"During the six weeks between his death and your finding him, Kedzara Twigg Chandler was answering his online emails and personal messages, impersonating Jacques Bonnier, or *Frenchtoast*, as he was called.

In addition to the events surrounding his death, Bonnier was deep into dealing cocaine. It appeared his online business was legitimate but he also used it as a front for illegal drug sales. All the wines and beers, as well as locations, referred to people and places for shipments and purchases. We found two kilos of cocaine in the bottom of an otherwise empty aluminum briefcase."

"What about the information we gave you about the bombing in front of the Top of the Turret Residence Tower the day Arthur

Symington was killed? She admitted to arranging those murders. Have the New York police been successful acting on that information?"

"Yes, sir, we gave the information to the New York City police that Kedzara Twigg Chandler confessed to Miss Hamilton. Working on those leads, they found that Ms. Chandler called the same New York cell number on May 21, 1999 and again on December 24, 2004. The number belongs to a suspected New York terrorist, Hanaz Rad, known to the New York State police and America's FBI, but they had nothing actionable on him until now. Fortunately, Hanaz Rad kept the same cell number all that time. He used it to do business under an anglicized name, John Bradley. His brother, Dawid, called himself David Bradley. Homeland Security in the states picked Hanaz up and under interrogation, he rolled over on his brother. The pair admitted to the murders and in a plea bargain, named a suspected terrorist in Finsbury Park who goes by the pseudonym, Ra'id, as their contact.

Under warrant, detectives searched Rad's warehouse and found a stockpile of explosives and detonators, as well as a computer with names and information about terrorists in the New York City area. They also found a shoulder-fired missile launcher and a box of programmable rockets. Apparently, they used that weapon to bring down the Learjet. Normally it's difficult to connect current murders to a cold case such as the plane crash, but with the information you provided, we pulled it all together.

We have questioned Norah Twigg about the timing of her daughter's visits. She was very cooperative with police. Ms. Twigg said she always feared her daughter killed her husband and her sister-in-law. Her mother will inherit Chandler's estate, including the £150,000 we found in the house. We discovered a number on her mother's phone records placed on 18 December 2004, leading us to Ra'id. We've had this group under surveillance and this may be the break we needed, actually.

Although hired hit men were the killers in the states, we are certain Kedzara Twigg Chandler was behind all of it. This wraps up quite a few unsolved cases. Unfortunately, Miss Hamilton, you and your family have paid dearly in these tragedies."

After Bowkler left, Barbara carried a tray with a pot of tea and teacups to the terrace and joined Peter and Hayley. Lizzie, Maggie, and Diva trailed behind Emily who carried a tray with a pitcher of lemonade, scones, and biscuits for midmorning tea.

"Heavens, I will never understand what was wrong with that woman. She must have been possessed."

"No, Mum, she was a psychopath and a murderer; a narcissist with no conscience and no feelings for anyone else; a sociopath for whom the laws of society were of no concern. In other words, she was absolutely barking mad. When we discovered the extent of her stalking and spying on me, I knew how mentally ill she was. I pleaded with her to get help, but she laughed."

"Peter, she must have loved you very much."

"No, she didn't, Darling; she was lustful, maybe, but love? No, that's something Zara could never have felt. She was ambitious and obsessed with wanting to possess me, so that she could be my wife for all the trappings that went along with who I am. Nevertheless, she saw me as Mr. Zara Chandler. She was bitter and vindictive when she failed to get what she wanted."

Miguel and Marisol called that day with exciting news -- Marisol was expecting a baby. They were both thrilled and Hayley was delighted for them. They wanted nothing more than a family.

"When I get back to New York, we must sit and talk about the future, Miguel. I have some ideas to discuss with you. I'll examine the terms of the trust I set up to make certain the future is secure for your baby."

"*Si, gracias*, there will be many changes, I know. When are you coming home, *méjita*? We worry, and we are lonely without you and Diva."

"I know, Miguel; soon. It will be soon. Miguel, what has become of Dream-Girl? Is she all right?"

"She is gone, Señorita Hayley. The day she disappeared, the construction crew broke through to the entrance to complete the renovation. When she was leaving, the crew asked her where she was going and she said, 'I'm going home.' They asked her where home was and she said, 'None of your business.' She went onto the street, where a silver-haired man in a tan trench coat was waiting for her. He took her hand. One of the crew told Studs that he heard the man say, 'Come along, my dear. Your work here is done.' They walked away together and then a crewmember saw that she left her hat, glasses frames, and cigar. He gave them to Studs and he ran after her, but a passing truck with a huge mirror on it caught the sun and flashed in his eyes. After the truck drove by, they were gone."

No one could believe all the clothes she stuffed inside the doorway. She piled them high on supermarket carts and left behind a big cardboard box full of five-dollar bills. On the top of the box, she wrote, For the Homeless. *Señorita* Chris and I took the clothes and money to the Coalition of Homeless Shelter's office.

"Did you ever learn her name, Miguel?"

"You are not going to believe this, *Señorita* Hayley. The work crew saw her in the morning of the day she disappeared." Miguel chuckled. "When they asked her name, she told them to call her *Dream-Girl*."

It continued to be a pleasant late summer's day and Hayley sat on a chaise playing with the dogs and Barbara joined her for lunch. She had asked Emily to set out lunch of toad in the hole and spotted dick on the terrace. Barbara wanted to discuss the Christmas wedding and brought with her a stack of bride magazines and lists of caterers and wedding planners.

"Hayley, dear, I bought all the bride books they had on the news stand. We can look these over and then let's talk about what kinds of activities you can do here. Jessica suggested that you take over the paperwork for next year's festival."

The telephone rang and Emily answered from inside the house. She appeared on the terrace carrying the telephone.

"It's Miss Wyndham for you, Miss Hamilton," she said brusquely and dropped the receiver on the table.

"Thank you, Emily," Hayley chose to ignore Emily's snippy attitude and picked up the phone with a cheery smile.

"*Hi Chris*, I'm glad you called; there's so much to tell you."

Hayley's conversation started on an up-beat note while she told Chris all the news. Then the smile left her face and her voice took on a serious tone.

"What? When, Chris?" There was a long pause and then she said to Chris, "I'm extremely upset and disappointed that I wasn't warned. Why didn't you tell me before we left New York?"

There was a long silence while Chris told her what was happening in New York. She nodded, "Yes, of course Slick can have an exclusive interview with Peter and me when we come home." There were a lot of surprised, "you're kidding...that's wonderful...really? I'm very happy for her and I'm sure you like having Pookie with you in New York, too."

There was a long pause until Hayley said, "Certainly, Ben and Diane can stay in the penthouse until we return. Yes, we'll invite them to the wedding. Yes, of course; Pookie, too, and we expected that Matthew would be here."

While Hayley talked to Christine, Peter joined them on the terrace. He poured a glass of wine and sat under the umbrella. After a long conversation, Hayley finished talking to Chris and handed the receiver to Barbara.

"She wants to tell you herself what she's just told me," Hayley's voice quavered. Her expression had darkened over the course of the conversation.

"Hullo, Christine, Dear…Yes, I'm sitting…Oh, good grief," Barbara replied. She rose abruptly and braced herself against the balustrade. Her hand covered her eyes and she listened while Christine talked. "Thanks for telling me, Chris." She heaved a big sigh, "Yes, of course they can stay here at the house for the wedding. There may be some bunking up, but we'll manage. We've already booked all the rooms at the Cygnet for our wedding guests."

When Barbara hung up, she exchanged glances with Hayley. When she turned to Peter, her lips were pressed into a grim line.

"Well, Matthew went uninvited to see Chris in New York. She wasn't happy about it, but it seems she introduced him to Diane and Ben who are casting her mother's new Broadway musical, *Beautiful Dreamer*. Christine said that Ben *adores* Matthew and insisted that he try out. Evidently, he's a shoo-in for one of the lead roles. Who knew Matthew could sing and dance that well?

Diane invited Matthew to dine with them at the penthouse and while they were eating, detectives came by to talk to him. Apparently, someone murdered the girl who played Juliet in Sir Adrian's production in Utah. They believed he might have been the last person to see her alive.

Peter, do you remember the episode when the young woman claimed Matthew was the father of her child? He proved his DNA didn't match the child, but the Utah police found him through Interpol from DNA evidence collected from her bed. However, he had an airtight alibi for the time of the murder. He was on a flight to New York when it happened. I'll ask Edward to call Matthew and discuss this with him. Without a doubt, Matthew had nothing to do with her death, but we need to talk to him. This family always handles misfortune together and this will be no exception." She sighed and rubbed her forehead. "All four of them plan to be here for the wedding. We'll have a full house, won't we?"

"Barbara, please let me call Lippy about this. If the police should approach Matthew again, he shouldn't talk to them without an attorney present. His daughter, Brooklyn Capshaw, is a very successful criminal defense attorney and my father admired her. If you all agree, I'll call her after Edward talks to Matthew."

Everyone fixed their lunch plates and took a seat on the terrace under the umbrella. Peter sat with a frown of concentration wrinkling his forehead.

"Hayley," he spoke hesitantly, "this might be the right time to tell you that I have discovered a bracelet I believe is the same one your parents gave you on graduation day. I found it in a jewelry shop the day I bought your engagement ring. Someone who received it from Zara Chandler's mother had pawned it. If you don't want it now, Darling, I'll put it away for safe keeping."

"Peter! *My bracelet*? Yes, I want it. I very much want it."

"I've had the bracelet cleaned and the clasp repaired." He took it out of a jewelry box and fastened it on Hayley's wrist. She sat lost in thought. "Are you all right, Sweetheart?"

"Yes, Peter, I'm fine. I'm happy to have this bracelet again. I know it's mine, actually. See this tiny engraving along the edge, '*JAH ♥ EHT ♥ HEH*'? It's hardly noticeable." She sighed, "I'm wondering how long you've had this bracelet."

Edward walked onto the terrace with his newspaper. He greeted everyone, kissed his wife, and Barbara handed him his lunch plate and a glass of wine.

Hayley sat quietly, pondering these revelations and Peter took the sapphire ring out of his pocket. "What shall we do about this, Hayley?"

"Peter, I can't wear that ring. It's too great a reminder of Zara Chandler and all the senseless tragedy she caused."

He placed it on the table. "It's as if this is Zara's ring. She tainted it. This ring came from an estate and I've been wondering what happened to the former owners. I should like to trace it back. Perhaps I'll return it to Hatton Garden and talk to the jeweler. He said it had a dodgy history. I ignored him, but after all that's happened, it makes me wonder."

"Peter, please come with me to my studio." Barbara picked up the ring from the table. "I'll put this in the safe until then. Hayley, dear, will you excuse us for a moment? Edward, we'll return shortly."

"Peter, I wanted to wait until we were alone to bring this up. Today has been wickedly difficult enough without what I have to tell you. There was a legal issue with my diamond mines. I received a letter this morning from the mine's manager through my attorney in Namibia. Peter, you will have to go to Africa to assure that a dispute over a government agreement has been resolved to our benefit. They appear to have it under control, but I would prefer that you pay a visit. You are the only one I can depend on to take care of it for me...for the family."

While she spoke, Barbara took two matching blue velvet boxes from her safe.

"Amongst the most beautiful family pieces of jewelry are rings that I have always treasured." She opened one of the boxes and held out a diamond ring to Peter. "Your grandfather gave my mother's engagement ring and their wedding rings to me, Peter, and they are insured for five million pounds. He told me to choose the son I think should have them. I choose to give these rings to you. With my blessing, I want you to have this ring to give to Hayley, the woman you chose to be your wife."

"Yes, Mother, I remember this ring. How many carats is this stone?"

"Its eighteen carats, Peter, and it's a stone that is full of fire and perfectly symmetrical; it has no carbon and no feathers. It's pure, just like your Hayley. The side stones are three carats each. My mother wore her engagement ring from the time my father placed it on her finger until the day she died."

"I shall treasure it, Mother, and I think Hayley will, too."

Peter went to his mother's side. He gently kissed her forehead. "I love you, Mum. I'm so grateful for you and Dad. No worries about the African enterprises; we'll discuss it later with dad and I'll go when things at home settle down."

While Peter and Barbara were off discussing his trip to Africa, Edward sat with Hayley on the terrace reading his paper. Lifting the teapot to pour another cup of tea, she found the pot empty and placed it on the tray with a pitcher of lemonade and the cordless phone receiver. Walking toward the kitchen, she replaced the receiver in its cradle in the drawing room.

Emily was busy washing up in the kitchen and put water on the cooker to prepare more tea. Her thoughts were dark and ominous. *Too many changes; that pampered, self-centered, spoilt girl is upsetting the whole household. It was lovely when Doctor Peter came home to stay, but why did he have to bring her here? I'm waiting for the day she goes back where she came from, to New York City. I'll see to it that she stays there.*

Nearing the kitchen, Hayley heard the telephone ring and hesitated when she reached the doorway. Emily had her back turned and wasn't aware of Hayley's presence. She picked up the phone and was quickly absorbed in conversation.

"I thought it'd be you. Good of you to ring me, mate."

A pause...a caustic snigger, "Yes, Doctor Peter's going to marry the meal ticket."

Frost iced her voice, "If that bit of a knob wasn't an heiress, she'd be of no use at all."

She took a long drag on her cigarette, flicked the ashes on the stone floor, and ground them under her foot. "Yeah, he waited a long time to get his hands on the full monte; the bloody American trog's got tons of foldin' dosh. Like father, like son."

Her laugh was loud and coarse. "Crikey, hooked good and proper. She's a blinkin' cabbage and never suspected a thing, the sad cow. She'll learn…"

She snickered, "The Barbie Doll must be in bad straits; she's not letting her get away. What do I mean? She's got flippin' bride books clutterin' up the terrace and herself right in the middle of it all, planning a Crimbo wedding. They fancy having it here in the Chapel.

Blimey, if she thinks I'll allow her bloody caterers in my kitchen again to impress that bleedin' twit and her lot..."

Emily snorted smoke through her nose. "No, Matthew's not been back since the bleedin' heiress caused such a ruckus between Doctor Peter and him. The Barbie Doll's pissed, but it was that rich bitch's fault. I have good news for Matt that I overheard. Can't wait to tell him that he's got readies he doesn't know about...yet. Yeah, some kind of trust they're keepin' from him."

She paused, listening. "Oi, that's bollocks; I heard Matthew's in New York. He's got that Hollywood bloke, Christine Wyndham's daddy, wrapped around his little finger.

Yeah, Matthew called...talked to me...yeah, I promised I'd help him sort it out," she sniggered, "and he told me there's bugger all money left." *Raucous laughter*, "At least I'll know where my paycheck's coming from."

Another pause... "Blimey, heard Peter knew who the killer was before they left New York. Yeah...-bloody twit didn't know! Yeah, don't know for how long. I don't want her under my feet," she grumbled in her gravelly, cigarette-sucking voice. "*Crikey*...in all the years this family's had non-paying guests, this is the first time it's like we're running a cheap hotel. I can't wait until she's gone. If she comes back, I'll have her *guts for garters*."

Hayley gasped; the tray fell from her grasp and clattered at her feet. The pitcher broke and when she abruptly turned to leave, she slid on the spilled lemonade, twisted her body, and fell on the stone floor.

Startled, Emily spun around with a frown and hung up the phone. Seething that she had been overheard, she pierced Hayley with dark, accusing eyes.

"*You wicked, stupid girl!*" Emily glowered at Hayley, her voice shrill, "Look what you've done; you've shattered Mrs. Gabriel-John's beautiful heirloom lemonade pitcher with your meddling." She lowered her voice afraid she might be overheard. Her head reared back like a cobra ready to strike and she hissed, "Get out of my kitchen and stay out. I'll bring more tea. You're a pathetic cow; go and sit somewhere out of the way and continue to be useless."

Furious, Hayley pulled herself up from the floor. Slightly unsteady on her feet from the fall and the jolt to her wound, she limped back to the terrace, picked up Diva, and sank into a chair. Shock and confusion overtook her. Trembling and in pain, she slumped forward with her eyes squeezed tight against gathering tears. She felt her heart racing in her chest and a slow, burning anger welled in her.

How dare that woman talk to me in such a demeaning tone of voice? And there was no way that she could have known about Peter, Matthew, and Ben Horowitz unless she'd been listening to my phone call! I'm such a fool. Has this all been a colossal charade to get access to my money? Were there signs? I didn't see the signs! Am I so naïve and trusting of this family that I have allowed my love for Peter to blind me to avarice and deceit? What have I gotten myself into?

Peter and Barbara walked back to the terrace and Barbara took Hayley's hand in hers. "Now, let's get started, shall we, Darling? We have a Christmas wedding to plan, but first, Peter has something for you. We think you'll be pleased."

Emily sauntered onto the terrace with a tray and set a new teapot on the table. Smug in her sense of power over the family, with her lips pursed into a smirk, her brows raised, her sly eyes narrowed, she pinned Hayley with a triumphant stare. She swaggered back to the kitchen, marching to the tune of her inner delusions, her head bobbing from side to side in righteous self-satisfaction.

EPILOGUE

"Revelations come when you're in the thick of it,
pitting yourself up against something larger than yourself."
~Frank Langella~

Seven Valleys Estate
Wolds-on-Thames, Oxfordshire
August 2005

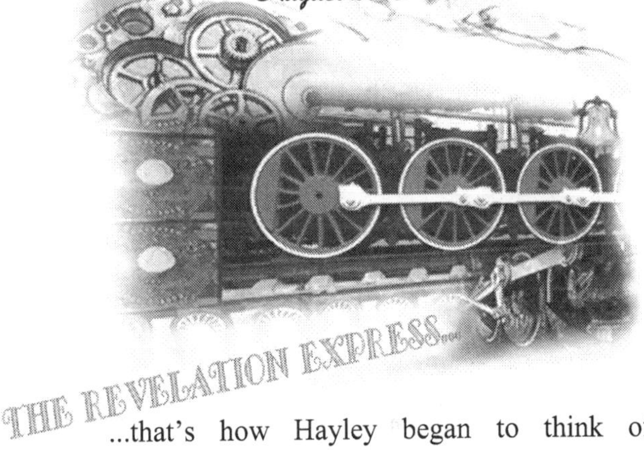

...that's how Hayley began to think of this extraordinary day. It was as if they had boarded a speeding train that barely slowed down at every station, so that someone with a new disclosure could hop on.

I'm free...fate has handed me a pardon. Hayley breathed deeply and slowly exhaled.

Bowkler told us Zara Chandler is dead. Chris's phone call was astounding. I had no idea they had kept so much about the threat of Zara Chandler from me. Peter still hasn't told me when he knew. My bracelet...for how long had Peter known about it without telling me?

Patricia, Marisol and Miguel, Matthew, Dream-Girl. So much has happened and there were so many revelations that my mind and emotions are spinning. It's too much to take in; there's so much to do in New York when I return, too many changes to anticipate, and too little time.

And now...there's the Emily problem.

Barbara touched Hayley's hand, but she didn't respond.

"Hayley? Did you hear me, dear?"

"I have my Grandmother's diamond engagement ring for you, Hayley," Peter said. "I think you'll be pleased."

Hayley's voice was a whisper, "I'm sorry, Peter, I cannot accept an engagement ring. Not now," she glanced up at him, "not until I've had time to think. I'm calling off the wedding, or at least, postponing it."

"What? Why, Hayley?" Barbara looked stunned. "Are you not happy to have the wedding here? Is that it? Is it the chapel? Would you rather have the wedding in New York? That's certainly..."

"No, Barbara. It's not the chapel; of course not. The chapel is beautiful. Perfect. No, it's just that...I need more time and I'm troubled by something Chris told me."

Her words sent Peter into shock. When he could speak, his voice sounded strained, "What? Hayley, whatever do you mean? What could Christine possibly have said that would make you want to postpone our wedding?"

"I told her about Zara Chandler's death and she told me that you suspected she was the killer before we left New York. She said Dream-Girl drew you a picture of the red-haired killer and from that drawing, you felt sure it was Zara. You knew you were taking me into danger when we left New York for England. You never told me she had stalked you, that Tom Leighton said she had stalked him, or that she had stalked *us* in New York. On top of that, Tom told you she swore to kill my mother. I'm angry, Peter, at both you and Christine. You both knew and you kept me out of the loop. Why, Peter? I had every right to know."

"I wasn't sure and I thought I could protect you. I didn't want to frighten you. It was for your own good. Chris and I thoug--..."

"No, Peter, Chris says she didn't know until *after* we left New York and got to London. Yet, you still kept me in the dark. Did you think if you told me I wouldn't leave New York? You didn't give me a choice and I resent that. It was pure selfishness, or at least poor judgment, on your part. I trusted you, Peter, and you let me down. Withholding that information left me vulnerable, unsuspecting, and powerless. I'm not sure you know me at all. I'm not sure I know myself anymore; all of this tragedy has had an impact on me. I've changed, but this I do know -- I can't relinquish control over my life – neither what I am, nor what I have -- not to you, not to anyone ever again. Knowing this, you might not want to marry me."

"I'm sorry you feel that way, Hayley. Please believe me, everything I did, I thought was in your best interest. I may be guilty of poor judgment, but I am not selfish."

Hayley stood up and turned away from Peter. "Barbara and Edward, you've been so kind and generous. I'm already far too indebted to you and it appears that I've overstayed my welcome. Therefore, I must leave. You must think me a terrible ingrate, but I want to go home, please, as soon as arrangements can be made."

"My dear," Edward's voice sounded calm, but on his face, one could see his bewilderment. "None of us always uses the best judgment. You're upset and angry, Hayley, and rightly so. I agree that Peter has a lot to account for, but not in a million years, could you ever overstay your welcome. We consider you a part of the family. Won't you reconsider such a hasty departure, get some rest, and at least stay until Peter can explain his motives and reasoning? Perhaps the two of you can come to an understanding."

"It's not just Peter's keeping me in the dark, Edward, there are other issues I have to think about, too. I've let too many personal responsibilities slide while I've recovered. There are things at home that badly need my attention and I must protect my interests. My life may appear to be simple, but it isn't. Most of all, I need to be alone for awhile, to sort out some truths, you see."

Peter's hands trembled from the shock. "*Truths*? What truths, Hayley? The truth is that we love each other. What else matters?"

"I must reassure myself that what I have been led to believe really *is* the truth, or I must expose deceptive motives to protect myself. That's why I need to leave now."

"Deceptive motives? What in blazes are you on about? No one has led you to believe anything that's not true." Peter stared at her, dumbstruck. His voice was harsh with emotion, "You can't mean this, Hayley. I'm completely gobsmacked! Why? What's happened? For God's sake, and let's discuss this. I'm really trying to listen, Hayley. Please explain to us why you've ... had this change of heart. I love you so, we all do."

Hayley interrupted Peter and spoke softly, "Let me be perfectly clear; I love all of you, too, but how I feel about you is not the issue. It isn't a change of heart, Peter; it's a change of plans. I love you deeply, even though I'm disappointed in you...*and Chris, too.*

Please understand; this is all quite painful for me. Because of all that has happened since we decided on that date, I believe December is too close to arrange the wedding; it's too short a time. There is too much to do, you see. Maybe a year from this December would give us all enough time to accomplish everything that needs to be done and to make proper decisions."

"Hayley," Peter said miserably, sitting down and holding his face in his hands. "*Over a year from now?*"

Peter's mind swirled in confusion. He raised his head to look at her. "Hayley, of course you can return to New York anytime you want, you aren't being held captive here, but I must go with you."

"No, Peter, there's no reason for you to go and I'd prefer to go alone. I'm going upstairs to pack and ring the airline for a flight." Hayley stood up and said, "Please, Edward, will you drive me to the airport, or shall I call for a car?"

"*I..I..of course I will, Dear*, but first, please take a moment to consider the wisdom of what you're about to do. I'm not sure you really want to fly home alone. Perhaps you'll allow Barbara to accompany you."

"That's a good idea, Edward." Barbara looked at Hayley, "What is on...Darling, that's *blood* on the front of your dress! *Edward, she's bleeding and her clothes are wet!* What's *happened* to you, Darling?" Barbara reached out, but Hayley pulled away.

"Hayley...darling, we don't understand." Tears streamed down Barbara's face. She turned to Edward and went into his arms.

"Hayley, please sit down. *Please,"* Peter said. "What could have happened during the fifteen minutes I was gone from your side, and what was so terrible that you are willing to do something so rash and impulsive when you are obviously unwell?"

"No, Peter; I'm all right." She placed her hand over the spot of blood. "It's just a..."

"I'm concerned about your fragile state of health. This has been an unsettling day and I think you really need some rest. It's not the time for you to be leaving. You are obviously not ready to travel. Dad, please ring up William to come and look at Hayley's wounds. I would prefer that he tell us if you are ready to travel, Hayley. And before you do anything, or go anywhere, we need to talk."

Hayley ignored his comments. Holding her side, she turned away to leave the room, but glimpsed Emily lurking off to the side of the open doorway. She turned to face Peter again.

"Whatever you don't understand, Emily can explain to you, actually. Ask *her* for the truth after I'm gone. She holds all the answers...*don't you Emily?*"

"All right, now I'm *thoroughly* confused. My God, Hayley. What does Emily, *of all people*, have to do with this?" He looked at her as if she'd lost her mind. "Our Emily has always shown the utmost loyalty to this family."

"*I see*. Well, then, I want to add that perhaps *your Emily* is not the person you think she is. I realize she has been with this family your whole lifetime, but the truth is, I wonder if you *really* know her."

Hayley sighed heavily and started to walk toward the doorway. She saw that Emily had gone. Halfway through, she turned; her face glistened with tears and her eyes held sorrow when she met his.

"Yes, Peter, so you must ask your Emily. She knows all about the secrets and lies."

"Hayley gasped; the tray fell from her grasp and clattered at her feet. The pitcher broke and when she abruptly turned to leave, she slid on the spilled lemonade, twisted her body, and fell on the stone floor."

Author's Notes

In a World Apart, took several years of research to assure historical, logistical, and procedural accuracy, as well as authenticity when switching between fiction and fact. I want to thank those who helped me here in the states *(you know who you are!)* and in England, my beloved friends –

Averil and Reg Rhodes, Geraldine Pass, and Dr. Peter Haydn-Smith.

I especially want to thank Carol Marie Decker, my best friend, an English Literature major, who as my editor, sat for hours helping me to pull apart manuscript puzzle pieces and assemble them to fit. She let me drag her around New York City and all over England and Europe doing up close and personal research.

--Therefore, I am dedicating this book to--

~A brilliant and sweet angel~

Carol Marie Decker

In a World Apart

Is the first book in the series --

Bound by Destiny

The series follows the lives of Hayley, Peter and his family, Christine and her family, their friends and their associates. Each book introduces new people who stir up trouble, upset their equilibrium, complicate -- and possibly threaten -- their lives.

In a Perfect World, the second book in the series, will take the reader on a worldwide rollercoaster ride with Hayley and Christine through Europe on a fashion venture, with Matthew to Broadway and Hollywood, and with Peter and Edward deep into Africa on a mission for a covert British consortium.

In a Secret World, the final book in the series, finds Seven Valleys Estate the center of turmoil and change, with many unanticipated entanglements and challenges that Chris, Matthew, Hayley, Peter, and the Gabriel-Johns family never could have anticipated.

12319521R00240

Made in the USA
Charleston, SC
27 April 2012